NO MAN'S LANDER

STRONGER STILL

THESE TREACHEROUS TIDES

D. N. BRYN

STRONGER
STILL

Printed in the United States of America
First Printing, 2023

Print (paperback) 978-1-952667-87-9
Print (hardcover) 978-1-952667-86-2
Ebook 978-1-952667-85-5

For information about purchasing and permissions, contact D.N. Bryn at dnbryn@gmail.com

www.DNBryn.com

Edited by Chih Wang with CYW Editing.
Cover design by Laya Rose.
Published with The Kraken Collective.

This work is fictitious and any resemblance to real life persons or places is purely coincidental. This book may not act as a guide for hippocamp-related situations resulting from excess of corelium.

THESE TREACHEROUS TIDES SERIES BOOKS

Our Bloody Pearl
Prequel

Once Stolen
Aurora Cycle Book 1

Odder Still
Aurora Cycle Book 2
No-Man's Lander Book 1

Stronger Still
Aurora Cycle Book 3
No-Man's Lander Book 2

Ever Death
Aurora Cycle Book 4

Untitled
No-Man's Lander Book 3

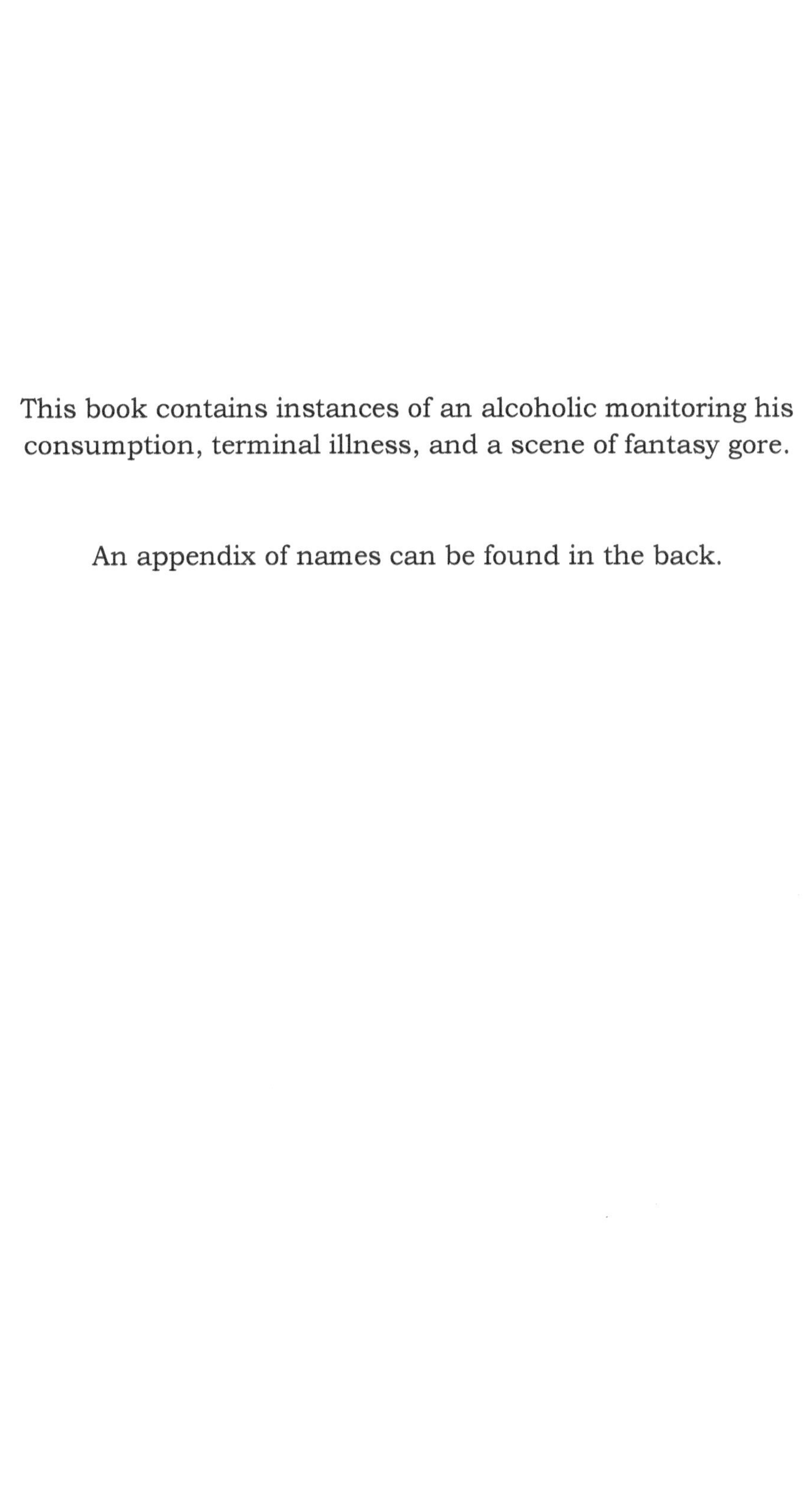

This book contains instances of an alcoholic monitoring his consumption, terminal illness, and a scene of fantasy gore.

An appendix of names can be found in the back.

To anyone learning to untangle the good of their family from
the harm, without suffocating beneath the weight of it all.
You are not alone.

And to my brothers.

CHAPTER ONE

their city to sink

I TAP MY REMAINING fingers against the ferry's railing—six nails and two stubs; the dark, rainbow-laced strands of my aurora tissue crisscrossing like fishnets over them. The motion makes no sound, lost to the waves or the wind or just the phantom reality I seem to originate from. The ferry chugs along without regard to it all, tossing steam out the funnels on its roof as it slowly closes in on our destination. The city of Venalt looms before us, a mass of uneven buildings that seem to rise straight out of the enormous Altice Bay.

Tavish's hand drifts across the railing, jerking back as my nails accidentally meet his skin. "Och." His diamond voice is as sharp and brilliant as ever despite the four hundred miles south that we've come from the old seat of his family's power. "You're having a time of it."

"It's nothing." I grunt, trying to shift my focus from my anxious fingers to the mild, salty wind brushing under my heavy cowl and through my braids. It only makes me all too aware of how the fabric of my slit black robe doesn't rustle, even when the scarlet trim flares and dances over the tops of my boots. The strings of my high, lace-up collar twist just as silently. Through the lacework of the sheer fabric, the visible aurora-made fishnets on my chest look like nothing more unnatural than colorful threads against my brown skin. My fingers go back to their soundless tapping.

Tavish doesn't need to hear them to look unconvinced. "You're certain?"

"Really, it's nothing," I repeat.

Lavender meows in disagreement and pokes her silvery-grey head out of the pack on my shoulder. The chubby little cat gives one look at the rolling waves and pulls back inside with a soft, grumbled growl as she repositions herself. She's taken to this lifestyle better than I expected. Better than *I* have, at least. Though, I'm composed partially of a hermit who spent his whole life in nearly the same place, so I suppose that's a low bar.

"Is it now? You're not even the slightest bit anxious?" Tavish's brow pinches. He looks like the picture of a princeling even after six weeks spent on the road, telephoning our news to every city established as having an aurora, sending letters and radio messages where the long-distance wires haven't been laid, and becoming a traveling enforcement when our messages are ignored. His ginger curls twirl gracefully around his ears, his crisp silver-and-blue suit a perfect fit over his plump, poised body, and his plaid half cloak arranged just right to hide the sauce stain he acquired on his right shoulder a few days ago.

I want to grab his face in both hands and kiss him just for looking like this—for looking like this and agreeing to be mine. But right now that want is blanketed by exhaustion and my thrumming anxiety and something tight that's beginning to feel a bit like guilt. Tavish chose to come with me, chose to be mine. But here I've been, dragging him from place to place with more and more rush and less and less joy, and perhaps it hasn't worn him down yet, but it's certainly wearing *me* down. "I just wish we knew what we were up against here."

"Our letters might have simply been lost or misdirected. With their telephone lines damaged and so few ships coming to and from the city, their mail system must be strained." Tavish picks at the edges of his finger—not bloody yet but starting to redden. "Besides, it's been nearly a decade since my brother and I last visited. Things could have changed. They may not even have the aurora anymore—the coastal one nearest here went missing a few years back—or it might have already faded away."

"Then we'd have come for nothing."

Half of me—the human half that merged with me to become this new form, both human and aurora all at once—uncoils his subconscious from mine, leaving our minds running just separately enough that we can think our own thoughts for the moment. Within our shared mental space, he nudges me gently. *'We're doing all we can.'*

His voice in our head feels huskier and warmer than my aurora one. His statement should calm me. But it doesn't. We tap at the railing all the harder, our hands aching to bounce something between them despite the stubs of our right fingers proving time and time again that they just can't quite manage it anymore. *It hasn't been enough.*

'No,' he agrees with a rush of pain and sorrow.

The death of the aurora we lost in the city of Zarencia still echoes in our head; the way its melodic vibrations turned into a lament as it faded away, still grasping at us, its energy snapping out too suddenly for us to replenish as its people clutched their remaining few ignits like it was their lives on the line and not the aurora's. The other dozen auroras whose cities and countries and caretakers we've convinced to save them don't make up for it.

My human half feels the sentiment as though it's his. *'It's not supposed to be enough.'*

The truth of that pounds in me like a heartbeat: steady, eternal until death, and perhaps a bit past death as well. Doing a certain amount of good is not a free pass to stop caring the rest of the time. It's just becoming so hard to care this much and not have the power to solve every problem, to fulfill every need.

What if we fail again? It's a whisper in the back of our head, just as much mine as my other half's.

'*We have to try anyway. We don't have a better option.*'

Our agreement slips us back into one person, no *we* any longer, only an *I* made of two parts so thoroughly woven together that no thought or will or want can be attributed to either of us any more or any less than the other, the way two mixed paints become a fully unique color. The more time I spend like this, an absurd compilation of two individuals with two pasts and one future, the more I piece through the gaps of my hazy aurora memory. I still can't quite recall my aurora life before the mangrove, not in scenes or even flashes, but I have a sense of who I was: Of wanting something fully and aggressively at odds with the world. Of being willing to die for it.

Behind us, two uniformed guards shout, "Hippocamp sighted off starboard!" and "Get everyone inside!"

"These hippocamps were the animals causing the telephone line damage and the lower number of ferry crossings?" I ask Tavish.

He turns toward the cabin with me, his cane clicking before him. "Aye. We don't get them as far north as Mara, and they're usually rare even here, but when they do come out, they're said to be vicious things."

One of the guards waves us and the other three parties toward the windowed cabin at the ferry's center. "For your safety, please proceed indoors until we've reached the harbor."

As the other passengers hurry toward the cabin, I catch the grunt of a nearby woman—human, by the looks of her— to her friend, who could be a very dehydrated finfolk or perhaps some other species I'm unfamiliar with. "Seems there's just more and more of the bastards at every turn."

The pair continues to mutter in concern as they find seats in the nearly empty ferry cabin. One of the guards climbs the top of it, perching among the steam stacks to scowl at the waves while another continues to motion Tavish and me inside. Confusion tightens his features as he focuses beneath my cowl.

I tug it down a bit farther. Part of me yearns to see the shock on his face, the recognition now that, for the first time in my life, I'm someone worth knowing of—even if much of the world still thinks I'm an overexaggeration or a straight-up myth. But this doesn't seem like a good time to roll the dice on whether his final reaction to me will be awe or fear.

This hippocamp must worry him more than a stranger with rainbow tips pointing his incisors and flashes of color gleaming in his eyes, because he quickly turns his gaze back to the sea, hand hovering over the pistol at his waist. I give a final look at the choppy waves with the city looming ahead and follow the other passengers inside. The guard closes the door after us.

Across the barely populated room, a woman scolds her son in hissed shouts.

Tavish flinches at her raised voice. He tucks himself against the cabin wall, his back straight and his chin held high. "It's a bit odd."

It takes me a moment to pick up his train of thought. "The hippocamps?"

"Yes—them coming this close to the city, being willing to attack a ship this large. Though I suppose I hadn't exactly taken the common ferry during visits here as a teenager. Alasdair was arranging trade agreements, after all, and Sheona was there. We had to look the part. Well, he did. I had to be silent and pretend Mother hadn't sent me along just to get me out of her sight." He quiets in a way that holds weight, as though his emotions are trying to be loud enough to break free of the sound barrier. A slow, trembling breath leaves him. "I suppose we'll never get to conduct *that* wonderful ritual again."

You don't regret killing her, do you? I want to ask. Or perhaps, *Does her death still hurt, even after all she put you through?* But those feel like too big of questions for ferries and hotel rooms, as though in order to utter them, we need to be settled and at peace, not scrambling in a panic from one city to the next, never staying more than a night or two anywhere. "Why did you stop coming?"

"Apparently Venalt decided branching into ignation wasn't worth the price if they were only receiving it as a loan." The tension in his body releases slightly as he thinks, his unfocused gaze adding to his contemplative expression. "It was peculiar, though. Alasdair seemed to be getting along so well with everyone that last trip. He spent an entire weekend talking through design possibilities with one of their brightest engineers—she's the daughter of the family I addressed our letters to, in fact. I was sure he'd converted them all to the idea by the end of it."

He only names Alasdair as the star of this scenario, but I can't imagine he wasn't wooing the city alongside his older brother, even as a teenager. Though perhaps I believe that only because I never saw the two of them together. The Findlays did have quite a way of cutting each other down.

Now there's only Tavish left, the strongest of the diamonds.

"But the city chose not to work with your family after?" I ask.

"As far as anyone told me. Mother could still blame my exclusion from company affairs on my youth then, and at sixteen, I still believed her."

"She was a silt-breather."

"Aye." His lips twitch, but I can't tell if it's up or down. For a moment, he seems to struggle to find something to say, his mouth moving soundlessly before he finally settles on a rush of "Do you think the hippocamps have left us?"

A gunshot answers him. Four or five more fire in rapid succession, overlapping in a rain from two different weapons. The other passengers go quiet, edging away from the windows. A tremor runs through the boat, and a man outside screams.

Tavish's face pales. "What was that?"

"I'm going to check. Hold her majesty." I shove Lavender's pouch at him, already halfway out the door before he responds with a weak insistence that I be safe.

The Venalt harbor is so close now—mere minutes away—but minutes might be too long.

Water spills across the deck on one edge where the railing has splintered beneath the mass of an almost equine creature with a sharklike tail where a horse's back legs would have been. It's grey but for spotty, white, porous ridges along its neck and back. Its stubby front legs dig into the flooring, using armored, two-toed hooves that are twisted and sharpened into talons at the ends. It bites down on the foot of a screaming human guard, its pointed teeth jutting in crooked layers out the sides of its severe, equine-shaped face. With a heavy jerk, it tugs the man back toward the water. He catches the splintered rail with both arms. His companion—a harpy, I think—struggles to reload their pistol, the crown of white feathers along their head and arms flaring and shuddering every time their clawed fingers fumble. Something snaps: either the screaming guard's foot or the wood.

A rush of determination and anxiety courses through me. Beneath it lurks my old indifference: this isn't my fight, these creatures aren't my enemy. But it's my world—a world I care about. And that makes it my fight.

I sprint across the deck in three great strides, sliding against the railing as I wrap my arms around the falling human guard. With a groan, I lock the thumb of my partial hand into his pants and drag him back toward the deck. The harpy leans around us, firing at the creature still clamped onto the human's leg.

Each shot makes me cringe. It's just an animal—a hungry, aggressive, dangerous animal, but my monstrous pets waiting for me back in the Murk have been the same at one time or another. Killing the hippocamp for doing what comes natural to it isn't justice. Most of the bullets skid off the crocodile-like armor that covers its body, though. The one that does embed between the plates only makes it bite down harder. This time, it's definitely the bone that crunches, blood welling around the creature's teeth.

My new boots have a slight heel on them, courtesy of a very attractive boutique manager in Eyrr; if I can kick at the eyes of one of the hippocamps just right, it might startle enough to release its prey. My massive one-eyed croc, Sheila, would've given me death stares for a week for this, but it's less destructive than a bullet, and another snap of the creature's jaws could cut the man's foot off.

I swing my leg over the edge of the boat in preparation. Before I can kick, a faint rhythm hits me from the direction of Venalt, catching in my chest and making my aurora threads vibrate. No one else seems to hear the peculiar song—no one but the hippocamp.

Its eyes roll back and it seizes up, a sound like a waterlogged shriek coming from it. It releases the man's foot, dropping fully into the sea with a splash. As the boat continues to chug onward, its bow cresting into the harbor, I spot the hippocamp's head breaching the surface behind us, watching. Just watching.

The song continues to sweep softly through me. It slides into the background, fitting itself just left of my heart, a steady secondary beat that aligns lightly with my own. I stretch out with my aurora threads, searching for its source. The singing aurora seems to shift through a fog somewhere within the bowels of the city ahead. It reaches back, weaker than I, but no less inquisitive. We can't quite lock hands, though, still too distant to touch.

But it's here. And for now, it's alive.

The harpy drops to their knees on the deck beside me, putting pressure on the other guard's wound as the man hisses through gritted teeth.

I drag myself away from the edge and stand. "Can I help?"

The harpy doesn't even lift their head. "Are you a doctor?"

"No." It feels useless just to watch—all this power in me and I can do nothing.

The harbor cradles our ferry as we chug toward one of the long docks that extend from Venalt's magnificent promenade. The city's ornate structures seem to float on the deep-blue bay, stones of a burnished tan forming majestic, multistory buildings; archways and pillars and domes dominating everything with their red, gold, and marble accents. Water channels twist through the city, just as plentiful as the streets and bridges.

Even with most of the structures pressed together, each one maintains a unique form with differing heights and slightly altered styles: lines of archways with clover patterns cut atop, verandas held out by gracefully curved supports, flower boxes of blooming vines that spill down the sides of buildings, and rooftop gardens of fruit trees. Everything seems fashioned in multiples of three, from the geometric, carved patterns to the window bars on the external metal elevators that drop straight into the water once empty of air-breathing passengers and return with seated mer.

In the channels, motor crafts zip around slim boats with upturned bows and sterns, their drivers pushing them forward with long poles. Far larger ships of a similar style fill the port we're aimed toward. One of them pulls past us, sleek and fast, bearing cargo strapped to its deck. Another watches at the edge of the port with cannons out, manned by the same uniformed guards I spot along the city's edge, all warily watching the water with the help of small barricades and large guns.

Tavish emerges from the cabin with the other passengers, apologizing as his cane bumps the sides of boots and calves. We echo the familiar call we've exchanged since first meeting, but when he says my name, his diamond voice sounds more anxious than normal, and my reply of "Here" comes softer and gruffer than I mean it to.

I glance through the group that awaits us on the dock, a scattered mix of two-legged species and a few mer in wheelchair-style arrangements. "Who lives in this city, other than the harpies?"

Tavish makes a noise in the back of his throat that could be a laugh or a snort. "I'm not exactly the person to ask. Every species is the same dark on dark to me unless you set them against a strong backlight, and I've only been physically intimate with a few of them."

"A few in this *city*?"

His lips peek up at the ends. "Only one whom I got very far with. What was I meant to do at sixteen in a foreign city with no responsibilities or recreation, except try to sleep with someone?"

The soft tease that enters his voice makes my heart warm. I drop my nose into his hair, my lips brushing his temple. "Anyone I should be jealous of?" I lower my voice, curling my words around the edges. "Anyone *I* should try to seduce?"

"Well . . ." Tavish smirks. The ferry's gangplank slams down with a sound like a gunshot, and his expression drops as he jerks so hard his head smacks my nose.

Three people rush on board with a gurney, shouting for the little crowd of passengers to stay back, but I keep watching Tavish, my chest tightening. "Are you all right—"

"Would you retrieve the luggage, please?" He cuts me off.

I stare at him a moment longer, but he seems stable, his chin raised and his fingers locked around his cane handle. "Okay."

By the time I balance my light duffle and Tavish's two massive suitcases with my missing fingers, the injured crew member has been carried off the boat. Tavish and I move slowly up the dock, the other passengers dispersing ahead of us. They all seem to be locals with known destinations.

"I thought Venalt was meant to be a tourist city?" Based on what little I heard of it back in the Murk, people came from across the continent for its engineering feats and great wealth of art, their open acceptance of all species, making it a safe and peaceful escape. I think of the ferry crewmember with his mangled foot. Perhaps *safe* is no longer the right word. "Is the threat of the hippocamps really that bad?"

Tavish's face pinches in thought. "Perhaps. I certainly remember the docks being louder. Busier, too, I imagine."

"Odd."

Despite the lack of tourists, the place still boasts a wider array of sapient species than I've seen almost anywhere else these past six weeks. A pair of satyrs with their slightly bowed humanlike legs and curling horns argue over a catch of fish with a harpy whose flowing top reveals his long arm feathers ruffling in agitation. Three short people with pointed ears and cat eyes shove a cart past them, veering it too hastily toward the dock's edge. A mer slips out of the water to catch their spilled box before it can make a splash. Along them all rush the always prevalent humans, infiltrating themselves into the cracks of every community possible.

"What is this species called that's pixie-like but stouter?" I lower my voice, feeling a little rude asking so close to them, but a lot ruder not knowing in the first place.

"Ah, the kabalos. Three of the greatest thieves alive are known for being kabalos. Strange, how their greatest engineers and leaders and artists never seem to be known for their race, isn't it?"

My skin crawls, the slight hints of my Murkling facial features a stark contrast to my otherwise river-born appearance, neither of them letting me find a home that didn't squeeze me between the margins. "We can never just stop, can we?"

"I'd say the bias was only natural, but we clearly aren't born with it," Tavish says, his smile bitter. It slips into a sigh. "This city does better than most, though. Their nereids' community happily took in a fair number of finfolk when things first went poorly for them back ho—" He seems to catch himself on the word, his voice losing its strength as he quickly transitions to "back in Mara."

I cringe. If I hadn't dragged him along with me, how close would he be to finding a new home by now?

As we reach the end of the dock, we step from wood to stone to something else entirely. It runs in lines through the flooring's massive tan slabs. Shimmers of gold and streams of scarlet curl through the opaque and almost porous material.

"Do you know what this is that supports their stonework?" I ask.

"It's called corelium," Tavish replies. "These waters produce it naturally in great chunks that sit at the surface. It's incredibly strong yet floats even when holding quite a bit of weight. Mother initially wished to trade the ignation for it flat out, but her offer was too steep, and apparently the hippocamps have a kind of obsession with it—they consume it during their mating ritual or something."

"They eat the corelium? But it's so solid." I glance back out to the sea, the thrum of the aurora's song still humming in my chest. That must be another reason why it's keeping the predators out.

"Something in their saliva breaks it down, I believe? I'm sure someone here has a better explanation. What we are truly in need of, though, are directions."

Glancing along the nearest buildings, I find a sign for a tourism center. Beneath the words in large, bold font are the three most prominent linguistic variations—one which mirrors closely to the Murk's local languages—but they must have been put up a few generations past because even the more isolated communities like those bordering my no-man's land learn the trade tongue as children now. The sign's metal is studded with clovers, and the vines from the flower box in the window above it creates a manicured border. I spot a map through the open doorway.

The harpy woman at the front desk startles from her book when we enter. A confused but eager smile spreads across her face. "Welcome. What can I do for you?"

Tavish straightens his already perfectly fitted suit jacket. "Where might we find a directory? We're looking for the home of Benetta and Agnese Viscardi."

"Ah, I don't know the house myself, but I can tell you Benetta Viscardi passed a few years back, and her wife before her, I think?" She taps the spine of her book to her lips: a religious text, it looks like, titled *The Three Great Prophecies and What They Mean for You*. "They used to live in one of those big places just outside the foundation's edge, though—the whole loop is a really nice spot if you're here long enough to check them out."

Tavish hums softly. "Is their daughter, Fiordelise, still here?"

The woman's enthusiasm dims for barely a moment. "Chancellor Fiordelise, now; got elected by the Institute last year. You can find her there, if you manage an appointment."

"What about a hotel? The Grandavair, perhaps?" Tavish asks. "We'd like to refresh."

I cringe at the implication that this will take us long enough to need a place to sleep, but with all I've dragged Tavish around, perhaps a day of rest *is* in order. "Nothing too expensive," I add.

"The last of the bigger hotels closed last month, but there's a couple little places still open. The one off Opaque Channel and Stiletto Street would be closest to the Institute."

"Thank you," Tavish says, his brow only slightly creased.

As he walks out, I pause at the map of the city. I find the Opaque Channel—one of the six primary channels with dozens of smaller ones intersecting them—and Stiletto Street, then work my way inward, up the Celeste Channel to an outlined patch of the city, a little off from the midpoint, with *the foundation center* scribed in delicate letters. What Tavish has informed me is that the city's three governing bodies sit equidistant along its borders: the Citadel, the Basilica, and our destination, the Institute.

We find one of the small hand-propelled boats—gondolas, the sign informs me—and I pay our way with the small silver coins we traded for on the coast. Each time we switch currency, our once-overflowing purse seems to shrink exponentially. What we have left barely jingles.

Tavish waits to one side as I load our luggage. "If you would." He holds his arm out. "As much as I love these channels, I'd prefer not to go swimming at the moment."

"Later then—some midnight streaking?" I tease, taking his hand and helping him into the boat. "Have you gotten to shift at all since Alfhouat? You must be dying for it."

He stiffens, and his jaw works. With one hand, he finds the selkie brooch attached to his collar, the ignation shimmering softly within. "No, I'm fine. We'll be busy, and then we'll be gone. I'd rather not have to . . . fit it in."

"All right." I don't want to feel guilty, but I do, the sensation tingling in my fingers and tugging at my gut.

Tavish sets Lavender's pouch in his lap and leans back against the boat's cushioned side. His thumb drifts toward my leg, lingering against it in a way that reminds me just how long it's been since we found the time to fuck. "This is nice," he whispers.

"The trip must remind you of Maraheem, being on and near the sea again?" There's certainly something about the smallness of the boat and the tight channels that make me think of the rivers at home.

Tavish doesn't respond.

I stare up as our gondola slips beneath a covered bridge of sweeping tan archways and embossed stone sprouting sculptures so precariously that it seems they'll fall on us at any moment. "There's so much rock here, though, it hardly seems like a city built on one spec of a submerged knoll."

Our driver holds aside the veil of vines that drops from the far edge of the bridge, and we pull back into the morning sunlight, the high buildings on all sides once again. When I lean over the side of the boat, I find a mirror world gleaming below, merfolk swimming between structures that go down two and three stories in places, dark sea beneath them. Swirling bioluminescent lights glimmer between sealed electrical bulbs, giving their waterlogged undercity a hazy, sleepy feeling where it tucks into the shadows of the buildings above.

Lavender rustles her way out of her pouch to peer at the water with me. Her tail flicks back and forth as she watches two mer-children play—nereids, I assume—snatching and throwing their spear-shaped toy with their pair of thick, tentacle-like legs while they accent their spoken mer language with simple hand motions.

I kiss the top of the cat's head. "Those aren't your kind of fish, your majesty."

She gives an annoyed *merp* as I scoop her to my lap, but settles there in a happy ball, tail still flicking as I pet her.

We watch between the buildings as we pass tighter channels with doorsteps right on the water, a small second-story park of orange trees in clusters of three, and a wide stone square with market stalls erected on one side and a great cathedral domed in gold on the other. Through the gap of another large channel, I spot a section of buildings that lean slightly, caution signs barring off the flooded walkway.

"Is that usual?" I ask our gondola driver.

He shrugs, giving a hard push of his pole to a side of the channel. "The Institute constructed each corelium block to take just enough weight off the city's main supports, but the

Basilica kept adding new artistic embellishments without talking to them—sets off all their careful planning, the Institute says. They've been trying to tear that one down, but there's a historical grotto built into it by the Basilica's fourth chancellor, so the Basilica throws a fit every time they touch it."

"The Basilica?" I repeat. "That's the religious government branch, who deals with art and humanities?"

"That's it, yeah." The gondola driver catches us before we can bump into the end of the channel, bringing the gondola to a smooth stop against the side of the street. "They've been at it for decades—all three of them, even the Citadel. Amazing this city even floats still. Though, I imagine it won't for much longer."

Tavish's head jerks toward him. "Why do you say that?"

"Well, the hippocamps, of course. Once our aurora dies, they'll come for the corelium. Only the old foundation center will be left." He fiddles with the horn-shaped pendant on his necklace, letting the boat drift. "It'll be chaos when it goes down, but we orthodox followers of the Divine Three, we've been preparing. It's the first three of the great prophecies after all. Once the city sinks, the savior will raise a glorious new capital that will span the Nereidian Sea and become a shining guardian of commerce and culture." He smiles, a tooth missing on the left side. "So don't you worry about us. Go enjoy this age of the city while it's still here."

A shudder runs down my spine. I collect our luggage, Lavender included, and step out of the boat. Tavish almost trips following me, but I pull him up the rest of the way, my aurora strength making even his heavy bulk easy to lift.

He straightens his outfit with care. "Have we reached the hotel?"

"I assumed we'd be stopping there after."

"You took us straight to the Institute, then?"

"I think. I found the nearest channels on the map. It should be just past this block." I feel defensive suddenly, though I know I shouldn't, some ugly need to be justified rubbing up against my guilt. "Their aurora is dying. We aren't here on vacation."

"Their aurora is under the protection of their three chancellors—the most powerful people in the city, and not the kind you can barge in on looking like you spent the morning on a ferry and still expect to be taken seriously. Well, you probably can, but not me." He tugs at his half cape, pulling it a hair to one side and then twisting it right back the way it was. "I need to freshen up first."

"You already look immaculate." It should be a compliment—I mean it as a compliment—but in the midst of my exhaustion and stubbornness, it comes out a little exasperated. I press my fingers to both sides of my nose. The motion feels lopsided by the missing digits on my right hand. "Please, I just want to be done with this."

From down the street a woman shouts. A door slams in her wake. Tavish stiffens, his fingers curling around his cane. "If you want to go now, then go." He sounds tight. "But I desperately need a bath."

"Tavish—"

"You should meet with Chancellor Fiordelise. If we're already here, you might as well." Maybe he means the look he gives me as something comforting, but it seems half a grimace and half a flinch.

"You're sure?"

"Of course I am. Why else would I keep saying it?" His tone turns a little snippy.

I react to it like oil to a flame. "Fine. Go back to the hotel, I'll join you later."

He makes a sound that might be an acknowledgement or just a general huff, and strides down the pathway that wraps the foundation center, somehow managing to have picked the right direction.

With each step I want to call after him, but I feel a weight on my chest, metal pulling me into the ground. I'm too tired for this. Too tired for all of this.

'You're depressed,' my other half corrects.

Shut up, asshole.

'I love you, too, silt-breather,' he says gently.

I breathe, because I know he's right. The pointed, empty fatigue that comes with my depression has been creeping up on me the last few days, making nights easier to slip away into and mornings harder to rise from. If I can just get this over with, then there will be time for the rest both I and Tavish desperately need. Rest and a bottle of wine, and maybe appetizers on a veranda with Lavender in my lap and Tavish's head on my shoulder.

But we have an aurora to save first. Or I do, anyway, Tavish already lost around the bend. The lack of him just makes my heart sink further.

Through the ache in my chest, I can still feel the soft melody of the city's aurora. It's closer through the fog, a reassuring presence. Despite the fragility of its vibration, there's a strength there too. It'll live long enough for us both to take a breather.

I secure Lavender's pouch on my shoulder and collect the luggage, turn my back on the city center, and set off after Tavish. With how worn Tavish and I are growing from this aurora-saving process, I feel a bit like Venalt's aurora isn't the only one fading.

CHAPTER TWO

aurora ambassador

WITH MY MISSING FINGERS, it takes me a fair amount of juggling to keep our luggage and Lavender's pack supported as I walk. And walk I do—down the path, over a bridge, up a stairway, over a second bridge, along a sweeping veranda, down an elevator, and along another path. By the time I reach the hotel, I still haven't caught up with Tavish yet. Or else I've passed him.

When we first left Maraheem, every separation made me fear all the worst possible outcomes, but the further away we've come from Lilias's bruising heel, the more that anxiety has dimmed. Tavish is capable of dealing with most kinds of trouble that might come his way. More capable than I feel at the present moment, standing in the hotel's small foyer with a suitcase under both arms and a cat making unhappy sounds from the pack on my shoulder. A single chandelier lights the room, dim enough that it's hard to spot the chips in the elaborate molding and the places the gilding has peeled away on the lavish but dusty furniture. The host squints as he stares into the shadows beneath my cowl.

"Yes, a Mr. Tavish K. Findlay checked out room thirty-six. He said his companion would be paying."

I count out the coins for a single night and collect the key. As I climb into the building's internal elevator, I smile at the host with my aurora-enhanced canines. He balks, but the contraption quickly rises out of his view.

The theatricality of it all gives me a sliver of joy that passes in an instant. Being this—the only human-bonded aurora—may have the perk of shocking and thrilling and uneasing people, but it comes with the responsibility of every other less mobile and verbal aurora's safety. And as that weight on me grows, so does my fatigue, until a long rest back in the Murk appeals more than these dramatics. I just need to find the strength to keep going until this is over, whatever it costs.

As though my exhaustion hones my senses, my gaze snaps to the soft blue glow of the tiny ignit in the elevator's motor, sealed away behind a locked wire casing. If there's one in every elevator in the city, Venalt shouldn't have any trouble using them to keep their aurora alive. Once they know.

We sent so many letters, I protest.

'To a dead couple Tavish barely knew, at a house they no longer own.'

My own rationality only agitates me further.

I find the suite Tavish reserved. The door opens to a small room fashioned with half panels of wood beneath soft green wallpaper with leaflike curls and two broad windows, their sheer curtains pulled. A deeper-green sofa and love seat crowd a coffee table near the door to the bedroom. Tavish stands, undressing beside a round, three-chaired table with six-pointed starbursts swirling along the edges. His drenched curls cling to his head, three shades too dark.

The door squeaks as I close it.

Tavish jerks away from the sound so harshly he bumps over the nearest chair, spilling the wet clothes he's draped onto it. They quickly form a small puddle beneath them, his brooch peeking through the rumpled fabric. He scrambles for a flip knife tucked in the lining of his soggy pants.

The fact that he's carrying one—that I've never seen before—startles me so thoroughly that it takes me a moment to speak. "It's just me."

His shoulders relax. "Did you see Chancellor Fiordelise?"

"Not yet." I set the luggage down, along with Lavender's pouch. Part of me—not an aurora or a human part, but a bitterly scared part—wants to ask if he fell into the channel, but an equally scared part doesn't want to embarrass him further. "You were right. We're both stressed and tired. That's hardly the best time to be telling some poor chancellor that the way to save her aurora is to give it back the power they're running their city with."

Tavish inhales. "Aye. Of course."

His arm still shakes as he sets his knife carefully on the table, like he's not quite sure what to do with it now.

All of me catches on that look, on the confusion and worry, as though the cord that's tangled us together for this long turns his fear into my pain instantaneously. The bruises along his sides healed weeks ago, but I can still recall them fresh as the day Lilias's boot pounded them into being, the rib she broke leaving him to sleep funny for over a month.

I press a hand to his shoulder, trying to make my tone teasing. "Were you planning to stab me with that?"

"I figured it would be easier to draw than the cane-sword. I was wrong, clearly." It sounds so much like a defense.

"All right."

"It was a shite idea."

"All right," I say again. *No, it wasn't* was the better response—I can feel that in every pinched muscle of Tavish's face. But he's also correct; the little training we've found time for has been with his cane-sword, and he seems just as likely to hurt himself with this knife as anyone else. I scoop up the sopping pile of his clothes, neatly draping the fabric back over the chair before nudging the brooch into his hand. "Here."

He doesn't press the brooch to his skin, just holds it, face tipped away from me. "Would you run me a bath, please?"

"All right," I say a third time, like it's the only reply I have the energy for. I don't know what else to tell him. The moment I leave the room, though, it feels like I should have said something more.

The tub sits in an alcove beneath the bathroom window, small but sturdy. I can't quite feel the water temperature as I run it. By the time I flop onto our bed, I'm not entirely sure what I set it at. I almost get back up to check. Because I care. I care that Tavish is safe and happy. I care that the auroras live. I care that this world keeps spinning, and that I'm here in it.

But there is so much of that and so little of me.

I cringe as Tavish trips over the luggage I left in the walkway.

"Good fuck, Rubem!"

"Sorry," I call back. It takes so much effort just to be loud right now, but I prop up on my elbows anyway. "I can move them?"

"No, don't bother, it's . . . " He never finishes the sentence, meandering past me into the bathroom like he's lost in whatever hasn't been said.

We both are.

And I can't figure for the life of me what happened, nor where exactly it started. Is this new, or has it been creeping up for days, days of stress without a proper romantic moment nor even an improper sexual one? Or perhaps it's nothing but an odd mood, a lack of sleep and space and good drink, and it'll all work itself out with one decent night in a hotel that isn't chipping or leaning or warping or sinking. Perhaps I won't have to say anything about it at all.

I peel the two halves of my mind apart, and it feels more like unraveling this time.

'*Are we losing it?*'

Probably. But we'll manage. We have to.

I can sense the song of Venalt's aurora fluttering through me, soft yet solid. I close my eyes and let the vibration fill me up, slowly knitting me back into one piece. It still feels as though a hollow remains behind, an empty spot in my chest where something should be: Life, energy, fulfillment. Alcohol.

I could have picked up a bottle of wine somewhere on the way. It seems like too much effort to go out for it now. So I lie there, drifting, like a buoy lost to sea.

Distantly, I hear the bath drain, then the clinking of Lavender's food being poured, and a little later the bed shifts as Tavish lies down beside me, not quite close enough to touch. He smells of the hotel soap: something floral, almost bitterly so. It irritates me, and I take a minute to realize that I miss his old honey-tinged scent. He must have run out of that cleanser at our hostel stop yesterday, or perhaps in the days before and I've only just noticed.

I try not to overthink it, but the only other things to focus on here are the gentle sound of Tavish's breath and the way he feels so near, yet so far—he and this city's aurora both, with its song still pouring through me, soft and stoic.

"How do they treat their aurora?" I've seen it every way imaginable since Maraheem: the auroras worshiped in temples and kept as pets; revered, protected, traded, and objectified. We took the liberty of repossessing a few to better places, but most were happy enough—happy to return to a passive, continuous slumber as soon as their energy deficiency was met.

Unlike me.

It sends a chill down my spine every time, knowing how very alive I have been since crawling out of that mangrove, and not being entirely sure why. Perhaps it's the same reason I'm also a man who hid for his entire life, content with peaceful seclusion, until an aurora convinced him that his own peace was worth little if the rest of the world suffered. Perhaps there's no reason at all.

"Hm?" Tavish turns toward me, an arm propped under his head. His bathrobe falls open, revealing one of the little scars that run beneath his nipples.

It draws my gaze lower, my fingers itching to slip between the fabric and trace the curve of his stomach. The last time he moaned for me echoes through my mind so strongly that both halves of me shiver. But I don't know if I have the energy to follow through, and I certainly don't have the right to demand of him what I can't currently give back. Besides, I just asked him a question. "Do you know how Venalt treats their aurora? How do you imagine they'll react to this—to me?"

"I suppose I never rightly paid attention. They were a commodity to me; I hadn't questioned what people chose to do with them." His unfocused gaze drifts right over me, not seeing the way the rainbows twist through my eyes or gleam across their lids when I blink. "I don't ken these people as being overly compassionate toward it, though. It was on display far back when they first erected the city, and they had some kind of dispute about it upsetting the general populace, so they tucked it away, out of sight and mind."

"Who has it now, then?"

"Venalt's three government branches all share ceremonial control of it, but it's kept within the Citadel. As the director of their armed forces, I suppose they're the most equipped to protect it."

"Why are we not seeing *their* chancellor, then?"

"Because I've no connections to their chancellor. And the one in control when I was here last was a notorious ass, too stubborn to meet with my brother and too irritable to be worth the trouble. According to the Institute, that's a trend with them."

I snort. "And what does the Institute think of the Basilica chancellors?"

"Gaudy, vapid, and overly religious." Tavish's lips quirk, and he snuggles farther into the bed. Closer to me.

"And you don't ascribe to their biases at all?" I tease, leaning in.

"Not even a bit." He smiles fully then, lips pursed.

I lean in to kiss him, and at the same moment he sits up, leaving us bumping forehead to chin. He startles, catching himself in a barrage of "Sorry, sorry" that overlaps with my own horrified apologies.

"I should have—" I start, and at the same time he says, "No, that was my fault, I was in my own head. I thought you were getting up."

Those are two different explanations, I don't point out, because he cups the side of my face clumsily and presses his lips to mine, soft and warm. Then he's gone, staggering to his feet, robe clutched in one hand.

It was an honest mistake, something that's happened a dozen times before. But this time it makes my cheeks burn, and a lump forms in my throat.

"Trenches, it's getting late, isn't it?" he says. "We should go soon. To the Institute."

My chest seems to fall out of me, an airy cavity that makes me sicker with each breath. "Of course. That's why we're here."

"To save the aurora," Tavish agrees, turning away.

Its song vibrates softly through me. "To save the aurora."

A long shadow hangs off the Institute, encasing us in its thrall. Behind us stretches the rest of the foundation center, the Institute's patio of marble giving way to a central space of lawns lined in trees, park paths cutting neatly through them. A few blankets lie across the grass, families and couples relaxing in the late afternoon quiet, but it seems empty compared to the rest of the city, almost ghostly. A little like me.

At the foundation's direct center stands a circular structure, its pillars overwhelmed by vines that crawl across its cracked dome, shadows lurking within. It looks hopeless and forgotten compared to the Institute building that gleams bright and tall in front of us, with its massive domed roof and the sheer feat of its presence dominating the landscape, all arches and columns, angles and great windows, bridgeways between towers and rooms held out by curved supports. The whole place seems to protectively hug this third of the foundation center, ready to strangle at a moment's notice. A series of stars with six spindly points, three long and three short, adorn the giant archway over the building's main entrance.

I stall as we reach the threshold. Every time, this grows harder, not easier, because every time, the auroras I find are closer and closer to death. And every time, my heart breaks a little more.

Again, I tell myself. *Once more. And, if we have to, once more after that, and after that too.*

Tavish squeezes the arm I've been guiding him with, such a gentle, knowing pressure that it seems he must be trying to reassure me after our tension earlier. The thought fills all the cracks in my chest. I step with him into the building.

Dozens of halls lead from the massive, domed foyer, stairways wrapping up to the higher level's verandas, their great stone bulk seemingly unsupported. The sheer scale of it nearly eclipses the stone counter before us, where a man in a crisp grey suit and square spectacles surveys those leaving. The building seems to be mostly cleared out for the day, the last few stragglers making their way across the expansive space.

So empty like this, the size and arrogance of it reminds me eerily of my time in the upper city of Maraheem, its quiet quarters filled with wealth few had the opportunity to enjoy. But this place, despite its flagrant flaunting of power, feels well loved and far more relaxed, with the gentle wearing on its stones and the happy chatter of those leaving for the day.

That pleasantness doesn't seem to extend to the man behind the desk though.

His eyes narrow as we approach. "The Institute will be closed to visitors shortly. Do you have an appointment?"

Tavish plants his cane in front of him, as princely as ever but now a prince in a palace once more. The effect is dazzling. "We're here to see Chancellor Fiordelise Viscardi."

The man looks more bemused than impressed. "The chancellor does not take appointments after lunch. If you wish to schedule one, I can have her secretary contact you in the morning."

"We are old friends of the family, surely—"

"I'll be certain to mention it tomorrow."

A flush pricks in Tavish's cheeks. His little finger trembles against my arm. "If you would only phone her."

"I think she'd really like to see us," I add, pressing a hand to Tavish's arm and leaning against the counter. Hooking my cowl with my thumb, I slide it back a few inches, my teeth bared in something not entirely a smile. "See, as I hear it, your city is going to be overwhelmed by vicious, corelium-eating monsters as soon as your aurora dies. I'd prefer we avoid that. I, in particular, would prefer it by any means necessary."

The man swallows, his gaze darting from my teeth to my eyes. He lifts a handkerchief like he might clean his glasses before quickly putting it back down. "I'm sure she can fit you in," he squeaks a little as he says it, clearing his throat after. "She'll be working in her private apartments by now, but you can bring it up with her secondary—first story, final left hall, turn to the right, it's the last door."

"Phone ahead for us," Tavish says, sounding not like a question or a demand, but a fact.

The man quickly spins the numbers on his phone.

As we turn the corner, Tavish releases a soft, vibrant laugh, red still lingering on his cheeks. "You think you're quite the dashing rogue, don't you?"

I grin. "You enjoy it even more than I do."

"I enjoy it exactly the right amount, thank you." He smiles cheekily and nudges me in the side with the end of his cane.

I catch it, sliding my fingers over his with a soft growl. The way he looks now, his lips pursed and his chin raised toward mine, I could almost believe our kiss at the hotel hadn't been an awkward mess of apologies. Like this, I could slip my hands farther onto him and press him against the pristine marble wall of this empty Institute corridor. I could fit my mouth to his so perfectly we become one person and draw my legs between his until he groans, hot and dark, "Good fuck, Ruby" playing from his red mouth.

But we're here to save Venalt's aurora, to make all the wants we've been denying worth it in the end, and I can't distract from that now. So I just hold my fingers over his, guiding him down the hallway until we reach the door at the end: simple wood in a stone frame carved with geometric patterns.

The room inside looks like a smaller version of the central space, a domed skylight letting afternoon sun wash across the secretary's marble desk. The chair behind it sits empty, but a short woman—a kabalos—with dark skin and hands that never seem sure what to do with themselves, directs us a few doors down to the chancellor's private apartments.

The tanned, olive-skinned satyr who answers looks every bit the sturdy middle-aged ruler, probably only a few years older than I but inhabiting her midthirties like she belongs there. A simple circlet rests in her hair, the silver metal forming a cutout of a bursting star just above her brow, three long points and three shorter ones, all of them spindly and thin. Loose brown locks spill from under it, and her small horns curve back into spirals. Her white shirt is tucked perfectly into her pleated dark skirt, the matching suit jacket buttoned twice below her bosom.

The hard lines of her lips pull even tauter, making them nearly vanish altogether, and her stern nose tips up. As her gaze lands on Tavish, though, the expression falters. "Dair?" She whispers. Then she blinks and shakes her head. "No, you're his brother, aren't you? I'm sorry, I've forgotten your name."

"Tavish K . . . " He makes a sour face and finishes, "Findlay. It's a pleasure to see you as well, Fiordelise. You're a chancellor now, it seems?"

"And you're alive." Her brow lifts, the thick, unkempt lines making her expression all the more severe. "I'd heard the Findlays were all killed during that rebellion last month."

"Just most of us," Tavish says, each word sharp and crystalline.

Fiordelise sighs. "You've come here regarding our aurora, I hear? And you've brought with you—"

"Me." I smile and nudge my hood back with only slightly less dramatics than in the central chamber. "Rubem of No-Man's Land. Pleasure to meet you, Chancellor Fiordelise."

The chancellor's face pales. She nods. "Why don't you both follow me?"

Beyond the door, the atmosphere changes drastically, the corridor so averagely sized that it feels constricting compared to the large chambers we've just come through. Wallpaper of geometric patterns gives the space a homely feel, and music flows from farther in. Fiordelise directs us to a very different kind of office than her formal one, the large wooden desk at its center strewn with diagrams, shelves filling two sides, and a grand clock ticking away in one corner. A set of large windows overlooks a small channel where a gondola floats idly.

In the next room, I spot an older child or perhaps a very young teenager playing a pianoforte, her wavy brown hair pulled up in a high ponytail beneath her tiny horns. Her fingers drift a little clumsily across the keys, missing a note here and there. Fiordelise closes the door with a soft click. The girl's song fades into the background like the aurora's, the two overlapping but not interfering.

Fiordelise takes a seat behind the desk, Tavish across from her. I grab a chair from the side of the room and flip it around to sit backward on it, leaning just enough to tap my nails on the desk's wood.

"Tavish, I would like to hear of what happened in Maraheem." The chancellor's voice shifts, her whole composure slipping into something soft, almost fearful. "Is your family truly . . . Is Alasdair . . .?"

Tavish's expression remains neutral, but his hand tightens on my shoulder. "I am the last Findlay."

"I'm sorry." It doesn't sound like a mere pleasantry from a decade-old friend, but a genuine consolation borne of shared sadness. "If you don't mind, how did he die?"

"They slit his throat." Tavish swallows. "I don't think he suffered."

"I did always tell him if he kept acting as though the world was his, someone would try to wrestle it away eventually." A sad laugh leaves her, like the petals of a flower falling. "Well, it's too late to change what's been done. He always was who he was and—bless that man. Bless his proud soul." She lifts her gaze to the ceiling and taps across her chest three times. When she looks back at us, she appears calmer. At peace.

The expression seems to slip into Tavish, peeling away his tension. He smiles. It makes my heart swell to see and makes it bleed that I have to turn the conversation away.

"Chancellor, you have an aurora here in the city?" I ask, even though it's clearly not a question.

"Yes." Her eyes narrow, a flicker of something unidentifiable but dark sparking through them. "And you will leave it be." She bares her teeth, leaning forward on her elbows. Paper crinkles under them. Even with the full three feet of desk between us, her presence seems to loom over me, matching my intimidation claw for claw. "I know plenty of you, Rubem of No-Man's Land. You stole an aurora in Roekia and two more in Geviso. Another disintegrated while you were with it in Zarencia, and Maraheem's all vanished the night before you left—even those rebels seemed not to expect it. I don't know what you're doing to them, but you can leave our aurora and our city alone."

The indignation that sears through me splits me in two before molding me perfectly back together as both halves of me hiss, "I have done nothing the auroras didn't ask of me." I press my palms to the wood, trying not to shake under the memory of their deaths. It vibrates in me, through me, out of me, until it feels like a song, the tune mixing with Venalt's aurora's into something dangerous and grieving.

Venalt's aurora reverberates, sending me echoes of comfort in return.

I breathe, letting them in. There will always be someone new who doesn't understand me, who won't give me a chance to prove myself; aurora or human, it makes no difference. I have to put that aside and focus on what I've come for. "I'm not here to take your aurora, unless that's what it wants. I'm here to stop it from dying."

Fiordelise's harsh expression pulses, her ears turning red, but she pulls back ever so slightly. "We have that covered already, thank you. Weeks ago one of our trade partners brought news of how returning the ignits to a weakened aurora will heal it. We've conducted the necessary preparations."

"Oh?" Tavish's fingers drift, finding my shoulder after a moment and settling there. "If that's true, then we're glad to hear it." The careful placement of his *if* reveals almost as much as the hope that slips into his voice.

Hope I wish so ferociously that I didn't have to crush. But one stretch of my threads toward the source of the city's aurora tells me that while alive it might be, it's not healthy. In a city full of ignits that it has spent its life producing, whatever preparations these people have made are not enough. "If you're already taking action, then why is your aurora still so sickly? I know you have ignits in your elevators, your motorboats—your electricity is fueled by them, I wager, and in a city strong enough to try investing in ignation twelve or so years ago, that's just the start. You could have your aurora thriving again already. So what's stopping you?"

It's only half a question, because I've only seen one answer so far, twisted into different shapes and hidden within sparkling exteriors, but still always the same motive at the root of it all: greed. It comes in both the arrogant, jealous kind that makes the rich grab for more, and the fearful, stubborn kind that causes otherwise kind individuals to turn a blind eye in order to keep what little they have, but always, always it is still just greed. Just the value of possessions and of power raised above that of life.

I want so badly for Fiordelise to prove me wrong.

But all she offers is the tightening of her lips, a stony wall sliding over her features. "We have the situation handled."

"Handled," I repeat. My fingers tingle and twitch, and I snatch a hippocamp-shaped paperweight out of a line of them beside Fiordelise's desk phone, tossing it into the air with my left hand and catching it again as it falls. The motion still leaves my right hand fidgety, the stubs of my smallest fingers bouncing against the wood.

"Your people believe their city will sink soon." Tavish leans against the desk, his manner almost conspiratorial and his phrasing casual.

"Those who do have been listening to the Basilica for too long." Fiordelise's nostrils flare, and her gaze darts out the windows. "As I've said, we know what needs to be done. You"—she looks at me—"may let Venalt take care of itself."

I toss the figurine again, giving it a spin as it flies. "You say you have your aurora's situation—should I say, death—handled, but tell me, what exactly are you at the Institute doing?"

"We are doing what's necessary to keep our city functional."

"That's not an answer."

"You are not my government—you are not even a resident of this city—you are owed no answers."

"I'm an aurora. I can *feel* yours hurting. *Dying.* And it sings for the protection of this city even while you're letting it suffer. I don't care who your government is or how mighty your city thinks itself, that is still my business." In my aggressive toss and throw, my hands slide back into a familiar old pattern, launching the paper weight from one to the other. My finger stubs flail, the empty knuckles beside them stinging in a phantom pain as the figurine catches on my partial thumb and tumbles across the desk.

Chancellor Fiordelise picks it up with such bridled emotion that she trembles. She runs her finger over the edge of the hippocamp's tail, where a chip is missing. "I think you have done enough damage here as it is."

I feel the dismissal in her voice, in Tavish's gentle tug as he whispers, "We'll try the Citadel next."

But I nudge him off, pressing a fist to Fiordelise's desk hard enough to rattle it. "You may sentence your aurora to suffer while you enjoy your ignits, but the ignits won't last either. They will be dying soon too."

"I'm not the one who doesn't understand that!" Fire flares in her cheeks. She rises so suddenly that her chair scoots out from under her, slamming into the encroaching shelves. "I will see you both out now."

A bang echoes through the room half a second later, turning her final word in on itself as red blooms from a tiny hole in her stomach. She stumbles back, slumping into her chair with a stunned inhale. Her gaze drops to the quickly spreading blood.

She mutters, "I—I think I've been shot."

And her eyes roll back.

CHAPTER THREE

the meaning of a bullet

FIORDELISE'S ARMS GO LIMP as her head lolls, her chest still rising and falling in sharp gasps. The red seeping from her stomach nearly covers the small bullet-sized ignit lodged there. Its fierce pink glow tinges the blood with a fuchsia shine that seems too bright and festive for murder. Someone must have shot it through one of her office's great windows.

Unlike an ordinary bullet, its work isn't finished yet.

I've never seen this color used to kill before—never seen it at all, outside a few rare glimpses—but I wouldn't wish the unmaking that's coming for her on my worst enemy. The chair beneath me clatters, and somehow I'm on my feet, the world spinning.

Tavish grips his cane so tight that it trips him up as he tries to pull his sword blade free of its sheath, turning in a circle like he might run through the shooter by chance. My mind leaps to the knife tucked into his belt. Two weapons, in case the first can't protect him. Three weapons, if you count me.

I grab his arm, almost getting a sword to the face for my effort. "The shot came from outside!"

He doesn't quite loosen his hold on the cane-sword. "Is she dead?"

"Not yet." Though, every moment we stand here, the ignit continues to churn out its energy. Soon it will start killing her with more grotesque, clinical certainty than the bleeding. Unless we do something.

Tavish echoes my thought. "Help!" he shouts, his crystal voice resounding hollowly for once, not cutting through walls and wills as it should but bouncing blindly around the room. "Someone—someone should call—"

I scramble for the desk phone, only to realize I have no idea what to dial. "Call who?"

"I don't know, but we have to help her!" Tavish's face is so white it seems he's the one bleeding out and not the woman in the chair across from us. Already the scarlet that oozes from her stomach has faded, the liquid going clear around yellow chunks and red goop, the individual parts of the blood solidifying together. The wound itself seems to grow, little by little, the muscle at its edges peeling away to strips of protein as the fat concentrates to a buttery mass, her body slowly unmaking itself into its composite parts under the pink ignit's energy.

It's a rare ignit, one used in civilized places to separate out pollutants or salt for water purification, or in less civilized ones as a tool of torture, unmaking hands and feet with more ease than any blade. But never have I seen it kill before. The horror builds in my chest like a painful tearing, as though I'm the one being deconstructed and not Fiordelise.

An ignit deactivator. If we can find an ignit deactivator—

I turn around the room, like one might just appear for me.

A thud sounds from behind the desk. "A little assistance, please?"

Tavish is at her side, pushing his stripped coat to her stomach, the composite parts of her blood smeared across his hands. His hands. Pressed to her stomach. To the ignit.

A whole new kind of terror launches through me, catching in my chest before spilling its way to my feet. It springs me forward. I crash into Tavish, shoving him away from Fiordelise.

He shrieks and his whole body shakes. His hand dives into his jacket. Before I can quite register what he's done, he slashes at me with his knife. I lean forward on instinct, reaching for him. The blade cuts through my shirt fabric and slides into flesh, the pain spearing between the ache of my heart and the burning of my lungs.

"That's my chest," I wheeze.

He freezes. "Oh, good fuck. I'm sorry."

I wrap my fingers over his as I nudge them off the hilt. "So you *were* planning to stab me all along, I see?" The joke hides my pain. From the first day we've been together, he could recognize me by my silence, and now he's stabbed me for it. That hurts more than the blade itself.

Tavish lets the knife go.

I pull it from my chest, the sharp agony fading as I knit my aurora flesh over the opening. It leaves a scar of black and rainbow marring my fishnet crisscrosses and a fresh dose of fatigue for both my body and my mind—far more than would have plagued me had I healed a wound like this six weeks ago.

"I'm sorry," Tavish whispers again.

Fiordelise continues to be unmade beside us, fat and liquid still sloughing off the now fist-sized hole in her stomach.

The door to the piano room flies open.

Fiordelise's daughter trembles behind it, her baggy pants tucked into stockings at the knees and her suspenders lopsided over her puffy sleeves. With both hands she clutches the pot of a thorny plant. She looks between the knife I hold and her clearly injured mother. Lifting the plant, she screams a battle cry that's equal parts terrified and terrifying, and swings her makeshift weapon at me.

I duck and catch her by the wrists, kick the pot from her grasp. It crashes to the floor. She screams again, struggling fruitlessly.

I bundle her arms against her sides and toss her at Tavish. "Don't stab this one, just hold on to her."

"Rubem!" he protests, looking horrified. But he manages to grab her, finding her arms and wrapping his own around them. They're near in height, but she's no match for the sheer mass of his body, even fumbling as he is.

I turn back to Fiordelise. There's no time for a deactivator now. The pink ignit continues to conduct its careful separation. It wallows in a hole the size of my fist, lumpy yellowed fat circling one side and ribbons of meaty tissue on the other. Crystals of compounds I can't name form a sparkling line between them. Water drains from the edges.

My stomach heaves. I swallow the sensation down and thrust my hand into the muck. The pure fat slides against my fingers. I gag, but I close my eyes and press my fingertips to the small ignit, attempting to draw its energy into myself. Nothing changes.

Fiordelise seizes. Her head tips back and her body jerks, the pink ignit still bright and active inside her.

Panic clamps down on me. The last time I did this, it happened as a reflex, my demand for its energy greater than my natural instinct to create the ignits rather than destroy them. I try to remember the process, the feeling—that need for the power to fight harder, to be more, to be enough to convince the human in me to save us all. Now I'm here. Not saving, but failing. Still not strong enough.

I need to be stronger.

The ignit disintegrates.

I feel its power pulse into me, a gentle thrum that fills me like a cup of the best merlot, turning the world bright and settling the anxiety in my nerves. The remnants of pain from the stab that I sealed over in my chest fade away. My other-dimensional threads reach, so close to being able to connect with the Venalt aurora that I can nearly melt right into its thoughts, its emotions coursing through me with curiosity and confusion and desperation as it reaches for the fresh energy inside me, not quite managing to take it.

Fiordelise goes still. I lean just a bit closer despite the stench of her wound, but with each passing heartbeat, my hope wanes, then crashes. Her chest doesn't rise again.

"Fuck." I yank my hand out of her corpse. The energy from the ignit still pounds inside me.

Fiordelise's daughter lets out a sob. She has one arm half-free of Tavish, raising her shoe like a weapon. Tavish must sense the change because he slowly releases her.

She drops the shoe, her chest heaving as her hands bundle into fists. "Mom?" she whispers, so hoarse it's barely a sound. "Mom . . ."

As though reality takes her word as truth, it's not Fiordelise's body I see anymore, but my own mother, lying broken in a pool of blood as the blossoms from the tree above her scatter down in the breeze. The grief burns in a way that's no longer fresh—has not been fresh in nearly three decades—but feels upturned somehow, like an old scab ripped off a half-healed wound to reveal the still-broken flesh beneath.

I force myself to bundle it back up. This is not my mother, just a woman bent on denying her aurora's salvation. A woman who made Tavish smile and raised a daughter eager to fight for her. That's all I know her as—a mere impression of a person whom I had meant to get what I needed from and then forget about. Now the basic components of her organs cling to my hands as I sign her a vacant, stuttered death proclamation.

Someone shot her. Someone planned this.

Fuck.

The hall-side door flies open, and the brown-skinned kabalos who brought us to Chancellor Fiordelise's office enters—Iseppa, I think her name was. Iseppa's short hair comes free from behind her pointed ears as she jerks to a stop. Her brightly painted lips part in a strangled breath, and her already wide, darkly lashed, catlike eyes seem to grow farther. She screams, shrill and high, waggling her manicured nails once before turning and charging back down the hall.

I look from the gore on my hands to the corpse before me, then to Tavish's knife still at my side.

"This could be worse," I mutter, a taunt to a universe whose only graceful caresses have always come before a slap, and I half expect fresh bullets to begin raining on us. But nothing stirs, just the rough draw of our breaths in the small, cluttered space.

"She's dead?" Tavish whispers.

I feel like I've been here before, and like I'm somewhere else entirely. Too many bodies, too many times Tavish has had to utter that same question. At least this time it's not his family lying still and limp—just the last person in the world who might have said something good of them, the last person to see them the way he did. He was given a single soft moment to mourn with someone who understands, and then this. A caress, then a slap.

His face crumples in time with my thoughts.

"Tavish?" I whisper.

Fiordelise's daughter still stares at her mother's body, sobs breaking free of her chest like parasites.

The trembles start in Tavish's fingers, working through his arms and into his shoulders. Each breath he drags in seems shallower than the last. He pulls his knees toward his torso, brow pinching as he presses his forehead to them. His lips quaver, but nothing comes out.

"Tavish." I drop beside him, rubbing my slick hand clean, and pull him into my arms. The wood on one side and Fiordelise's body on the other suddenly seem to bend toward us, tugging at my lungs with greedy fingers.

I scoop Tavish up, half carrying, half pulling him around to the far side of the desk, where the stink of Fiordelise's death isn't as strong. Something should be done for her daughter, but I am likely the last person she'll let help her. The moment I set Tavish down, he pulls at me, one fist curling around my shirt and the other clutching my cape like a blanket. His whole body shakes in a way that brings back flashes of Fiordelise's seizure. Flashes of my mother. Of Tavish, bloody beneath Lilias's boot.

The pain in my chest feels unbearable.

"I have you," I whisper, rubbing gently up and down Tavish's arm, pressing my lips to his hair and rocking him slowly. "I'm here." And I know, so thoroughly and fully, that I want to keep being here, with him, for him. I want to be better at this, despite the stress and the fatigue. "I'm here."

His only response is to stay.

As we sit there, backs to the wall, Fiordelise's daughter picks up her shoe. She sniffle hiccups, her shoulders jumping with each sharp inhale, and the shoe falls again. Her face pinches as though she's trying to force back her sobs, her freckles bunching into each other. Slowly, she lowers herself to the ground, pulling the boot into her lap instead. Her fingers tug at the thin laces as though she's not really seeing them.

I have to do something for her. Find someone who can comfort her, cover her mother's corpse with a sheet, turn back time so that I think to disintegrate the ignit the moment it enters Fiordelise's body.

But I still have Tavish in my arms. He flinches as the door to the room bangs into the shelf behind it, two new people barging through. They both wear the dusky-blue uniforms of the guards at the harbor with a pin of a triangle beside the small, colored badges on their jackets.

They draw their batons, pointing them at Tavish and me, but as their gaze tracks over me—the rainbows shining in my eyes and the points of my canines—they balk. One of them looks almost excited while the other tightens, his knuckles turning white around his weapon. In any other circumstance, both reactions would've benefited me; people who love you or fear you are less likely to attack. But being the only witnesses to a chancellor's death makes me rather wish they'd ignore us entirely.

And she *is* dead. After everything I witnessed in Maraheem, that shouldn't strike me so hard, but my mind keeps circling back to it, like I'm figuring it out all over again.

"Are these the ones, Mrs. Collari?" the first guard asks—a satyr with small horns, far more upright than Fiordelise's, the bow of their legs obvious even beneath their pants.

Iseppa Collari peeks around them before quickly nodding. "That's them! They were hovering over her—her—oh, gods—" Her gaze bounces over Fiordelise's body, arms lifting. She gives her hands another air shake, like she's trying to dislodge her emotions out her fingernails with a final soft, wailing "Oh."

The satyr pats her shoulder, and the other officer steps toward Tavish and me. "We're taking you in on suspect of involvement in the death of Chancellor—"

I can't believe this, can't believe it so much that they get through the first two lines of their speech before I manage to cut in, "We didn't kill her!" The words fit a familiar pattern on my tongue, but the statement blurs into the background noise, not a demanding slice like Tavish's but the shocked and scattered anger of a tired fool. "We tried to *save* her."

We tried, certainly. The pink ignit's energy still thrums through me, the release of it too late, too fumbled. Her death was not my fault, but perhaps I was the only person who could have saved her. The knowledge of that roars in my skull alongside the ignit's power, a furious gale that feels like a recoiled whip.

"You can tell it all to the investigators." The satyr nods to their second, who pulls out a pair of cuffs so similar to the ones the guards use in Maraheem that my vision wavers for a moment. "And your companion, too."

My companion.

I feel Tavish's hand on my leg the same moment I glance back at him. He shakes his head, or perhaps his head just shakes, a wisp of his voice coming out. It sounds like my name, desperate and pleading.

"Can't you see he's having a panic attack," I growl, placing myself purposefully between Tavish and the officers.

They stall, and the fear of one seems to spread to the other. The satyr extends a shaky palm toward me. "Now, if you both come quietly—"

I move before they can finish, uncoiling on instinct, hot and fast. Sweeping their batons to the side, I rip the cuffs from the officer's hand. "What's happening now is that you are not touching him until he consents to it, or I will snap every limb you place on him."

The officers stagger backward.

I step after them, and step again, and each time I twist the handcuffs, one edge braced between my half thumb and palm, my fingers through the metal loops. The ignit's energy floods through me, pulsing along my aurora-threaded muscles. It blazes. The metal cuffs snap, then snap again. I toss the pieces at the officer's chests. They flinch from each hit.

Their terror ripples through them, tense and defensive, but instead of breaking them down, it pulls them taut.

"Fuck," the satyr whispers.

The other draws a pistol.

With the ignit energy flowing through me, I could eat the first bullet easily, perhaps even the second and the third, but I don't want to risk any after that. I still have an aurora to save here, in this stubborn city who just murdered one of their chancellors. And Tavish, panicking. Gods, Tavish. My fist tightens.

The officer with the gun hisses, "Don't move!"

"Stop that!" Fiordelise's daughter stands, her shout sharp enough to cut despite the sob in it, her arms over her head like her own voice is too loud. She sniffles, her eyes puffy, but she draws down her arms, and her chin lifts. "They couldn't have killed my mother. There's a hole in the glass. It—it broke inward." Her shoulders tremble in a little inhale, and she points to the window, at a tiny, crack-lined gap barely visible in the evening light. "Whoever shot my—they shot from outside, and these people were both always in here."

The way she stares down at us is eerily familiar, her lips pulled into a determined line and loose strands of her wavy hair dancing along the sides of her lightly freckled face. The knowledge prickles down the back of my spine with a discomfort that makes me shut the thought off before I can carry it to its conclusion. It's a look, that's all. A look and a voice, and it collapses a little as the girl's lower lip wobbles. She runs the back of her hand aggressively under her eye.

"So, they couldn't have killed her," she says, softer now. "You can stop fighting."

"Smart girl, Matthia," comes a masculine voice from the doorway, wetter and gruffer than the land species that speak the common tongue. The nereid rolls his modified wheelchair into the room, his pair of tentacle-like legs coiled beneath him on a soaked sponge. By the water that still glistens on his dusky, silvered skin, he must have recently surfaced from the underside of the city. The short flares of orange-tipped fin on his head drip as he pushes them out of his face. He wears nothing but an embroidered sash, his badge far larger and fancier than the officers. "She's almost right, too. Just because they couldn't have fired the shot, doesn't mean they couldn't have killed her in the end, but it certainly makes it improbable." He gives me a quick sizing up, his gaze tightening; then he turns to the officers. "By the Three, Camillus, put that damn gun back before someone sensible reports you."

The officer with the gun stammers, "But he—he—"

"Made you break regulation? That's it? Are you a fucking teenager, blaming your bad calls on everyone else, huh?" The nereid says it so flatly that his lack of emotion becomes one all on its own, his insult followed by something that definitely includes the words *these gods-damned kids* under his breath.

Flushing, the officer slips the weapon away. "Sorry, Commander."

The nereid grunts. He squints at the kabalos, wrinkles appearing around the edges of his icy-blue eyes. "Iseppa."

Her expression clouds. "Commander Favaro."

"Zuane will do." The nereid gives Iseppa a smile as stiff as a board. "Escort Matthia out of here. She's seen enough, I should think."

Matthia protests, but her voice shudders, and when Iseppa scurries across the room to collect her, she follows numbly, one shoe still clutched in her hand. She looks back only once. Zuane waits until she's gone before he wheels himself to Fiordelise's body, the officers in tow.

With the threat evaporated, the leftover threads of ignit energy seem to knit into a net to catch me from collapsing, leaving me floating in a haze of shock. I refuse to let my gaze catch too long on Fiordelise's body as I twist toward Tavish. He leans against the shelves, his head tipped back and his breathing more even. With each inhale, he draws his fingers tight, releasing them on the exhale.

I return to him on silent feet, humming softly to let him know I'm here. That I'm me. Just in case that's what he needs to identify me now.

He doesn't flinch when I run my fingers through his hair, brushing his curls out of the way. A heavy sigh escapes him. It only rattles a little.

"Your anxiety is coming back, isn't it?" One of us has to say it, it might as well be me.

He turns his head away. His lips part, then press back together. A bead of liquid appears along his bottom lids, turning into pools. One tear overflows, but he doesn't brush at it, just stares endlessly onward, his expression impenetrable, unreadable even to me.

Something wells inside me, a bright, hungry thing, so full it could burst. I mean to say that I'm sorry, that this is my fault, that I should have done something differently—saved the auroras faster or let him make a home somewhere while I traveled—but wedged between his utter vulnerability and my utter inability, the truth comes out instead, words that have been creeping up on me, but neither of us have said out loud yet. "I love you."

They sound too small, too brisk to have so much meaning, to be a thing that devastates my chest and scares me half to death. I love Tavish. Of course I love him.

And now I've said it.

He freezes, as soundless as me for a moment, then another. His mouth opens, and closes, and the next inhale he draws is shallower again, hitched. Panicked.

Oh gods.

I feel as though I've done something brutally, violently wrong, torn my own heart from my chest, and now there's no way to put it back in again, the organ growing stiller and colder with each second that Tavish clutches one knee, wearing an expression like I've shot him. And still part of me hopes for his face to slowly alight and his reply to come in a breathless affection, because this was not, even after the day we've had, at all how I would have expected he'd respond.

Zuane interrupts us.

"You say you were here when the attack happened?" His flat voice plows over my terror. He finagles his chair away from the desk, leaving the officers to finish jotting notes while one of them talks quietly over their radio.

I have to swallow twice to work through the ache in my chest, and even then, my reply comes out stiff and hoarse.

"Yes. A pink ignit, small as a bullet. The initial wound didn't look too bad, but you can see what it became."

Zuane's head bobs, and his nose wrinkles. "Nasty thing." He glances over the scene one more time, his jaw pulsing. He swallows. His voice takes on an edge. "They sure knew what kind of statement they were making."

"What kind of statement was that?" Tavish asks. He sounds almost like himself. With a hand on the shelves and the other on his cane, he pulls to his feet, only wobbling once.

"That the Institute needs to give up their ignits," I answer, trying not to look at Tavish as I say it, and not to look at the body either. Now that Tavish's anxiety has passed, the visceral nature of the death seems to hit me all over again: the way the slick of Fiordelise's unmade gut clung to my hand and her daughter's sobs wracked me as if born of my own lungs. "There are a few reasons they might have picked an ignit in place of an ordinary bullet. They might have wanted to cause Fiordelise the most pain possible as she died, but she passed out at the mere sight of her own blood, so she hardly felt anything, and if they'd been hoping the gore of her death would shake people up, then they wouldn't have killed her in such a private space. Why else shoot your enemy with the very thing she's hoarding except to make a point on just that?"

"Well done." Though Zuane says it just as flatly as everything else, I swear his lips twitch at the end. "That would be my conclusion, yes." His gaze darts back to me. "Since you two were the only ones who saw her die, we'll be needing statements at the Citadel."

I smile, a slight threat to the motion. "And if we'd like to return to our hotel instead?"

To Zuane's credit, he has the good sense to be afraid, yet wears that fear with a strength and maturity his subordinates clearly lack. He tips his head, lifting his hands in a placating gesture. "Think of them as eminently obligatory statements. We'd much prefer your cooperation here; I believe enough of our handcuffs have been martyred for one day." His gaze sharpens. "And I did say you were *probably* innocent in the chancellor's death. The more you work against our finding the culprit, the more—well, you know how that saying goes."

"Unfortunately we do," Tavish cuts in. His thumb strangles the top of his cane, but his expression remains impassive, his smile so shallow it hurts to look at.

"Tavish," I say, pleading, even if I'm not quite sure what I'm pleading for. To talk with him, I suppose. To climb into his chest and see why his heart is beating out of time with mine.

But he ignores me, body and soul, his attention fixed on Zuane. "Chancellor Fiordelise was a friend of the family. We are happy to help in any way we can."

"Good." Zuane grunts. His gaze lingers on me. Then he spins one wheel, managing to turn his chair nearly all the way around in the small space. It bumps a set of folders. One of his tentacle-like legs shoots out, propping itself against the shelves to tip the wheelchair enough that it slips past the block and out the door.

We follow him, Tavish one step ahead of me. His cane brushes back and forth before him. My spontaneous confession still bounces around my head, echoing between my ears like a haunting breeze. I love him. Of course I love him. I've loved him for days or weeks, for my whole life, perhaps. From birth, there was a space in my chest carved in just the exact shape of him, a dark hollow filled perfectly by his light, a nerve that only connects when he cradles the severed ends.

But maybe he was not built to hold me in the same way, and I simply missed all the signs. As I cross the room after him, I nudge the broken handcuffs with the toe of my boot. It feels like I've set us on a course now, the fork in the path chosen, for better or for worse.

CHAPTER FOUR

an interrogation of two

COMPARED TO THE ELEGANT architecture of the Institute building, the Citadel is solid and discreet, as though it gains power simply by existing. A short wall surrounds its base, and its tall, slim windows barely let in the last of the evening light. No massive foyer greets us, just a long corridor, lights pointing upward from ridges built into its tight, high walls, everything made from simple sheets of stone. The officer at the end nods to Zuane.

Footsteps and wheels echo as we turn each corner of the labyrinthine space single file, the hallways barely wide enough for the occasional approaching staff member to fit by without the awkward brush of shoulders. Where the Institute felt pretentiously old, this reminds me of something primordial, like each stride carries us further into the bowels of a great beast which has dwelled here since the beginning of time and will remain until the world crumbles. I try to keep track of our turns, building myself a mental map, but slowly the corners and doorways start to overlap in my mind.

I move closer to Tavish.

Zuane finally pulls back a metal gate of interlocking metal diamonds that rattle like wind chimes as he shoves it to the side and directs us into a work space of stiff wooden desks, city maps and protocols hanging on the walls. A circular brazier casts the chamber in disjointed light, leaving the doorways and halls that branch off from it dim and shifting. Two uniformed Citadel members lift a hand from where they work, but most of the desks appear empty at this point in the evening.

We move through a few more halls, shorter and less intimidating, and Zuane opens a door to a small, enclosed room with a table in the middle. At least its benches look padded. He motions me inside.

"You can wait here."

Tavish tries to step in, too, but Zuane holds him back. "Just your companion, for now."

The edge of Tavish's cheek twitches. He smiles, so poised that it seems he planned this. "Certainly. You'll want to know if our stories match, after all."

They leave me there.

The door clicks behind them. There's no lock on this side, no place where a key might fit, but when I try the handle, it doesn't budge. My fingers clench around it, fear turning them into a vise. Instinct tells me to break the lock—despite the way my aurora strength has been declining over the weeks, I could manage it easily using the last of the pink ignit's power—but I breathe through the impulse. If there's any chance that the Citadel will work with me to save their aurora, I should probably not go destroying their holding cells. Besides, this could all be perfectly normal.

Perfectly normal for a situation where one of the three heads of a sovereign city is murdered in front of you.

I lean against the door, pressing my head into my hands. In the middle of the commotion, the emotional exhaustion of falling apart didn't fully hit. It slams down now, raking through me in waves that seem to catch on the inside of my ribs and the back of my skull and twist my organs into nauseated knots. Cushions be damned, I slip to the floor. I need a drink.

Want a drink, I remind myself. This is a want now, and I've been careful to maintain it as such, to never let so much of the poison build inside me that its presence becomes my norm. But that want still bulges like a tumor, begging to be made use of. Because, while I want a drink, what I *need* is something that will make me no longer feel as though I'm spiraling my way into the ground, grave dirt piled up above me.

I came here to save Venalt's aurora, and now I'm in the city's interrogation room, waiting to be questioned about a murder. Tavish could still turn this entire situation to our advantage—might be doing that even as I sit here moaning on the floor. But even his beautiful words can't work through all problems, and this day has thrown him so thoroughly that he must be just as exhausted as I am. Just as torn up.

I love you.

It could have all just been too much for the moment, but his lack of response feels more and more like a returned slap than a shocked coincidence. I try not to regret it. No matter how much it might hurt right now, I can never regret loving him.

The door whacks against my back, jolting my head forward as someone tries to open it with a curse. I grunt and fumble to stand. The back of my skull aches. And the center of my chest, though I presume one of those things has no physical cause.

"Depths beneath," Zuane mutters, wheeling himself into the room. As he stops beside the table, his boneless legs uncurl to pull himself onto the bench. "Well, sit."

I perch across from him.

"Your companion says your name is Rubem . . . Rubem Findlay?"

I almost choke on my reply. "No." Rubem *Findlay*.

I love you.

They should fit together, those two concepts. I love you, therefore we become a little more of each other. But it doesn't feel like I can even begin to claim that right now. "No," I repeat. "Just Rubem. Rubem of No-Man's Land." It's who I am, more than ever before—not Rubem Veneno from the rivers, or the Rubem named by his Murk-born mother, but a wanderer, an outcast. I am the barred and battered territory in the middle of a war zone, claimed by none but ravaged by all.

"Right, then, Rubem." He laces his fingers together. "What were you meeting with Chancellor Fiordelise about?"

"Tavish was an old acquaintance of hers, and I wanted to know why your city's aurora is still dying. We were having a civilized discussion about that when she was shot."

Zuane doesn't write my statement down anywhere.

I narrow my eyes. "Do you have lawyers here? Am I supposed to get one of those?"

"Venalt has a legal system, yes. We could certainly find you a lawyer, though it would take at least until the morning. But, let's be frank here: your companion is from one of those big families they murdered in Maraheem a few months back, and you—you're that aurora everyone loves to hate?" He leans back just a hair, as though sizing me up. "I didn't think you were real; no one ever seems to have you in proper pictures, do they? It's not the first time the sudden loss of an aurora or the fall of a city has been blamed on something too fantastical to be true. It's not the first time, either, that a series of absurd events have all been attributed to the same outrageous cause because there was someone at each point along the way who took advantage of it to bury their own truth."

Being a fable, I can appreciate, especially if I get to vanish back into my obscurity at the end. But being an excuse? Not so much. "And what do you think now?"

"Now, I think that if I make a call to the governments of Zarencia or Fis or Roekia, they'd be happy to send me new handcuffs."

I try not to let him see the truth of it on my face. Tavish could have used his political knowledge and charismatic instinct to turn the question on its head, taken the tip of it for his own quiver. The best I can do is cross my arms and bare my teeth, not the threat Tavish would have created, but an invitation. "Would you like to try it?"

Zuane makes a sound of gruff contemplation. "You *are* the aurora, yes?"

"In part."

"Then you'll be dying here soon, too, if things keep progressing as they are."

"Dying sounds so casual, doesn't it?" I spread my fingers on the table, just near enough to Zuane's folded hands that I see him flinch. "We aren't dying, strictly speaking. We're being killed—not quite the way someone killed Chancellor Fiordelise earlier, but in the case of your aurora, just as purposefully."

Zuane doesn't argue. He slowly curls his hands closer to himself, splaying them down to mimic mine.

I smile. "You're looking a little dry around the gills, Commander Favaro."

"Zuane is fine, really."

"Commander Zuane."

He draws his hands back farther, palms resting against the edge of the table. "You said there was a pink ignit, which is indeed the only thing that we know of that might produce a wound like Fiordelise's, but I saw no ignit on the body. Did you consume it?"

"If you know to ask that, then you must have at least given your aurora *something*."

"Did you consume the ignit?"

"It's not there anymore, is it?" I tap my nails—the remaining ones—against the metal. "I think I'd like that lawyer now. Or, better yet, you have that fancy pin and title, you must work with the chancellor of the Citadel, right? Tell them I want a chat. If they come talk to me, I'll answer whatever you want."

"I'm trying to work with you here."

"Then work with me."

Zuane holds my gaze. His thumbs bounce once; then he shoves off the bench, back to his wheelchair. The wet sponge squelches beneath him. "I'll see what I can do."

"Bring me Tavish and a drink while you're at it?"

His gaze catches on my incisors as he pulls the door close behind him. At the click of the latch, all my energy and aggression founders, the lack of an immediate threat leaving me even more dead inside than before Zuane came. I have fucked this up. I'm not sure how yet, but the positively ripe knowledge of it rots like a decaying thing inside me.

This small, isolated room seems suddenly too exposed. I slump off my seat, pulling myself into the shadows beneath the table. My long legs barely fit, and I prop them on the far bench. I pull up my hood before leaning my head back. The position gets miserable as I linger there, a piece of metal poking the back of my skull and the floor pressing against the bones in my ass. But moving anywhere else feels impossible.

I close my eyes. My thoughts drift anxiously back to Tavish—they had never left, not truly—but as I rest, I focus more and more on the gentle vibration of the aurora's song cradling around me. It sinks in, soft and alive and alight. I feel nearer to it here, so close I can pinpoint its physical direction, beneath me and a little to my left: right below the building.

It dozes, the sensation of its dreams woven beneath its song. That gives me pause. I've felt auroras slumber before—it's their natural state, the one they all try to return to once they have the energy to fully relax. But this feels different. Venalt's dying aurora drifts turbulently through a state of consciousness that's reminiscent of the way I sleep now that half of me is human.

I reach for the aurora, brushing the edge of its threads hesitantly.

Reminiscent, yes, but not the same. Where my rest involves the dual parts of me creating a space of unconsciousness, and the other sleeping aurora I've come into contact with were single, lonely minds drifting within themselves, this one feels different. A mix of both and yet also neither; not two sapient individuals intertwined but also not a single consciousness. Through the veil of its slumber, I sense its self in a way I haven't with others—gentle and tired, but vastly protective and hurting in a way I can only begin to comprehend, my deep and painful feelings for Tavish only a soft echo of the fire inside it. That knowledge feels intrusive.

I pull back, leaving it to dream. No point in waking it when there's nothing I can do for it yet.

I unspool into my halves, letting the touch of the human around me become a near physical thing I can bask in. He holds me, and I him, his presence in my mind nuzzling. I lean against him, reminding us both that we are not alone. Together, I know we lose track of that—we are so much a single person, with our actions, thoughts, and emotions fully in line, that there isn't even an echo of the other—but in the quiet and the melancholy like this, we can appreciate again how he chose me, and I chose him. Until the day when the world I come from drains the last of our life from us, that will never change.

'Did we know this aurora, before you came here?' he asks.

I don't think so. But the more I drift back through my hazy memories, the less certain I am either way. *I don't think I would remember, if I had.* I strain, trying to stretch around Venalt's aurora without grabbing hold, to see the scope of who it is without intruding on its intimate self. It takes a slow shape, one that's more energy than space. Like the others we've encountered, it doesn't spark any familiarity.

As I curl back into myself, I pause.

'Do you sense that?'

It's so faint.

The vibration is barely a flutter, like a third heartbeat between mine and the singing aurora. But as soon as I think it, we seem to deafen this new presence, the two of us too loud to hear anything else. I keep listening, keep reaching, but it doesn't reappear.

Distant voices echo down the hall. Something thuds on the level above us. Our left hip goes numb all the way down the leg to our heel. And still I can't find the third presence.

It's nothing. An echo, or an aurora on the mainland.

'It's nothing,' I repeat.

I almost believe it.

No one comes for me. No one comes for so long that the lights embedded into the little clefts of the ceiling shut off. I pull myself out from under the table, hitting my head on the top twice and the sides once before I manage to make it to the door. My fist echoes crudely in the small space.

When no one answers, I call for Zuane, then call Zuane a silt-breathing bastard. That gets no response either. I switch to something less juvenile and slightly more important, shouting that someone had better check on Lavender if they plan to keep me here much longer, even though I know we've left her enough food and water for another day at least. Tavish's name rises to my lips, but it only escapes in whispers.

No one comes.

I never expected them to, I realize. My palm presses to the knob again, feeling at the resistance. If they were planning to set me up a meeting with the chancellor or even another interrogation, why not answer my calls?

'Because we scared them?'

Probably. Stupid dramatics.

'We loved every moment.'

Shut up.

We laugh, a soft, echoing thing that bubbles in our chest, masking the fear and doubt and exhaustion. Despite my annoyance, I can't bring myself to break out of here quite yet, not if it means I'll have to go through whatever chaos it'll create that much sooner. After another round of stumbling, I curl up on the bench. I dream of Tavish.

I love you.

The lights wake me with the sour tang of agitation already building at the back of my throat, their bulbs blinking back to life as the interrogation room door slams with such ferocity that I jolt upright. The shift drops me off the edge of the bench. I land with an agonizing silence that makes the pain shooting through my hip and shoulders seem like it's mocking me.

A plate of food sits just inside the closed door. Indignation pounds in my skull so hot that there's half a second where I think I might cry. I drag myself to my feet and bang my fist into the door again. This time I swear I hear people somewhere beyond. Still, no one answers.

I go motionless. Closing my eyes and pressing into my aurora senses, I focus on the noise from beyond the room—on the fluttering vibrations they produce. It feels wrong to be seeking something not of the aurora realm, but even my human half's world uses motion to create sound, and tuning myself to the music of it sharpens my already exceptional hearing. Whoever deposited my breakfast is moving away from me, almost out of my range, but still I manage to pick up a piece of their conversation.

"Commander Zuane's too scared to move him, I think. All that aurora nonsense is getting to him. But he's looking for a way to deport the other one back to the mainland as soon as possible."

"The selkie? Isn't he a witness?"

"Apparently his testimony is useless, and he keeps demanding to see the chancellor. Zuane just wants him out of the way."

My blood runs cool at the thought. If Tavish wants to stay on the mainland, if he wants a break from all the rushing around—a break from me—then I will force myself to accept it, but the idea of someone dragging him away from me against our will sparks fear and rage in my chest, as though the lingering excess of the pink ignit's energy is forming a storm in my chest.

Through the constant, subtle song that floods the city, I feel its aurora react. I'm still lingering in this half reality that connects the human world to the aurora one, so I reach out my threads toward the source of the song. Almost immediately I brush against the aurora's presence.

It feels far weaker than yesterday, the deterioration so startling that it pulls the air from my lungs. My head goes light, and I lean against the wall to keep from stumbling. It presses at me in return, like a pet searching pockets for treats, unable to quite reach inside and connect with my energy.

Hello? I ask.

It stiffens, the vibration of its song skipping like a scratched phonograph record. Curiosity flashes through it, mixed with desire. It can't hear my thoughts any more than I can hear its, but this close to it, I can feel that it wants me to come. Feeble and helpless, it can sense my still-flourishing energy and my mobility, and its intrigue and desperation morph to form a playful begging.

I want to, I try to tell it, returning its longing with my own.

I gather part of my remaining strength and press it gently toward the suffering aurora as a gift. Before it can reach the aurora, the energy reflects, slamming back into me so hard it jars my teeth. Even like this, our aurora halves so near, there's a disconnect that comes from never having been physically connected. I know it's possible to transfer energy without that touch—have had it poured into me from auroras over a mile away—but all my attempts to do the same always fell short. I am too grounded to this reality. Too human.

I have to go to it.

I press my forehead to the door. Once I break free, I doubt the Citadel will even pretend to hear us out about their aurora's safety. But they were barely pretending before.

And the longer we wait, fretting and eating their food and doing nothing, the more time the aurora suffers and the more likely Zuane finds a legal route to deport Tavish from the city. Venalt's aurora tugs at me, its wordless desires rubbing against my own. It's anxious and a little aggressive, and more than anything, it wants to meet me. It wants my help.

That's what I came here for, not to bow to bureaucracy, but to save an aurora. I send it back an affirmation. *Just wait, not long now.* We don't have long if Zuane really does plan to get rid of Tavish and me.

I cup the door handle, carefully knitting my aurora power along my muscles, and shove. The metal resists for a moment, then something snaps within the lock. The handle slams down. The energy it draws out of me seems larger than it should be—or maybe their lock is simply stronger than the usual, or my restless sleep was more draining than I thought. The subtle fatigue that hums in my bones worries me though.

I slip out of my bland holding chamber into the empty hallway beyond. Doors line both sides. I try them one by one, finding more interrogation rooms like mine, none in use.

I try not to panic—of course Tavish would never let them keep him in such a harsh place—but with every empty room, my anxiety grows. I note a small camera mounted at the top of the hall, its wiring taped to the ceiling. The Citadel building was clearly constructed long before the recent creation of wire-transferable film, and it seems they didn't bother to have the Institute adjust the wall's structure to hide their security addition. If the cameras are working, they might lead me to Tavish. If the people behind them don't spot *me* first.

But I can't help taunting them through the camera, making a show of tugging up my hood and holding the stub of my fingers to my lips. If it's my dramatics they hate, then dramatics is what they'll get. No one in this section of the building seems to notice, though, the distant babble of voices maintaining its constant ebb and flow as I follow the camera's wiring down the hall.

It leads me into a converted storage space with a series of giant boxes and a screen as blank and empty as the chair in front of it. The side of one of the boxes sits open, revealing a generator compartment with an empty gap for an ignit. I press my fingers into it, spilling a bit more of my waning energy. It leaves me with a slight malaise that sits in my muscles and taunts me, but the screen lights up with a black-and-white image that sputters every few seconds.

It automatically shifts through the connected security footage. Corridor, workplace, corridor, empty cell, then a quaint waiting area with Tavish sitting on a sofa. The way my heart jumps, brandishing an excruciating mixture of joy and pain at the sight of him, makes it hard to think as I scrounge back through my memories of last night, finding the shadowy impression of a similar room off to the side of the central work space.

I head for it, holding my breath as I dart behind a row of desks. When I reach the right door, I quickly flick the outer lock and slip inside.

Tavish lounges on the sofa, his expression bored and his pinkie fingers tapping incessantly. Or trembling. The way he draws breath, small and sharp, it must be the latter.

I need to say something to him, tell him I'm here so he's not caught off guard, but the words lodge themselves inside me, caught halfway between my first *I love you* and his lack of response. My body acts anyway, reaching out. My fingers find his shoulder, a soft motion that draws across his neck, thumb brushing off his jaw.

He goes stiff. Shooting from his chair, he grabs me with both fists, pulling us together. "Good fuck, Ruby."

The words come out in a sound near a sob, and he presses against me like I'm something necessary for life and not a man who's dragged us around until we're both verging on collapse. The guilt barely has time to hit before he murmurs again, four small words—four, so, so much better than three—that make everything in my gods-forsaken life up till now worth it.

"I love you, too." His lips find my neck, my jaw, the crooked edge of my chin, one hand pushing beneath my cowl to weed into my braids. "I should have said it, and I'm sorry, and I—" Then our mouths are locked, his head tipping back and his arms pulling me down to accommodate my height. He kisses me with all the hunger and desperation of a starving man, his tongue pressing inside my cheek and his teeth dragging over my lower lip.

It's hot and fast and perfect, leaving me tingling and throbbing after. That ache echoes in my chest, though, with something more solid than my blinding lust. He loves me. He's safe, and he's here, and he loves me. It's all I've ever wanted and so much more. "Tavish—"

"You're not hurt, are you?" He grasps at my shoulders, then my arms, traveling to my hips and chest, as though he's checking that I'm still in one piece in a way that only stirs my need for him further.

I grab him back, holding him gently by the wrists. "Tavish."

"Commander Zuane claimed they had you safe somewhere, but when you didn't come for me all night . . ."

"I'm fine." I chuckle. "If they already didn't like me, I figured breaking out wouldn't help matters much."

Tavish's brow lifts. "Them already not liking you was the exact reason I assumed you'd break out immediately."

"I thought you'd prefer I give you the chance to sway them with your pretty words first."

"Oh, absolutely. I'm surprised, not offended." He presses through my loose grip on his wrists, fitting his palms into the crests of my collarbones. "And either way, I love you," he says again with soft vulnerability, the kind that asks for the same in return. "I love you."

"Thank fuck. I mean, I love you, too." I lace my fingers over his, the stubs fitting perfectly into the crooks of his knuckles. "But you seemed to be pulling away?"

"Aye, I know. I've been concealing some of my troubles from you, and I can explain that, I think—I've given it plenty of thought while trapped in here—but I do love you. Is that enough to start with?"

"Always." This is what we've been missing: chests ripped open to reveal the bleeding hearts within. Tavish and I—we're going to be okay. I know we will. "But we'll have to talk later. Right now we should probably deal with the fact that the Citadel is going to like us even less now than ever, and we still have a job to finish here."

Tavish's lips crook up. "What do you suggest?"

"I got to do some of my own contemplating while locked away," I say. "And I think it's time we steal Venalt's aurora."

CHAPTER FIVE

not so singular

THIS ISN'T THE FIRST time we've stolen an aurora, and those experiences seem to have paved the way for us, making the start of this endeavor the easiest one yet despite our bizarre circumstances. It certainly doesn't hurt that the department's main work space is cleared out for their lunch break, and the entrance gate is wide open. I lead us in the opposite direction from the building's entrance, guiding Tavish by the arm down a few of the buildings' tall, tight hallways before stopping in a random empty corridor.

"Do you know where we're going?" Tavish whispers.

"I'm about to find out." I hope.

I plunge headfirst into my threads, calling back to the city's aurora, who has been waiting impatiently throughout all of this. *Can I come to you?*

It gives an acknowledgement, its curiosity overwhelming. I can almost hear the words that would accompany it: *yes, come, please, now.* Its weakness worsens with every second we linger, making it all the more determined and desperate. Through our strained connection, it flashes images at me: the building's front entrance, a right-hand turn, a door, and onward. Its original path as it was taken to its current home in the building's basement, I assume. Each glimpse is barely an impression—a hallway with a unique statue, the clipped base of a corner brick, an old blue stain still lining the cracks of the floor—but a sense of direction comes with it, orienting me.

I follow its guidance. Tavish holds to me, each of his steps making a gentle swoosh where mine are entirely soundless. As we move through the convoluted hallways, their geometric structure of tighter and tighter honeycombs becomes clear, letting me guide us along the most external route possible through mostly empty corridors. Each person we meet still forces us to slow, Tavish mimicking lighthearted dialogue of how excited he is that my father has allowed us to visit him here.

I try not to let the mentions of a second parent—a parent who isn't my long-dead mother—distract me. It's difficult to forget an adolescence spent dreaming that my long-lost parent would reappear to admit how wrong they were to leave my mother and me and to bring me somewhere I would be cherished instead of insulted. The dream turned bitter half a lifetime ago, but on rare occasions, I find the crust of it still clinging like a calcium deposit to some dusty corner of myself, so tightly fastened I need a pickaxe to clip it off again.

Tavish must sense the shift in my mood because the next time three staffers pass us—two in uniform and one with casual robes over a suit—he cuts out his speech entirely. We catch the tail end of their conversation in its place. By the sound of it, it's half gossip, half genuine worry.

"I hear Chancellor Teodor hasn't left her quarters in weeks, that she's relaying all her orders through the commander."

"Well she's not visiting us, I can tell you that. Our office is only getting memos at this point."

As they round the corner behind us, Tavish's grip on my arm tightens.

"What is it?" I whisper.

"Did they say Chancellor Teodor?"

"Yes. Why?"

His lips pucker. "I just knew a Teodor, is all."

"Is this going to—"

"No." He cuts me off, his diamond voice softening around the edges. His grip loosens with a gentle squeeze. "It's a long story, but I doubt it's the same person. She'd barely be older than me—candidates aren't even considered for chancellor until twenty-eight, I believe."

Tavish drops the topic as we pass a corridor echoing with chatter, but I can't ignore the pucker of his brow or the slight red that's come into his cheeks. I almost ask for the long story here and now, when the Venalt aurora tugs at me. Its mental hall map cuts out. I stop.

Our connection wavers, the aurora heaving from the effort of this simple communication. I can feel my worry echoing into it. The thrum of its song sputters here and there, and this close to it for this long, I get a sense of how much energy producing the constant vibrations takes out of it. It's overwhelming. And the aurora is running low—so low that it can't both sing and send me its memories at once. It reaches out in all directions, its annoyance tinged in fear as it meets with only me. I feel its conflict like it's my own: the need to protect its city from the destructive teeth of the creatures surrounding it fighting its desire to keep its connection with me.

I want so badly to punch every last one of Venalt's leaders for letting it suffer this way. It's their city this poor aurora is saving, their people who will be torn apart while it sinks. *Take me to you, and I'll help,* I plead, even though it won't hear the words.

It returns a slew of emotions: protective yearning and anger and determination.

Please. I send it a glimpse of the auroras I've met in the past, their strength returning as fresh energy is poured into them.

"Ruby?"

I jerk my vision back to normal as Tavish whispers my name. Beyond his voice comes the approach of what sounds like a full brigade in the high, echoing chambers. We don't have much time. *Please.* I press my urgency and fear toward the aurora, begging it to understand. *This may be our only chance.*

After a final moment of hesitation, the aurora's song cuts out. It slams me with the rest of our directions.

With Tavish on my arm, I jog us down the final few turns, into a nook in a dim hallway that seems to lead nowhere. There's a solid door where it seems a wall should be. I use a rush of my aurora strength to snap through both of its hefty locks. The next step I take feels too light suddenly, and I grab onto Tavish to stop the wave of vertigo that hits me. It clears quickly, but the fact that I'm this drained in the first place unnerves me. All I've done since my last sleep was break a few locks. And power a small generator. And send a wave of emotions and images at an aurora I'm not connected to.

Maybe this drop in energy isn't so unnatural after all.

The aurora's song returns in stammers as I pull Tavish down the broad stone steps beyond the door. My vision shifts naturally, the walls turning crystalline and my body going ghostly, until I can see the cords of light wound through me, so white that they leave black imprints behind. As we descend below the ground floor, a dim light flickers ahead, growing until it's bright enough to draw me back to my human sight again.

"Do we have a plan?" Tavish hisses.

"Get the aurora. Leave."

"Am I supposed to carry you *both*?" Tavish grabs me as he says it, barely keeping me from dragging us both into a tumble as I miss a step. "What if it's hosted in a tree, Rubem?"

"A tree underground?"

That doesn't seem to console him much.

But as we round the final curve and the Citadel's basement opens before us into a massive, shadowy expanse, smelling faintly of mold and swamp, rot and rust, I realize how utterly and inconceivably I'm wrong. The Venalt aurora's host is no plant. It's not even an invertebrate.

Its serpentlike body basks in the underground lagoon that takes up half the basement's space, its extensive tail the size of a tree trunk. Coils upon coils of it disappear into the darkness. Thick coppery scales armor it, with black patterns along its sides and a tinge of green that flickers through them as it shifts in the light of the mounted wall bulbs. Between the natural colors, though, are scales flashing rainbow on black, and others ashen where the aurora within it is dying. A host of little leathery fins flare from its sides as it lifts not just one but three giant necks that bear intimidating viper heads, emerging like a hydra from the same central serpent's body. A split tongue darts out of each wide mouth, and its two rainbowed eyes—the leftmost eye of the leftmost head and the rightmost of the right—center on me.

Our aurora threads brush properly for the first time, and through them it pulses: *'Welcome, one whose home encompasses the world. I've heard much of you.'*

"Fuck," I say in return.

CHAPTER SIX

confinement and conpulsion

VENALT'S AURORA BLINKS, OPAQUE lids sliding up from the bottom of its eyes and drawing back down again. Though the serpent heads display little emotion outside of their mild curiosity and inherent creepy stare, I feel the aurora's laughter mixed with a flutter of something animalistic, intelligent but primal in a way that reminds me of my massive crocodilian, Sheila.

So this is what I sensed in the odd quality of its dreams. It *is* like me, two individuals woven together. But unlike me, half of it thinks not in the words and higher logic of this world's sapient people or the very imagery-based thought patterns of the aurora, but in the pure sense and impulse of an animal.

Tavish tightens his grip on my arm, tipping his chin toward the sound of the aurora's shifting. "Ruby?"

"It's all right—we're fine," I reassure him. "Or all right in a sense anyway—we found Venalt's aurora and it's not guarded. In another sense, I suppose this decimates my idea of bringing it back to the hotel."

'How hilarious.' It laughs into my head again as it continues brushing its threads against mine, its obvious exhaustion at odds with its good humor. *'I would squash the place.'*

At the same time, Tavish asks, "It's not a tree, is it?"

"No. More like a gigantic, three-headed snake."

'A leviathan, this species is called. Though not commonly do we have three heads. I am special.'

It is special indeed. "Give me a moment, I think I'm still in shock." The wonder hits me full in the chest as I say it; I'm not the only time an aurora has bound with an intelligent host. This serpent is different from a human, certainly, but it moves and thinks and breathes the way no aurora's host I've seen has. And I'd never even known of its existence until now.

Venalt's leviathan aurora stares at me, cocking one of its heads. The heat of its attention comes with more of that subtle humor, soft and intrigued. *'Not all the wonders of the world go flaunting their presence at every—'* Its voice cuts off as a shudder runs through it. The rainbows that gleam in the darkness between its scales ripple in and out, its song mimicking the motion in the sputtering quality of its vibrations. The aurora lowers its necks back onto the stone outcropping, eyelids slipping up a few inches as it finishes, weaker, *'—every turn.'*

My fury with this damned city flares, catching in my chest like a warning. I pat Tavish's arm once to signal my leaving and jogging toward the lagoon. My boots splash in the puddles that form where the stones are uneven, slipping where a moldy substance has built up. The state of this place fuels my anger further. I crouch beside one of the aurora's rainbow eyes.

As I do, I feel its tendrils reaching out to me, into me, tugging at the energy that flows along the edges of my being. It takes only tiny morsels, but I feel its hollow hunger, how desperately it needs more. *'You don't have the sickness yet? If I draw from you, can you recover?'*

I don't respond in words. Pressing my palm to its scales, I push into it the way I had tried to earlier. This time, it works. Each drop of strength drawn out leaves a hollow behind, as though it's stripping away pieces of muscle and bone, of lung and blood. My head turns light again, blackness coming in around the edges. I drift my knees, leaning my torso against the massive aurora, arm looping over it. It vibrates like a purr.

For a moment, all I hear is the thrum of its song beating through me: its heart and mine. And then a third heartbeat, weak but near . . .

Tavish's hand appears against my back, his voice questioning. "Ruby?"

"I'm here," I mutter. My exhaustion seems to be stabilizing into something harsh and pounding yet bearable, but leaning against the aurora like this reminds me so much of the monstrous pets I left back at home, and I'm remiss to move.

Tavish grumbles some variation of "You better be."

The aurora laughs. It feels stronger than before, though only barely, like I've dropped a bucket into a dry riverbed. With every thrum of its song, what I've given, it starts to drain. I brush my fingers gently over its forehead. "You can't keep producing such huge, constant vibrations like this." The song stops the hippocamps from approaching the city, I know, but if Venalt won't care for their aurora, they don't deserve its protection. Even as I think it, I can feel the aurora's objection rising, but I fight it anyway. "We'll get you free from here—anything you need from us—and find you ignits someplace that appreciates you. You can live a good life wherever you wish." Though with how few ignits are left in most places, I can't guarantee it'll be long. A few happy years have to be better than this, though.

It closes its eyes fully, irises still mostly visible through semitranslucent lids, as all three of its heads sigh, but its emotions press against me through the threads of our aurora halves, terrifyingly vibrant. *'The hippocamps must not reach the city. All the people here . . .'*

Its love burns like a kind of rage, its commitment to this city so strong it seems that the dedication alone should be enough to produce boundless energy. But if physics worked that way, the world likely wouldn't be reliant on ignits. It hisses, a sizzling sound that bleeds through my head so loud it takes me a moment to realize it comes also from the creature's mouths.

'The people here are mine,' it finishes.

Maybe I don't understand how it can feel that way for a specific place, a group of people, not when my human half's ancestral groups worked so hard to force me out, but I know what the depths of its care can look like—feel the mark of that love in my own affection for my pets and, deeper still, branded into my aurora flesh, even if I don't quite know where it came from. But this aurora cares, cares so much, when the very people it seeks to help don't seem to care themselves, don't even bother to ease its suffering.

It takes in my emotions the same way I sense its own, and it seems not to need my thoughts voiced in order to understand. *'They don't know that I feel it as I die,'* it snaps, then corrects itself as thoughts of the chancellors come to mind. *'Most of them don't know, and the few that do, only barely. I have been here since near the beginning, in hidden waterways beneath the foundation, growing along with it for hundreds of years. They have never seen me—have never seen any aurora in a host whose pain they can relate to. Don't judge so harshly.'*

"Then why don't you show them? Show the city exactly who they're hurting!"

'I would scare them,' the aurora replies, its statement so fierce that it nearly covers the fear that vibrates from it. *'They were scared already, when I first grew big enough to eat them, they were scared—they wanted me moved. A less dangerous host. But this body that's big enough to eat them is big enough to protect them, too. So I stay here, and no one knows. No one can know.'*

I want so badly to tell it that it's wrong, that if they truly understand how much their aurora loves them, then they'll adore it with the same unadulterated ferocity, but I've kept too many large and dangerous pets and seen the pain of too many disregarded auroras to believe that. I cringe at the thought of how my human had my own aurora ripped from its old host before he knew it to be a sapient, the memory surfacing with such strength that Venalt's aurora must feel it. But still, I cannot be any less furious with the city's people. I will judge them just as harshly as I have judged myself, and that sentence wasn't light. "You are too kind to them."

'They are mine' is all Venalt's aurora says in return. I sense one of its heads move behind me, twisting around Tavish. It nudges his side, its nose fitting against his torso. *'And this one is yours?'*

Tavish yelps, then releases a shaky laugh. "Ah, yes, hello. I'm . . . Tavish. It's a pleasure."

'Luca,' the aurora murmurs in my head. *'The pleasure is mine, little morsel.'*

I repeat the name out loud for Tavish. "Don't call my boyfriend edible, please. Whichever sense you mean it in."

'But he is edible. In both senses.' Luca sounds just playful enough that I don't try to grab the aurora by the nostrils and give it a sterner warning.

I cringe—*it* feels like the wrong pronoun for a being that identifies under a proper name. None of the other auroras have had them, except for me: for Rubem. And I have a gender that corresponds to that name, to the original human who used it and to the full person I've become. Perhaps all the auroras I've met have, too. That thought makes me feel like a creep for taking this long to realize it. But then I'm half aurora, so if that half of me didn't notice anything potentially amuck until now, perhaps none of us care much about pronouns.

Across the room, a low glow emerges in one of the stairwells: inactive ignits pressing against the thin fabric of a bag. It's hard to make out the person who carries them, their form merely a shadow leaning on a thick case as they descend, each step slow and silent.

I stand as Luca gives an excitable squeal in their mind so loud I can feel it resonate through our still laced threads and straight into my human bones: *'Look who I've found!'*

The newcomer drops their bag of ignits in shock, but they hardly seem to notice, stepping with agonizing slowness into the light of the dim basement bulbs, their long, dark hair gleaming like silk and pale skin nearly glowing. "Tavish Findlay." The words sound whispered in the hollow space. "You've grown up just fine."

I don't see Tavish's face as he replies, but his voice drops, low and tight and hoarse. "Hello, my darling Teodor."

CHAPTER SEVEN

his darling Teodor

IT TAKES MY MIND no time at all to place that name: Teodor, the "long story." It's easier still to guess what that long story entailed. Something burns, hot and jealous, up the back of my neck. I swallow it down. Whatever Tavish had with Teodor, it doesn't change what he has with me now.

But I still scrutinize his past lover as though my subconscious is searching for the pieces that Tavish must have found delight in, not quite comparing them to myself, but in the least, wondering.

She, Tavish said, though this human has a genderless kind of beauty, flat chested beneath her flowing white shirt, little buttons tying up the front all the way to the top of her throat, where it ends in a looped bow, accentuating her long neck. The fluttering of her crooked cape with only the topmost of its five latches connected does nothing to disguise her long limbs, bringing her nearly to my own height. I spot no fishnets. Our shared love for roguish finery only extends so far, then.

Beneath her ethereal looks, her bones appear a bit too knobby, shadowed circles pulling down her dark eyes. When she bends to retrieve her fallen ignits, she moves like she's made of porcelain. Even in the low light, her pale skin comes across as more sickly than natural pallor. The shine to her long, black hair as she crosses the space between us can't mask the thinness of it, the way it seems almost to be fading out with each flutter. She leans on a cane far sturdier than Tavish's, the top twisted into a padded handle and the bottom cushioned to be as soundless as her bare feet on the smooth stone.

Tavish stares through her with an intensity to rival my own, a blush on his cheeks and a curl of his lips that looks scared and desperate, as though he's hoping she's everything he remembers and terrified she isn't. I try not to stare at him in the same manner as he clears his throat and says, "Chancellor Teo does have a brilliant ring to it."

"Fuck off." Her androgynous voice sounds a little too husky for her tall, lithe frame.

Tavish laughs, though it comes across strained. "Why, if you cared so much, you should have come visit me." The words have a forced cheeriness atop their cutting nature. This is, after all, the person who kept us imprisoned since last night—or at least chose not to stop it. "You could have at least had dinner brought by."

"You—*you* are the aurora ambassador's fancy prick Commander Zuane wants deported?" Teodor shakes her head. "Who would have guessed! You come back for the first time in twelve years, and I only hear of it because you're watching my colleagues be murdered and breaking into my basement."

"He is trying to *deport* me? I suppose that's better than execution," he grumbles, like mere extradition is an insult. When his attention flashes back to Teodor, though, it sharpens to a point. "I would think as *Chancellor* Teodor, you would have a more invested interest in your own city's turmoil."

"I've been a bit busy dying, darling." It could have been a joke if not for the physical evidence of her sickness.

Tavish's aloof expression wavers, a glimpse of horror peeking through. "Are you truly . . ."

"It's been months coming, something like tuberculosis." She snorts, the sound turning into a quiet cough that she seems to try very hard to suppress. It makes her words waxen. "If you're going to mourn, do it when I'm not still here."

"I'm sorry," Tavish says.

My heart wants to break for him, but it can't, not yet, not while there is another living being dying in this room, and it could easily be saved by the woman in front of us. "Now what, then?" I ask. "You try to lock us back up? Send us away?"

"Frankly, I was happy to leave you both there for as long as possible, and knowing just who you are only makes me more certain that was the right choice." Teodor's gaze finds mine, her eyes so black that her irises seem to bleed into her pupils but for the hint of grey that runs through splices of them. "You're a threat to the flimsy stability of our city, aurora ambassador. Tavish as well, with that lovely mouth of his."

"It's been too long, Teo."

I can't quite read the inflection in his voice: *It's a shame we've been apart this long*, or *We've been apart too long to make this work*. Or maybe it means neither of those things, and this is just what you say to an old lover you parted with on amicable terms over a decade ago. I try not to let it make me snippy.

Which is decidedly not why my statement comes out like a dagger. "We aren't leaving, if that's what you expect."

"You may be strong, but you are one aurora in a city of—"

'*I want him,*' Luca shouts, loud enough that it seems to echo through my skull. The aurora slides farther from the lagoon on its long, serpentine tail, sliding a coil of itself around me as it hisses. '*He* is *strong. He can do what you cannot!*'

Teodor glares at the massive aurora without a hint of fear.

"Tavish and I made a point to *meet* Luca—how many others can claim that?" I rub the side of its nearest face as I say it. It nuzzles into my touch. "If you give a damn about your aurora, you will work with us, not against us."

Teodor's wide nose wrinkles, her full lips pressing together. She must have more Southern ancestry than her pallor gives her credit for. "You did get here, so I assume that Luca guided you in some way. He can be as stubborn as a bad algae when he wants to."

He. I can't tell whether it's the aurora's preferred pronouns or just the host body's sexual identifiers, but I don't feel any negative reactions from Luca as Teodor says it. Which helps my aurora gender conundrum not at all.

Luca does stick out all his tongues, though, flicking them at Teodor affectionately.

The chancellor huffs. "Don't you pull that, you scaly monstrosity. You're no judge of character—you know exactly four people who are still alive today, and you don't care that two of them can't decide whether or not it's fine if you die."

'They're mine.' The assertion is just as fierce this time, but somehow it manages to be a grumble too.

Teodor scowls. "Go back to bed if you're going to be like that."

'Maybe I will,' Luca snaps through the threads, his two upright heads jerking back as a look comes over their faces that I swear is the serpent version of disgust.

"Fine."

'Fine.' Luca lays down his heads and promptly slides his eyelids closed, though I still catch the faint shift of the pupils behind them as they continue to track Teodor.

It occurs to me only then that, without an aurora, Teodor has had no idea what Luca has been saying for their entire argument. She's learned to read the massive snake's emotions through body language alone. After all the great, scaly pets I've had in my life, it doesn't seem unreasonable, but it's rare to find anyone willing to put in that much time and effort. It gives me a sudden respect for this chancellor . . . even if she's locked Tavish and me in a cell for a day, and Tavish keeps flushing over the sound of her voice.

As Teodor approaches Luca's third head—the one that isn't supporting me or quietly resting beside Tavish—she releases a sigh. The sound turns into a deep, silent cough. Luca nudges her so gently that his fear is obvious even without the emotions vibrating off him through our aurora connection. Teodor places a hand on his nose. "He looks strong today. I assume that has something to do with you, aurora ambassador?"

"He was far too weak when I arrived."

"Dammit." Her voice catches. She glares at Luca afresh. "Why didn't you wake me, you fool?"

'I tried,' Luca murmurs, his voice in my head but his attention only for her. He nudges her again, a soft vibration running through the throat of that head alone. *'You didn't hear.'*

Teo groans. "I thought I sent a memo for Commander Zuane to bring you one of the remaining ignits this morning, but with Chancellor Fiordelise's death, everything has been a mess. It's my fault still, I should have . . ." Her gaze wanders absently, like she's searching for a solution. A tremor racks through her, and she coughs again, quiet as ever. It doubles her near over, Luca supporting her under one arm, and her cane on the other. As her hacking continues, she yanks a handkerchief from her pant pocket and holds it to her mouth. She bundles it up again almost too quickly to see, but I catch a hint of something dark.

'You have to take care of yourself, too,' Luca says, so gentle and pleading that it changes the tune of his song for a moment, lifting it into something achingly sad.

Whatever anguish this city has inflicted on Luca, Teodor isn't a part of it—not willingly anyway, her own suffering coming between what she wants and what she can do. And it makes me all the more determined to step in, to find a way to save Venalt and their aurora in her place. She doesn't have the strength or the power herself. But maybe I do.

Of the three of us, I'm not dying yet.

"We're not here to cause trouble," I say. "But we do want to help Luca. I won't let another aurora die if I can stop it."

'The city,' Luca pushes.

"And saving Luca will save the city, too," I add.

Teodor's mouth opens, and I can already see the answer on her face: an *I understand* followed with a *but.*

Tavish beats her to it. "If you think we have enough skill and drive between us to be a danger to your city, then make use of us instead. Turn us into an asset." He doesn't let her answer yet, plunging on like a whistling bullet, seeking and hungry. "Is your city truly going to sink if the hippocamps reach it?"

"Undeniably."

"And Luca is the only thing keeping them at bay?"

Teo doesn't answer as quickly this time, her lips pursing. "Another aurora could learn his song, but it would take time, likely weeks or months, and strength to rival Luca's, and they would just end up in the same position as Luca in the end—trapped in a place without enough access to ignits."

"I could try anyway. I haven't started the fading process yet, so I don't need ignits." The words are out of my mouth before I weigh their implications: us, here, helping Luca sustain the city until who knows when. Not being there for any other auroras who might need me in the coming weeks, but being here for this one. Being here for a whole city— better yet, being here, in one place, to let Tavish feel settled for a moment. To let *me* feel settled.

The moment I think it, the idea latches, a tight, dangerous thing: What if this could be the place for us? It hasn't felt like home at first sight, but what city ever could be, after the Murk and Maraheem? Maybe it would be enough for us, so long as we're here together.

My heart struggles to hold on to the thought, to try it on for size, but I shiver from its mere presence, and it's all I can do to bundle it away. One step at a time. There's no use getting up hopes that will just be crushed in the end.

Teodor stares at me, Tavish with his brow furrowed and his mouth soundlessly open, and Luca prodding gently against my emotions, as though testing if I'm authentic.

I give a laugh, wishing I had something, anything to toss around. "Only if nothing else can be done, though. I'd much rather storm the Institute for every ignit they have."

"That's a thought." Teodor keeps staring at me.

'No, you know I don't like that,' Luca retorts, a small hiss accompanying it.

She scowls, but lets the subject drop.

It feels like a miniature revelation to know that Teodor would take greater action in this, but Luca doesn't want her to, and she listens to him. I feel Luca lurking around the thought as he turns his attention back to me, but he chooses not to comment on it, nudging my side gently instead. *'Can you vibrate more than your emotions, home worlder?'* The final phrase is an odd mix of language and emotion that takes my human brain a moment to assign words to.

No. Or at least I've never tried before.

I don't truly sense the flicker of hope Luca has been giving off until it cuts out. *'Then it will take too long to teach you the song.'*

I feel deflated. *Are you sure?*

'This is my city. I can keep protecting them.'

That's not really an answer, but Teodor's questioning "Will you try?" snaps me back to attention.

"He says it won't work. It would take me too long to learn."

She rubs a hand to her face, groaning. "I suppose you do truly want to help him?"

"More than anything in the world."

"Then I'll let you stay—if you follow my lead. I do *not* need Tavish's genius and your strength tearing through my city."

"Am I merely a genius with a beautiful mouth to you?" Tavish asks.

I have to stop myself from shooting him a scowl he won't even see. "We'll play by your rules, if that's what it takes."

Teodor nods. "Let's sit down, then. Luca, are you well enough to join us?"

'More well than you are,' Luca grumbles. He gives her a bob of all three of his heads, though, the motion a little out of sync.

"This way, then," she says. "We have a lot to talk over."

CHAPTER EIGHT

the dead versus the dying

AS TEODOR SETS OFF across the basement, Tavish takes my elbow like he belongs there. I hope he doesn't feel the relief it gives me, the way I doubted him despite knowing it was ridiculous. He squeezes my arm, a soft smile on his lips.

We move back toward the large stairwell Teodor entered through. Nothing but the drip of the surrounding water, the click of Tavish's cane, and his soft footsteps mark our path, I as silent as ever and Teodor . . . Teodor is barefoot, her cane cushioned on the bottom. The echoing nature of the large, empty room must cover whatever sound she makes.

As we ascend the steps, Tavish finally breaks the quiet. "You care very much for Luca."

"I do." Teodor seems to hesitate, but she glances back at Tavish, and her expression softens. "Luca's the reason I fought so hard to become chancellor despite my age," she explains. "It had always annoyed me that the Citadel basement was closed—for being structurally unsound, it was said, but that seemed ridiculous, since the Institute built this structure originally and all their work is immaculate. One day, my birthday actually it was, I got a bit too drunk and said fuck it all and found my way in. Discovered Luca. He seemed so lonely."

'*I have an entire city, thank you,*' Luca grumbles in my head.

But I feel the way his heart aches and the way he tries to tuck that out of my senses before I can see it. I don't push after him. I don't let him pull too far away either. His hurt is viscerally familiar, a stab that brings up a lifetime of human memories and those from my aurora time in the Murk, of the loneliness I felt there, as well as the ostracized impressions of a deeper aurora past I can no longer remember.

You are not alone, I whisper.

Luca seems to mull that over from a distance as the stairway turns into a wide hall, the ceiling low and walls still the same rugged, unkempt stone, though graciously no longer covered in water or slime. A large wooden gate sits on wheels to one side, and Teodor rolls it out of the way to reveal what looks like the back of a tapestry. When we push through it, I realize that's exactly what it is: a faded scene of a woman on an island of shining corelium with her palm pressed to the nose of a hippocamp-like creature—equine face and arching neck, sweeping tail and stubby front legs—but without the teeth and armor. A distant relative to them maybe, or an old fairy-tale imagining.

The room itself is small and simple compared to the rest of the building, much like Fiordelise's personal chambers were. Long, stained-glass windows let in light along the top of the wall and in gaps between shelves and cupboards. Where Fiordelise's held books, Teodor's contain the full plethora of everything else on the planet and then some. Teeth and tusks, crystals and little toy models, laundry hanging from fancy weapons covered in dust, and three different globes with slight variations in size and style. So many blankets and pillows pile beneath the four-poster bed's curtains that I'm not sure there's even a mattress below them. Under the mess, I swear the floor is covered in a collection of overlapping ornate rugs.

It feels cozy and warm and loved, a chaotic disaster perhaps, but one that turns a collection of random objects into a home. Even if Teodor isn't my type, I can see what Tavish loved about her. What anyone might love about her, regardless of romantics.

I whistle. "Quite a lair you've got here."

"Commander Zuane always says this place is so messy you could hide a hoard of ignits in here and no one would notice." She tosses her ignit bag to one side as if to prove her point. It's immediately buried in the clutter.

I laugh. "I've seen a hoard of ignits. It was far more organized."

She notices Tavish still lingering in the entrance, his cane bumping aside a lacy pair of underwear. "Shit." She looks like she might try and grab them, but a tremor runs through her, and she stays where she is. "Just be careful where you walk, Tavish. Or turn. I haven't had the energy to clean in a while."

"If you're doing so poorly, should you not be handing the reins to someone else? Enjoy what time you have left." It seems to hurt him to say it, his long-lost love returned just in time to be lost again.

Like he'll lose me to the aurora fading, sooner or later.

Teodor waves a hand at him dismissively, then seems to realize what she's doing and stops. "Zuane has taken over most of my duties. I'll enjoy my time once I know Luca won't be following me." She grunts. "I don't know about you, but I'm going to be needing a drink for this."

"Only one?" I laugh.

She looks back at me, a slight tug of her lips breaking through the flat expression. "One bottle."

"I think you might be the only sane person in this city."

A laugh breaks out of her, succumbing to a cough a moment later. Once she wrangles it back into submission, she uncovers a drink trolley from the eccentric clutter, pulling it just far enough out to look through the lower shelf of half-empty bottles. "You've been meeting all the wrong people."

"Like Chancellor Fiordelise?"

She cringes. "Exactly." She brings back a whiskey and a bourbon with a pair of glasses. Her brow lifts as she extends the bottles. "Just don't leave your lipstick on the rim."

I almost take one, but I can feel myself pulling apart at the thought, so I shake my head. "Start me with a glass, thanks."

"Suit yourself." She pours Tavish and me a whiskey—mine a bit fuller—and keeps the bottle of bourbon, taking three long gulps as we both find seats in the mess.

Luca pulls one of his heads through the secret passageway and settles it just inside the room. He licks Teo's ankle as she flops onto a clothes-covered chair. She smiles at him.

It snaps something inside me. I down my glass in one go, letting the burn ignite me, and slam it onto the arm of the chair harder than I mean. "How are the people here letting this happen—to a living being, to someone whose entire life is about protecting them—to—" *To someone like me*, I almost say. But this is about Luca. This is about Venalt. I breathe out. "Even if they don't know that Luca is sentient, or they don't care to learn, it's their own damn city that's going to sink. Can't we make them care about *that*?"

"What about that prophecy the gondola driver mentioned?" Tavish asks, cupping his whiskey in both hands. He hasn't even sipped it yet.

My skin crawls at the thought of the prophecy. While I was alone in the cell, it had slipped my mind, but the more I think back, the more my stomach turns. Prophecies themselves have never bothered me, but the ones I've grown up with have been simple, personal predictions that can shift over time and continuous action. The gondola driver's enthusiastic rant about the foretold destruction and resurrection of the city feels insidious in all the ways it disregards the pain it would cause in the meantime. "They can't really believe some better city will rise from the corpse of this one, can they?"

"Some do—or want to, at least. Some believe we can fight the hippocamps off, or that the tales of them consuming the corelium are exaggerations. Which they're not—a few of our scientists went out with samples to test. Three of them didn't come back, and the other two are lucky to have their remaining limbs." Teodor shakes her head, cringes, and takes a long swig of her bourbon. "Some think they have time to wait and see how things play out, that the Institute will hand over the ignits once the situation is dire enough, not realizing it's been that dire for weeks."

"And the Institute?" I roll my fingers over the rim of my glass. "I know they rely heavily on their ignits, but what use are generators and motors if there's no city to power?"

Teodor grimaces once, then again as she takes another drink. "Chancellor Fiordelise was too stubborn for her own good. We're hoping the interim chancellor, Iseppa Collari, will see reason, but at this point, I'm willing to apply pressure where hope doesn't pay out."

Apply pressure. I see Chancellor Fiordelise's stomach rearranging itself into its component parts again, her body seizing, Matthia sobbing her name. That was certainly a kind of pressure. And if Fiordelise wasn't working with the Citadel to save Luca, then the only way to overcome that might have been to replace her with someone who would.

But motive doesn't make a murder. Teodor holds her bourbon bottle with frail hands, staring into it like it might tell the future. It remains uselessly silent in all regards.

I glance toward the ignit bag Teodor has dropped in the mess of her collection, only the soft glow of blue and red revealing its position. If I strain, I can feel their power gently thrumming, calling to me. How much more does Luca feel it, as weak and tired as he is? I try not to think of the time when I'll start fading, start needing the ignits just to stay alive, but the reality of it still shivers down my spine. "Is that all the ignits you have left?"

"These, and a few others." Teodor nudges the bag for emphasis. "When he was healthy, Luca made primarily blue ignits, with an occasional pink or red. They had little use in weaponry, so most were distributed to the Institute for their engineering projects, with a few to the Basilica for religious services. The ones we had in the Citadel were for our security system, and the handful no one else had filed claims on yet."

So few. It's as I thought and somehow worse all at once.

"Has the Basilica offered their ignits?" Tavish asks.

"Of course not. I'm the enemy—the war to their peace, the justice to their mercy. Besides, they're too busy praying for guidance." She looks at her bourbon, growls like it's the Basilica, and takes another long drink.

She's downed more of it than even I could have. It makes my skin crawl with conflicting desire and disgust. I tap my glass against the arm of my chair as if enough vibration will signal its refill. I have to force myself to loosen my grip. Slowly, I set the glass off to the side. My craving doesn't leave, though, my eyes gliding back to the bottle, the light buzz that's growing at the base of my skull, so soft and warm that I can almost believe this would all be a little bit better with just one more glass. What harm would that do?

You know the harm, I shout, splitting apart so frantically that it hurts. *You've been here before. You can't go back, not when Luca's life is at stake and you might be the only one who can save him.*

The other half of me withdraws in guilt, nothing to say to that, only misery.

I wrap him up, holding him. Through the threads I've tangled with Luca's, I feel Venalt's aurora do the same, curling around both halves of me with both halves of himself. I sink into him, focusing on his presence, on our two— three?—no, two heartbeats soft and slow. "Tavish and I can go to the Basilica in your place. Even if their ignits will only tide Luca over, we'll get them."

"No offense, but last time you and Tavish met with a chancellor she ended up dead."

I look at Tavish, hoping he might step in with his diamond voice and give Teodor a hundred reasons why we need to be trusted with this, but he picks at his cuticles, mouth clamped so tightly shut his jaw looks strained. I'm on my own, then. I give Teodor a grin and a shrug. "Well, now we're meeting with you. When you're alive after we leave, we'll be fifty-fifty on dead to not dead chancellors."

Teodor blinks. A rumble starts in her chest and ends with her coughing into her handkerchief. As she finishes, she wipes a bead of moisture off the corner of her eye, and her breath comes in ragged, but she still manages a smile. "Fucking depths, man. You and Tavish must make quite the pair if that's your very best manipulation tactic. Balances things out, I guess."

I'm not sure how to take that. But I need her to agree. I need to be able to do *something* for Luca. "Just let me talk to them. I have none of your political baggage. If they see you as the enemy, then I can be a neutral party." I don't say the rest of what I'm thinking: that their prophecy is causing people to accept—maybe hope for, even—the city's sinking. And that could make them just as guilty as Fiordelise.

Teodor shakes her head still, but she bounces her shoulders and takes another long drink. At the end, she lifts the bottle like a cheer. "What harm could it do? Perhaps, from you, they'll listen. Badger them a bit—but words only." She looks pointedly at me as she says it.

Which is hardly fair since I've only killed three more people in my life than Tavish.

"I don't need any genuine criminal charges strapped to either of you, or else I *will* have to lock you up somewhere." Teodor finishes her bourbon, setting the bottle to the side. She positions her cane as though she means to stand, but when she puts a bit of her weight on it, she winces and gives up. "I'll talk to Commander Zuane, stop them from dragging you back in, so long as you don't make a ruckus. Keep out of the Institute though. Zuane is pissed enough at you both as it is, I don't need you stirring up more trouble there while he's trying to conduct his investigation."

"Thank you." I nod and try not to look too unruly, not like a man who has stolen multiple auroras, aided a rebellion, and watched one of Venalt's leaders die yesterday.

My gaze drops to the mostly full whiskey bottle. Tearing it away, I rise and wave a hand between the tapestry Luca still has his head beneath and the room's main door, half-open to reveal another small, similarly over-decorated room. "Should we . . .?"

"You can leave here directly through the basement. Luca will show you the passage. It has a secret doorway if you need to return through it—I'm sure Luca would like that."

"Of course," I say. At the same time, Luca vibrates, *'He should come back soon. I like him.'*

It's so open and honest that the statement seems to lodge in my chest. *I like you, too, my friend.*

He purrs with delight. *'We can save my city.'*

Yes, I think we can. And I feel almost hopeful about it all.

Luca pulls his heads from the room, and the sound of his scales brushing against stone echoes as he draws himself slowly back down the steps. I wonder if the rest of his body fits on the stairs or if his tail is so long that it still drapes into the water even when his head is with Teodor. He hesitantly offers me the faint impression of coils upon coils wound through the entire foundation's underwater passages.

It's an almost overwhelming scale, so much grander than any creature I've known in the Murk. *Impressive.*

The emotion he sends back is half embarrassment and half pride.

As I turn for the exit, I press my fingers to Tavish's arm, waiting for him to rise before looping it through mine. He lets it go, grabbing my hand instead. He squeezes, and it almost covers the tremble running through him. I can't guess at the cause of it—Teodor, or us, or all of this, his loss and his future and another city on the brink of collapse—but my heart aches for him all the same.

His attention shifts toward Teodor, and his cheeks go pink. "It was nice seeing you again."

"Was it?" There's a tipsy edge to her voice that wasn't there when she spoke of politics, and a streak of red to her ghostly cheeks that looks sickly compared to Tavish's blush. "I did think maybe you'd write after Maraheem fell—ask me to take you in or something. But I suppose you found someone to *actually* elope with this time."

Tavish's expression softens, but his grip on my hand turns into a vise. "You don't still hold that against me, surely."

Her anger seems tight and small, like a thing held close to her chest, spilling free only now that she's lost control over it. "I waited for you. I went back and forth on that boat thirteen times. Thirteen fucking times, waiting for you, because you said you'd be there. But you'd said a lot of things, didn't you?"

"I was sixteen. I was scared." His voice sounds so even compared to hers, a crystal thing built of logic and sharpened with just the right edge of emotion that I want to believe he was innocent in all of this. But as good as Tavish is, I know that innocent is not a thing he has ever been.

"And I was seventeen!" Teodor's rough voice cracks, and she coughs a few times before retaining it in a hiss. "I was seventeen, and I was so in love with you that I was willing to give up my perfectly happy life and my parents and my massive inheritance and everything I'd ever known to save you from your mother, and you just left me there without a fucking word and ran back to her." Her voice goes so hoarse and her skin so pale, she seems like she's nothing but a veil spread over aching bones and a decade of harbored anger.

"When Maraheem fell, I knew you weren't dead. Tavish K. Findlay could talk a blade into breaking itself before it cut him."

Tavish holds himself so stiffly that it turns his breath sharp and short. "I'm sorry."

"Keep your apologies." Teodor drags herself to her feet with her cane, waving her free arm uselessly, then dropping it. "I got over you. I'm fine."

Tavish lets me go, the tension seeming to dispel from him like a deflating balloon, leaving only the trembling in his pinkies and the hard line of his jaw. His diamond voice wavers. "Teo . . ."

"Get out. I don't want to hear it," she snaps. But as Tavish turns, she adds, "Just—I have to know—did all your pretty words finally make her love you?"

"No." He keeps his back to her, but his chin tips, both hands clutching the top of his cane. "I was the one who killed her. You didn't ken that, did you, darling?" He leaves with his cane clashing in front of him, not pausing even as he slams his shoulder into the edge of the secret passage, nearly yanking the tapestry off the wall to push through it. It hangs lopsided as it settles behind him.

"Fuck," Teodor mutters.

The curse seems all my brain is capable of producing, too, my heart fighting between anger and suspicion and not sure who to aim either at.

Before I can figure it out, Teodor groans and slumps back into her seat, dropping her head into her hands. Teodor, who's slowly dying. Teodor, whose best friend suffers the same fate unnecessarily, abandoned by the people he refuses to stop caring for. Teodor, who just relived the traumatic ending of her first love because the man who hurt her has appeared in her city without warning and tangled himself in her co-chancellor's death.

"I made a fine damn mess of *that*," she says.

"You did."

"Take care of him." She sounds almost sincere through her misery. "But also take care of yourself."

I have to draw a breath, then let it out before I can properly manage, "You too." I find I genuinely mean it. "Get some sleep. And don't drink too much."

"What's the alcohol going to do, kill me?" She smiles without humor and lifts her fingers. "See you soon, Rubem of No-Man's Land."

"See you." The farewell makes me feel no less awkward as I push into the tapestry, Teodor coughing raggedly behind me. Tavish's usually poised strides sound cumbersome now, a few slips and curses and slams of his cane interrupting them. I catch up to him as he reaches the bottom of the stairs.

"I'm here," I whisper.

He takes my arm.

I can feel him trembling through it, each inhale a little too shallow. "If you're going to have another attack—"

"No." He tightens his hold on me. "I just want to go back to the hotel."

I don't fight him.

CHAPTER NINE

only option

BUT I SUPPOSE YOU found someone to actually elope with this time.

I can't get the statement out of my head. It slings back and forth like a battering ram all the way up the elevator to our hotel room, echoing in the sound of the keys and Lavender's disdainful mew as we enter. Tavish has stopped shaking, but there's something off about him still, something in how he moves, a little too precise, each comment measured and poised in a way that feels like a wall between us.

He takes his suit jacket off, turning from me as he carefully drapes it over a chair. "You should say it—whatever it is you're thinking."

But I can't yet, can't quite put into being the fullness of my emotion. "Did you love Teodor?" I ask instead, leaning onto the counter of the tiny kitchen and crossing my arms. "When you left her behind, did you love her?"

Whatever he expected from me, it must not have been this. His head shoots up, mouth opening. "Aye, I loved her. I always will."

"Then why didn't you tell me about her?"

A flush draws over his cheeks, and it's not the red of a long-maintained crush, but the stark color of his embarrassment. Maybe this whole time, that's what it always has been. "I kenned that what I did to her would have scared you. I didn't want to risk that."

"You didn't want to risk scaring me off? Why would that scare me? I'm not Teodor." The statement is too close, though, too close to what I want to—need to—say, that it breaks the words free. "But you're still you. You still wanted to stay in Maraheem, every minute leading up to its fall, even when you knew that I wouldn't, that I couldn't." I breathe in and breathe out. It feels like a hurricane. "Did you come with me after your family's death because it was your only option?"

He swallows. "You *were* my only option—the only decent one, anyway. I have no one else, and starting off in a new city alone, after everything that had happened, felt unthinkable."

Pain rolls through me, so sharp and startling it takes me a moment to realize: I didn't expect his answer to be yes. I asked for the reassurance that he had wanted to come with me with the same fever that I had wanted him to come. Instead, he's slapped me in the face. "You used me."

"Trenches, Ruby." Tavish runs a hand through his hair, his unfocused eyes finding the ceiling, but his diamond voice holds, perfect and cutting. "Aye, a little, I suppose, but not like *that*. I cared about you. I wanted to be with you. What does it matter that the universe had to nudge me a bit?"

I hear the truth in his voice, feel all the ways my accusation doesn't line up with our reality. But I also feel all the ways it does, all the truth that backs my anger. And it hurts, hurts so much that I can't look at him yet, can't find words that don't turn into barbs the moment they form on my tongue.

This was supposed to be different.

This night was supposed to be us opening up to each other, figuring out where we are together after the covering up and the confessions of love. Reconnecting on a new level.

But now all I can think is how close I was to being another Teodor to him. "If not for Maraheem collapsing, would you have even considered being with me at all?"

"I . . ." He goes quiet, so quiet that I swear I can hear the tightening of his brow, the subtle draw of his breath like thunder. He's thinking; I just can't tell whether he's trying to decide on his answer or trying to decide how to say it without breaking me.

"No," I say. "I don't want to know. Just—fuck this. I'm so tired." I toss up my hands, turning away. Each silent heartbeat feels like a mockery as Tavish doesn't fill it. My vision tunnels, a rush flooding through my ears. I force my lungs to open, to mutter something that sounds like "I—I have to go. I'll be back—but I need—"

I can't finish my sentence, can't do this a moment longer without saying something I'll regret. I push through the door. As it slams behind me, I feel a bit like I've flung myself out in pieces.

I have half a mind—half both my minds—to slam right back through it, but the anger and pain are too fresh, and my fear so palpable I can taste it metallic in the back of my mouth. I need the space to think and compose myself. This will all seem more reasonable after a walk. And a drink. My feet carry me around corners and stairs, and out through the hotel doorway, along the curve of the street. After a gaggle of teenagers in a boat stares at me, I yank up my hood, keeping close to the buildings.

As my initial surge of emotion fades, the world comes back into focus: the mild sea breeze chilled around the edges; the early afternoon sun creeping in between the high walls, reflecting in silver ripples off the clear blue channel water; the golden flecks in the corelium sparkling against the red; the city's subdued tan and white stones contrasted by the deep-green and auburn vines draped down the sides of the buildings and tangled along cords strung between; the delicate detail of every doorframe, every flower box.

But all that becomes merely a backdrop to hollered greetings from the tops of balconies and jokes passed between boats. The strum of a string instrument descends from a high window, the chitter of birds and the squawk of gulls sailing overhead. My own silent footsteps seem merely to be drowned in a fuller orchestra.

I move idly over bridges and up stairwells, down tight, wrapping paths with tiered door stoops, somehow always keeping the hotel—keeping Tavish—a few blocks away. I pass three restaurants and two bars before I realize that I've been here before: wandering a foreign city, thoroughly alone with a future in chaos, and what I want more than anything is the notion of acceptance—someone with a free smile and too many wrinkles who will welcome me in just long enough to make me feel like I belong. What I'm looking for is Ivor Reid's place back in Maraheem. But he's hundreds of miles away, maintaining a city still on the brink of a second collapse.

I follow the next whiff of food indoors.

The small place is tidy, plants in the window and metal chairs ornamented in stained-glass flowers, half-filled with lunch customers on their way out. A number of their usual items are crossed off the menu chalked behind the counter, but I'm not here for their food selection in the first place, and by the trouble they're having traveling back and forth from the mainland, I imagine most places are low on the same things right now. I find an empty stool at the bar and dig through my pockets. No wet leaves this time, but the lint has accumulated again. I pick a few of our final coins out of the mess and order something called the Three-Quarters Prophecy that sounds like it has enough alcohol to kill a small leviathan.

The bartender—a satyr woman around my age, her horns twisting more outward than up—pauses after she sets the drink down, staring at my hooded face with a furrowed brow. Her eyes dart away, and she touches a small horn on her bracelet, strung beside a little three-leaf-clover pin.

I wrap my hands around my glass, the rainbow crisscrosses that mar my skin twinkling against the drink's gold and scarlet hues. "Do you believe this whole prophecy business—the city sinking and returning again stronger and all that?"

"The three great prophecies?" She pauses. Her fingers slide along the edge of the counter. "The city will sink. And once the second prophecy comes to pass, it will be raised to a glorious pinnacle." She tones her words a bit like a song. "I want to believe it, isn't that almost the same? I want to have hope that if this all comes down, it's not the end, you know?"

"What if we don't survive until that better end, though?" I venture softly, trying to make it a gentle nudge, but the emotion sinks into my words, clogging them up with an anger and pain that aren't about this city at all. "Maybe you should leave now, before everything falls apart."

Her gaze darts back to me. "Maybe," she says. "But what if I give this all up and the aurora lives and the city stands? Or it does fall, but we aren't harmed in the process, and the prophecy comes to pass, and we get a stronger, safer place from that momentary collapse? I'd have just walked away from what I love most in the world."

"Huh."

She gives an awkward smile and moves a few steps down the bar. Trying to slip away from the conversation, probably. Or just from me.

I don't blame her. And now that I'm no longer standing outside our hotel room, seething and in pain, I don't blame Tavish either.

I'd have just walked away from what I love most in the world, the bartender said.

Like an explosion, the things I care about have turned from a pinpoint to an expanse, but at the center of that, of every future I see myself in, Tavish has slowly made a home. Six weeks with him should be too little for such a total rewriting of my life, but six weeks of seeing him break and bleed and pull himself back together, of him setting his most vulnerable pieces in my hands one by one feels like an eternity.

I turn my glass, lifting it and setting it back down. Its mixed reds swirl like the corelium, sparkling with a faint touch of flecked golden glitter.

There were a hundred thousand ways Tavish could have twisted his admission. Ways he could have framed it that would have made him look like the victim. Ways he might have used it against me. But he had given me the truth, even though it made himself look bad. A bloody chunk of his heart, and I'd thrown it back in his face because he was right. It did scare me.

Drinking myself into a stupor might substitute the fear for a while, but no amount of alcohol will fix this. That's up to me.

I nudge the full glass across the bar, pressing another small coin beside it, and leave. As I pass through the tables, my chest twinges; we have so little money left, for me to spend it on something I don't even drink. I could still down it.

My feet stutter, but I push myself forward, over the threshold and out the door.

I retrace my steps through the city, stopping up the street from the hotel to dip into a flower shop. The door slides soundlessly open, blasting me with the scent of its wares. They run in racks, about two dozen freshly cut bouquets neatly arranged to hide the empty spaces between them. They must all be from gardens within the city. Between the vase displays hang glittering trinkets: the star of the Institute, the triangle of the Citadel, and the clover—the Basilica—along with little horn pendants.

"Her poor daughter," the seller bemoans from the front, their tone a mix of empathy and gossip.

I don't recognize the kabalos purchasing a bundle of white lilies from them until she replies with genuine ferocity, "They won't get away with it."

It's Iseppa Collari, the woman who first found Tavish and me with Fiordelise's body. She was Chancellor Fiordelise's right hand, and now, the new interim chancellor of the Institute.

I bare my teeth as I mosey up to the counter behind her, leaning against the edge of it as I ask, "Who won't get away with it?"

She squeaks and raises her lilies, nearly smacking me with them.

I lift my palms. "Peace."

"Serves you right, sneaking up on people like that." She releases a sharp breath, something that I think she intends as a huff but rings more of fear than the arrogance she tries to paste across her features as she delicately rearranges the bouquet in her arms. "Weren't you meant to be held at the Citadel for questioning?"

I wonder if they put flowers on graves here. If they have graves, in a city with no soil. "There's only so much you can ask a simple witness. Contact Commander Zuane if it worries you."

Her nose wrinkles. "*Zuane*." She enounces his first name the way he gives it out: flat and gruff. "That asshole had better pull his act together."

"Well, there's something we agree about," I grumble.

Iseppa gives me a longer look, her gaze narrowing. "He's spent so much time lurking around the Institute all month. Like he thinks he might steal our ignits just by being there. Sweet-talk them right out from Fiordelise's nose or something." She huffs. "That's none of your business, though."

I lean toward her, just enough to make her flinch back. "The ignits *are* my business."

"You aren't getting them," she snaps, lifting her bouquet as though she might shield herself with it.

"We'll see about that."

Her eyes narrow. "I still think there's something off about you, aurora-man," she mutters, and whirls toward the door.

I let her go then, watching it close behind her. As much as this whole situation itches like a scab I desperately want to pull off, revealing the wound beneath, there's something more important waiting for me at the hotel. I turn back toward the counter.

"Do you have just the petals, by any chance . . ."

CHAPTER TEN

most in the world

THE HOTEL ROOM FEELS dark by the time I return, the tight, tall buildings cutting off the afternoon light and the half-drawn curtains casting hazy shadows. The soft squeak of the door closing and the plunk of my takeout bags on the table are buried beneath hoarse sobs, wet and rough and tired, like they've been forced over gravel. Each one spears into me, a knife for every extra step I took away from here.

Pushing back my hood, I slip around the couch where Tavish curls, a pillow beneath his chin and Lavender pressed against his thigh. He trembles as he inhales. Red rims his eyes, lids swollen, and his curls jut at odd angles. Despite it all, he's still the most beautiful person I've ever seen. And I never want to see him like this again—never want to be the cause of his pain.

Something jolts inside me with the momentary dread that maybe he wouldn't hurt this much if he never came this far with me. He has other options now—better options. But he has those options, and still he's with me. However we came to be here, he chose it, the way the people of this city are choosing to hope for its salvation. The way their aurora beneath chooses to protect them. The way I want to choose Tavish no matter the effort it asks of me or the pain it might occasionally inflict.

I set down a final bag beside the couch and settle onto it. As the cushions sink beneath me, Tavish's breath catches. He freezes just for an instant, then finds me with a hand. I let him pull me close, wrapping him up in my longer limbs and pressing my face to the top of his head.

"I'm sorry," I whisper, and it sounds as rough as his sobs.

"You're sorry?" Tavish gives a wet laugh, burrowing against my chest. "You do ken which of us has been a conniving arse?"

"All I know is that you're conniving and I'm an ass." I tangle my fingers in his clothes, even my half hand doing its best to cup his curves, to prove that he's here still, and so am I, so we will keep on being. "You're already forgiven, always." I pause, then add, "It's all right if you wouldn't have come with me back in Maraheem had things been different. Things weren't different. You did come. And you're here now."

Tavish doesn't unwind himself from me, but he lifts his head, letting me see the pinched, vulnerable look on his face. "I would have stayed behind, not because I didn't want you, but because I wasn't brave enough to—to be my own person, be someone who was free to travel the world for love. I couldn't have forced myself to be rid of my family that easily, not without all that happened."

Anger sparks in my core, and this time it's not toward Tavish but everything that has forced Tavish into this place: his mother keeping him small, his father willfully ignoring it, his brother using it to take the spotlight, even his sister hiding in her library under her own burdens instead of working with Tavish to free them both. "I understand. And it's not your fault."

"It is my fault! They were my choices." The edge burns out of his words as he continues, "I should have told you about Teodor. I was scared—scared I'd lose you—because I know that you've been left behind all your life, and I couldn't bear for you to think you might need to leave to keep from me doing the same to you. Because I love you, not because you're my only option. I may be blind and have anxiety, but I'm fully capable of paving my own way in the world, if you haven't noticed." His voice goes huffy. "I made connections in half the cities we've been to—the high minister of Alfhouat even offered me a job. I bet that I could talk this hotel's owner into paying me to live here if I wished."

"I'm sorry, you're right," I say, my heart stuttering a little with joy at the pretentiousness of his grumbling. "I never doubted that you could be making a life of your own. I acted as I did because I was scared, too."

"Both of us, oi?" Tavish's mouth quirks. "We're cowards."

"Well, I suppose *scared* isn't actually the right term. More like terrified? Absolutely completely wrecked by even the smallest chance that you might not want to do this again." I cup the side of his face and tip his chin up, but he slams his lips into mine before I can kiss him, pressing himself against me so firmly that he slides into my lap. He's eager and questing, as though he's exploring whether this version of me is the same one he kissed in the Citadel waiting room and in that Maraheem laboratory and a hundred other times. I'm not the same man, not quite, and Tavish seems to realize that, pausing thoughtfully, our lips still brushing.

"Do you really think I'd be here with you if it wasn't what I wanted?"

"No—yes." I cringe. "Maybe. You've had a rough go of things recently, and this isn't exactly the life you're accustomed to."

"And is it for you? I'm not the only one who left a home behind, who has to bear this stress and fatigue. I'm not the one who has to watch as we pass through cities that refuse to save their auroras from a sickness that's coming for him too." Tavish's hand clutches into the fabric of my shirt, like he can hold me in this life forever that way, turn both of us immortal. A lump wells in my throat, so tight and hot that I can say nothing as he continues, "I want this, Ruby. I want to be here with you, whatever that takes." He smiles, small but aggressively sincere. "It hasn't been all bad. Remember that little restaurant in Roekia and the walk we took along the river in Eyrr?" His lips twist into a smirk. "The way we fucked on the train over the mountains?"

I flush straight through my core. The rest of that trip is a haze, but our sex—that, I think I'll remember until I die. "Damn, it feels like a century ago." I lean back, pulling him against my chest. "Was that the last time we did it? What happened after that?"

"I don't quite ken it, really." He lays his head on my shoulder, his nose tangling in my braids and his curls lapping at my chin. "You were depressed those two days after we arrived in Geviso, and I . . . I don't know. I felt like I was, well, not the cause perhaps, but at least another burden instead of a solution. My anxiety was worsening again, and I suppose I withdrew. It felt safer for you if my problems weren't in the way."

My chest aches with such a pounding pain for all the hurt he's been facing alone that I swear he must feel it through my layers of fabric. "You think that after all that you do for me, you could ever be a burden?" I tip his face back up, turning mine to let my lips brush his forehead. "And even if you did nothing for me, could give me nothing but your baggage, I'd have wanted you with me still. Would I be here if I didn't adore you just as you are?"

"You *are* an absolute dobber sometimes," he says, but he melts against me, and the last of his tension abandons him in favor of a full smile that presses into his tear-reddened eyes.

I run my palm up and down his back. "Can we talk about your panic attack?"

"Aye, if we must." He groans. "I don't understand. I was fine. That first week or so, I felt normal, and now every sharp bang or scolding parent's voice, and I think I can hear her." The *her* is so obvious, his voice hitched and twisted in a way only Raghnaid Findlay could inspire. "When I look back, it's her I feel in all that pain Lilias inflicted on me—for some damnable reason, it's her I think of, as though every terrible thing that's happened to me is her doing, and will keep being so, because she's there, inside me, telling me I was too weak to avoid it, too useless to overcome it."

My heart bleeds for him, and I wish I knew exactly what to say to take his pain away. "She was always wrong about you. You were strong then, and you are now, too. This isn't weakness." I draw my fingers up and down his back, rhythmic and soothing. "She's gone. And she's not coming back."

"Because I killed her." He turns his face against the couch as he whispers, "She had to die."

"You did what needed to be done. But that doesn't mean you can't feel for it. You didn't just save a city, Tavish. You lost your entire family, even Sheona. That's not the kind of thing people walk away from unchanged."

He draws in a tight, sharp breath and lets it out. "I'm not sad over her death, though, is the thing. It's that—trenches, I miss them, all of them." He utters it so softly it sounds like a prayer. "Even her. Like some kind of fucking addict. I just want it to stop."

I realize how still I've grown the same moment he does.

He rubs his thumb against my shoulder. "But then, I suppose it's only natural to keep craving that attention after living with her for so long. If the anxiety she branded me with doesn't make me weak, then this must not either."

He says it for me more than for himself, I think. I almost want to tell him that I left that drink at the bar, but the glass of whiskey from Teo's and the wine in the bags on the table shame me out of it. I press my lips to his, quick and soft. "It doesn't make us weak," I say, and I try so very incredibly hard to believe it, for both our sakes.

Silence stretches between us, yet it feels not stiff, not painful, not awkward, but peaceful: a thing filled instead of emptied. I bask in the stillness, letting it slip into every part of my chest that has been scraped out over the last week. It feels like waking up.

I can see a thought working through Tavish, picking a soft flush along his cheeks. He exhales, almost a laugh but a little more worried than humorous. "I promise this is not simply because we met Teodor today, but . . . Good fuck, and I'm supposed to be decent with my words." He breathes out again, seeming to center himself. "If we're in this all the way, for the unknowable future at least, is it just the two of us, a monogamous relationship? Are we happy with that?"

I snort, more from his terrible execution than the concept itself. "Are you asking if you can sleep with Teodor?"

"No, trenches no. I'm still wildly attracted to her, I'll give you that, but our relationship sailed a long time ago. If I can pick up the pieces enough for us to be amenable, it'll amaze me." He pulls his hands together, one nail shoving into another. "I merely figured that while we're here, we might as well talk about it."

I catch his fingers, kissing them for good measure. "You're right. And I love this—this is enough for me. I don't really know yet if I'd be all right adding a third person to it. I can't say I'd be very comfortable sharing our relationship with someone I wasn't also fond of, and right now I'm still just learning how to be with someone at all after so long alone. But I also can't say I'd be opposed if it would make you happy."

"I'm already happy."

"Are you, now?" My chest warms with such affection that in this moment, I could climb inside him and let his light brush against mine.

The thought thrusts the two halves of me apart so hard we blink a few times, trying to search for the source of the bizarre notion. It's aurora, definitely—something specific to aurora physiology, though not the physiology I'm accustomed to in this world—but whatever memory it comes from slips away like ash as soon as we wrap our fingers around it. We plunge back into one as Tavish brushes his hand along the lines of our jaw, both halves of me utterly content to focus on him and him alone for now.

"Though," I say, soft and languid as his touch shivers over me. "Since you're one person, and I'm two people, we're technically already in a polyamorous relationship."

Tavish cups the back of my neck. "Huh. I hadn't thought about that."

"Is it weird?"

"Oh, undoubtedly." He returns to tracing his thumb down my collarbones and along the crisscrossing aurora flesh of my chest and spreads his palm against my sternum. "Is it . . ." he starts, then stops. "So you're . . .?"

"Hmm?" I brush his curls off his forehead.

He takes another moment to gather his thoughts, but the delay feels content and contemplative, as though he's not the least bit worried of the question or the answer, only explaining it properly. "I suppose what I want to know is, you're Rubem—the Rubem I met on that beach in Falcre—*and* you're the aurora?"

"Exactly."

"How did we never talk about this?"

"I thought it would scare you."

"Good fuck."

"I know."

"But, I couldn't tell the difference." His voice goes clipped at this, a knife turned inward.

"I think that's how it's meant to be." I draw my hands down his back, just to let him feel me, know the me that's here is the same one who loves him. "I don't have memories that verify it, but I get the sense that this process isn't as unique as we thought—or, it is, here, but for the aurora, back wherever they fell from, what I've done—what we've done—it's something sacred and wonderful. And it's meant to be like this, only works properly when both individuals are aligned in such a way that when they become one, they aren't two contradictory fighting consciousnesses, but two people who already want to grow into the strengths of the other, that each can become more like the other without losing anything true or good of themselves."

"So, you are *more* you like this?"

"Yes. Or at least, I'm more of the Rubem that the Rubem you met decided he wanted to be, and more of the aurora that the one who found him chose to become. The Rubem you first met would never have traveled the world like this, but the more he felt of the way his aurora cared, the more he wanted to care like that too. And then we got me."

"No wonder it's so rare, then, for an aurora and a human to bond, if it has to find a human who fits them this perfectly."

"Even more so because the aurora has to want to live like a human, too," I explain. "Most of them—all those I've met, except possibly Luca—don't have any interest. They want only to shift from peaceful dream to dream, and bonding with a host's consciousness—with a host who has such a deliberate and intelligent consciousness in the first place— prevents that."

"Do you have another name, then? An aurora one."

"I did once, but it's gone now. I like the name Rubem, though—all of me likes it." An awkward laugh comes out, unbidden. "It still breaks my mind a little bit. The whole process felt so natural, but when I think about it too hard, it is—what did you just call this?—*undoubtably weird.*"

"You were always an odd one."

"I get odder the more you know me." I repeat the words like a prayer, smiling.

Tavish probably doesn't recognize it as a phrase I used to describe myself when we first met, certainly doesn't know how often my aurora half repeated it while trying to convince my human side that we didn't have to be enemies, but he must hear the affection in my voice because he smiles back.

His brow scrunches. "Do you still use the same pronouns? Do auroras have genders?"

I groan. "The fuck if I know."

And I wait, tense, as though my aurora half might drop a gender on me—as though my aurora history might drop one on us both. The most that comes is the soft sensation of something less firmly masculine, along with the suspicion that the pronouns my human half has always used might have overlapped with my aurora ones without fully encompassing them. I think also that my human half's pronouns might never have fully encompassed his gender in the first place. That maybe he has always been a wider, more ambiguous thing than *man* or *male* could properly describe. I'm not certain, but I do know that I am no less as I am now, only more. And that I'm content.

I exhale. "I feel right in my body, and I'm happy with how people perceive and refer to me, and how I perceive myself. That's enough, I think."

"That's all gender is, just being happy with who you are in the world and how it relates to you," Tavish says gently, and finds the edge of my lips with his own. He shakes his head as he pulls back, like he's dislodging something. "You're really two people in there?"

"Two people who both think you're the most handsome man alive." I press my lips to his hand again, outlining each knuckle, then tugging up his shirt sleeve to nuzzle his wrist. "Or am I just making this weird?"

"I don't believe it's quite my kink." He laughs. "But it's you now. And I do rather like you."

"That's it, just *like*?"

"I rather *love* you, unreservedly." He drags his fingers gently across my throat and my chest to the bared slip of skin from where he stabbed me in Fiordelise's office, making me throb in places so deep that I think he's trying to pull my desire straight to the surface. "And I'd rather like to show you just how much I do."

I feel myself respond with a bone-deep desire and an awful boner. "Please," I murmur, pausing to just breathe him in. The floral hints in the hotel's soap have worn off, leaving him smelling not of honey, but still of something so indescribably him, sweet and dark and wonderful. It takes far too much willpower to sit up straighter and slide Tavish partway off my lap. "But before I forget, I brought you something, Well, I brought you two things—one of them is lunch, or dinner, whatever we're at now—but the other one is just, I don't know, romantic, I guess."

"Rubem N. Man's Lander!"

"That's not how my name works."

Tavish gives me a little shove. "Shut up and offer me your romantic present already."

"As you wish, my princeling." My princeling. I don't know when it turned from *the* to *mine*, but we don't fit together any other way now. Everything we've just done proves that. I lean over the couch to collect the small sack I brought in earlier. I stall once it's in my hands, not entirely sure what to do with it, but Tavish runs his fingers down my arm and snatches it away.

He hums softly and presses a hand in. His brow crinkles. Then his face blooms with joy. He pulls out one of the rose petals, drawing it delicately across his lips. "You scoundrel. You didn't pull them off the flowers just for me."

"No, they came that way. There's a blossom intact on the table, too, but I figured you could enjoy them more directly like this."

He throws the petal at me, laughing. "You just want me to fuck you on a bed of roses like a romantic fool."

"Gods, yes." I tug at his tucked-in shirt, pulling it free from his pants until I brush skin.

A vicious smirk takes over Tavish's face that probably forecasts a fair amount of begging in my future, but fuck is it worth it. As though to prove just how this night will go, he dips his hand beneath my shirt fabric to treat my nipple like his plaything. He tugs hard enough that I make a hollow sound, my body in desperate need of that hand somewhere a bit lower. But when he lets go, he scoots back entirely, setting the flower petals to the side and sweeping himself to his feet with a smirk to fit a most pompous princeling. "First, though, I'm starving."

"You're a conniving ass, and you should be ashamed of yourself!" I shout.

He laughs.

As he tries to scamper toward the table, catching the edges of the furniture in an attempt not to hit anything, I grab him from behind, kissing his neck until he melts against me, moaning. It turns into a groan when I finally let him go.

"Who's the arse, now?" he grumbles.

I grin, pointed rainbow incisors and all. "Dinner first."

Our early dinner tastes as amazing as breakfast, but far better, for the only stress involved is the way Tavish brushes his fingers into my arm every ten seconds. The alcohol is better, too—better than any of Teo's whiskey or fourth prophecies could ever be—not just because it's wine, but because this time I'm drinking it in a contented celebration and not to drown out or glaze over any darker feelings. It also helps that Tavish keeps rubbing the tops of his bare feet against my ankle.

We finish dinner and then what comes after finishes far faster than it deserves. The late afternoon glows through our curtains as we lie, still half-clothed, on the couch, scattered rose petals pressed between the cushions. We graciously balance out the rush by taking our time to collect the flowers and carry them into the bedroom for a long bath and an even longer, more proper tangle through the sheets, complete with enough begging to make my deep voice hoarse and enough bliss to carry me into another world entirely.

The suite is dark by the time Tavish rolls off me, panting and sloppy, a lazy smile on his face. I tip my head to give him a slow, lingering kiss, the kind that carries into our dreams. Lavender leaps between us, purring as she curls against our stomachs, and for the rest of the night, I can almost forget the corelium holding us up and the hippocamps swarming the waters beyond, Luca's song thudding just left of my own heartbeat.

CHAPTER ELEVEN

the dead versus the dead

THE CHANCELLOR OF THE Basilica makes us wait in the building's long central structure for nearly an hour, but I can almost forgive them. Engravings, stained glass, sculptures, and patterns ornament every inch of the high walls and arched ceiling, dictating scenes of peace and war, of landscapes and animals and plants, of nearly everything in this world and some things that most certainly aren't. All of them flow toward the three massive, gilded statues in the center of the building: a finned snake that could be a single-headed leviathan, a winged lion, and a marine equine creature that looks like a soft herbivore cousin of the hippocamps.

Worshipers and meditators sit on cushioned benches along the walls and unroll mats from canisters to kneel upon. A melodic chanting rises from a group of them in tasseled robes, filling the space with a hauntingly beautiful song that makes my heart lift and my body loosen. These gods are so different from my own that I can't begin to imagine my Southern deities of monsoons and sun and mist ever existing in a place like this, but just the peace and reverence of it brings them to mind—and reminds me of how very little mind I've actually paid them since leaving the Murk, as though they cease to exist beyond the boundaries of the swamp. For now, that seems best. They are a part of me I'll have to face again someday, but I just can't bring myself to do it yet.

With or without them, I can still bask in the Basilica's beauty.

The majesty of it all transcends my aurora splendor so thoroughly that with my hood up, no one seems to notice me. It feels nice to blend into a group again, especially when this one is even more dramatic than I am. I walk Tavish slowly through the structure, explaining the décor to him as I bounce a few coins between my remaining fingers. He's less enthused by it all, but in a relaxed way that leaves him napping on a bench, his expression peaceful.

While he rests, I reach for Luca. Neither of us have untangled the threads we wove when we met, and I find him instantly, his massive form still lurking beneath the foundation center. He thrums a happy greeting and draws off a sliver of my excess energy. I can feel the power he's pulled from me alongside what's left of the two small blue ignits Teodor gave him last night, all pounding in the rainbow-strewn flesh of his aurora. Still, the ashen pieces between them seem larger today.

How many more ignits are there at the Citadel?

'Teodor had eleven. So nine now.'

It hits me again just how much energy Luca is using for his song—far more than the average aurora. *That's mere days' worth.*

He sends me back an acknowledgement that's so mournful it peels away all the peace this place has instilled, and replaces it with a desire to storm past the fancy gates that bar this side of the building from the private wings, and take the Basilica's ignits by force—or better yet, to storm right out, across the foundation's central park and into the Institute. Luca's emotions turn vicious at the thought. *'I can't take from the people.'* Fear tinges his words, fear that isn't pointed at me. *'They're mine.'*

You're scared of them?

'No.' He's telling the truth—I can sense it, even as I can sense there's more he's hiding beneath his reply. *'You won't steal enough ignits, even if you tried. You're one person who doesn't belong here. They'll notice you. You'll be stopped.'*

You might be able to do it, though. You're large enough that they couldn't fight you.

'No!' He retaliates with a snap through our connected threads so strong it hurts in my aurora flesh. It brings the fuller truth with it: he's not afraid of them, but of what they think of him. Afraid they will do more than merely not love him, but will hate him, too.

It hurts: the mix of his pain and the pain that I feel for him. I breathe. *Fine, I won't steal anything.*

'Fine.' He must sense my displeasure, though, because he coils grumpily away, as though turning his back on me. But he doesn't untangle us.

I pace the length of the bench where Tavish naps, twisting and tossing my coins. If the Basilica only owns a handful of ignits, then they alone won't keep Luca alive much longer. But with how few he has currently, even doubling his stores would be worth a meeting, especially if it gives us time to solve this as peacefully as Luca would like—not that peace itself wasn't already yanked off the table by shooting a pink ignit into Chancellor Fiordelise. And if it's the Basilica who killed her . . .

One of my coins nicks my thumb wrong, dropping past my hand. I jerk to catch it, but only end up losing the other two in the process. Their clattering jolts Tavish awake. As I scramble to collect the coins, a Basilica staff member appears.

He wears a modern robe-suit combination a bit less ornate than the staff conducting their religious ceremony near the main statues but just as beautiful. His gaze hops from the slight veins of rainbow beneath the skin of my cheeks to my eyes half-hidden beneath my cowl. His throat bobs as he folds his hands loosely in front of him. "Chancellor Alvise is just finishing their meeting. If you come with me, they will see you shortly."

Tavish climbs to his feet with a tiny yawn. As soon as he's standing, though, his usual poise takes over, his smile effortless and a pride-laced charisma clinging to every word from his diamond voice. "Perfect! Thank you."

Just as *shortly* has meant *someday* for the last hour, it must also mean *immediately* to the Basilica, because Chancellor Alvise rushes up to us as soon as we're through the golden gates, all but holding their circlet in place over their white head feathers as they jog. The middle-aged harpy's flowing robes are cut open from wrist to shoulder bone, letting the rows of their long arm feathers flutter freely, the top set of pure white lying above one of deep grey. Everything else on them is gilded in some way, greys and blacks covered in a shimmering gold that accents their olive skin and makes the yellow ring around both of their slit pupils blaze from behind their glasses. So many earrings ornament their ears that the lobes have stretched, and their bangles jingle with each step.

Their voice is almost a shock in comparison, informal and youthfully excited. "So sorry to keep you waiting like that—our director of the children's house keeps wavering on whether to send the poor dears across to the mainland or not—I don't know what she thinks I need to weigh in on for that." Alvise doesn't quite meet our gazes as they speak, as if they need to be looking elsewhere in order to focus. They make a queasy sort of hissing sound. "I am the chancellor, I suppose that's why. Anyway, anyway, come along—I heard you already spoke with Teodor and the late Fiordelise, did you?"

"Aye," Tavish replies. "We didn't mean to leave you for last, but our schedules accidentally dictated the order."

"Oh, please, I'm not that important." Alvise pauses, then their feathers ruffle and they correct themselves. "I'm a little bit important, but no more than the other chancellors. You don't have to coddle me about it or anything, I promise." They glance at him just long enough to wink, and the soft wrinkles around their eyes multiply in a way that's endearing instead of aging.

I try not to like them too much—even as vibrant and apparently honest as this chancellor is, the Basilica could still be responsible for the whole mess Luca is stuck in—but Alvise's easy manner puts me at ease all the same.

Tavish smiles, and for all the world, it must look calm and sincere, but I know the way he beams at me behind closed doors, and this is a presentation, even if there's hints of truth beneath it. "Don't undersell yourself, Chancellor. The director of the children's house does want your opinion after all."

"Of course—whatever would she do without me there to nod and confirm that her choice is fine?" Their expression doesn't change as they plunge onward. "I do miss the children, though, so much easier to talk to than adults. Bless their hearts—the adults, I mean. Don't know what gets into most of them."

"They grew up?" Tavish suggests.

Alvise looks thoughtful. "Hmm, yes, I guess so."

The corridors tighten as we walk, not quite as ostentatious as the central Basilica but no less gorgeous for it. A kabalos waves at Alvise from atop a dolly filled with buckets of what appears to be gold flakes, and the human pushing it gives a bow. A similar interaction is repeated with every person we pass, cheery greetings paving our way. Alvise responds to them all with an overwhelming smile and a gaze that never latches for long.

"Anyway, anyway, what've you come for? Someone said ignits?" They look at my chin as they say it.

My impulse is to grin with my aurora-lengthened incisors and ask why they want Luca dead so badly, but the innocent sincerity on their face makes me hesitate. I swallow, looking to Tavish. "Something like that," I say, hoping he hears it as *Fucking save me.*

He steps in like my own personal knight. "We're concerned about the fate of the city and its aurora. As we understand it, the vibrations the creature produces are the only thing keeping the hippocamps from sinking Venalt, but we met with the aurora yesterday, which seems to be doing poorly. I imagine that doesn't bode well for the city." He pauses, humming as if a new thought has just occurred to him. "Though, I hear there's a prophecy about the city having a miraculous rebirth of some kind? Perhaps this place is not so doomed after all?"

"The first three prophecies, yes! They provide a beacon of light in these darkening times by telling us that everything will turn out okay in the end, though most of us here at the Basilica believe we shouldn't encourage the prophecies' fulfillment. The Divine Three don't ask us to bring dark times upon ourselves just because things will get better after. That would be malicious, especially in a situation like this, where the outcome doesn't just affect oneself."

"You're not hoping the city will sink, then?"

Alvise looks genuinely distraught at the idea. "Oh, divine ones, *no.*" Their expression shifts as they pause at an elaborate door, opening it a crack to glance in before letting us through behind them. "The observance chamber should be quiet for a bit—no one is using it until the noontime ceremony."

A giant skylight overlooks the spacious, circular room. A series of tall, spindly pedestals sit at its center, bearing a set of three ornate objects—religious paraphernalia, I assume, fashioned from the triangle, clover, and starburst of the government branches combined. Each one bears three slots with ignits in them: one blue, one red, one pink.

Alvise tuts as they grab a cushion from the side of the room, planting themselves on it with their legs crisscrossed, hands on their knees. "Anyway, anyway, the prophecies do claim that a new, glorious city will take the place of this one, sure, but it doesn't promise that won't come through death and struggle and heartbreak, which would be cruel to bring upon ourselves purposefully, not to mention the potential for misinterpretation at every turn—what if we literally sank the city only to realize that it was a metaphor for some other situation all along? And there's the second prophecy to consider."

"The second prophecy?" I ask, setting out two more cushions. Tavish accepts his with a chaste kiss and sits down, making it look like a throne instead of a simple pillow on the floor.

"Yes, of course, can't have one and three without two! First, the city will sink, and third, it'll be raised to a glorious pinnacle." They speak the words with far less reverence than the bartender who told them to me yesterday, but with a bit more wistful introspection, as though the prophecies are a thing to be dissected apart in order to admire. "But second is the savior. Before the depths can claim the city, the golden will rescue it from annihilation, and from their work will come so on and so forth, third prophecy, et cetera. The need for someone to conduct a valiant rescue does seem to imply something unsavory in the meantime, and why would I ever hope for that?"

"No, you're right. That would be cruel indeed." Those same words could be a barb, but Tavish says them so gently and consoling that they become a blessing instead. "To keep the city from being overrun, though, your aurora will need a constant supply of ignits. I know it's a lot to ask, but if you could part with yours for the sake of keeping Venalt afloat . . ."

"I think we should, certainly, but it's a delicate situation. Very few people in the Basilica want the city to sink, but there's a large fraction who believe that we shouldn't stand in its way either. The aurora must be dying for a reason— should we really interfere with that?"

"Yes." It comes out as a growl, both palms planted into the cushion as I lean forward. "They're dying because we're using their ignits irresponsibly!"

Alvise cringes, their face closing up and their posture pulling back. "Don't shout at me, please," they mutter, staring into their lap as they wiggle one of their bangles back and forth. "I wasn't aware of that. But you're their ambassador, if you say it's true, I believe you."

Tavish's fingers graze my arm before he takes hold of it, squeezing it gently. "We know it's not common knowledge, which is why we've been trying to spread the word."

Alvise nods. "If we're causing their deaths, then that sounds like something we should make an effort to fix."

I try to smile in a way that isn't intimidating, but it turns into a grimace instead. "Then will you help your aurora?"

"Oh, I don't make those kinds of decisions." Alvise laughs. "I just run a third of the government, apparently."

I want to strangle them—politely, in a way that doesn't particularly hurt them, but still, strangle.

"You must understand, I never thought I'd be interim chancellor for this long," they explain. "I only let that bloody fool put me down for it because he swore he'd live another three decades, and I was the one he trusted most, and no one would feel hurt if I took it, because I'm not a threat. Everyone loves me. But everyone loves me because I *don't* make big decisions, see, and I don't make big decisions, because I'm just not cut out for that. Never have been, never want to be." They wave a hand like they're tossing the conversation out the door. "Oh, why am I telling you both this, you don't care. You just want the ignits, and I—damn. I do very much hate this."

"Interim Chancellor?" Tavish asks, sounding for all the world like he's merely curious and not reflecting a thought that's setting off alarm bells in my head.

"Oh dear, yes." Alvise's feathers flutter, and they give a hiss, deep and low but more stressed than angry. "Really, I'd hoped we'd arrange a vote to decide our next chancellor by now, but everything is stalled to the deepest depths with the hippocamps blocking so much of our trade and our tourism nearly dying out. It's been four weeks of exchanges with the Citadel just to arrange for more guards on the ships."

I try to mimic Tavish's subtle questioning, but I sound a bit more like a sledgehammer. "What happened to the Basilica's last chancellor?"

"Chancellor Domenego? A terrible accident. The sectioning of the roof collapsed in his private chambers. He'd finally let the Institute come examine it, and they'd told him it was growing unstable, but they'd assumed there was more time before it was officially unsafe. Apparently they hadn't calculated for the ornamentation Chancellor Pollonia had added to the beams a few decades back."

An accident with a roof the Institute had just investigated. My mouth goes dry. Alone, this calamity might have passed undetected, but with another chancellor deliberately murdered in the same month, I can't help but see a connection. I draw my next question out, almost afraid of Alvise's answer. "What was *he* planning to do with the Basilica's ignits?"

"Give them to the aurora." Alvise bobs in their seat, shaking their head. "But Domenego hadn't announced it publicly yet; it was just a few people at the Citadel who'd been told, I think. He knew there would be a backlash from within the Basilica—the prophecies, of course, I already explained all of that. And these ignits have been with us since the very beginning; they were the first ones our aurora produced, dedicated to the Divine Three for granting us a solid foundation after we floated through the sea for so many desperate months. Our people will want to know how come the Institute isn't offering up any of their ignits when they have so many more than us. The Basilica's supply might not be running elevators or generators, but we serve just as necessary a purpose here—whatever the Institute seems to think. A city doesn't thrive without beauty and hope and love. Maybe the Institute lights our houses, but who takes care of the orphans, funds the hospitals and trains their doctors, feeds the hungry, puts on the art festivals that draw in boats of our tourists? And we don't rub it in anyone's faces! Or, well, I'm rubbing it in your face now, but you aren't from here. Though, maybe that's worse." They suck in a breath and let it out like a laugh. "Sorry, I got carried away, I think."

I lift my brow, trying to overcome the sinking feeling in my gut. "You really don't like the Institute?"

"As people go, I'm sure they're fine. But they're so frustrating. Pigheaded bastards. Bless their hearts, though." They lock their thumb and first fingers together, extending the other six, and tap the back of their hands to their chest. A blessing, maybe. Or a curse. "Anyway, anyway, I know you came for the ignits, not to hear me ramble about the Institute. And I want our aurora to have them, I really do. But . . ."

I'm hit by two rushes at once: rage and understanding, both so strong they feel as though they're ripping me apart. My lungs tighten, my head spinning. *How can they sit here and do nothing?*

'We did nothing for a long time, too.'

And we changed! While they . . . I swallow, sinking against the other half of myself. *They might do the same, but it's their choice.* Still, it makes me nauseous. *Why does everyone get to make the wrong choice for so long?* We both ask the question, but neither of us have the answer, not apart and not together. We ripped each other from our homes. We almost got a pair of teenagers killed and murdered a group on a beach for simply following the instructions of a ruthless family. We've made more wrong choices than good.

What if someone had stopped that?

Tavish smiles at Alvise, and I can see our frustration and guilt are mirrored in him: in the pain he saw inflicted on his home, and the parts of that he enabled. "Did your late Chancellor Domenego put his intentions into writing?"

"There was a letter—I believe the Citadel has it still."

"How hard would it be to fulfill his last wish in his name?" Tavish asks, like he's suggesting we go out for drinks, not manipulating a third of the government through one overhesitant harpy. "No one can wrong you for respecting the decision your predecessor made."

"I couldn't." Alvise's feathers rustle, their expression apologetic, but slowly their brow tightens, lips pressed together. "Actually, I could. That could work. That could actually really work. It's not even my decision, after all, it's just what he'd already chosen to do but didn't have time to complete." They stand, grabbing the skirts of their robes to keep from tripping on the hem. Their bangles rattle. "I'll have word sent to the Citadel. If they can find me that letter, I can probably get the ignits to you imminently."

It should feel like an achievement, but half of my mind is still fixated on everything else that's wrong: two dead chancellors, the Institute's ignits still locked out of reach, Alvise only helping us on a technicality. The weight of it all pulls away the energy that's been fueling me, leaving an exhausted twitchiness in its place. At least there's still a bottle of wine left at the hotel.

A bottle of wine I absolutely should not be drinking in this state.

Forcing a smile, I help Tavish up and follow Alvise toward the door.

"We cannot thank you enough for agreeing to this," Tavish says. "I'm sure your aurora will be incredibly relieved, too."

"Relieved? Can our aurora be relieved?" Alvise pauses, their hand on the knob. "I had the impression it was just a dormant sea snake?"

A rifle of anger stirs in my gut. They're one of the people who should know. Even if no one else does, they should.

Alvise should understand who their decisions are hurting, by gods.

'*Don't,*' Luca shouts through our threads, so hard it rattles me. '*Don't, home worlder, please,*' he repeats, softer.

We're going to talk about privacy later, I grumble at him. But I give Alvise a smile in place of the scowl that's trying to burst through my cheeks. "All creatures have feelings, don't they? Aren't your gods a set of animals? One of them looks like a snake, too."

"Those are merely our visual representations for the deities. Their real forms are either incomprehensible, or they've never been seen, or they would impose undesired expectations on us as mortals, depending on which theology you're following." They open the door, giving a cheery wave when someone outside calls a greeting, before turning their attention, if not their gaze, back to me. "But we all agree that living things, regardless of relative sapience, are to be respected. I do hope the aurora finds peace in this, if that's a thing it can find."

As with the other aurora I've encountered, I don't feel the urge to correct their use of Luca's pronouns the way I do with his sentience. Gender nonsense.

"I'm sure the aurora will," Tavish replies.

Through my threads, I feel Luca beam.

CHAPTER TWELVE

the figment of a home

"THE BASILICA COULD STILL have killed Chancellor Fiordelise," I say, dusting the remnants of lunch off my hands.

Tavish and I sit at the edge of a rooftop garden overlooking the plaza where we purchased a cup of breaded and fried meatballs, its stalls bustling despite their reduced options. The leaves of the small potted fruit trees around us reach toward the sun high overhead. Honeybees buzz quietly through them, competing with the distant rumble of voices and motors from the nearby channels to fill the air with an ever-present hum.

"Aye." Tavish sucks crumbs and grease off his fingertips with a kind of reverence that gives me visions of those same lips on my hands and my—I clear my head, trying to focus on what he says as he continues, "If the Basilica realized the Institute had tampered with the roof that killed their late Chancellor Domenego, they might have murdered Fiordelise as revenge. Or perhaps as a ploy to save their own ignits by trying to force the Institute to elect a chancellor more willing to surrender theirs."

The whole situation makes my head hurt. "But who wanted Chancellor Domenego dead in the first place? It only makes sense that it was someone from the Institute, but was it Fiordelise giving the orders? A random engineer taking it upon themselves to commit the sabotage? Someone else entirely—maybe someone who just wanted to make the Institute *look* responsible?"

Tavish leans against my shoulder. "Would anyone from the Basilica understand the roof structure enough to make it fall on their own chancellor?"

"That begs the question whether this kind of sabotage is feasible in the first place. Maybe we're spiraling here?" I sigh. "It could have all been an accident."

"I don't believe that, and neither do you. There's something nefarious going on, we've kenned that from the beginning."

"You're right." I rub my hands down my face. "Somewhere in this mess, someone actively *wants* the city to sink. There's too large an effort to keep the ignits away from Luca for it not to be foul play. But we don't know who's working to sink the city and who's just reacting violently to their efforts, so what the fuck are we supposed to do about it all?" The question leaves my throat tight and my head numb.

"What we are doing, I think." Tavish gives me a weak smile, but a warmth fills it, as though he's trying to channel hope into me with that look alone.

It almost works. I give his shoulder a little shove. "We just keep tumbling from one mess to the next until we hit a nerve, then?"

"Oh, I fully intend to saunter between messes, but you may tumble if you wish. So long as you tumble back to me after." He leans, bumping his chin to my shoulder and nuzzling across my ear before finding my cheek with his lips.

Smiling myself now, I turn my head and catch his mouth in a quick kiss. The path before us is no clearer, but at least its darkness is easier to face with Tavish at my side. That's a kind of hope all of its own.

Tavish shifts his leg until his knee presses against mine, solid and comforting. His shoe brushes my boot. The pristine, shining leather that comprised it in Maraheem now has scuffs and clinging dust, a nick in one side of the toe from a rock he tripped over during our escape in Geviso.

I keep glancing back at that shoe. It looks worse for the wear, yes, but there's something almost appealing about it now, turning it from a spotless decoration to a well-loved necessity.

Tavish traces it along the side of mine. "I've been thinking, and I want to know, how do you feel about Venalt? From what you've seen of it."

"It's beautiful."

"And beyond that?"

"The city has none of the egregious wealth gaps of the old Maraheem or some of the other places we've been through, and outside their bureaucratic nonsense, the people seem good-natured and less prejudiced than most, if a bit caught up in their prophecies. And it is beautiful." I pull out one of our few remaining coins to bounce between my knuckles. I wonder if Teodor would grant us a commission for the work we're doing. We probably should have been asking for one all along if we're to have any money left to establish ourselves somewhere once this is done.

Tavish hums. "They have a thriving mer community with well-tended waters and a wakeful aurora in a similar state as you."

"They do."

The knowledge that once we're through with our travels, we'll have to find a place to live that suits us both hangs between us, growing larger by the second, but neither of us seem capable of eclipsing its height, of carrying its weight, not even together. Or perhaps it's the together part that's the hardest: the admission that one of us might want something the other does not, and the sacrifice that will surely arise from it. Worse still, there's always a chance one of us might not live long enough to make that sacrifice at all.

A satyr shouts from across the rooftop garden, their sharp tone aimed at a child with one hand clapped on a tree's ripe orange. I swear Tavish flinches.

His shoulders remain tight as he sighs. "Perhaps this place is too . . ."

"Too what?"

He hesitates before carefully explaining, each word precise and a little cautious. "When we first left Maraheem, I figured my heart would be drawn to the cities most like it, and at first I think I was. But perhaps I don't want that after all? Being somewhere that will remind me of home, it will simply—simply remind me of home."

My chest twists as I think of walking through the tight, vapor-strewn streets of Maraheem's lower city and seeing just enough of the Murk in it that it made my longing to return nearly unbearable. "I understand." Trying to crack through his growing tension, I nudge his shoulder gently. "Venalt is about to destroy themselves. That must count as two marks against them, maybe even three."

"Unless we do something about it?"

"I thought we were already doing that." I mean it as a tease, but it comes out a grumble instead. "If we ever end up in another city where the people are solving their problems through murder, let's not care enough to stick around, please."

Tavish laughs, but there's a strained edge to the sound, a deflation where relaxation should be. "And here I was about to suggest we go looking for more death."

"How about a walk instead? By the time we've finished, someone might have found that letter for Chancellor Alvise, and the Institute might have been bullied into following the Basilica's lead, and Luca might be saved, and we can forget all about homesickness and murders and ignits for the night."

"I like your plan infinitely better."

I help him up. Arm in arm, we set off.

Traipsing through the city benefits our moods, if not our situation. Describing the sights to Tavish, taking them in myself—even the people's mix of fear and admiration every time I'm recognized as the aurora ambassador—makes me feel a little less like I'm sitting and watching the world fall apart. And, for all that I can't quite see the city as my home, it truly is a beautiful, wondrous place. With each new bridge and vine-strewn channel, majestic dome and tucked-away garden, I let myself fall just a bit more in love with it, even if it's a shallow, rudimentary sort of affection that feels flimsy compared to the heat that burns in me for the Murk. It's still something, something more than I've felt for any other place we've visited.

But that feeling darkens as we reach the edge of the city.

The barriers that the Citadel has constructed along the sea-facing streets look pathetic and too few, and those within the channels are floating, swaying messes that appear ready to fall apart if hit by a strong wave. Barely a ferry's length away, a hippocamp paces. Each time its head surfaces, its dark gaze seems to find mine, as though it knows I'm the one keeping it at bay for now—me, and Luca.

And I wonder if it knows, too, that someone is trying to stop us.

We wait back at our room for word that the Citadel has retrieved the late Chancellor Domenego's letter for Alvise. Despite our hotel host's continual assurances that he'll bring us a message if someone calls for us, complete with a share of groveling that matches my increasing frustration, I spend the rest of the day returning to the lobby in regular intervals and checking in with Luca through our threads nearly as often. Nothing comes, though, not late that afternoon nor the evening, and when I call the Citadel the next morning, the only information Commander Zuane's secretary can give me is that they're "working" on it. Luca's responses are no more comforting: Teodor is in bed, and he has a measly few ignits left. He draws a little more off my replenishable energy to supplement them.

I pace the hotel lobby, distracting myself by trying to pick apart and replicate the vibrations Luca uses to keep out the hippocamps, but that venture is just as frustrating. Each chord I manage only feels more and more hollow as I attempt to build them into a song, as though I'm missing some fundamental step in the process. Luca watches quietly through our threads. He stays just distant enough that I can't tell if his silence is judgmental or despondent or if he's merely more exhausted than he's letting on.

Tavish puts up with about an hour of my miserable frustration before insisting we go find lunch at a café. As genuine as the suggestion must be, the place we settle on after an indecisive hop up and down the nearby streets has a menu that's greatly reduced, metal chairs that squeak as my knee bounces, and nothing in sight that's small enough for me to reasonably toss. The food seems to take three years and a day to arrive.

When we return, our hotel's elevator has an out-of-commission sign blocking off the doors, so we trek up the stairs in silence. The curtains of the lone window at the end of the hallway have been closed, and the lightbulb in the wall sconce across from our room flickers. A chill runs down my spine as I slip the key in. I turn it, but no click comes, no pressure there to be relieved. It seems to all be building inside me instead.

"I swear I locked this . . ." I hold my arm out, gently nudging Tavish behind me as I open the door.

The room looks exactly as we left it but for a piece of paper that now flutters under last night's half-empty wine bottle. I tug it free erratically, knocking the bottle over in the process. The cork pops off, and wine spills across the table to drip in soft, rapid plunks onto the floor. It feels like the fluttering of my heart as I focus on the note. A single word has been pasted across the center in black ink, each letter taken from a newspaper heading: *LEAVE.*

Beneath, tied in a piece of string, is a tiny cat's claw.

The tension in my chest turns into fear, drawing up visions of blood smeared across a deck and puddled on a ballroom floor, one pet lost and a love who nearly joined it because Lilias wanted what I couldn't give. Gods, don't let this happen again.

"Lavender." Her name comes out as a breath, like the mere thought of her hurt has knocked the wind from my lungs, but I raise my voice as I rush through the suite, calling for her in hoarse roars. I drop to check beneath the couch, behind the love seat, in the crack of the counter and the wall.

Tavish follows my voice, adding his own without question.

My heart thuds faster with each empty pillow and bag and nook, pounding through my ears and blurring my vision. It feels like Lilias creeping up behind me, pressing her knife against my ribs, asking me if I care enough. I can't have failed again. I can't.

"Lavender!" I shout, dropping to my knees beside the bed.

A small mew calls back.

I paste myself flat to find her cowering in the space beneath the dresser, her legs and tail tucked tight and her blue eyes massive. A tiny line of blood pools in the crack of the wooden floorboards. I let out a sob, going limp. "She's here," I whisper, then, louder. "She's in here!"

I press my hand into the space, drawing it through her fur gently, coaxing her out little by little. The gouge where her claw has been torn off has stopped bleeding, but she holds the paw itself gingerly, whimpering when I touch it. She refuses to leave my lap, clinging there with her remaining claws when I try to move us to the bed.

"Good fuck," Tavish mutters after I explain, followed by another series of curses and a drag of his hands through his hair that's so violent his fingers tear at a tangled spot in his curls. They shake when he brings them back to his lap. "And they want us to leave? That's the entire message?"

"Just that word."

"We won't, though." Tavish states it, not a question but a vow, as though this is proof he needs for himself, determined despite the panic I can see welling in him. "We saved Maraheem. We saved so many auroras. We are strong enough."

"We are," I agree. Too many times, I've let other people threaten me into places I didn't want to be. I overcame Lilias in the end. I can overcome this too.

But I can't help worrying that by the end of whatever storm Venalt is brewing, it'll ask for more of me than even Maraheem did.

CHAPTER THIRTEEN

standstill

IT TAKES HALF AN hour to calm Lavender enough to wash and wrap her paw, and another half hour to convince her to curl up in her traveling pouch. She spends most of our trip to the Institute giving spontaneous cries to confirm we're still here, and screams when we enter the crowded detective wing with such gusto that I have to take her back into the quiet outer corridor while Tavish relays the information to Commander Zuane. By the time Tavish returns, she's giving weak purrs and concerned mews beneath my constant petting.

"He'll look into it," Tavish says, "but he didn't seem to have high hopes. There's not much security in that hotel to begin with, and the note was free of unusual fingerprints."

I grunt, though I expected as much. "And the letter Chancellor Alvise needs?"

"He says the Citadel lost it."

"Tell him to search Fiordelise's apartments." It's such an absurd hunch that I almost feel weird saying it out loud, but Tavish quells the insecurity instantly.

"I did—I thought that if she was at all involved in the late Basilica chancellor's death, that she must have stolen it somehow. But he claims her quarters were investigated already, and that if there was a letter from the Basilica found, he would've heard of it. I think he was laughing at me then. Or trying to decide whether to throw me back into that waiting room—it's so hard to tell with that tone of his."

"Fuck him," I grumble.

Tavish crinkles his lips. "I'd rather fuck you, if it's all the same."

Through the dredges of my frustration and fear spills a soft laugh. "I'd like that. But if late Chancellor Domenego's letter isn't here, then it seems we have work to do."

My fist makes no sound against Teodor's apartment door, so I call out for her, perched against the wall with Lavender in my arms. The moment I proposed this, Tavish volunteered to check on Luca instead. After our last meeting, I don't have the heart to tell him I can feel Luca just fine from here. He deserves the respite. I miss his stabilizing presence, though, as I stand alone in the tall, tight Citadel corridor outside the chancellor's apartments.

Teodor answers with an annoyed grunt, deep bags beneath her eyes and her arms crossed, but her expression softens as I tell her what happened—from the note in Tavish's and my hotel room to the missing Basilica letter. She invites me in. I set down Lavender's pouch on a chair beside the door, and the cat surprises me by hopping out. She limps through the disastrously filled space like the excess of hoarded objects are her new toys and presses up her back into Teodor's palm as the chancellor bends down to stroke her.

"Make Zuane search Fiordelise's apartment again," I say. "I know it sounds like a stretch, but with her decision to withhold the ignits and then her violent death, she has to be a part of this somehow."

"It *is* a stretch." Teodor sighs. She turns deeper into her foyer, gingerly stepping between the gaps in the clutter, where the ornamental carpets peek through.

I push after her. "But you'll do it?"

"I'll consider it." She grimaces, wobbling, and catches the back of a chair. Her gaze drops to the bag sitting atop it, a soft red glow peeking through the fabric. She stares at it with a desolated longing. How many ignits are left in it? Three? Four? "I'll consider it *strongly*, but when I'm rested enough to think straight."

"I can search instead. Everyone here is so busy, let me—"

"Absolutely not," Teodor snaps, loud enough that Lavender's ears twitch.

The intensity of her reaction surprises me, pulling at the vague suspicions I've been harboring toward all of Venalt's government. From what I know of Teodor, I can't imagine she'd hurt this city, much less Luca, but that doesn't mean she can't be involved in this mess somehow. Or she might just be a completely innocent bystander too confined to bed to realize her government has fallen apart until two other chancellors are dead.

Every new theory feels like a pink ignit churning in my gut, trying to separate the facts from the chaff. But no provable truth emerges. Teodor remains a tired, snappy leader in a broken city with no obvious proof of anything.

She grunts at my expression and adds, softer, "Don't meddle in this, please." Her legs wobble. "I'm letting you wander the city and talk to Alvise, but if I suspect you might start doing more harm than good—"

"Letting me?" It's half indignation, half snarl, a sharp-edged thing that would make Tavish proud. I bare my teeth with it, my hood falling the rest of the way from where I'd already pulled it back.

Instead of rising against me, though, she caves, her eyes closing and a tight, small noise leaving her. She sways again. This time, one of her knees gives out.

I spring to catch her, pulling aside the ignit bag to carefully lower her into the chair. She lets go of me as quickly as she can, pressing her palm to her mouth as she coughs. Her body seems to curl into itself, as defenseless as her city.

I ache for her. I do not need another person to fear for, but the pain and desperation that pulses through her—this one single person who has loved Luca and fought for him through everything—makes me hurt just the same. My mind screams with the impulse to press my own energy into her, to lift her out of this state. But she's merely human, skin and bones and the flesh between: a bit of stardust waiting to return to orbit. My aurora power will do nothing to delay that.

I lower myself until I'm looking up at her, trying to soften away my harsh edges. "I'm trying to save Venalt, not destroy it. I promise."

"I know," she whispers. "Luca trusts you, and trust is not a thing that comes easy to him. That means something to me, whether I act like it or not."

Looking at her now, her gaze lowered and her body drawn back, I see a mirror of that distrust. I see someone who's been hurt before, burned before. Someone a little like me.

Her eyes rise to mine, dark with a hint of ashen grey in the pupils, and her mouth opens. She draws a breath, but she doesn't speak. Quietly, she shakes her head.

I understand somehow—I want to say more, too. I just don't know what.

"I need to rest," she finally mutters.

"Will it help?" It seems that is all she's been doing, and still she looks one bad step away from falling out of this life. "What you have, it's really . . ."

"Fatal? Yes." She coughs again. "At my stage, most of my peers would be suffering in style on a terrace at some coastal sanatorium, but here I am dealing with troublesome aurora ambassadors and a city that seems ready to kill me before I can even die properly."

"This—this is it? You just give up?" It hurts to say—hurts to think. "I heard they're testing some kind of new antibiotic on patients with symptoms like yours in Lindfel. It hasn't been perfect, but isn't it worth trying?"

The smile that tugs across her face is so sharp and sad and broken all at once. "I don't think there's an antibiotic that can cure this." She exhales, tipping her head back. "I always figured I'd die young. I was the queen, the empress, the goddess of wild shit, so many schemes that should have killed me, so many plans that never should have worked out. But this . . . this wasn't what I pictured." A laugh escapes her, the perfect match to her expression. "Guess we never really know when we're going, do we? We can accept it or not, but some things can't be changed, right?"

"I suppose not." But it doesn't feel right at all that someone like Teodor, someone with so much left to give to the world, should be ripped away from it like this. *It'll be me soon.*

The thought shears me in two, but my human half can offer no more comfort to me than I can to him, no more comfort than either of us can offer Teodor or Luca. *'When we start to fade, we could find a place willing to spare us their ignits.'* It's a halfhearted consolation, one he believes no more than I. *'We could be all right, for a while, at least.'*

Where would that be? Not the Murk, not here, not any of the places we've been with auroras of their own to care for. We barely found places for the ones we stole, and they were easy, peaceful creatures that haven't gone around offending people at every turn.

We don't have an answer. Perhaps Teodor is right: there are some things that can't be changed, only accepted. But where does that leave us? A chill runs down our spine.

Where does it leave *Tavish?*

Dread and guilt tightens in our gut.

Teodor releases a stunted hack that slams my halves back into one, as though I need all the fortitude I can get to keep moving forward. Her eyes close. Resting like this, she looks like a skeletal haunt, more dead than alive. Each shallow breath she takes wheezes slightly.

I force myself to turn away. There's nothing more I can do here, not for her and not for myself either. But Luca I might still be able to save.

I find Lavender perched on the head of an unsightly grey, waist-tall sculpture of a winged lion. She protests as I scoop her up, wiggling and mewing pitifully.

A hand clamps on my shoulder. "Rubem."

As I wheel around, I almost crash into an exhausted Teodor. My heart skips, and I jerk backward, knocking soundlessly into the statue. "You startled me."

It's these damned carpets and the clutter; they must have masked Teodor's footsteps. No one else can possibly be as unnaturally quiet as I am; all my life like this, and I've always been the only one. It's just whimsy and homesickness making me think that Teodor might share the trait.

I laugh, a hollow noise that doesn't quite fill the room. "It's ironic, I'm usually the one doing that to people."

"You are rather quiet, aren't you?" Teodor's eyes narrow. It seems almost like she'll say something more, like I'm not just imagining how silent she is when she walks and sits and coughs, but then she focuses on the unhappy cat in my arms, and she moves the conversation on. "I was going to say, it's fine if she stays here. I'll keep an eye on her."

The thought of her watching over Lavender floods me with a relief in such stark contrast to my earlier unfounded suspicions that they feel almost comical; however Teodor might be involved in this city's messes, she has nothing to do with threatening us. I let the cat back down, leaving her with a container of her food and a head scratch. "You be good, or the mean Citadel chancellor will lock you up."

"Funny," Teodor grumbles, though a hint of a smile graces her lips. "But Rubem . . ." She sighs. "I *will* deal with this when I can. The Basilica's letter, the threat against you, all of it. Don't do anything troublesome in the meantime."

I bob my head, but as I close her door behind me, trouble is exactly what I plan to do.

CHAPTER FOURTEEN

something troublesome

LUCA'S BASEMENT IS AS dark and damp as last time, the steady drip of water and the tap-tap of Tavish's cane fighting for a hollow audience.

For all Tavish's insistence that he would be checking on Luca, the aurora isn't even in sight, his presence currently curled through the deeper dregs of the foundation nearby. I clear my throat as I approach, and Tavish only startles for an instant before turning to smile in my direction.

"Teodor claims she'll look into things once she's feeling up for it, but I want to check Fiordelise's apartments at the Institute ourselves. Preferably now. Before she wakes back up."

I expect Tavish to respond with every reason why this plan is impossible and reckless. Instead he smiles. "Aye. Then we will."

"You're serious?"

"I think you're right. We can't merely stand around and expect that this will come together, and we are the only ones I trust not to have an agenda—at least, an agenda outside of Luca's salvation. It's either this plan or else we start stealing ignits, and the former feels slightly less illegal, considering the apartment's resident is dead, and it's a job that the Citadel should already be conducting. Besides, whoever sent

141

us that note wants the city to sink, and our best bet is that Fiordelise was involved, for better or worse. I'd like to ken what she was up to."

"I doubt they'll just let us waltz through the front doors of the Institute to get there though. Not after last time."

"No, it's not likely." Tavish's jaw begins to move to the slight, thoughtful rhythm that signals he's chewing on his tongue. "Perhaps we can avoid them entirely? Do the chancellor's apartments there have a back door?"

"Teodor's suite only opens to the interior of the Citadel, so I'd assume the Institute ones are the same."

I think of the channel behind Fiordelise's office, but while moving in and out of the foundation circle a few times, I've noticed those adjacent waterways are all gated. As I sift through our potential entry points, I feel Luca lurking in our conjoined threads, already a bit groggier and less responsive than this morning. Before I reach for him, I'm careful to dam all thoughts of Teodor's commands—and my reservations with the Citadel in general—as far back in my mind as I can.

You're wrapped along the tunnels beneath the foundation, right?

It takes him a moment to focus on me. His tightening threads draw off some of my energy, and I press a little more after to help him along. The water of the lagoon parts as his thoughtful answer comes. *'This is where I live, yes.'*

And the tunnels stretch from the Citadel through the rest of the immediate area? Could we use them to get to, say, the inside of the Institute?

'Yes. Those exist—I know them.' His head pokes from the surface on the pool's far side, his mind fluttering with a sudden burst of vigor as he leeches off my thoughts. *'You want to know what Fiordelise was doing before she died? You think she stole the letter Alvise needs.'*

The emotion I get from him is so muddled, I can't tell if it's agitation or excitement. *Can you help us?*

He hesitates, but then whatever he feels shifts slowly into enthusiasm as he thinks it over. *'I can. There is much water, though.'*

I grimace. *How much?*

'Most of it.'

"You're talking to the aurora again?" Tavish whispers.

"Yes—sorry, I can translate if you're uncomfortable."

He laughs. "You're allowed to have conversations without me in them. I know you'll share if it's important."

"How do you feel about swimming beneath the foundation to sneak inside the Institute?"

"In this?" Tavish's nose wrinkles. "It smells delightful, of course, but are you sure I won't also come out of it with three heads?"

Luca rumbles, his laughter vibrating through his body as well as my mind. *'I was born like this!'*

"Luca says you should be honored to join his three-headed ranks."

"Well, in that case." Tavish grins and unbuttons his jacket. He draws a folded waterproof bag out of an inner pocket before tucking the jacket into a neat square and loading it in. The rest of his clothes follow one by one.

I add my boots and cloak, pausing at my shirt before stripping that off too. "With all your technology, I'd think the selkies would develop waterproof clothing, like the mer."

He goes still, and at first it seems like a thoughtful contemplation, but the tremble that edges his pinkie as he twists it around his brooch makes me wonder. "We're no mer. We have to take our clothes off to transform anyway," he finally says, folding the last of his clothing slower. "Before my grandparents' time, there was a long tradition of wearing the skins of regular seals as cloaks with ties that could hold to the wearer even after transforming, but that died out when the first rudimentary air locks were installed in Maraheem, after the families like mine kicked out all the real merfolk who lived there." He hands me his bag and cane with more force than is strictly necessary.

I try to lighten his mood, softly nudging him back before tucking the cane into a loop in my pants and slipping the bag over my shoulder. "Well, I for one would like to see you in a sealskin."

He snorts. "You don't think it would conflict with my current fashion choices?"

"Your most current fashion is being very deliciously naked, so I see no issues." I kiss his cheek with a playful growl.

The corners of his lips lift.

Luca actively avoids my thoughts with the force of a freight train, and I sense it's less to do with Tavish's state of undress and more with how the sight of him is drawing to mind our previous evening, kindling a fresh fire in me that's just dying to be stoked. For poor Luca's sake, I douse it instead. I can come back to it later, when we're far enough apart that he can ignore me, and I'm far enough from here that I can fully give myself over to the longing.

Tavish moves to the edge of the lagoon, and his half smile turns into a grimace. The ignation in his brooch alights in a flash of rainbow. His bones snap, caving and twisting, skin stretching and face contorting. He drops to the ground, shaking himself, and fur sprouts through his flesh, settling as he finishes the transformation. With an unhappy wiggle of his whiskers, he plunges into the water.

'Are we ready, home worlder?' Luca thrums to me.

I crouch beside the lagoon. Tavish was right to worry that its grime might give him another head. As I slip off the edge, I send out a quick prayer to whatever gods are listening that I don't emerge from this with any more consciousnesses than I already have. The water rushes in, eerily temperate compared to the coolness of the channels throughout the rest of the city. It comes nearly to my chin before my feet hit a slimy stone surface. My toes curl, heels lifting instinctively.

Tavish waits at the center of the lagoon, just his nose above the surface. His whiskers twitch as I approach. I brush the top of his head and press my nose to his. It's still odd, seeing the seal and knowing that beneath that fur is the man I love, with all his brilliance and his graceful strength, but I certainly don't find it disagreeable. And he does make for a very nice pillow in this form.

The water rolls as Luca swims around us, his small leathery fins extending to help guide his serpentine motions. He dips down, vanishing from sight again. Through our threads I feel him dart into a tunnel, his large body leaving just enough space for Tavish and me to follow.

I slip beneath the surface after him. Tavish tails me through the underwater gap in the stones, the tip of his snout pressed to my back to keep from losing me. Even here, it seems, I'm nearly a ghost, my body making as little vibration in the water as it does anywhere else.

Beyond the tunnel, a darkness too deep for human eyes sets in. I shift to my aurora sight, coating everything in an outline of hazy silver as it turns the world to a shrouded grey. The ceiling feels too close above, Luca's thick body too near below, and even with my sight, I knock against them by accident. I recoil with each collision, the tightness of my chest growing along with the sense that the walls are closing in. My lungs begin to burn as my brain screams that this wasn't just a bad option, but a deadly one, too.

The moment the tunnel opens, I burst upward. I breach the surface so fast that my head bonks the ceiling a foot above. The air is stale, drenched in an earthy, mold-ridden scent, and through the cracks between corner stones, I can make out the roots of a tree reaching down into the water, something fungal growing along them. I close my eyes as I breathe, hoping I won't consume all the oxygen here in a single go.

Tavish rubs his body against mine, nuzzling into my stomach questioningly. I stroke his back and lift his nose to the air to prove that I have enough to breathe so that he needn't fear for me. He snorts into the cramped, damp space, and his whiskers flutter.

"Terrible, I know."

Luca nudges me through our threads. *'They're all like this, but no worse.'*

I can handle it.

I *can* handle it, but it takes effort, and after the next submerged tunnel, I turn my thoughts to Luca in a vain attempt to distract myself. *That thing you've been calling me: home worlder. When we first met, you said something like that, only longer?*

'One whose home encompasses the world? That is who you are, isn't it? Those who you wish to save are everywhere.'

Maybe it's his leviathan host's idea of home that he's drawing from—an instinct that makes all that resides in its realm feel worth protecting, and therefore everything worth protecting feels like home. *That's not how it works for sapient species here.*

As soon as I think the word *sapient*, it feels wrong. Clearly this aurora's host is no less a sentient thing than me. I shake the conundrum off: a philosophical quarry for a different day. One where I'm not currently drawing my fingers along the underside of a submerged tunnel, counting the seconds until we reach the next pocket of air, my lungs screaming at me and my head pounding.

'You are not home with the people you love? Seems foolish.' Luca huffs, and through him I feel the sensation of his snake heads hissing.

It brings other senses with it: a wave of animalistic perception that must be the way he views our surroundings. It's so foreign compared to my human interpretation of the world that I almost inhale the disgusting foundation water as my brain tries to turn Luca's sensory exhibition into something I can understand. Through it, I feel the water rushing past Luca's scales, the bulk of his body extending through the foundation so far beyond us, the pulsing of his muscles carrying every coil seamlessly forward. I receive flashes of something that mixes taste and smell and the layers of heat that he sees in congregation with his aurora vision. It brings with it a tumbling perception that runs beneath his thoughts, preoccupied by every vibration in the water and scent of potential prey and the heartbeat of a child running across the top of the foundation above.

It's so very different from the way that I function, the way I *think*, even when my two halves were apart. I can't imagine the courage it took to forge a permanent bond with a creature this far removed from the usual brain function of an aurora, what might have propelled Luca to take that risk.

How did you choose this host? I ask as we settle into another pocket of air.

'*No choice. It was a blessing from the three.*'

My lungs still burn, the oxygen in the cracks here not enough to fully sustain me, but I force myself to duck under the water once more as Luca continues swimming. *Were you living in something else before this, then?*

'*Yes, in a grass that dwells within the sand and sun and shallow water. Venalt's ancestors found me. I was on the other side of the sea, and they carried me with them in their raft-boats, all floating together. No city for them then, just the boats.*'

It sounds so like my own experience before leaving my mangrove and that of every other aurora I've met. But the peace that resonates from Luca doesn't match with the feelings of depression and frustration that finally led to my own waking. *Did you enjoy that, living in a half dream?*

'*Yes. I was happy.*' His words come with a soft, wistful tone, bundled around a deep longing. '*They would give me stories and laughter, and sometimes I grew them ignits. But they did not need the ignits to be happy then. I was theirs. They were happy for me just to be with them, and I was happy just for that, too. The things we loved were only each other, so we were home there.'*

I see flashes of Luca's memories as he narrates, most of them the subtle, drifting sort that I have from my time in the mangrove: the caress of the constant breeze, the sensation of bobbing gently on the shifting sea, the soft glow of festivities, and the salt of a mother's tears. They loved Luca, not even in the distant caretaker way that the Murk loved the aurora half of me, but as a priest loves the sacred, and an albatross, the sky. Luca was the thing they centered themselves around, this old tribe-minded people who sailed their homes through the mild Nereidian Sea, and they cared more for his safety than they did even their own. *What happened?*

'Some of them became no longer happy. I loved them still, but I was not enough. They began to take from the coast cities instead of trade, until the coast cities came and took back.' His speech wavers in my mind, the words slipping beneath the stronger waves of his visual memories, all scattered and shifting like a nightmare: blood and screams, a child's fingers wrapped through Luca's fronds, a growing darkness that spreads like a panic. *'It happened while I was too far into dreams to move or to help. I woke—like I am now, like you—to find only the pain after. And so many dead, all those who'd talked to me and braided their pearls into me. They kept me safe, hidden beneath their bodies while I was sleeping.'* Luca's emotions flood me, powerful as the day they were made, intense rage and grief and love, and something I recognize all too well: guilt.

I want to wrap around him, to tell him this wasn't his fault, he could have done nothing more for them—but I don't believe that about any of my past, even the places where it's actually true, and I think he already knows it just as well as I do. Instead, I lean into his presence, grieving with him for every aurora we've already lost, for my poor caiman whom Lilias killed to threaten me, for the people who died in his past and in Maraheem and in the Murk and everywhere else we've been, for the woman whose rooms we're about to intrude on. Death is made no less final by whether it was preventable or not.

As we continue through the tunnels, up to another tight air-topped chamber, I ask, *That's when your people came here, isn't it?*

Luca pulls two of his heads out of the water beside Tavish and me. 'Yes. *They found the foundation rock, lonely in the bay. That is when the Divine Three gave me this host. My leviathan half lived in its tunnels, still very young and much smaller but already strong enough to protect the infant city as it grew with me. With the corelium it slowly did—it grew strong, too. And me always with it.*'

I can feel the point where his mind skips, scooting past the place in the story when this new form's strength became worrisome to the people, and the chancellors decided to move him out of their view, slowly excising him from their thoughts and their heritage. Slowly creating this version of the city, in which a people who once sacrificed themselves to protect their defenseless aurora now sacrifice that same aurora even as it protects them.

'Finally the hippocamps came,' Luca continues, as though he needs to finish now, to reach this cruel, twisted ending in order to make sense of the rest of it. *'Two first, then four. I was strong by then, strong enough to create my song.'* He releases a soft hiss, a twitch running through his black, rainbow-strewn patches. Ash shudders off the dying strips between his scales. *'But now the sickness takes my strength, and no number of heads can fight that.'*

The force of his love for Venalt hits me then, like a crashing wave or the sinking teeth of a hippocamp. But the moment I feel it fully, I realize it's been building inside me, seeping into my pores throughout this whole conversation. With each memory, each scent, each emotion, he's slowly been carving his love into my soul. It's such a bright, beautiful thing that it feels nearly blinding. Weighted against the whimsy I experienced while exploring Venalt earlier, that was a drop compared to this ocean of love, this, a vibrant, fulfilled thing and that, only the hint of a vague concept.

I can't dislodge it now that it's sunk in, as if it's just as much a part of me as my love for the Murk—just as much my own as it is Luca's. It echoes between us, capped in devastation at the thought of the hippocamps' invasion, until all I can do to keep this feeling from consuming us both is divert our attention away.

Was your bonding to the leviathan mutual, the way mine was? Can a creature like that choose an aurora back?

'*Not like yours, but still reciprocated. I had no need to force my aurora self in. This place was my leviathan's already; it wanted what could help it protect its territory. I could help, make it live longer, grow bigger. So it let me bond.*'

That leviathan is so clearly still a part of his consciousness. I can feel it in the current of Luca's thoughts, the way they tumble with more sensation and instinct than mine, their emotions denser, less malleable. Even his language betrays it, the choppy, slowed pace of the storytelling as he struggles to put that many words to things that his brain no longer naturally categorizes with language. *It's changed you, hasn't it?*

Luca thinks for a while before he answers, guiding Tavish and me from tunnel to chamber to tunnel again as he does. '*Maybe,*' he finally decides, '*Teo thinks I am immature and stubborn and too forgiving. I think she is impulsive and gives up too easily and holds too many grudges. I guess we are both stubborn, then, and lenient, then, and ignorant about some things. Your sapient species and leviathans are just different, and so I am just different. But I am happy. I can protect, like this. So, I am happy.*'

I'm told that's the best we can be, just to find happiness with who we are in the world and—

One of Luca's heads whirls around, shooting past me and snapping up the skinny form of an aquatic weasellike creature squeezing itself out of a crack in the wall. He downs it in a pulsating swallow.

The sight makes me want to laugh, even as my lungs protest the thought. *Does your ability to eat wriggling pests in one go also make you happy?*

'*Very happy. They taste good.*' Luca's two unoccupied heads lift, both tongues bobbing out in amusement. '*I'll save you the next one.*'

Both the aurora and the human halves of me shudder at the thought, which only intensifies Luca's glee.

We stop in three more air patches. The swim takes us longer than it would have to cross the foundation from above, but avoiding anyone who might try to stop us is worth it. Finally, Luca pauses us in a room with a high ceiling, a maintenance shaft ascending on one side.

'*You can go up here, but I don't know where it leads.*' He motions to it with a head, then to the other end of the room, flashing me his leviathan sensory interpretations of each as he does: metal and cracks, water and warmth. '*One tunnel farther along is a direct entrance to the basement of the Institute, which opens very near the chancellor's rooms—I used it to meet with Chancellor Anzola when they were creating the first corelium supports into the city, but I was a lot smaller then. I can't fit anymore.*'

We'll keep going. I press my palm to his nose. *Thank you.*

He makes a soft, happy sound in my head, pressing into the touch. Then his song stalls as he goes utterly still. My heart skips, but the vibration picks back up with a happy enthusiasm. '*Teodor is awake! I'll tell her what you're doing.*'

No. A rush of panic rolls through me, stronger than I anticipated. Whatever deadly tangle these chancellors are in, I can't just assume Teodor isn't a part of it, no matter how much I might respect her, or even like her. I can trust her with Lavender and Luca, but not with this city. Nor with what she'll do when she finds out I've gone directly against her orders.

I try to find the right words to explain this to Luca, but I feel his understanding just as firmly as he must have felt my wariness. I brace myself for a defense, an accusation, an argument. Instead, Luca's presence around my threads draws back to form a shield. Through the cracks seeps his acknowledgement, his own worry flickering in and out of view. I hold my breath.

You know something about her. You agree with me.

'*No!*' His shout is such a forceful spear that I can't tell how much of it is a lie through the pain that shoots across my skull. Despite his denial, he withdraws, curling around a thought, a fact, something he doesn't want me to know.

I press into the space, my threads clutching him as I try to glimpse it.

With a frantic yelp that resonates as distressed hisses from his three leviathan heads, he shoves me off. His own aurora presence snaps away from mine. He drags his threads back with him, cutting them all off from mine so violently I feel them snap in places. The pain of it rattles me.

Fuck. My chest aches as the weight of what I've done slams into me. I reach out, threads lengthening and hand extended. "Luca—"

He pulls himself below the surface and coils away. This segment of his body vanishes through the tunnel from which we came, wiggling backward in anxious, frantic bursts. It carries his aurora presence with it, bundled up tightly within himself again, near enough that I can still feel the vibrations he projects outward—his song with hints of grief and betrayal mixed in—but too disconnected from me to sense his thoughts or the intricacy of his emotions. Too far away to reach out and apologize.

I want to swim after him, but he vanishes, his presence a murky haze now that our threads are no longer connected. There's no chance that Tavish and I will find our way back through there alone. As much as I hate to let Luca flee like this, hurting and afraid of me, we have to continue.

We've come this far to help his city—his city that I now love with his own deep, unmanageable affection. And to help him. To find Alvise's note and get him another week of life. Before Teodor comes to tell us off.

I brush my hand down Tavish's furry back.

"We're almost there," I tell him, and I dive for the tunnel toward the Institute.

My lungs begin to ache as the tunnel continues. Warning signals flash in my mind, constantly drawing my attention back to the solid rock looming above me. My chest aches as my lungs scream for oxygen. They plead for me to start burning the energy my aurora flesh has saved to keep them satisfied. But I only have so much of that, and I might need it still.

Tavish presses against me. I wrap an arm around him, focusing on his solid form, the soft fur and supple rolls. My mind begins to slip, no up or down, no time or space. But I feel Tavish beside me and keep kicking.

When the tunnel finally opens, I let him go, bursting upward. The moment the air hits me, I breathe—too soon. Water slips in, making me cough and sputter as I fight to keep from going under. In an instant Tavish is there again, holding me up. I clear my lungs enough to stop the burning and press a kiss to the top of his head, his fur slick beneath my lips. His whiskers rustle.

I squint toward the basement's door. Even in the ghostly veil of my aurora vision, its stone outcropping appears far cleaner and better kept than the Citadel's, with a metal ladder extending into the lagoon on both ends. A piece of massive machinery takes up most of the space both in and out of the water, its pipes and pumps and fans all whirring along. The city's main generator, perhaps.

I nudge Tavish and head for the ladder up to the outcropping. The moment my feet hit the stone floor, they form puddles beneath. I do my best to gently squeeze a bit of the grimy foundation water out of my braids and pull half of them up in a bun, where they'll likely stay damp and gross for hours, but after the disgusting dip they just had, they'll need a good washing when we're back at the hotel anyway. As I pull on my shirt, the sound of movement makes me pause. It dies down too quickly for me to pinpoint its origin, somewhere ahead or to my left: either beyond the closed basement door or around the side of the generators. Another one of those creatures Luca snapped up in the tunnels, perhaps.

Collar still unlaced and cloak half on, I turn back toward Tavish, only to find he hasn't made it up the ladder yet. He swims beneath it, his seal nose tapping against the bars and his whiskers trembling. Flickers of rainbow shoot across his brooch and jump like lightning along his fur only to cut out in a sputter of grey before they can transform him properly. In a flare of colorful lightning, the brooch's power overcomes the ashen damage. His bones crack and his fur draws in, limbs expanding and face contorting back into his voluptuous, freckle-strewn human shape, every curve and crease where he left it last.

But as Tavish clutches to the ladder, naked and shaking, I still feel as though the world has fallen out from under us. Like the aurora and the massive yellow ignit from Glenrigg, the ignation in his brooch is fading. Dying. Will soon be gone.

"Tavish?" I ask.

A shudder runs through his shoulders, and he snaps back, his diamond voice high and tight, "I am *fine*."

From beyond the basement door, a haughty feminine voice replies, "Hello? Who's there?"

Tavish's brow tightens, and as he climbs onto the outcropping, he hisses Iseppa's name.

"Fuck." I finish tugging on my cloak and help him scramble into his own clothes, but I can hear the patter of Iseppa's feet.

"If I find he's snooping around again, I'll—" she mutters from just behind the door, her voice turning so low that the threat sounds like a jumble of grunts and huffs beneath the rattle of keys.

"Go, I'll distract," Tavish whispers.

Leaving him here to be interrogated by the Institute and potentially called in by the Citadel twists at my gut, but of the two of us, he might be able to talk some sense into Iseppa. And without the handheld reading device he lost somewhere along our mountain crossing, he won't be much help in finding the missing letter from the Basilica anyway.

I peck his cheek and sprint soundlessly to the door, a series of wet footprints trailing me. At least it's dark in here. I scoot off to the side of the entrance. The door shoves open, Iseppa's short figure silhouetted by the distant glow of the lights from the floor above. As she fumbles around the wall for a switch, I slip silently by her.

She startles, but from the basement Tavish distracts her with a soft "Hello? Iseppa, is that you? I seem to be rather lost" in such a tone of casual bemusement that I have to stop myself from chuckling under my breath.

"Why you—" Iseppa stammers. "Why are you—"

I leave the rest of their conversation behind to sprint up the stairs, a ghost in the night.

CHAPTER FIFTEEN

orphans both

I'M DEBATING WHETHER TO break the lock to the chancellor's apartments or sneak out the window of a nearby room to enter from the channel side when I find the front door already cracked open, an argument spilling out.

"She's an orphan now—isn't that the home's job in the first place?"

"They're under no obligation to accept her until her great-aunt on the mainland has been informed and denies guardianship."

I slip into the hallway, catching the flash of someone in a Citadel uniform pacing past a woman in Basilica robes in the room beyond. Their words prickle across my skin. They're here, arguing in Matthia's home about what will happen to the child like she's a mere inconvenience with no feelings and no say in how the rest of her adolescence will go. I hope the poor girl isn't also forced to listen to this.

With one eye on the end of the hall, I sprint soundlessly to Fiordelise's office. The late evening sun no longer hits the windows, but pieces of it reflect off the buildings beyond the channel, leaving just enough light to see in. The far door is already closed, but I can still hear the continued bickering of the two beyond it through the hall.

"What about moral obligation? Aren't you supposed to be humanitarians or something?"

"The children's home is stretched too thin already; she will suffer more there than—"

"Oh, sell a statue or something."

"Who do we sell them to when your Citadel won't send anyone to help us ship them past the hippocamps?"

"We might have the personnel for that if we didn't have to play guardian for random orphans!"

"She's a witness, isn't she?"

"A witness you won't let us bring back to the Citadel."

"That's no place for a child."

"Then make the children's home take her already!"

I cringe with each new exchange, until I can't bear to listen to their argument a moment longer. Quietly, I close the door to the hallway. It dims their voices to a murmur.

At least now I can think.

However much I might dislike Zuane, he was telling the truth about searching the place. In the absence of Fiordelise's body, small flags mark the glass on the floor and the seat where she died. Her papers lie in neat, labeled piles across the table, drawers emptied and even some of the books rearranged. My heart immediately sinks. But I came all this way, I can't just turn around now. The Citadel might have missed something.

I shuffle through the organized papers, carefully keeping them in their original stacks. They look like plans for a shift away from ignit usage, with diagrams for steam-powered vehicles and a generator with a set of massive stacks and an elevator system that's all pulleys and cranks and counterweights. Nothing out of the ordinary, especially if she was on track to offer her ignits to the Citadel after all.

Perhaps I was wrong, and she had nothing to do with the roof that collapsed on the late chancellor of the Basilica. But she tried so aggressively to steer me away from the topic of ignits, to convince me the city had everything under control without giving out any real details. That didn't feel like the argument of someone with active plans to follow my suggestions.

I nudge a few books around and glance through the drawers. The longer I work, the more my exhaustion bears back down on me, what little remained of my enthusiasm and adrenaline being worn away by each dead end. With a grunt, I sit beside Fiordelise's chair and drop my head into my hands. My still-damp pants cling oddly to my thighs, but I don't have the energy to pick at them. What did I think I'd find here? I uncovered Alasdair's murderers by sheer accident. Investigating—thinking—understanding people—that was never my forte.

You scared off Luca, disobeyed Teodor, sentenced Tavish to an entire conversation with Iseppa, and for what?

No other voice contradicts me, the guilt holding me together like glue.

To my right, the door swings open, letting in a sliver of the continuing argument over where Fiordelise's kid should go before shutting again almost as quickly. Matthia stands there, hand still on the knob. One of her suspenders dangles off her shoulder, and she clutches what looks like it was once two different plush animals sewn together three decades ago. She hides the plush on her body as best she can and glares at me.

"You," she says, staring down her nose like I'm some kind of bug she's still trying to decide whether to squash. If not for the red, puffy rims of her eyes and her hair frizzing out around her tiny horns like Tavish's curls after a bad day, she might even be frightening.

"Me," I agree, tipping my head back against the shelves. I plant my palms on either side of my body, but I can't muster the strength to get up. Or maybe just the will. Instead, I pat the floor. "You want to sit?"

Matthia looks like I'm suggesting we eat slugs. She tucks her plush animal closer, and her gaze flickers back to the door she's still holding. Something passes through her expression like she's shattering all at once and then sealing herself right back together again.

It hurts to watch, hurts because she's so young, so undeserving of all this pain that life decided to thrust upon her for nothing she's ever done, and it hurts because it was me there once, eyes red, passing back through the place my mother was killed and wanting to feel a piece of her there even if it meant carving out gory chunks of myself as sacrifices. It was me once, and is me forever. Some wounds heal, and others permanently scar, forming you into the person you'll build the rest of yourself on, however beautiful and terrible that person is.

I exhale, long and slow, and stare at the ceiling. "What's your plush's name?"

"It's not mine," she says, so fast that even if she wasn't tightening her hold on it as she spoke, it still wouldn't have been a convincing fib.

"Of course not." I nod. "Animals own themselves. We just take care of them sometimes."

She snorts and mutters, "It's just a plush." But she gives its misshaped head a pet as she leans against the door, slowly sliding her way down. "He's the Underbed Monster. Mom named him. I tried to throw him away last year, but she found him again. She said I *had* to keep him." She pulls her knees to her chest. Her pants ride up above her high socks, too short for her growing frame. "Why are you here?"

I thought your mother might have the letter I need because she maybe possibly murdered the Basilica chancellor doesn't seem like quite the right thing to tell a grieving kid. I settle on a more amiable "There's a lot of tension between the Institute and your other two government branches. I thought if I knew more about your mother's plans, I could do something about it."

"Why would you care? You're not from Venalt."

"If everyone keeps arguing, then your aurora might die. I care about him. And I do care about your city, too." Whether or not that was all Luca's doing, it's true now.

Matthia nods slowly, watching me like she's trying to decide if I'm real or not. "If the aurora dies, the hippocamps will come take our corelium to make their nests. You know that's where we got it from: from them. They reuse it every mating season and leave it floating along the surface after the eggs have hatched, to come back to it later. But then we started taking it when they were gone. So now they'll take our city, and it's not even their fault." She gnaws on the inside of her lip. "We'll have to put everyone on the foundation center, with tents and stuff. And a lot of food. If we fill the basements, we can hold supplies for everyone for, like, five months and build boats for families, and the families in the boats will build the city again."

It sounds like someone else's idea in her young mouth. I lift a brow. "Was that your mother's plan?"

A blush rises beneath Matthia's light freckles. "Yes."

The fact that Fiordelise was making preparations in case Venalt sank doesn't mean she was actively trying to reach that outcome. But it does feel suspicious with everything else I know of the situation already.

I consider asking Matthia if her mother spoke more of the city falling, but the way her face slowly crumples, her shallow breath interspersed with sniffling, I can't risk destroying her further. She notices me watching and pinches her lips together, scowling away from me.

"It's all right to hurt." I don't try to smile, don't even gentle the words—they are what they are: the truth. "My mother was killed when I was a little younger than you are. I know it feels worse than anything else you've ever been through before, because it is worse. It hurts. I bet you're angry, and scared sometimes, too, and that's also all right."

Matthia sniffles, wrapping her arms over her knees with her face covered behind them. She looks so small, gangly legs and all. "Everyone says it'll get better."

"It will, in some ways. You'll reach a time when you'll be happy again, and you'll feel safe and at peace, and have other people you care for as dearly as you cared for your mother. You can let that happen—you're not forgetting her or loving her any less." I feel more than hear my voice hitch, the knot in my chest half joy and half pain. It took me so long to reach here, to escape my isolation and learn to care for my melancholy. I hope it takes Matthia months, not decades, that she will have people who can guide her through it the way I didn't. Rising onto my knees, I snatch one of the paperweights on Fiordelise's desk—the little hippocamp-like one with the chip from where I dropped it last time. I roll it between my fingers, tracking the motion of its tail back and forth, letting it distract me from the uncomfortable well in my chest. "No matter how old you get, though, you'll still miss her. Some days when you think about her, you'll just remember the love, and some days you'll feel all the pain again, as much as you do today, and you won't ever stop wishing she could be with you."

"I don't want to keep missing her! I want her back," Matthia snaps. She drops her head into her arms, shaking.

"I know, kid." I don't tell her there are pieces of her mother she will forget, that in ten years she'll be a fresh adult wishing she'd written more down or had better pictures or made a phonograph record with the sound of her mother's voice, because if she does all those things just to try to fix the future pain, it will only break something new in its place.

Matthia's crying slowly quiets, but tension remains in every molecule of her frame, from her taut shoulders to her curled toes within her woolen socks.

I tuck the paperweight into my pocket. "Can I come sit with you?"

Her head lifts. She stares at me for a moment; then she nods.

I scoot around the desk chair, settling against the shelves at Matthia's side, offering comfort the way a cat does: a solid presence without any force behind it. She doesn't know me well, and like a wounded animal, if I push her trust too far, I think we'll both end up suffering.

She lays her head back on her arms, staring toward the bullet hole in the window. A strand of her hair tangles in her mouth the way Tavish's so often does. "Are the people who did this going to kill me, too?"

"No. I don't understand everything about this situation yet, but I am positive that no one is going to hurt you. No one is going to let that happen."

"How do you know? We don't even know who killed her. Or—or why. Nobody knows anything. Or nobody tells me anything." She glares at the floor, but through the anger I see the same foundation as her fear, a grief that will keep infiltrating everything else until the residue of it becomes a part of her, the gold sealing her cracks back together. "You don't know they won't just kill me, too. The government can't decide if they're going to send me away or not. They could choose to leave me here, and whoever did this might come back."

"Do you want to go somewhere else, somewhere safer? To the mainland, to your great-aunt, maybe?"

She jerks nearly upright with a shake of her head. "I—I don't even know her. She's really old and she lives in the mountains."

"You'd rather stay here in Venalt? Even if it's dangerous?"

"I think so. I've never been anywhere else." She pushes her stray waves away from her mouth and nibbles on her pinkie. Her nails are bitten down to nothing, a few with the skin around them torn back like how Tavish's get when he's stressed—like his are currently. "Unless my dad came back. I'd go anywhere with him."

The addition hits me like an anvil to the chest, reminding me just how much I once hoped, bloody and raw, for my second parent to return. "Do you know where he is?"

Matthia shakes her head. "Mom mostly wouldn't talk about him. Once she said he loved me, and he had a good heart, but he was a fool who didn't know how to act on it. I think she was drunk then." Matthia sniffles. "But if he loves me, he could come get me, right?"

"I . . ." My voice catches, a tight, off-kilter thing that wants to curl up between my ribs and sob itself to sleep. "If she said that your father loved you, then he did, but it's complicated." I can say it, speak the words, know that it has to be the truth, logically, and yet they sound like nonsense. Sound like the way a knife thuds into a heart.

Matthia feels them no differently. "It's not complicated!" she demands. "He would come get me if he loves me. And if he isn't dead, too."

That's not a conversation I'm ready to have in this moment, much less one Matthia is, her eyes wet and her absentminded nail picking turning aggressive and ugly. So I try my best to redirect her. "Where would you go, if you did travel? You know, I've seen a lot of this continent in the last month. Venalt is very pretty, but there's some pretty neat places out there too. Towns made of towers that hang beneath cliffs, castles that burrow deep into the ground, underwater cities full of selkies."

"Is that Maraheem?" She seems to perk up, if only a little bit. "Mom said it had a war."

"A really tiny one, yes. But sometimes a group of people have been hurt for so long that fighting back is the only way to get peace for everyone."

"I'd want to go there, then. Selkies get to be *seals*. That's cooler than funny architecture." She watches me out of the corner of her eye, tracking the patterns of rainbow-filled darkness that crisscross my chest in the gap of my shirt where I haven't found the time to lace it back up, and over my hands where the sleeves fall back. "You're the aurora everyone is talking about, aren't you?" She points to the fishnets. "That's what they look like."

I give her a teasing smile, showing off my rainbow-tipped incisors. "How do you know that?"

Her eyes roll toward the ceiling as she huffs. "I read books, of course. Mom got me a rare-creature encyclopedia last year, a really special, expensive one by this supersmart adventurer satyr who lived, like, two hundred years ago, when no one wanted to let satyrs write books, because other people were stupid and thought our brains got squished by our horns. It didn't have a lot about auroras, though. I just know they're weird, and they function like a single-body fungal parasite, but they're not made of cells like any fungus, or any other type of living cell either. And no one knows where the energy for the ignits they make comes from. But I guess most of them don't actually make those anymore." She pauses, looking at me again, her eyebrows tight. "Are you going to die like our aurora?"

The question sends a burst of panic through me. Because the answer is yes. Yes, I'm going to fade, and then, unless something changes beyond my control, I'm going to die, and there will be so very little I can do about it without hurting another aurora in the process. Someday, sooner than later, I won't be here, not to love or to protect, nor to be loved in return. There's so much I'll be leaving behind: Tavish and my pets, Luca and Teodor if they live long enough, the auroras still dying around the world—even this city itself with its government too caught up in its hostility to solve anything.

I want so desperately to be here for them, for a lot longer, at least.

It occurs to me that I don't even know what happens to an aurora when they die in this world, or what effect that will have on my human half's soul. Whether I can transition to an afterlife or will merely be wiped from existence. Whether the halves of me will complete this journey together or be ripped apart. At the sheer weight of its unknowability, my fear turns into an overwhelming dread that latches into my bones, and it's all I can do not to think on it too hard.

None of this is a thing I can tell a grieving eleven-year-old either. Instead, I give Matthia a shrug that doesn't cover my feelings in the slightest. "Someday we'll all die. But hopefully neither of us for a long time."

She nods. Carefully, like she's worried she might hurt me, she pats my shoulder. Coming from her, so broken and young and reminiscent of my past, it feels like the nicest thing anyone has ever done for me. She props her plush on her knee after, fiddling with a stitch that's coming loose along its chest.

"You should get someone to fix that, or it'll break."

"Someday everything breaks." She holds the plush out to me, though, like I might fix it for her.

I take it gently, not the least bit sure of how to repair a stuffed toy. Up close it looks even odder, three button eyes and too many limbs, a few coming out the wrong places—a proper horror show. But by the wear and tear on it, it's a well-loved one. The padding inside has gone bunchy and stiff, but mixed in with the fluff, there's something genuinely hard. "He has a lump," I say, handing the toy back.

"It's always been there. Mom said it's his heart. And he's mine, so it's my heart, too."

"That's cute."

"It's stupid. Mom was stupid." By the fresh gleam in her eyes, I don't think she really means that.

The sun seems to go out all at once as the last of its rays are blocked from the edge of the channel. In the dimness of the room, the quiet feels like a living thing. I shudder. Matthia must sense it, too, because she scrambles across the floor to tug on the reading lamp. The light flickers once, then streams to life, flaring its yellowed glow through the room.

She picks it up, carrying it back to the floor with her. As she settles beside me, the light reflects off the underside of Fiordelise's desk. I shift closer.

"What is it?" Matthia asks.

I scoot under the desk enough to run my fingers along an odd crack, a bit too wide for an average plane of wood. When I push it, the whole panel springs. "There's a drawer here—did you know that?"

"Can I see?" Matthia clambers over. Any hesitation she once had about my presence completely evaporates as she wedges herself into the space with me, holding to my shoulder to get a better look.

Together, we pull the first pile of papers out of the drawer. We spread them out on the floor; more blueprints and architectural drawings, like the ones on the desk. These range from individual structures to large sections of the city, all of them resoundingly similar in style to the Institute building.

"That's not Venalt," Matthia says quietly. "It is, but it's not. There's no corelium."

"She redesigned the whole city . . ."

"Mom said if it sank, then we could build it way better the next time." Matthia stares at the plans, slowly chewing on the inside of her lip. "These are so good, though. Why did she hide them?"

"I don't know," I mutter, even though as I draw the second bundle out, I think I do.

My heart sinks at the sight. I don't have to spread them out to recognize them: seven letters; my sloppy, spiraling handwriting marking down Tavish's perfect words, extra blots of ink in each of the dozen places I had to pause to ask him for a spelling. Fiordelise received our letters, every single one. She knew that ignits would save Luca long before the traveling merchant told her. And she hid it away in her secret box with her plans for a rebuilt city.

Beneath our unanswered correspondence sits the last of the hidden drawer's contents, the one that pulls together everything else I know so far. The typed memo reads: *Chancellor Domenego is planning to give the Citadel his ignits. Do something.*

Fiordelise did something all right. She worked to make sure Luca would die and the city would sink, not to achieve an end to a prophecy, but to give herself the opportunity to build a better metropolis from the foundation out—one she'd painstakingly designed piece by piece, far more logical and self-sustaining and in line with the Institute's ideals than the current Venalt. And someone killed her for it. Her death to stop the death of an aurora—or to try, anyway.

There's no letter from the Basilica stashed with it, no proof of what Chancellor Domenego was planning to do. But maybe this will be enough. It has to be enough.

From the other room, the Basilica staffer shouts at the Citadel office, "Where is she?"

"You lost her?"

"Matthia!"

The kid looks at me, her face a question of fear and confusion. Maybe she hasn't put all the pieces together yet—she probably doesn't want to—but she knows something here is wrong. And she doesn't know what to do about it.

I wish I did.

Frantically, I begin stuffing the papers into a stack small enough to fit back into the drawer. Matthia joins in, her smaller hands moving faster than mine. Even with us both working together, we barely get them into a semblance of a pile before the door to the living room bursts open for Matthia's temporary guardians. Through it, I can hear the echo of something worse coming down the hall.

"No, no, Tavish, if you are so convinced that this letter the Basilica needs is somehow in Chancellor Fiordelise's office, then I demand we look," Zuane says, his dry voice twisting the irony in.

As he finishes, the hallway door opens as well. Zuane looks, understandably, none too surprised to see me.

I grin at him. "You're late."

CHAPTER SIXTEEN

every intent

MATTHIA'S TEMPORARY GUARDIANS—A Citadel officer and a Basilica staffer—stand, stunned, in the near doorway, their gazes darting to the hall entrance where Commander Zuane in his nereid wheelchair enters with the most disgruntled-looking Tavish I've ever seen. Zuane opens his mouth, but at the same moment, the Basilica guardian seems to pull herself together.

She shouts at me in horror, "Get away from the girl!"

"How did you get here?" adds the officer acting as Matthia's guardian. "This room is off-limits!"

Still on my knees before the paper mound, I hold my palms calmly out the side, grinning in a way that I know doesn't come across as the least bit compliant, but dammit, I can't help it. "Now, now—"

Matthia grabs my hand. Her small fingers curl over the stumps where mine used to be, and her nose lifts, her shoulders pressed back. "I let him in," she says, bright, sharp words that slice every protest from the room, as if she's the Divine Three all merged into one, speaking her will into the universe. As if she's . . .

No.

My chest tightens. She can't be. I want to believe it, for Tavish's sake and for Matthia's, but that doesn't make it any more than an eerie coincidence.

Zuane snorts, giving Matthia a long glance before shifting his gaze to me. "Just thought you'd come ruffle through my crime scene, did you?"

"Why might I feel the need to do that?" I shrug, the rainbow in my aurora flesh shimmering. Behind Zuane, Tavish presses two fingers to the bridge of his nose like this whole situation is slowly killing him.

The officer leans down to get a better look at the papers. They curse. "Sir, there's a secret drawer beneath the desk. These must have been inside it."

"We found them," Matthia explains, and I think she means to try to shift some of the blame off me, but it seems to do exactly the opposite.

Zuane's flat expression cracks ever so slightly. "Fucking Fiordelise. Package them as evidence." He shifts his gaze back to me. "And you—you're coming with us."

"Again?" I growl.

Tavish interjects, his diamond voice cutting through the rest of the commotion like a blade through a chest. "That will be entirely unnecessary. Rubem is here on ambassadorial duties from Venalt's aurora. He has a right to conduct his own investigative measures."

He gives no indication that he's lying through his teeth, but Zuane looks prepared to ignore any number of truths if it will put me back in a holding cell. "What this is, Mr. Findlay"—I almost miss the flinch Tavish gives when Zuane snaps his name, but the way his pinkie quivers, then tightens is unmistakable—"is trespassing and tampering with Citadel affairs. If you wanted to collapse an entire investigation, this is how you do it."

Collapse an entire investigation wide open, I want to snipe back, but I only discovered the drawer in the first place because a grieving eleven-year-old found comfort in pulling a lamp off the table to sit on the ground with it. I settle for a more dignified "I think you'll find this does quite the opposite."

"And how do I know someone didn't send you here to plant it as evidence? Or to steal parts of it as a cover up?" He scowls, or at least I think he does. "If you haven't destroyed anything with your own ignorance, I'll be amazed."

Tavish scoots into the room in front of Zuane, imposing himself into the space like he belongs here. "Have you not finished your examination of the room yet? You left it open for a child to enter, didn't you? What can someone possibly ruin that your people had not missed entirely? If they abandoned evidence here in the first place, then perhaps they're not properly conducting their jobs."

Zuane visibly straightens, rising to Tavish's level of sophistication like he's been tugged there on puppet strings. "Our staff is preoccupied defending this city from hippocamps, Mr. Findlay"—Tavish flinches again—"an effort in which anyone here is free to be of use if *they* wish to risk *their* life and limb."

Tavish doesn't have to lift his voice, only his chin. "Are you implying that a blind foreigner fight your battles for you, Commander?"

"You deliberately misunderstand me—"

"Or that it's the job of the man whose fellow aurora has kept your city powered and safe—cities across the globe, powered and safe—for centuries, but which your people seem determined to let die while they squabble?" Tavish continues. "Or is it merely that you hope the untrained civilians of your city will pick up arms in your place?"

"Of course not!" Zuane snaps, frustration and something almost like fear cracking across his feature as his head fins ruffle, the spikes along his arms flaring. "I mean only that we are understaffed in a city ill-designed to support our work to begin with, not when it would rather boast architectural feats and artistic monuments in place of anything remotely defensible, and then blame *us* for not having the ability to do our job." He draws in a breath, his fins relaxing as he lets it back out. "While that's not your fault, we will still need Rubem to accompany us. The chancellor would like to see him."

Tavish's mouth goes stiff. He picks at the nail of his wobbling pinkie finger. "Who am I to deny Chancellor Teodor."

I feel his worry in the base of my chest, doubled down by everything I now know. We can't avoid Teodor for long, but I also can't let the only evidence we've found—evidence that might prompt the Basilica to give up their ignits—go wandering from hand to hand, where it might wind up anywhere. Anywhere, including wherever the Basilica's original letter did. "There's a memo in there that Chancellor Alvise needs to see. I'll see Teodor after it's been delivered."

"A memo?" Zuane stares at me. "Is this the statement you were so certain you would find here?"

"This one's related."

"I am happy to hand over the specific declaration Chancellor Alvise is seeking after an examination, but anything else you've uncovered must be recorded as evidence."

As Zuane speaks, the Citadel officer presses Matthia out of the way to scoop up the stack of papers, using gloves to shuffle them into a bag.

"This one is just as important as the memo we were seeking!" I try not to sound like a whiny child, but my efforts only turn the statement into a growl, equally ridiculous but twice as threatening. I reach for the memo, the robust, grey-toned paper obvious at the top of the stack. "If Alvise could just see it—"

The officer jerks the memo away from me.

Zuane takes it with a huff. His lips curl.

"I can deliver it!" the Basilica guardian volunteers, hand raised like this is a game.

Zuane cringes. "Aren't you watching Matthia? Poorly, I might add. No, I'll have a courier from the Basilica contacted. They can retrieve this from our offices in the morning."

"Retrieve what?" Through the crowd slowly gathering in the apartment hall, Iseppa pushes her way forward with a shrill squeak. "What is all this?!" She manages to sound both stunningly confused and explicitly accusatory, throwing her hands up in a defiant flick as she converges on the commander.

"This is still a crime scene, Iseppa," Zuane says, clearly attempting to resume his air of logical indifference and just as clearly failing.

"Like the deep it is," she curses. "You couldn't care less that Fiordelise died—and I think we all know why."

"The Citadel wants to find Fiordelise's murderer as much as anyone." A spark of emotion shoots through Zuane's tone, too fast and clipped to pinpoint. "Desire alone does not solve a case."

Iseppa scowls. She gives the memo in his hands a passing glance before snatching it away so hard the lower corner tears. As she reads, she mutters, "This is about Chancellor Domenego."

"It's also evidence." Zuane tries to grab it back but collides with the officer's attempt as Iseppa slips free of them.

Something in me snaps. Whatever else the memo means, it also represents days of Luca's life. Days they're waving around like children. Selfish, squabbling children playing with an aurora's life—a city's life—like it's a game, choosing to sacrifice everything instead of relinquishing the upper hand. It reminds me so excruciatingly of Maraheem. Of Raghnaid Findlay, staring down her nose at the world. Of every aurora who had to die to stop her from crushing the city in a wild attempt to retake it.

I can feel my frustration turning into rage, then to something brighter, something that vibrates in every thread of my being, aurora and human alike.

Matthia's hand tightens around mine. I squeeze hers back before pulling free. When words have failed, then comes me.

I bare my teeth and launch myself over Fiordelise's desk. In one quick motion, I snatch Iseppa's wrist and twist up her fingers to free the memo without tearing it farther. She shrieks, and Tavish says my name so perfectly calm it can only be a mask. Zuane shouts. His officer lunges for me.

Tucking the memo to my chest with my whole hand, I duck the officer's grasp and slam past like a battering ram. With his tentacles wrapped firmly around his chair, Zuane grabs at me. In a burst of aurora power, I wrench him off and plunge out the door.

"Rubem," he shouts after me.

"This memo needs to get to Alvise!" I call back, sprinting down the hall and out the apartment.

The officer charges after me like a stampeding peccary. My lead slips as my muscles protest, human and aurora flesh alike twitching from an exhaustion I have no right to be feeling with all the energy I should still have stored within me. I push past it, running down the long marble halls and into the Institute's massive foyer. It seems twice as large as the last time I was here, the white floor polished to a slippery shine, the dispersed lighting of crystal lamps giving every curve and corner of the ridged walls and ceiling a shadowless feel and leaving the few clusters of gossiping Institute employees slightly disembodied against the ethereal glow of it all.

Half a ghost already, I sprint through on my silent feet, making it nearly to the entrance before anyone seems to notice. The officer stumbles into the foyer behind me, alternating between talking into a mobile radio and shouting after me. I'm far enough ahead that it makes no difference.

I slip out the front of the Institute at a full sprint, so fast and free that I don't stop in time to keep from running straight into a group of Citadel staff. They startle for barely an instant. Then four pairs of hands grab for me. I hold the memo closer, elbowing and twisting, shifting my weight to throw off the attacker at my back and swiveling to ram my knee beneath another's legs. As the next officer slams a fist toward my chin, I shove his blow away, darting in to land one of my own.

A gun presses to my side.

There is a moment were the halves of me split, each evaluating our own side of this: my human remembering the mortality of this host body and the devastation a bullet can do when fired this close to the flesh, my aurora calculating how much energy we've used to deflect longer range bullets in the past. Together, we recognize that we don't have the strength to defend this time. I plunge back into one consciousness. Instead of taking the bullet, I jerk forward, slamming my palm at the barrel to drive it away.

As I do, someone behind me cracks their heel against the backs of my calves, and someone else slams a fist into my side. My knees cave, hitting the stone with a flash of pain. I grunt as my aurora flesh twists to soak up the impact. The agony subsides, but it leaves a familiar panic in its wake.

My instincts scream at me to do something, anything—hide or beg or fight back with tooth and nail—my body's impulses honed by an adolescence of bruises and insults. I snarl as hands latch around my arms, someone's fingers gripping my braids. The more they push, the more I push back, blind in my rage and the swimming of my vision. Through it all, I feel the paper crinkle in my grasp. The back of my mind flares a warning, but it gets lost in my own anger, lost beneath the weight of all these bodies so desperately pushing me down, again, again, again.

Not again. I've had fucking enough.

Heat rushes through me, blazing from my aurora flesh in crisscrossing pulses that turn the world to a shimmer and a scream as the Citadel officers all reel back, sizzling like they've been electrocuted. They twitch and topple, curling up as they moan. For a moment, it feels right, feels like winning.

My arms wobble, waves of energy and fatigue, of relief and fear, swaying and stabilizing me in cycles, but with each cycle, the exhaustion takes over a bit more of me, my guilt destroying my triumph.

The officers just lie there in whimpers: two humans, a satyr, and a harpy. One looks nearly old enough to retire and another young enough to barely be out of school. They're just people. Just people in pain.

A frightened scattering of workers peek through the Institute entrance behind me and cluster at the edges of the wide path in front. An onlooker in a medical uniform slinks by me to kneel beside one of the fallen Citadel officers. Commander Zuane bursts out of the Institute, his wheelchair churning, Tavish panting behind him.

I remember the paper crushed beneath my palm.

I should stand. I should run all the way to the Basilica and demand to see Chancellor Alvise immediately. But there's already a crowd coming toward us down the path that wraps around the lawn from that direction, and I know it's too late.

What's done is done.

"What is the meaning of this?" Chancellor Teodor shouts from the front of the group. Her husky voice doesn't cut like Tavish's or Matthia's, forcing her to repeat the question louder once the hush has settled and all eyes have turned toward her. It rattles then, an eruption that matches her expression.

She moves with steady slowness, her limp barely visible as her cane settles soundlessly on the stone. It's almost eerie how quiet she still is, even without her plush cushions and bare feet to pad her way. Each step she takes is lost beneath whispered breaths and the rustle of clothing, silent as the grave she seems so close to inhabiting. It makes the back of my neck prickle.

Chancellor Alvise trots behind her, their feathers ruffled and half their jewelry missing, as though they were pulled from their home partway through removing it. Their usual bubbliness is hidden beneath an anxious confusion. They keep behind Teodor like the Citadel leader is a shield.

Teodor seems more a battering ram. She heads straight for me, her gaze bouncing from Zuane to the officers slowly pulling themselves together at my feet. "This is pathetic," she hisses. "You are all pathetic."

"Chancellor—" Zuane barks.

"Do you have leave to speak, Commander?" Teodor barks.

For all the fury that's now eating up Zuane's expression, his cheeks brighten a shade and he looks away.

Teodor turns her attention fully on me.

I can barely hold myself up any longer, no strength and all weariness. No valor and all guilt. All me, broken despite my every effort. It seems only the pinprick of Teodor's gaze that keeps me from sinking the rest of the way to the floor.

"You," she says.

"People seem to be aiming that word at me a lot lately." I breathe out, then in, and something comes with it, a laugh or a sob; my heart, flayed and battered and no closer to the vague sense of success it yearns for.

She shakes her head, her voice lowering. "You are just the sort of person who would fall for Tavish."

A smile creeps onto my face, an inward, bitter thing. "I wasn't always." The words go from smooth to caught to smooth again. "I don't suppose you'd accept an apology?"

Like each movement is fought for, she uses her cane to squat slowly down. In the bright cast of the light from the building behind me, I spot a flash of the ashy-grey ring in her irises before she drops into my shadow, turning them an inky black through and through. "Apologies are for those who intend to change."

I swallow. Slowly, I unclench the memo. It's wrinkled, a few letters beyond repair, but it's still legible. "What about this, then?" I offer it to her. As she takes it, I add, "You said you'd deal with it all, I know, but I couldn't let them keep squabbling over Luca's life like that. My pain has been disregarded too many times to watch it happen to him."

She rolls her thumb over the memo, flattening it into a rumpled version of its old self. "Luca isn't too happy with you right now."

"That, I do fully intend to change for."

"All right," she says, as if there's no more to it. "Can you stand?"

I grimace. "If I have to."

She nods. I'm the only one close enough to see the flash of pain that twinges her features as she pushes back to her feet. I rise to help her, and she lets me before handing Alvise the memo.

Alvise's brow shoots up. Slowly their chin bobs. "It's not what we were looking for, but yes, yes, this will do."

Teodor stares at them. She coughs once, stopping so quickly that it seems it might simply be an encouragement to the interim chancellor except for subtle clues like the rigid way she holds her back and the fact that she hasn't inhaled since.

"Oh, right, yes, I'm supposed to do something now," Alvise mutters. They give the memo a wave, their two remaining bangles jingling. "This is proof—or, proof of proof, or so forth—that it was Chancellor Domenego's final wish that the Basilica's sacred ignits be donated to the cause of keeping Venalt's treasured aurora alive. In his memory, the Basilica will be fulfilling that pledge despite the hardship it imposes on our faith, because Chancellor Domenego believed that this was the only morally acceptable choice, and it has therefore been elevated to a mandate by the Divine Three."

I can't imagine that it's procedure for Basilica announcements to be shouted in front of the Institute to a random crowd of staff, a few gaggling civilians, and four downed officers who are only now sitting up, but I can see the genius of it a moment later as all eyes turn to Iseppa, her small frame silhouetted by the Institute building. Her raised chin wobbles. She lifts her hands and lowers them again with a breath.

"The Institute's dedication to honoring the Divine Three through our understanding of their world and our use of their physical laws places us under that mandate as well." She closes her eyes, giving another little wave of her fingers. "So, we'll also be donating ignits to the Venalt aurora, whatever is needed for its survival, as I'm sure Chancellor Fiordelise would have wanted."

I almost laugh at the thought of this being Chancellor Fiordelise's desire, but then the magnitude of what Iseppa—what Alvise—what Teodor, through my near failure—have all done finally sinks in with a relief so great I want to laugh.

Luca! I shout, all tired joy. My heart drops as the call echoes outward without response, Luca avoiding it so thoroughly that I'm not even sure he can sense me reaching toward him. But at least he'll be safe. Whatever happens, I can rest easy knowing that.

Teodor extends her hand to me. "I'm not finished with you."

I grunt. "Clearly. But you really should be in bed in your state."

"Rubem All-Worlder, don't you dare tell me what the fuck to do."

As I turn to look for Tavish, to let him know of my departure, I find Iseppa and Alvise beginning an uncomfortable conversation about the transfer of their ignits, in which Alvise rambles good-naturedly while Iseppa attempts to steamroll them at every turn, mostly failing due to Alvise's cheery obliviousness. Tavish works his way past the crowd at the Institute entrance, dispersing most of them with his cane and clanking it against Commander Zuane's wheelchair more often than I imagine is strictly necessary. It leaves only Zuane in the backlight of the Institute's massive doors, his face veiled in shadow. I swear he scowls at me still. As I scowl back, every light in the Institute and across the foundation circle and beyond the edge throughout the city suddenly goes dark.

CHAPTER SEVENTEEN

the opposite of ghosts

THIRTY-NINE OF THE FORTY ignits used to power the main generator are gone. An Institute staffer brought us out the final one, the fist-sized blue stone dim from the overuse of keeping the generator running as long as it could after the rest of the stones were taken. As Teodor took it, her fingers trembled in the hastily lit candles brought over from the Basilica.

The time between then and now feels like a ruthless eon of anxiety, my strength coming and going in spurts as I silently pace the length of the Institute's foyer under the scrupulous gaze of three different officers and Teodor's sharp, suspicious glances. The foundation circle is closed off, and reports trickle in for the gathered leaders, interim and not, with alarming certainty: all the remaining ignits in the foundation circle are gone, from the dozen pink ones used in water sanitization to the clusters in the Basilica's sacred artifacts. One group of Citadel officers retrieves an ignit tracker from the depths of their storage but the already highly imprecise tool—useless for most inactive ignits— reveals nothing.

Under Tavish's guidance, all three acting chancellors begin emergency preparations for the powerless city and send out ignit search teams. One of them quickly returns from beyond the foundation circle with even more harrowing news: around the city, other ignits have been taken from elevators and boat motors and backup generators. It's almost too much to process, the sickening emptiness in my chest growing by the minute.

Teodor seems to weaken in time to it. As she fades, so does the polite but distant demeanor she presents Tavish, until it seems like she's ignoring him for fear of what she might say if she starts paying him any amount of attention.

If Tavish notices, he doesn't show it.

As he finishes with another round of delegations, I steal him off to the side. "I'm taking Teodor back to her rooms."

"Aye, please."

"That bad, is it?"

"I can feel her glowering."

I chuckle. "Technically she's scowled no more at you than at anyone else, but I do see what you mean." Gently, I add, "You know, you could try talking to her, she might . . ." The way he shudders makes me trail off.

"No. It's fine," he mutters. "You take her back to the Citadel."

I squeeze his arm. "Keep an eye on things here while I'm gone. But safely."

"Not sure what good that would do us, considering the state of my eyes."

"I love you."

"Aye, you do." He smirks. "Now go help Teodor."

I kiss him, soft and a little longer than I should, considering how recklessly it makes me want to pull him off into a storage room and try to forget that we had put the world back together for barely a minute before it fell apart into twice as many pieces. I was so close to having made a difference. If I had not waited so long, had pushed harder, had done more, then Luca might have had the energy to sustain himself for months instead of a single, feeble, blue generator ignit that's more a taunt than a boon.

Teodor protests as I take her arm. "I can get home when it damn pleases me."

"You could. But you could also, as the esteemed and highly terrifying chancellor, be forced to physically escort me back to the Citadel for being a terrible nuisance criminal. The fact that I don't want you to die tonight is arbitrary."

Teodor hesitates, but a tremor runs through her chest. She tucks her body forward, coughing quietly into her arm. Each hack grows stronger, until everyone in the room should hear it, but still it's silent, as though her existence is out of phase with this reality. So much like her footsteps.

Like my footsteps.

The thought makes me shudder.

She presses a handkerchief to her mouth. In the dimness of the distant candles, what comes out looks black as soot. "I guess you probably shouldn't be allowed to pace ruts into the Institute's floors," she mutters, and something twitches in her cheeks, her gaze darting. "If I have to take you back to stop you from making trouble . . ."

"The very worst trouble."

"We are still going to talk about that."

"As long as you get to sit in a chair for it." I smile, and because I can't help myself, "With bourbon."

"Damn you." She loops her arm through mine, leaning half on me and half on her cane.

"I think that's your job," I tease.

She laughs, soft and hoarse, and lets me lead her into the dark, ignitless night, the world caving in around us both until we're two wisps on the breeze, two silent ghosts fading into the night. And I think, perhaps, we might have more to talk about than she realizes.

The basement lagoon is empty, but I sense Luca sulking beneath the foundation, unaware that he's been saved and damned all in one breath. By the time I set our single candle on one of the many random end tables of Teodor's room, she bypasses the chair entirely and collapses into her pillows, soundless. *Soundless.* I still can't believe it. Her chest rises and falls in bursts, and her eyelids flutter, but she waves a dismissive hand toward the cluttered bar cart.

"Is there vodka? This esteemed, terrifying chancellor feels like it's a vodka night."

I slip into the bathroom with a glass, dragging aside the clutter in the sink and filling it from the tap. Teodor makes a face as I return, her expression deepening when I thrust the cup at her. "This humble prisoner counters your demand with an offer of water."

"Get out," she says, but she downs it between coughing spurts. I take a sip of something I think might actually be gin before handing her the bottle. She grabs my arm as I try to pull back. "You hurt Luca. You went to the Institute. You found that damn memo. I really don't know what to do with you."

"I don't know what to do with *myself* sometimes." Sighing, I climb onto the bed beside her. Its overly plush mattress sinks so much that Lavender almost slides into me from where she's curled at the edge. She takes advantage of the momentum to roll sleepily across my lap, stretch, and then plant herself between my thigh and Teodor's.

"Did you find anything else in Fiordelise's office?" Teodor lets me go, taking a swig of her drink and offering it back.

I want to accept. I know I shouldn't—I've done so well, or better, at least, than normal. But right now the world feels almost as dark as it looks. It clenches in my chest and closes my throat and makes me want to collapse inside myself, as though the thing within my ribs is a black hole. I have to fill it with something. As much as I know it won't last, know it'll only make things worse tomorrow, I need to feel just a little less like I'm dying right now if I want to survive long enough to see the sunrise.

The liquor goes down like a smooth blue fire.

I hand the bottle back, but I can already feel its grip on me, tightening like a noose. The draw of it makes me more reckless than the alcohol itself can. I scowl at Teodor. "What else did you expect me to find?"

She freezes, both hands on the not-vodka, and swallows nothing.

"Did you know that Fiordelise was withholding her ignits on purpose, hoping the city would sink so she could be the one to rebuild it?" I ask, giving Lavender a scratch on the head. She chirps softly and starts to purr, a happy, rumbling sound in direct contrast with the tension that vibrates between Teodor and me.

Slowly, Teodor nods. "Yes."

"And she killed Chancellor Domenego."

"That, I only suspect."

"Why didn't you do anything about it? You're the law, aren't you?"

Teodor flinches, her jaw going hard and her eyes harder. The flickering cast of our candle lights a vein of color in her pupils for barely an instant before it goes to an ashy grey, then to black. "The law needs due course. I couldn't arrest a woman on nothing but gut instinct."

I snort. "It sure seems like Zuane would be happy to do that to *me*."

"Zuane is rightfully pissed that you're running through his crime scene like a child in a playground." Teodor sips her alcohol slower now. "He doesn't show it, but this investigation has been hard on him. He feels out of control right now, so he's trying his best to take charge of the one problem with a solution, and that's you."

"A solution like locking me in an interrogation room again, huh?"

"You are a bit of a nuisance." Her lips twitch as she says it, bottle raised to them. A shudder rolls through her before she can drink, turning into a quiet hacking—normal quiet this time, not the uncanny silence from earlier. The silence so like my own.

I collect the bottle from her before she can spill it, supporting her arm as she leans forward to cough into her handkerchief. My frustration transforms at the sight of her misery. She has so little time left—she and Luca both, yet they give every possible moment to this city. To save a place and people they love. "I'm not the problem here," I say gently. "Someone is stealing Venalt's ignits. They're killing Luca, sinking the city. Fiordelise might have arranged for Chancellor Domenego's death and held back the ignits while she was alive, but she must have been working with a partner. Someone who left that threatening note in my hotel room. Someone who has the connections and followers to steal every ignit in the city in a matter of hours."

Teodor collapses back into the downy cushions, just as silent as my tapping hands. "They were all locked in Institute-issued cages, but the keys—Fiordelise would have had a master set and could have given them to someone. Whoever she did would only need twenty or so coordinated members, if they worked quickly and logically, portioning off the city between them. We had barely a few hundred ignits left for them to take."

"So their new leader could be anyone?"

"Anyone with knowledge of the guard system, access to the Basilica and the Institute, who would have been able to meet Fiordelise privately without drawing attention."

"Iseppa seems closest to her."

Teodor's eyes narrow, staring into the dark ceiling. "But she offered us her ignits."

"Only once pressured publicly by the Basilica's gift, and right before the power went out, when the generator would have already been relying solely on that one remaining ignit. She was suspiciously near the basement entrance, too." Too many mysteries, too many fractions. I rub my halved hand down my face. The places where my fingers should be tingle faintly with phantom sensation. "And the way she said that handing them over was what Fiordelise would have wanted, it felt like she knew it wasn't true."

"You just don't like her."

"I don't like Zuane either."

The low light nearly masks the shift in her expression, the slight twitch around her eyes and the bob of her throat. "I don't blame you. He's gotten to where he is by being a pain in the ass." She reaches across Lavender to poke my leg. "Kind of like you and me."

"Fuck off." But I find myself grinning, an unusual warmth blooming in my chest with an immaculate mixture of comfort and rightness. Like this is exactly how Teodor and I have always been, and the universe was just waiting for the two of us to slide ourselves into place. The thought brings a pang of fear with it. No matter how much I grow to care about Teodor, how perfect this moment seems, how much she's like me—like the family I never had—Teodor is dying.

And I can't stop that.

But I don't know if I can stop the affection that pulls like a cord between my heart and my gut, either, the shape of it slotting into me with such precision that I will have to start chipping away at pieces of myself if I want to cut it out by the root.

In the quiet that's lapsed between us, Teodor watches me, her eyes sharp and her expression tight. She draws a ragged breath, then another, and seems to come to a decision. Slowly, she lifts her palm, fingers flat, thumb pointing up. Her wrist trembles, but she holds it there, unease drawn across her features. "Slap my hand."

Now I'm the one staring. "What?"

"Don't ask questions, Rubem."

It feels like a weight has settled over the room. Lightning waiting to strike. An encroaching epiphany. It terrifies me suddenly, and I laugh, low and awkward. "Maybe you shouldn't drink so much."

"Rubem." She quavers, looking like she might run. She's just as scared as I am.

I slap her hand, not hard or soft, but the kind of playful patting motion I might make with one of my pets: a thing that's been perfectly silent all my life. The sound that rings out from our colliding palms makes me jerk so hard that Lavender scrambles off the bed. It fills the room, rattles through my head, my soul.

I stare at my fingers, wiggling them like maybe they've changed. But they're the same aurora-netted things, little scars and callouses scattering the dark skin, perhaps a few more wrinkles than last time I looked at them this hard. My gaze darts back to Teodor.

She beams. "Fuck, you really are one of us."

"Us?" But I already know the answer. Teodor is like me, and I'm like her. That makes there an *us*.

"Mom would call us astrals, the quiet ones."

"Ghosts." For how haunting the word is, my heart leaps as I say it. Ghosts. Plural. Not just me—or not just my human half—but more people with the same unnatural silence I've had from birth. A group to which I belong to. A people who might not kick me out for being different.

"Yeah, ghosts, I guess." Teodor sinks back into the pillows, still smiling. "Beings not quite here, people who don't fully mesh with the world, like we're always moving just a bit out of line. We're both pretty stable, though, compared to my ancestors—and yours, too, I'd guess. At least we can get by without most people noticing we're different."

"I'm from a place where silence is the difference between life and death. It would have been seen as a gift, if they didn't already have plenty of other reasons to hate me." My breath feels harder to draw. It hitches. "I thought it was just me, that there was something wrong with me. That it was—" I have to stop, closing my eyes as they smart, tears threatening, coming up from a well dug three decades before. "How many are there? How many of us?"

"I don't know. Before I was born, my mom tried to find others, and there were rumors—always just rumors that led nowhere. You're the first astral I've met outside my family." Teodor looks nearly as close to crying as I am. "I wasn't sure I really believed there were more until . . ."

"Me."

"You." It's not an accusation this time, but a blessing.

"How did we get it? Why are we like this, then? Does your family know?"

"Not entirely. The astralness goes back four generations with us, starting around the time of the ignit boon, but that first astral in our line would never talk about it. It was tragic, and it was caused by the boon somehow, but the way my mom would describe it, her grandpa would get too melancholic to say more. She said his sadness reminded her of homesickness."

Homesickness. That word stirs something in me, an emotion deep in my human bones at the thought of the Murk, but more than that, it makes my aurora half churn. I *am* homesick. I'm homesick for a place I can't remember, a world I know and love so thoroughly that it clings in rainbows to my skin and shines like brilliance through gaps in this reality. Yet I am here, in my human half's world, in a city that isn't even our own, giving my all for it, and for the single piece of it that resides in Luca.

And through it, I've found Teodor, forged myself a bigger home in the process. My home doesn't encompass this world, not yet. But perhaps it's getting there.

"Then one of my parents was as quiet as me?" Not my mother; she had the Murk's skill at silence but never the impossible inability to produce sound.

"Quieter," Teodor replies. "Whatever makes us like this seems to fade with every generation. My mom's voice would go in and out when she was upset, and her astral parent— my grandparent—had the things they held slip right through their grip, like they weren't even touching it. If I had a kid, though, they might not even be an astral at all."

"We really are ghosts." But ghosts are supposed to dwindle away, and it seems that we, at least, are returning, becoming more and more like the world around us with each generation. "When I slapped your hand, though, we made sound. So whatever stops us from interacting fully with the rest of the world doesn't affect our interactions with each other?"

"We're made of the same stuff, I guess."

The thought prickles where it should comfort. Beneath it, I find something else: terrifying and wonderful and everything in between. I almost don't say it. I almost don't want to know, to put that kind of expectation on us, but I can't live with it locked instead, either. "My second parent left my mom before I was born—they had to be astral like me, but that's all I know of them, not a name or even a gender. Is it possible if they had . . . if they were . . ." It catches inside me, and I beg Teodor to understand. The idea of my second parent seems too distant, a wisp of smoke I could never catch, but Teodor is here and real and *right.*

Her eyes seem to light, flickers of color in their depths and her cheeks going almost rosy. She props herself on her elbows. "You're what, in your thirties? And you're from the South? Alkelu?"

"Manduka."

"Oh." The glimmer fades. She taps her fingers absentmindedly, shaking her head. "My mom went to university in Alkelu before coming back here, and she—well, she made a time of it, that's for sure—but she was never in Manduka."

"And she was an only child? What about cousins? Younger aunts or uncles, or—"

Teodor shakes her head.

I don't realize how much hope I've collected until it all detonates like an ignit struck by an eruptstone, consumed from the inside out. We were almost siblings. Almost family. And it still feels like the right answer. "My mother never went more than a mile outside the Murk in all her life."

Teodor smiles, but it's a sad look, broken by a laugh. "It's a nice thought, anyway. I always wanted a perfectly terrible older brother to boss around."

It's a joke, I know it's a joke, but it lodges in my chest, right beside the admission that I have never thought about a sibling of my own, because I could never bring myself to imagine that there was someone, anyone like me, the boy trapped between two worlds and wanted in neither, creeping through them like a spectral criminal, a no-man's lander.

'A little sister,' I feel the human half of myself whisper, weak and envious. My aurora side responds with flashes that are more sensation than image: a brooding presence at my side, a sarcastic laugh that could brighten even the worst day, the way her voice would go flat when she'd snap at me, and I'd know it was just her love spilling out, that goddamned protective love that made her so stupid and bitter, her anger brewing hotter with each cycle, until I—

The old aurora memory cuts out, like a light turned off, leaving me panting and holding the duvet in both fists. It accentuates the gap in my memories, everything from before the mangrove sifting through my fingers as I try to grasp it again.

'You had a sister?' my human half asks.

I had a sister. I want to scream, to press my fingers through the shards of my skull and tear out the light hiding inside. *Why can't I remember her?*

The pain of not knowing—the pain of something darker, deeper that I did know once but now flutters somewhere beyond my reach—wrenches me, drawing trembles through my lungs and an ache in my jaw so tight it feels like the bone will crack. My other half, the human half, wraps me up, his presence strong and just as sad. All of my pain is his. And all of his desire to take it away is mine. I lean my mind into his touch, letting him whisper soothingly, *'I know. I know, my love. I know.'*

Teodor's hand closes around mine, snapping me back into one. "Hey, you good?"

I shift my fingers from under hers, trying not to make the motion seem like I'm pulling away. I don't want to *be* pulling away, but with the loss of my aurora sister still a fresh welt on my heart, I don't think I can bear Teodor making the same impression. I give her a weak smile. "Today's been a lot."

"Don't worry, I bet it'll be worse tomorrow," she says in a dry but gentle tone that brushes across that hole in my memories, making me shudder. Then she coughs again. Her fingers jerk back to lift her handkerchief to her mouth. It looks dark from edge to edge now. She curls her hand around it, tucking it against her chest. "You should get back to Tavish. Whoever left you that threatening note is still out there."

The little remaining warmth in my chest turns cold. "Are you going to be all right here alone?"

"I'll be fine. I have Luca."

But Luca is still curled deep in the foundation tunnels, and Teodor looks like she's wavering on the brink of death. "You shouldn't have pushed yourself so hard."

"Everything is pushing too hard these days," she grumbles. Her gaze drifts toward the not-vodka, but she doesn't reach for it.

I take a swig in her place before setting the bottle onto the nightstand. "Rest for a bit, at least."

"Only if you don't do any shit too wild while I sleep."

"Or you'll lock me up?" I try to grin, but my lips don't move right.

"Only for your own safety."

We sit in amiable silence—a together silence, the two of us astrals filling the space the only way we can. My gaze wanders the room once more. Every object is transformed by the dim candlelight, shadows deeper and hazier, a little more haunting. A little more ghostly.

There's a stack of ancient-looking books beneath the plate I set the candle on. I force myself to stand in order to move them, not wanting to risk the crisp paper catching fire while Teodor sleeps. As I set them to the side, though, I notice the stenciled illustrations of mythical creatures nearly worn off from the front of one. I show it to Teodor.

She grunts. "Found that in the library . . . or someone's library, anyway. I was trying to collect anything that might have information on hippocamps, in case they have weak spots we don't know about, but I never found the energy to read them."

"I know someone who might." I hold up the whole stack. "Do you mind if I . . .?"

Teodor makes a shooing motion. "Please. Though I doubt they'll find anything. These damn beasts seem unkillable."

Whether Matthia uncovers anything new about the hippocamps or not, I'm sure she'll appreciate the distraction. I make a plan to drop them off at the Institute for her after I find Tavish.

As I stack the books into my bag, Lavender finally leaps back onto the bed. She still looks indignant, but she curls against Teodor's side. The tip of her tail flicks.

Teodor gives her a slow pet before resting her trembling hand over the cat's back. "Do you want to take this fiend with you?"

"Her majesty looks happy enough here." Besides, it looks like Teodor needs the comfort.

She snorts. "In bed, at least. I woke to her hissing at that winged lion statue in the front parlor earlier. Not that I blame her. I'd have ditched it if it wasn't an expensive heirloom."

"I highly doubt you've gotten rid of anything before in your life."

"Occasionally, things are just taken away from me." Teodor's lips twitch, but the expression they shift through is harsh and sad. "If you don't feel safe returning to the hotel yet, you and Tavish are welcome to stay here too."

The thought of spending the night in our room sends a mix of fear and anger through me, but right now the anger wins. I challenge whoever left that note to return when I'm there, so we can be done with them. "I wouldn't dare. Tavish might die of guilt."

"All the better," she says, mouth twisted. As she watches my face, though, the expression falls. "You want to defend him."

"Of course I do. I love him more than life."

"Doing something for love doesn't always make it right."

"Which is why I'm not actually going to sit here and argue with you."

I give Lavender a head scratch. The royal nuisance turns her face so I can get in at just the right angle and protests as I pull away. She doesn't move to follow me, though. I pause, instinct urging me to give Teodor a more intimate farewell. But she's not my sister. And soon she won't be anything at all.

I turn away, leaving her the candle. By the time I reach the end of the bed, she's already asleep. Something hot and wet slides off my chin. My hands shake as I wipe it away.

CHAPTER EIGHTEEN

family matters

I RUN INTO A lurking Tavish as I leave the Citadel's secret entrance. He shifts awkwardly, looking as though he can't decide if he should enter or not. The tension floods out of him as I press my hand to his shoulder with a soft hello, but it just seems to rush into me instead.

"How did you get here?" I ask.

"I trailed behind a few of the officers returning for supplies."

"That's dangerous right now." I almost add, *and you know it*. But since he does know it, mentioning so would only be a further jab, and I'm not looking to fight with him over this.

"We're in danger more often than not. I have my cane-sword."

"When swords will ward off bullets, that might actually make me feel better," I grumble, and weed my arm through his. "You know, sulking out here is not going to mend your issues with Teodor."

"And invading her apartment will?" he huffs. His grip on me tightens, his body edging closer like he's looking for blood. "Not all of us can fix our problems by barreling mindlessly through them."

"It worked out."

"This time."

As we round the building, I guide us along the wide path that cuts through the foundation's central gardens. With the electricity out, the area is unusually quiet and dark, stoic trees silhouetted against the stars, branches rustling in a light breeze. The stone path beneath our feet reflects the night sky dimly, meandering between the park lawns as it carries us toward the dark silhouette of the old, lone building at the foundation's center.

Tavish still seems to stew, his pace agitated and the swish of his cane faster and more abrupt than usual.

I give his arm a tug. "Fine, tell me what other choice I had? Should I have just let them lose that memo entirely? Or waited for you to step in? I certainly couldn't have talked sense into them. Neither Zuane nor Iseppa listen to me—they both hate me, I'm pretty sure."

Tavish's nose wrinkles. "You could have started by not setting us up to have half the city's most powerful individuals dislike us. Because you are certainly right—they do hate you. And I don't blame them. You began your association with them as a spontaneous battering ram."

I let go of him, half tripping over my own feet as I try to process it all. "You're saying I did *what*?"

"You were needlessly aggressive." Tavish waves his cane like he's dictating an orchestra. It smacks me in the thigh.

I grunt, batting it lower. "Is that a demonstration?"

He sighs and tucks the aid under his arm instead. "I mean that when you meet someone who doesn't immediately butter you up, you have no idea how to speak with them in any manner other than confrontational."

"That's not fair!"

"But it is true! You can be quite the arse."

My left fingers curl and open, the missing lengths on my right hand protesting as they fail to do the same. I need something to toss, to throw. Me, confrontational? Me, whose human half has been kicked out of every place that should have been home until I secluded myself away to a strip of land no one else would have in order to satisfy them. Me, whose aurora half was shunned and dismissed no matter how hard I tried, how right I was, my sister the only one who ever truly believed in me and only as a courtesy. Something tight and wet bubbles up in me, threatening to drag in everything else.

Tavish's fingers find my arm, slowing me as they draw their way down. I want to pull back but for the gentleness in his touch, the way he slides his hand into mine, like he knows me inside and out and has stayed despite it all. He stops me with a final tug, the garden's central structure rising like a great domed shadow at our side.

"I love you, Ruby." The starlight crests his jaw and the curves of his cheekbones, leaving deep shadows beneath his manicured brows and between the soft parting of his lips. "I love you," he repeats, so soft that it could be its own whispering wind. "I kenned from the very start, when you broke down on the beach in Falcre, that the aggression you present to the world isn't who you are underneath. We all have aids in the way we approach people, just as we've aids for other areas of life. Mine are, perhaps, less hostile than yours, but no less harmful." He squeezes my hand. "But, you're still an arse, even if it's accidental."

"This is insult-Rubem day, is it?" With a groan, I lean against one of the columns that ornament the exterior of the deserted building beside us. My heart flutters in time with Luca's distant vibration. The song feels more mournful than usual. "Fuck. I really act like that?"

"Constantly." Tavish smiles as he says it, like it's not a moral failing, but an inside joke.

It warms me. That heat only reveals all the cold places, though, highlighting the rest of my faults and failings. "What else am I supposed to do? I don't have your fancy words or your voice or—" I fling my free hand up, motioning to something that doesn't exist. My sense of dignity, perhaps. "I haven't even been strong enough to actually fight back until now. If I'm a threat, it's because *threats* are all I have ever been able to manage. Who am I without even that?"

"I think I ken who you are, my aurora Rubem. And I ken how you feel, too. Perhaps we are simply too close to our own selves to see the fullness of us, sometimes, so we all need a little help along the way."

I breathe out. The next inhale feels a bit lighter. Still, we don't move, Tavish with his shoulder pressed to mine, and the quiet, secluded night enclosing us. He fiddles with his brooch, and his earlier tension returns as he chews on his tongue. Beneath his fingers, the silver ignation that curls through the crown-shaped device glows softly, hints of rainbow sparkling within. A single grey line draws through it like a worm.

My heart sinks in a flash of fear, my mind skipping back to the generator basement chamber. He struggled there. He struggled, and since he still transformed in the end, I haven't thought to pause to check on him. I feel like a wet rag.

"Oh gods, your ignation. I'm so sorry."

"Aye." He draws a sharp, short inhale. "I kenned it would happen. Maraheem took so very much energy for itself, of course its ignits—and its ignation—would be some of the first to collapse. And I just . . ." He seems unable to continue, his brow tight and his eyes nearly closed.

"I understand. Your brooch is such an integral part of your home and your heritage, your existence as a selkie." The irony twists in my gut: I'm finding myself, finding my people—or at least Teodor—and my identity, just as he's about to lose the last of his. Though it's only a matter of time before the single connection I have to mine dies, and a matter of time before I follow her. I'm just one step behind Tavish. My chest aches. "It's all right to mourn."

Tavish's clutches his fist around his brooch, hiding it from view. "It's fine, truly."

"It's not." I slip my hand over his. "But it might be again. It's just the energy the brooch gives out that transforms you, isn't it?"

As I speak, the edge of my thumb brushes the piece of ignation-filled jewelry. I've touched it a hundred times before, but it's as though feeling Luca's song—trying to replicate it with my own threads—has opened something in me, and when my skin makes contact now, a vibration echoes from it. What I sense is not as deep nor as musical as the thrum that rolls soundlessly from the Citadel basement, but it's there, waiting to be activated, to burst to life and transform Tavish cell by cell.

It gives me hope. "There must be another way to produce the brooch's effect. None of the other waves the ignits create are exclusive to them. We'll find you someone who can help you transform without it. Maybe even someone from the Institute?"

For all my desperate, mangled optimism, his expression still crumples, lower lip wobbling. I cup his face in my hands and caress away the glimmer that slides along his lower lid. "You are a selkie. In whatever form, with whatever means, anywhere in the world, you are still a selkie. It's a part of you as surely as I'm from the Murk even a lifetime after they've kicked me out. You are a selkie, and you always will be."

"What if I didn't want to be a selkie anymore?"

I stare at him. "What if you didn't—*what*?"

"I don't know. I should be miserable about this—I am miserable, I suppose—but perhaps the ignation going out is for the best. If my heritage were one of humanitarians and peacemakers, then perhaps I would feel differently, but as it is, this brooch is merely a reminder of my family and all the ways I wish I could throw them off. They're dead, yet here I am, carrying them with me. Carrying this . . ." His nails twist into the metal, and for a moment, it seems like he might rip it off, but he only drops it entirely.

I lace my fingers through his, wishing I knew how to siphon away his pain. "Not all that you carry with you is bad. Ailsa was your family. And Alasdair—perhaps he wasn't the most morally upright person in Maraheem, but he cared about you."

"Aye, well, love does not negate the harm you do, now does it?"

It sounds so much like something Teodor said. The bitterness and grief in his voice makes my chest ache. "I'm sorry. I'm sorry that you had such a silt-breathing family. You deserved so much better."

Tavish's breath hitches, but he lifts my hand to his cheek and turns his face into it as though the callouses and scars of my aurora-netted skin are the most comforting thing in the world. He leans into me as he does it. I press my lips to his hair, pulling him close. He droops, a tremble running through him. I hate to make him move, but he looks so weak.

"Come here," I murmur. "We can sit."

A few columns away, the wall opens in an arch where a small set of steps leads inside, and I pull Tavish over to the stairs. We settle on the stone with our thighs pressed together and the heat of him held to my side. I run my fingers over his curls, brushing them soothingly, but just as I think he's recovered, his misery seems to multiply.

"If we lose the ignits and the ignation—*when* we lose them . . . You're an aurora, Ruby." He doesn't seem capable of saying what he means, but the implication sinks into every tortured vowel, the diamond edge of his voice a mere memory.

"I'm not fading yet." I say it gently, casually, because anything else will break me. "And once the ignits are gone and they no longer pull energy from the realm the auroras fell from, then perhaps it will stop being taken from us, too, and the aurora will recover." My tone is upbeat, almost jovial, but it can't quite reach the panic that's hidden beneath my ribs.

Tavish releases a weak laugh, playing along. For how good of an actor he is, it's obvious my words are only giving him the barest of comfort right now. My panic grows.

"Or, who knows, maybe it won't even get that far. We know the ignit explosion carried Elspeth into the aurora's world; they could be fixing all our problems over there as we speak," I add, trying to distract us both, to distract him so that it might distract me too. "If anyone is the right mixture of smart and chaotically unwavering to figure it out, it's Elspeth."

Tavish pulls one leg up, resting his arm across it, and exhales so long I think he must be trying to empty his fear the way he's emptying his lungs. "You truly think Elspeth is alive still? That they can help us?"

I look up, past the domed roof of the building at our back and over the tops of the dark trees. A hundred stars twinkle across the clear night sky, the moon a mere crescent off in the west. I remember the bartender explaining why she was staying in Venalt. The hope she was clinging to. Maybe she's not so outlandish after all. "I want to. I want to believe it."

Tavish sets his head on my shoulder.

In the quiet of the night, there's only the sound of him, the softness of his breathing, and the light rush of his cane as he glides it absentmindedly along the stone. His half cape rustles against the back of his suit jacket with each small shift of his shoulders. Just by existing, he's more here than I'll ever be. At least when I don't snarl or snap or batter my way through things.

Maybe the sledgehammer of my aggression is an aid on two fronts.

"Did you know what Teodor was?" I ask, barely more than a whisper.

His brow shoots up, and he lifts his head. "A tall, husky-voiced grudge holder?"

"No, no, the—" Maybe I should have asked her if I could share her secret, but it's my secret, too, and I know that not only is Tavish worthy of it, but now he'll put the pieces together no matter how much I might try to distance Teodor from my explanation of my own unreality. "The fact that she's different from most people, quieter. Like me."

"Trenches, you noticed it, too? I always kenned she was, but then we were apart so long, I doubted it again, and now that she's sick . . ." Then a groan leaves him, starting low and ending in a whine. "I have a *type*, don't I? Good fuck, I'm *predictable*."

"Is that a bad thing?" I laugh. "I, for one, am glad. Rest assured I'm also questioning your judgment for having this particular type, but I'm the one benefiting from it, after all." I twist to catch his jaw in the cup of my palm, lifting his face toward mine. "I certainly won't tell you to stop being into me."

Tavish smirks against my lips. "I *am* particularly into *you*." He hums nonchalantly, his fingers drifting over my thigh, thumb fiddling with the knob of my hip in a way that makes me have to deliberately calm my breathing, and adds, "I do so love a good arse. You're not the only one who might resort to doing things with a fist. Or two, if they both fit."

I feel the heat hit my cheeks a moment before it disperses elsewhere. "Gods, Tav—" But I'm sputtering too much to get the rest out, Tavish laughing against the side of my neck. His hand fiddles teasingly with the seam of my pants before rubbing in a way that drags a desperate, guttural sound out of me.

"We're alone." His voice is all diamond again, glittering brighter than the stars, but he pauses from his fondling, leaving me aching against his palm. "We *are* alone, right?"

"If we weren't, you'd be dead right now." I groan. "No, I'd be dead. You'd be miserable. Then I'd reincarnate just to kill you, and *then* you'd be dead—ah fuck." I pinch my eyes closed as he presses harder, my body responding to him with such vigor that it feels like a betrayal. His other hand draws aside my cloak and shirt to hook the rim of my pants, but I grab his wrist. "No—no. Let me just—"

Tavish makes a grumble sound, but he lets go. "You are hardly any fun."

"Say that again when you're begging to come for the third time," I manage with mostly a straight face.

He smirks at me, tugging at his bottom lip with his teeth, and by the gods is he going to have to beg me hard for that third climax. Damn him, and damn all the wonderful sounds his fantastic stamina gives me time to produce.

I glance once more down the pathway we traveled here on, but the gardens are just as empty as before, their trees blotting out all sight of the government buildings. Pulling Tavish up, I guide him through the archway entrance to the building.

"Where are we, for reference?" Tavish asks.

"An old meeting place, I assume." Grass shoots between the cracks in the stone floor, and vines climb down through gaps in the tops of the walls. Perhaps it was a senate room before the government's branches ceased working together. Now though, the room is graciously empty.

Which makes Tavish all mine, and me all his.

I press my halved thumb to his chest and unbutton his jacket, then the vest beneath. My fingers pluck open his shirt, finding his smooth, perfect skin beneath. "But it's ours now."

"Good." In the darkness, I catch the edge of his lip's quirk as he finds my ass with one hand, the other grabbing the seat of my pants.

My knees go weak. The urge to give in makes me whimper, but I catch his arms. "No," I say, and I twist a growl into it, so small it feels like the rumble of a kitten, but it makes Tavish's smirk light up. I catch his lip between my teeth gently. "You can have whatever terrible fun you've planned for me after."

"Arse," he whispers, wiggling just a little, as though he might take back control at any moment.

I press my lips to his collarbone, his sternum, the soft base of his nipple, and the small, raised line that runs beneath, working my way slowly down his curves. By the time I'm on my knees before him, drawing down his pants, he's given in entirely, all moans and fingers massaging between my braids, and "Good fuck, Ruby, good fuck" becomes an accurate descriptor of the night as well as its perfect symphony. It is the best sound that could possibly have covered my astralness.

CHAPTER NINETEEN

swarm mentality

I STAY UP THE better part of the night, twitching back to full consciousness at each creak and rustle from beyond our hotel room. No one breaks in, though, leaving me to watch the gentle rise and fall of Tavish's chest and the quaver of a stray curl against his lips. As the first rays of sun spill across the sky, I finally drift to sleep with him.

By the time I wake properly, it's so fully morning it might as well be afternoon. The electricity hasn't come back on, but the city sounds rowdier than ever, shouts and thuds so loud that I close the living room window upon entering. It tells me all I need to know about the state of things: the Institute's emergency team couldn't find enough blue ignits left in the city to power their generator, which means our search party must not have uncovered the stolen ignits yet. My stomach knots.

Tavish left a note on the counter, his handwriting as delicate and perfect as ever, even if the first line of *gone to find* overlaps a bit into the *us food* below it. I throw my cloak on and head out. The streets and channels are even more chaotic than they sounded from our hotel. Half the populace seems to be packing everything they own into boats while the other half bars their doors against hippocamps like that will stop the flood once the city begins to sink.

It seems that hope doesn't last long once everything else begins to fall apart around it.

I find Tavish in the second restaurant down from our hotel: a café packed to the brim with unhappy guests and even less happy employees. Their entire menu has been replaced by portions of meals that can be made without burners and from unrefrigerated food, and their line for coffee worms itself out the door.

Tavish stands off to one side, his hip propped against the nearby table. Zuane, of all people, sits at it, his modified wheelchair pushed underneath and his dual tentacle legs wrapped around the back legs of his seat. He holds a nearly empty mug in one hand.

Even in the bustle, Tavish's diamond voice is clear and sharp against the rest of the commotion. When his name is called—simply as Tavish—he gives Zuane a farewell far more pleasant than the man deserves, and begins pushing toward the counter. I could catch up to him, but it seems like so much effort.

I take his place beside the table, crossing my arms as I watch him casually nudge his way through the crowded space, offering smiles and apologies as he goes. "You know," I tell Zuane, "I think he might secretly like you."

Zuane grunts. "He's a bright young man. I respect him for that." He brings his drink to his lips, downing the rest in one go. He cringes as he swallows. "But my opinions of Tavish are no more important than his of me. I must do what's best for the people of Venalt however else I might feel. That is my job."

It's one of the first nearly decent things I've heard the commander say, and it makes me want to snap at him all the more, something biting and petty like *I thought your job was to make my life miserable?* I grimace like I've just drank his bad coffee. Perhaps we've both been assholes here, but Zuane was genuinely just doing his job through all this.

"How do you decide what's best for them? You're one person. You could easily be wrong."

He surveys the room, and the corners of his eyes pinch. "I have tried to take into account as much as one person is capable of, to weigh the options accordingly, and to progress with whatever means are in my power. That's the best anyone *can* do." He taps his finger against the handle of his mug. "And something *must* be done. The path this city has been on for most of my life isn't one it can maintain. Something fundamental is broken within it, and if its populace are unwilling to take the burden upon themselves to fix that, then it falls to people like me." He finally lifts his gaze to meet mine, a hardness in his stare that might just be respect in the right lighting. "I think you'd understand that?"

I struggle to answer because he's right. And I hate that he is. I hate being the one person willing to stand up for the auroras, and I hate, just a little, that this mission has set me against Zuane, however unintentionally. Our goals don't even conflict; they're simply enough out of sync that we've been stumbling over each other in our individual attempts to help this city. "How does the ignit search go?"

"Poorly," Zuane replies. "No new readings have come from the tracker—the ignits must be inactive, as we thought, or dumped into the sea. We have found no useful evidence, and our witness reports are conflicting at best. A joint team is still looking, but there's little dictating where to start."

It doesn't come as a surprise—I didn't expect Venalt to solve the ignit theft any better than their other problems. But in this single case, I don't know if I can blame them. The only way to save Luca now may be a route that doesn't involve the stolen ignits at all. And if that's what it takes, then I'll find a way.

Across the room, Tavish accepts our breakfast with a gentle smile. Both halves of me, the human and the aurora, warm at his presence, at the fact that he's been willing to stand at my side through this lonely journey. But there is still nothing he can do to make this any less my singular burden.

'*Our,*' my human half reminds me.

Our burden, yes. But our burden alone.

Zuane pulls his wheelchair out from beneath the table and shifts himself into it. "Venalt's aurora is not the only part of this city that's dying. The people trying to desert it while they still can may have a point."

"But you won't be leaving."

He almost smiles at that, and I can see the weariness beneath the look. I wonder if he's slept at all since last night. "No. This city will sink, and I will still drag myself back to Venalt's defense, to make the decisions for it when no one else can."

I almost smile in return, the emotion beneath as worn and ugly as whatever Zuane must be hiding. As soon as he's gone, I take his seat.

Tavish walks right past the table before I manage to flag him over. He spreads out our measly lot with a slight huff: two buttered rolls, two whole apples, a pack of jerky, and a large mug of what Zuane was drinking. "The coffee is yours," he says. "I'm afraid any amount of caffeine will bring my shakes back."

It tastes just as bad as it looks, but I drink it anyway. "Any news from the chancellors?"

"Iseppa sent someone by to offer us a boat this morning."

"Iseppa?" My brow shoots up, my suspicion clear in my voice.

"Aye, my sentiments exactly." Tavish huffs, then grimaces, as though what he's about to say hurts. "But it might be best to take it. We could go to the mainland and beg Alfhouat or possibly even Eyrr to spare a few of their ignits for Luca."

My chest tightens, my aurora threads reaching instinctively as though they might latch me to Luca, to this city he loves. The thought of leaving it behind, even for its benefit, stirs panic in me. "I have to stay."

"Then I'll go for you." His hand nearly bumps over my terrible coffee before finally finding mine. He squeezes it.

Even with my fear still half covered by the shock of it all, my brain instantly lurches toward the thought of alcohol, and it takes deliberate focus to pull it back, as though I'm ignoring a flotation device as I make myself drown, drown in the thought of Tavish no longer here with me. I lean my elbow against the table, lifting his hand to my forehead. "You'll be gone . . . days."

A shared tension travels between us, binding us together. Tavish's thumb traces the wrinkles between my eyes. "I'll be safe, and you'll be here, with Teodor and Luca."

Two partial corpses. "It's so far," I whisper. In all six weeks we've traveled together, we've never been more than a few miles apart. Different cities feels like ripping him straight out of my dimension. "Is there no other way?" My gaze wanders him, as if I might lock him here with my eyes, and as it does, it catches on the soft silver glow of his brooch. His ignation. It's a ridiculous thought, but I have to follow it through. "When you came here as a teenager, you and Alasdair were offering to loan ignation to the city, right? So you must have brought some with you?"

They would have taken it back to Maraheem after. I may not have known the Findlays long, but I knew enough to understand that my bringing this up is merely a distraction, not a solution. I'm just trying to keep him here, even if it's by a minute, a moment, a heartbeat. Still, Tavish does me the service of considering my question. "We brought ten vials over the course of our visits, as well as the ignation in our brooches and an assortment of the smaller technology we run with ignation. Alasdair was in charge of it—I barely touched the stuff—but he was always so responsible. He would have had no reason to leave any here, and every reason to be sure that it all returned. Though, I suppose that was the trip when he lost his brooch. Or was it in Zarencia . . ." He shakes his head. "If there was ignation here, surely we would have heard of it already, or else it's as lost to us as the ignits."

It's the answer I was expecting even before I asked, but it still tears my hope away like it's flaying off a layer of skin.

"I have to beg the mainland to spare some of their ignits," Tavish concludes. "I have to go."

"I know. And I hate it."

"Aye." Tavish laughs, dry as the desert wind, his voice nearly consumed by the activity around us. "But we said we'd save Luca, and I know you'll not give up, so neither will I."

"All right." I force the word out before I accidentally swallow it. But he's right. If we want to keep Luca alive, even just long enough to get the entire city to safety, then we may need this. And a new thought occurs to me: whatever happens here, if Tavish is on the mainland, he will be safe. Without me, perhaps, but safe. Maybe that's enough. "All right," I repeat. "But I still wish you could stay."

He smiles, his sadness breaking through the forced display of hope. "So do I."

By the time we reach the harbor, the sky has gone splotchy with grey clouds, and a blustery wind whips in from the massive sea to our south. A static-filled, battery-powered radio announces the storm's progress as it crosses the water, coming up from Alkelu. No matter how many times they state that it won't land in Venalt until tomorrow, I keep feeling the need to glance its way, as though the first of the rain might appear on the horizon.

With the city's ignits stolen, half the boats lie dead in the water, useless corpses beside their steam-powered cousins. Of the functional ones, uniformed Citadel guards stand at bows and sterns beside far less professional-looking militia, pistols on their hips and blades in hand. When pitted against the solitary hippocamp attacks I've seen so far—or even the attacks of two or three—they might even stand a chance, if not for the sheer number of potential victims they carry. Crowded family groups overflow onto the luggage-laden decks, slowing the boats and sinking them deep into the water. Between the larger vessels float gondolas that look like they belong nowhere near an already choppy sea, piled high with roped-in belongings. A harpy child sits on the precarious stacks of one, clutching a blanket in one hand and what looks like a butter knife in the other.

My chest aches, both halves of me fighting my better instincts to grab the kid and run. I have to turn away entirely, just as I did from Tavish's ferry the moment he descended into its cabin, his cane held tight to his chest as he courteously nudged between the other passengers. From this distance, I couldn't see the telltale signs of his panic, but I could still feel it on the air like we're so fully entwined that even the wind serves our love.

Despite all the frantic packing of the morning, not a single ship has set sail yet. Both of the Citadel's functional ships and a fair number of towed boats block off the port's entrance, forcing the civilian vessels to line themselves up for an inspection and emergency briefing before their departures. Tavish's ship is among the first five preparing to leave.

Slowly, the Citadel line draws back for them, opening their way to the sea.

A spur of gondolas surge by the vessels, and a group of young harpies launches off the rooftops of the buildings along the harbor's promenade, doing their best with their insubstantial arm feathers to fly all the way to the escaping ships. Half of them can't maintain the glide long enough, plunging awkwardly into the harbor water instead. A cluster of nereids clings to the ship's hulls, some with weapons gripped in their teeth and others dragging along luggage that looks too heavy to hold for long.

I wait for the first hippocamp to emerge, fingers tapping faster by the moment.

The attack doesn't come, not at ten yards out. Not at a hundred either.

I shove my hands in and out of my pockets, finding the hippocamp-like paperweight from Fiordelise's office—it's a replica of one of the city's gods featured in the Basilica's central statue, I realize. Even the crude figurine looks so docile and soft compared to the creatures lurking somewhere beneath the boats, none of the toughened armor or spindly teeth. I flip the thing once, twice, three times, counting the revolutions.

Still, no hippocamps come.

With such a massive, wind-torn stretch of water between the boats and the slip of land on the horizon, the peace makes me more worried instead of less. *Where the hell are they?*

I pull myself up an extra foot on the pole of a lamp to get a better view, the wind flapping my hood free. The boats continue chugging slowly away. Someone on the dock shoves by me, casting a scowl upward. They startle as they focus on my rainbow-strewn eyes and the gleam beneath my skin, but the bustle of the crowd quickly takes them over.

From down the dock, a pair of familiar shouts rise above the chaos.

"What are you doing! Grab her!" cries Matthia's Basilica guardian.

"I'm trying," the one from the Citadel snaps back, shoving through a group of nereids in wheelchairs to lunge for Matthia.

She leaps the nereids' stacked luggage, knocking into a fishbowl with an unhappy-looking eel, and scuttles beneath a large trunk balanced by two human men. One of her suspenders waves behind her, and a thick book is tucked between her arms. Her hair bounces in a toppled ponytail so loose it nearly covers one of her tiny horns, stray chunks frizzing out around her freckled face. When the sun pierces it through a gap in the grey, it shines a brilliant auburn. As she weaves away from her guardians, she grabs at the arms of the nearest adults, targeting anyone in uniform. "You have to stop the boats! They don't understand!"

She's thrown off with grunts and pitying murmurs. She keeps trying to get someone's attention until her guardians are nearly upon her, and she darts away from them again, scanning the promenade. Her eyes lock on me. She shifts course.

I drop from the lamppost, bending down to take her by the shoulders as she arrives. "Matthia, what's wrong?"

Her guardians push through the crowd, one of them huffing and the other snarling, "There you are, you little pest."

I scowl at them. "You both can kindly fuck off," I say, hoping the addition of *kindly* pulls me out of the asshole category.

They look at each other. The officer steps forward. "We have to take her back to the Institute."

"I misspoke." I bare my teeth. "What I mean is, you can kindly fuck off, or I'll make you. That's not a threat, but a promise," I add, really hoping I don't have to make it true.

The officer swallows, paling, and the Basilica woman mutters, "Chancellor Alvise will hear about this."

"You go tell them," I snap. "Run along now."

With a final disgusted look, she huffs and turns, charging back through the crowd. Her companion follows her across the walkway, only to linger near the promenade shops, arms crossed and watching us through the shifting bodies and luggage. Good enough.

I turn my attention back to Matthia. "Are you all right, kid?"

"They won't make it." She still sounds breathless, but now it seems to come more from fright than exertion. "The hippocamps—"

"They haven't attacked, look." I try to help lift her, but she wiggles me off, shaking her head.

"No, they won't yet—there's never been this many around Venalt before, but when they've come together like this across the sea, my book says they do this, this thing, once there's enough of them. They act like singular predators when their numbers are fewer, but once there's a bunch in one place, their mating hormones drive them into a swarm mentality to make sure the whole population receives enough energy to build their nests. It's all in here!" She unfolds her arms to reveal one of the ancient books I brought her from Teodor's apartment, a finger tucked inside it so she can flip immediately to a worn page with scientific-looking hippocamp diagrams on one side. "So we have to stop the boats!"

"Oh gods." I press my palm to my mouth, phantom fingers tingling. All those people. Children. Tavish. Packaged with luggage and civilians, the boats carry too few weapons to fend off more than a stray hippocamp or two, much less a whole mob all at once. Oh gods.

I feel sick.

"We have to stop the boats," I whisper. Then I'm running, though I'm not sure where to, a radio perhaps—how many will still have charge left with the electricity down? If I can at least get in contact with one of the two big Citadel boats that still guard the harbor—they have their own power sources— they can warn the five vessels out on the water.

Matthia calls after me, shouting something about teeth, but I'm too lost in my own panic to go back for her.

I shove my way toward the nearest Citadel barricade, trying to keep Tavish's ferry in sight as much as I can. The first guard I come across, I grab with both arms. "I have to—"

All the anxiety in my gut turns violent as the waves around the distant boats seem suddenly to lift beneath them. From the sea rises armored equine heads and flaring tails. They throng the boats, dragging down anyone near the railing before the guards can even fire their guns.

My instinct is to fling myself into the water and release all my aurora energy just to reach them—to reach Tavish—visions of his blood smeared across a glass floor and his screams in my ears so real it takes me a moment to realize the last one is coming from the people around me. But even if I could reach them, I can't fight a whole swarm of hippocamps alone.

I ball up all my emotions like a cannon and shoot them in one mental cry. *Luca!*

Through the haze of the aurora veil, I feel him cringe away from my shout, trying to recoil from me.

No, no, not now. *They need you, Luca! They're dying.*

But he can't hear me—won't hear me.

I try to do what he's done with me in the past, even before we'd woven our threads together, and force at him a fuller thing than mere emotion: the sight of what's happening on the water. It seems to ricochet right off his consciousness, scattering into the abyss. Between my heartbeat and his, something else moves, echoing my sentiment back at Luca like a relay, but softer and fading fast. Part of it must land, though, because his song crescendos. His emotions flare with such intervals of fear and rage and love that I can't pull one from the other. Desperation follows it.

He doesn't want to reveal himself.

I can't save them alone, I cry, my gaze still fixed on the boats as hippocamps begin scrambling across decks, some with teeth bared and others clamped around the wounded, dead, and fighting alike. *Luca, I need you. They need you.*

His protective desire groans from him, filling my chest.

The city rumbles like an earthquake. I can sense the presence of Luca moving through the foundation's tunnels, his long body sliding faster than ever. He plunges out of the foundation and through the alleys of the underwater city. He's met with the screams of his people, nereid fleeing him in panic as the land-dwelling population scrambles away from the channel's edges—everything he has ever dreaded coming to fruition. I feel him hesitate, feel his dismay over their fear, his memories of when he was a docile plant, of gentle hands and loving laughter replaced by terror and abhorrence now that his host has three heads full of fangs.

I show him the boats again, inflicting the scene with the way those people must be screaming now.

His dismay hardens to determination. He charges onward. I catch sight of him as he bursts through the water beneath the harbor's promenade, all three viper heads weaving up and down in rhythm. I sprint along the dock, pulling off my cloak and shirt as I run and sliding out of my boots at the last moment before diving into the water alongside him. Luca shudders as I grab hold of one of his necks, his presence sparking with alarm. He doesn't throw me off, though.

Right now he loves his city more than he distrusts me.

The hippocamps' bodies are the size of my thumb at this distance, but their swarm sends a chill through my bones. It's bigger even than it appeared from the harbor, dozens upon dozens of the equine-sized beasts churning nimbly through the choppy water. They pass around the bodies of the people they've killed, red clouding the sea. The smaller hippocamps tear fresh chunks of flesh loose, gulping them down whole, while the larger ones leap onto the floundering boats for fresh prey.

Each undulation of Luca's body gains us speed as he swims toward them. His song sputters in and out, no longer the distilled calm that radiated through the city, but a pointed, sporadic thing. It hits a few of the hippocamps, sending the creatures fleeing out of the throng, toward the mainland, but far too many seem not to notice this trembling, fear-laden version of the vibration that kept them so firmly at bay all these years.

Luca heads straight for the large steam-powered merchant at the center of the five ships. Each hippocamp that comes too near receives a strike from one of his outermost heads. Most dart from his reach too quickly, his aim adversely affected by the speed at which he swims, but the ones he does catch receive a fang of poison, leaving them twitching in the water after.

My lungs burn, but I search for Tavish's boat in the fray. Its smaller form has made it a target more so than the larger merchant vessels, and the number of bodies already floating around it make me nauseous. I launch myself toward it. A smaller hippocamp darts toward me in the water, but I curl, catching its face in my fist, and hurl over it with a small burst of aurora strength. I surface beside the boat's hull, scrambling up the tail of another hippocamp to board.

Bloody water covers the deck. Luggage lies upturned and flayed, torn clothing fluttering damply in the wind. Someone sobs from under a fallen stack of crates, a hippocamp snapping at them as it tries to shove its head into their space. The cabin doors hang off their hinges, two of the windows shattered. The bloody corpse of a satyr dangles out one of them. Within is eerily still.

My knees go weak at the same moment my brain tells me to charge the cabin, to abandon and ignore all else in favor of finding Tavish, but I hold myself back from the impulse. Tiny droplets drizzle me as Luca rears out of the water, snatching hippocamps off boats and flinging them away. At Venalt's harbor, the Citadel's two steam-powered ships frantically try to disengage from their blockade and turn toward the swarm.

I grab a fallen sword off the deck and charge the hippocamp that's shoving its head into the toppled crate mass, grateful for my silent feet as they sprint me over the puddled wood with no more sound than the beating of my heart. On the ferry over, I hesitated before kicking the hippocamp that attacked us. A flicker of that guilt reemerges, but it's not enough to slow me, dampened by the blood and the bodies in the water and a love for this city and its people so thick and rage-filled that it's smothering. Still, I take no pleasure as I vault off the hippocamp's tail and twist to drive my blade through its eye socket.

It bucks, reeling backward. I twist the sword deeper into its eye socket, and it goes limp. Drawing the weapon free, I duck into the space the creature was assaulting. A teenage harpy crouches there, her ruffled white feathers stained red. I extend my free hand toward her and wiggle its finger stubs.

"Can you get out?" Like this, shirtless in the silvery-grey afternoon with my incisors sharp and my rainbow-crossed aurora skin gleaming faintly as it boosts my energy, I must look terrifying. I bend lower and drop my voice to something I might use on a scared pet. "Come on, let's get you somewhere safer."

She trembles, but her hand clamps around mine. I pull her out. She all but collapses against me at the sight of the deck, but she lets me guide her to the cabin.

Inside it looks much the same, death and destruction reigning. My heart aches, and I try not to see Tavish's damp curls in every hint of red, his suit jacket in every scrap of blue, to hear Lilias's voice asking me if I care enough. I take us down the stairs to the lower cabin.

The metal creaks as we descend. Halfway down, the harpy slips, pulling me with her. As we hit the floor, we come face-to-face with a hippocamp's open mouth. A shriek leaves the harpy, and she slams into me in her terror.

I grab her to keep her upright. "It's dead—it's already dead."

The corpse's gaping mouth looks stabbed straight through to the brain, as though someone had killed it just before it turned them into a snack. Blood still coats its teeth. I shudder.

Taking the harpy by the shoulder, I lead her through a small corridor that runs toward the ferry's center, my blade outstretched. A muffled sobbing reaches me, echoing mournfully through the bowels of the boat.

As we turn through the next doorway, a long, thin blade swings at us, accompanied by a battle cry that cuts like a weapon all on its own. My heart has a moment to leap before I'm forced to shove my harpy companion back, ducking the swing of Tavish's sword and coming up beside him. I mean to speak, but it comes out a sob as I pull him into my arms.

His tension transforms, his free hand clutching at my back like he might latch his nails into my skin. He straightens himself up as I pull away. Half of me wants to tell him how proud I am that he's holding it together like this, and the other half doesn't want to accidentally make him feel bad if he has an anxiety attack later.

Instead, I end up saying, "You're doing all right?"

"Aye, mostly." He seems to know exactly what I mean by it, because he continues, "The hippocamps don't remind me terribly of the lab or my mother. Or perhaps it just hasn't sunk in yet."

I know exactly what he means, that some combination of the lack of human enemies and the situation as a whole has let him detach it from his past so far. And I'm going to do everything I can to keep it that way. I glance behind him. "Is this it?"

The huddled group of about three dozen that he protects looks no better at fighting than Tavish, five of the adults already with serious wounds, the sixth lying motionless on the deck while a child clings to their arm. My teenage companion rushes a smaller harpy, scooping them up while sobbing. I try to ignore the way the child immediately asks for their parents—parents now likely ripped to pieces, their bones sinking into the churning sea that crashes against the high, round windows at the top of the wall.

"It happened so fast," Tavish replies. "The children were already below the stairs, and the rest of us—we were just closest."

I grimace. "The Citadel ships are coming. If we can get this group to the top of the cabin, they might be able to bring us back to the city."

The end of my statement is accented by the thud of a giant body as it slams into the window above us. I glance up just in time to catch the blur of grey that slides off it. The sea and sky beyond it clears, its endless blue only disrupted by the hull of the ship that floats on that side of ours and the occasional discarded chunk of a bloodless corpse drifting past. I spot the shadow of the hippocamp as it approaches this time, its tail thrusting and its stubby legs tucked in tightly. It slams into the glass.

The window cracks.

I curse. It's the only sound in a moment of bated breath, even the crying of the children giving way to the creak of the boat and the combined dip of the water and whip of wind through the window's small gap. Then the hippocamp hits again, and the top of its armored head shatters the glass.

CHAPTER TWENTY

the youngest findlay

THE WINDOW EXPLODES INWARD as the rest of the charging hippocamp's body bursts through it, the wood of the ferry's hull splintering at its sides. Shrieks erupt, and I shield Tavish behind me as glass and water rain down. The hippocamp bares its rows of spindly teeth, whipping its tail and digging its pointed two-toed hooves into the floor as it lunges for the kid beside their unconscious parent. It moves too fast for me to catch it in the eye, my blade dragging uselessly across the side of its thick, alligator-like scales. I kick my heel into the weak point behind its jaw, forcing its head to the side before it can take a chunk out of its prey. It rolls, swinging its neck in fury.

"Out!" I cry, motioning to the tight corridors toward the engine room. "Everyone out!"

I keep the hippocamp off our little group as they squeeze out of the room and into the small hallways, the teenage harpy helping Tavish carry the unconscious parent between them. The beast tries to follow us, struggling in the tight space, snapping and thudding. Someone—a child, I think— hands me a long metal pole, and I plunge it deep into the lead hippocamp's throat.

Water continues to pour through the broken window beyond its corpse, another hippocamp sliding through on the wave. The creatures won't need to struggle to catch us for long—the sea will bring us right to them.

I reach the engine room to find Tavish already herding everyone up the stairs, ushering them straight to the top deck in such a gentle yet commanding tone that they listen without question. They crowd in the center, waving and shouting for the nearing pair of armored and armed Citadel ships to rescue them.

To our right, the ships Luca has protected are still floundering, their survivors huddling on their deck amidst the ruins of their luggage. The final boat, a smaller sail-laden vessel, slowly sinks into the waves a few hundred feet away, eerily quiet but for the circling hippocamps. My chest aches, common decency meeting sparks of the intense love that Luca instilled in me—a love I still feel vibrating through him as he guards the other ships with all his strength, his coils keeping them from drifting away.

One of the Citadel ships pulls up at our side while the other circles around Luca to help collect his survivors. They stretch out a long gangplank to the ferry's top deck. The wood rattles and shakes, but it holds fast for the first of the civilians to cross.

I shake as I help guide our group over, but my fatigue is nothing compared to the exhaustion that radiates off Luca. His song comes in patters now, a few notes here and there. Each grab he makes at a passing hippocamp seems slower than the last, and when they sink their teeth into his tail, he barely manages to shake them off. There seem to be less of them, though, finally, scared off by the arrival of more weapons or simply too full to keep fighting, I don't know. But it won't matter how few there are if Luca fades out here and now.

I need to go to him—whatever barrier he's trying to put between us be damned.

But as I think it, someone from the nearest Citadel ship shouts my name. My heart skips. I turn back to it to find

Matthia hanging over the railing a few feet above the ferry deck. She waves at me.

"I need a tooth!" she calls.

"Matthia?" I shout in confusion. "Get away from the edge!"

She answers, but as she does, a massive turret-mounted gun fires from the second Citadel ship. The sound of it rattles across the water loudly enough to block out even her diamond-strong voice. She doesn't look so strong now, either, shaking as she watches the waves in horror. But her mouth sets in a determined line as she watches me, and I can almost see her mind turning with something chaotic and indistinct, only identifiable by the way it lingers in my memories: that terrible mixture of guilt and pain, of the way it makes irrational things seem like the only option.

She throws herself off the edge of the Citadel ship, awkwardly grabbing the ferry's railing. Her fallen suspender snares on a broken edge of metal and snaps off as she drags herself onto its deck.

"I need to get a tooth!" She waves a wrench at me and heads for the ferry's cabin. Her boots skid over the bloody water as she plunges inside.

Damn child.

Tavish is the only one left on the ferry roof with me, and I pause just long enough to brush his arm. "Go across without me—I'll be back!"

He nods.

I leap to the deck after Matthia.

It should be easy to find her, bring her back to our Citadel ship—this tooth business be damned—but as Tavish starts out on the gangplank, everything turns into chaos.

One of the hippocamps still attacking Luca finally latches properly to his neck, digging through the ashen aurora flesh. His leftmost head goes limp. He roils, trying to flip the creature off, and bumps the Citadel ship that's collecting his survivors just as their mounted gun goes off. Instead of hitting the hippocamp-infested water, the projectile arcs wide.

It plunges through the back end of the ferry's central cabin.

The structure turns into a splintered mass of wood and metal as it crashes down, the force of the collapse sending me stumbling away from the now-ruined entrance. The gangplank between the roof and our Citadel ship topples with it. Tavish drops onto the main deck, rolling once.

Relief floods me as he sits up, giving a croaked, "I'm all right."

But Matthia—

Matthia.

The ferry's crumpled cabin groans. The roof and walls have all dropped, supported only by the carcass of a hippocamp and a beam that's toppled over the cavity to the stairs. Through the gaps in them, I see Matthia's freckled fingers pushing uselessly. The whole thing rumbles above her—too many tons of wood and metal heaped in unstable bundles.

I scramble through the wreckage and press my hand to Matthia's. "Are you hurt?"

"N-no. I don't feel hurt. But sometimes that happens if you're in shock."

That she's quoting facts at me seems like a good sign.

She tries to shove her wrench into the cracks. "I—I told you, I need a tooth. A hippocamp tooth."

"Later, Matthia." Whatever this brilliant, foolish kid needs it for, it's not worth her life. "I can't get this off you without it collapsing. You'll have to go down, through the boat, and come up the other side." I feel sick just saying it. "I'll swim through to you, all right? You won't be alone for long. But you have to go now."

"There's water here. I—I can't hold my breath like that."

I realize it as she speaks, the sea creeping in around her knees as she stands on the fourth or fifth step. It sloshes over the deck behind me. The boat starts to tip.

Matthia screams like she's going to shout the sea itself into submission as she slips on the stairs. She plunges beneath the surface and returns sputtering, the waterline to her hips now.

Tavish—beautiful, brilliant Tavish—grabs my arm. Trembles run through him, and he clutches his brooch in his free hand like he's not sure whether he's trying to push fresh energy into it or break it to pieces. "Can I help?"

"Not easily. There's hippocamps in the water, and you'd have to find the hole blind—I'd have to go with you." There must be another way.

If I lift the fallen deck, I risk crushing Matthia in the process, and if I ask her to swim, I have to hope that with me pulling her the rest of the way out, she'll survive. If I had all the energy in the world, I could tackle my way in, grabbing her and taking the consequences for myself, but with the strain I feel now, I'd be unconscious before I managed to get her out again.

My gaze darts back to Tavish's fingers trembling against his brooch, the silver ignation shining through. The hope I've been trying to quell all this time rises again, along with the auburn shine of Matthia's hair and the diamond edge that her voice takes on when she's scared yet determined, and that look she gives that's so reminiscent of Raghnaid Findlay's that I shudder beneath it.

Another way.

"Give me your brooch," I tell Tavish.

He presses the metal wordlessly into my palm, no hesitation. He looks almost relieved. "It's better you use the ignation now before it all loses power, anyway."

A tight ball builds in the back of my throat. "That's not what I need it for." I turn my attention to Matthia, and with my heart in my throat, I weed the brooch through the gap toward her. "Hold this to your skin, Matthia. Do you know what it is?"

With her hair wet and dark around her little satyr horns, I can't find a strand of red in it; even her freckles seem blanched by her fear. But the more I look at her, the more I see Raghnaid lifting herself up from the ground, her desperation overwhelmed by her ruthless determination. "I think so," Matthia whispers.

"Just want it, kid." I press my own fingers against the cracks, wishing I could push them all the way through, take her smaller, shaking hands and squeeze them. "Want to swim out of here. And I'll be there with you."

The boat creaks again. With a final shudder, the caved-in cabin structure crumbles against the deck.

CHAPTER TWENTY-ONE

the second prophecy

THE FINAL COLLAPSE OF the cabin blows Tavish and me backward. Water floods around our feet. I expect hippocamps to glide in with it, my panic over our own fates crashing into my fear for Matthia, but Luca's heads lash around the ferry, snapping at the few creatures that haven't given up the attack yet. The Citadel ship throws Tavish and me ropes, but I ignore mine. I grab at the cabin wreckage, pulling it up chunk by dripping chunk as I scream Matthia's name. The sea quickly overtakes me, rising until I'm forced to bend into it, then dive after it.

My arms shake and my vision turns into a delirious tunnel. Matthia. Brilliant, strong Matthia, who held my hand and stood up for me, could be crushed or sinking. My eyes burn. I swim to the surface, taking one last gulp of air before plunging after the ferry. I grab the deck, pulling my way along its side until I reach the broken window. The corpse of the hippocamp I killed blocks it, pinned there by the rushing currents. I take the thing in both arms and shove. My lungs burn, but the corpse budges enough for the water to yank it aside.

I grab the window gap to keep from being pulled along after. Splintered wood digs into my palm as my halved hand fails to find purchase. With a burst of aurora strength, I heave myself inside the boat. The current immediately shoots me across the room, slamming me into the back wall. A small, lean seal wiggles there, struggling against the flow of the water. Tavish's crown-shaped brooch gleams on her chest.

My head spins, lungs fire and black spots assaulting my vision, but I grab her in my arms, blazing through the last of my aurora energy to shove us down and out of the sinking ferry. As the current releases us, a stream of bubbles leaves my chest. Darkness tunnels in. I should fight, but my limbs have gone too weak, my head empty and light.

Tavish will have Matthia now. The thought feels distant, but I cling to it. At least I've given Tavish back a piece of his family.

The world slips hazily past me, grey and black and blue. Someone calls my name. My body feels too heavy to respond, like it's turned into a solid around me. Around us.

We float, half leaning into each other, half engulfed by the other, like two trunks growing from the same stump, two carpets woven into one. I lay my head on the human's shoulder.

I'm tired. I think it and whisper it all at once, the words echoing in this odd nothingness space.

'That's my line.' He turns his face to mine, his chin pressed to my forehead. We sink farther into each other, two impressionistic paintings, two stained-glass statues overlapping. And we are, both of us, tired with a bone-infesting weariness that buzzes in the back of our mind even in this place of relative peace. This is not enough of a respite. Not nearly.

For a moment, I feel like we're choking again, water swarming in, turning into fire as it crashes down our trachea and sears up the back of our nose. From beyond us, a greater rest tugs, one that would take all this pain and weariness away. But we flinch from it.

We are not done yet, though a part of us—parts of us both—would like to be.

As though latching onto our refusal, a voice shatters through the haze. "There's still so many. I—I don't know what's happening now. The book didn't talk about this."

Our name is repeated after, our world shaken in a rough series of quakes.

We shy away.

I'm not giving up, I mutter, *I just need to rest a moment.*

'*I know, my love.*' He wraps around me, into me. Our hearts beat as one. Slow as one.

Perhaps it would be easier to slip away than we thought. *What if everything we've already accomplished is enough?* I think of the ignits we secured too late, of Fiordelise dead before I could save her, of all the bodies floating through the void with us. *What if we don't have to save them all?*

'*Do we believe that?*' he asks, though he has the answer already written inside himself.

I wish we could. My frustration burns in my lungs.

"Why isn't the aurora stopping them?" someone shouts— not someone I care about. But no, that's wrong; I am the one whose home encompasses the world. That thought—that title—sparks something in me, half determination, but half anger too.

They have it so easy, blocking out all the pain, the destruction and death, going on with their lives like they don't have a responsibility to help anyone but themselves. The feeling fades back to calm, to floating, a flutter of grey beyond near-closed lashes. *I'm sorry, I know that was you once.*

'*Don't be sorry for my past selfishness. That's my job.*'

I know he does feel sorry, so burdened under his guilt that it sinks like a weight onto us both. I wrap my arms around him, feeding him my affection, my pride. In six weeks he has done more than most people will their entire lives.

More than I ever managed alone. And for that, he deserves everything I can give him.

"Turn the ship around." Another cry, my name pressed between it like a whisper. One name, for two people. "We have to turn the ship around! To the harbor!"

'We're doing this together,' he corrects, returning the love I've given him with the same warmth. *'You deserve just as much of the credit.'*

Continued cries of our name grow like white-hot tendrils into this place, a penetrating thing that tries to insert itself into the safety we've made here. It wedges into my chest, where it aches, louder than the exhaustion. *Once more, my love?*

'Always,' he says, and we wake as one.

My lungs burn as water pours out of my mouth, every strand of my aurora flesh tightening to make the human cells cooperate. They react sluggishly, giving a second and third cough more stunted than the first. Someone thuds their palm on my back and holds my braids away from my face. I brace my palm against the metal beneath me and cough again.

"Rubem!" Tavish shouts.

Everything hurts. Phantom twinges pound through my fingers, and my head spins, but the bobbing sea comes into view, its deep blue meeting the grey sky on the horizon. People dash across the deck around me, all their voices blending into a single nonsense sound. Orange curls bob at the edge of my vision. I let my eyes close again.

Tavish makes a frantic sound, and a smaller hand presses to my forehead.

"I'm alive," I whisper, lifting my fingers. *Just barely.*

'We can rest later.' Those are the exact words my human half says, but I feel his deeper meaning: we can fall apart later. Together, the way both of us have fallen apart so many times alone. *'Later.'*

Asshole.

'Get up, silt-breather.'

"Rubem?"

Rubem—that's me now, isn't it? That's us. *Fuck*. I peel my eyes back open, pushing onto my elbows in one violent burst. My limbs feel like lead weights, and each breath comes in painful gasps, but I force myself to sit upright.

Tavish kneels beside me, his brooch in one hand. Matthia huddles beneath his jacket, the large garment like a tent over her spindly figure. She watches Tavish with a kind of wonder, like she's one-half of a magnet, and his brooch, his freckles, his hair are the opposite pole. Her fingers bob toward him as he leans back, and her throat clears once, then again. He decisively ignores her, turning away from her so purposefully that even his lack of vision can't justify it. But that will have to be dealt with later.

Because this attack isn't over.

Everything I heard in my half-conscious state clicks into place as the Citadel ships charge back toward the harbor, steam pouring in great gusts from their stacks. Between us and Venalt, the waves roil, heads and ridges and tails breaching the surface in a frenzy as the creatures charge the city.

Luca swims past us, releasing a great reverberation of grief and terror. But with each undulation of his tail, his fatigue grows, turning the last of his melody too rough and withered to affect the hippocamp swarm. I have half a mind to try singing the song in his place, damn my exhaustion and my previous failed efforts, but the very first vibration I draw forth makes the world slip in and out, as though all my senses forgot to exist in random flashes. I need rest. Or ignits.

Or something made from them.

My mind latches to Tavish's brooch on instinct, as though I can feel the subtle vibration of it calling to me from here. I can't recall the direct relationship, how many ignits Tavish claimed went into that small quantity of ignation, but it was more than we have left in Venalt, and so much closer than the foundation center, where those remaining few sit under lock and key. To actually consume it, though—the thought sends a shudder through me. The ignation in Tavish's brooch is his, whether he's enthusiastic about his heritage right now or not, and I can't take that away from him. Can't ask him to give it up for me again.

He may not have aurora threads to wind through me, but he seems to know my mind perfectly in this instant. With an unwavering grip, he presses his brooch against my palm. There's no hesitation, not even a tremble in his fingers.

It thrums against my skin, its gentle, dormant song just waiting to transform Tavish or Matthia. My love for him tells me to push it away, even as my instincts beg to consume it. "I can't."

"That's not for you to decide."

His voice is so steady, his words soft. But I shake my head, swallowing the lump in my throat. I pull my hand back and drag myself to the ship's railing.

Ahead of us, the hippocamps emerge from the harbor. They leap onto the clogged boats that still wait there, and tear their way across the crowded docks on their stubby front legs, teeth snapping and armored tails swinging. Through other windows and behind the Citadel's small, uneven barricades, uniformed guards and officers put up a valiant defense. Basilica medics drag back injured civilians while the odd Institute staffer helps assemble fresh defenses and hand out weapons.

In the midst of it all, Luca rises from the water, snapping up hippocamps and flinging them away. He pulls his body farther onto the promenade with each attack, wrapping along the buildings and winding himself around the column of a bow-shaped balcony half-encrusted in a fresh layer of gilding.

Atop it, Teodor bends over a long black rifle as the street is frantically cleared below her. Her gun bucks against her shoulder. On the dock a hippocamp drops dead, but the exertion throws her into a coughing fit. Each hack rattles the barrel of gold flakes she's resting her gun on, sending the tiniest trail of glitter falling over the balcony's edge. She shakes as she reloads.

We're so close now that the hippocamps ram into the sides of the ship, the screams and shouts from the dock echoing over their thuds and watery shrieks. But the rest of the boats make it difficult to maneuver. They push and grind to get out of the harbor while hippocamps rage across their decks.

Our vessel shoves through them and pulls alongside the nearest dock with such force that its bow crashes against the promenade, crushing through a layer of wood to hit the corelium street with a jolt.

Three blocks away, Luca continues his battle.

As he fights a group of hippocamps, one of them rushes him in tail-thumping lunges, aiming for the weakened base of his already torn-into left neck. It clamps down before Teodor can reload from her last shot. Two more leap out of the water to join it, tearing under his ashen aurora flesh to the leviathan meat beneath.

Luca shudders and tries lethargically to buck them off, but I can see the weight of his exhaustion bearing down on him as he turns to protect every other person in this harbor before himself.

"No, Luca," I whisper as in my mind I'm shrieking it, reaching for him with my threads. He doesn't have to dodge me, not anymore; he's so weak now that I can't even feel his presence.

Tavish wraps his hand through mine, his brooch still in it. "Take it to him."

I grimace, all the more so from the way Matthia stares at me beneath Tavish's jacket, like she wants so badly to snatch it out of our grasps and hold it as close as she held her ridiculous plush back at her mother's office. It's her heritage too. But her heritage is just as much a part of Tavish, and he will be here for her—and he *is* telling me to take it. So I do.

As I fit it to my palm, my aurora flesh molding to keep it there, Tavish asks, "How far away is he?"

"Three blocks."

"You're too weak for that." His jaw hardens, pulsing in a way that means he's biting his tongue. He slides the cane of his sword free, wrapping his other arm around me. "I'm coming with you."

The words spear some tender part of me. But he's right. My knees quaver, and without the railing, it feels like he's the only thing holding me up.

Together, we jump from the bow of the ship.

The impact of the promenade's stone floor rattles me. I lean against Tavish, and he holds me up, swinging his cane-sword in front of us as we charge toward Luca. Each step feels like daggers shooting through my bones, the constant thud of the ignation against my skin like a kind of siren song I have to fight to resist. If I take it now, I'm afraid there won't be anything left of it by the time we reach Luca.

My shouts of "Dodge!" and "On your left!" and "Luggage ahead!" are enough to steer us through the chaos of attacking hippocamps and the defending Citadel force, a handful of frantic civilians still trapped between. We duck around an overturned cart to let three Citadel guards distract an oncoming hippocamp. Another of the creatures emerges from down the dock, but a nereid I swear is Zuane crashes past Tavish and me, tackling its neck with his tentacle legs to pull himself around its head and shoot into the crease of its ear ridge. He gives us barely a nod before diving into the harbor.

A block and a half down, Luca still fights with everything in him, but everything is clearly so little now. His left head twitches and jerks like a dead fish, a small swarm of hippocamps tearing into the base of its neck. His right head tries sluggishly to pull them off, Teodor's bullets nicking off the creatures' armor, but he turns his center one toward me, two deep-yellow leviathan eyes gazing at me. He wavers, his eyes starting to roll back, his presence so far-gone that even this close, his consciousness is a wisp of smoke in a hard breeze.

One block away, then half. So close. We're so close.

From the water at our side bursts a hippocamp. Jaws wide, it rolls on the slick dock and launches itself the last foot between us. Between itself and Tavish.

I drag Tavish toward me just as the hippocamp sinks its teeth into him, tearing long streaks of red across his bare shoulder as it tightens its jaws. A burst of blood shoots crookedly through its eye socket. It jerks and goes limp, jaws still clamped around Tavish's flesh. He screams as the limp bulk of it pulls him down.

I feel like I should be screaming, too, like I should be bleeding, aching, torn open the way he is, but the world has gone quiet, so numb that it feels like this can't possibly be real. A ring fills my ears. My lungs shut down. And I think I've been staring—staring at him as he falls from my grasp, blood just beginning to pucker around the hippocamp's teeth—for a thousand years, a thousandth time I dragged him to a ledge and then didn't catch him, before a second hippocamp careens toward us from farther up the promenade.

Teodor cries out: she's still reloading—I don't know if I see it or she shouts it, because the hippocamp's mouth is gaping, its hooked hooves scrambling against the corelium floor as it lunges, not for me, but for Tavish. For the injured prey, the blood scent, the easy target. There's an instant where I can see the entire course of his death, every chunk of him it'll rip off, the way his blood will gush in pulses behind a frantic heartbeat until it slows suddenly to a gentle, constant stream, his mouth still open in a scream that has to be my name, will always be my name.

It's not energy that fills me, but something else, something beyond science: pain turned into power, horror into motion. It's the thing that Luca feels for this city, blazing full for Tavish. It's love.

I grab the hippocamp's jaw as it passes, curling the fingers of my whole hand into its lips and pressing my nails through the cracks in its teeth. Pinpricks of my aurora flesh shoot from my vacant knuckles and the stubs beside them, curling around the edges of the hippocamp's armor. We tear to the ground, sliding into Tavish's legs, but I hold on, hold its jaw open mid-bite. Spittle flies from its throat. Its tongue lolls with pulsing liquid within, pieces of lives caught in its teeth: a slip of fabric, an inch of skin, a bit of hair. I don't let go. It's turned away from Teodor, her rifle useless against it like this, but without the ignation, I don't have the strength to wrestle its head her way, only to keep holding on. I can feel Tavish's brooch pressed to my palm still, its dormant song pounding like my own heartbeat. Pleading with me. There could be enough for both of us?

Before I can choose—Tavish or Luca—a freckled hand drags furiously across the creature's neck, over the crest of its head, and down its face, smearing a trail of blood from two fingertips. It stops at the hippocamp's eyes. Tavish's blade descends. Life leaves the creature. Its tail, draped over the side of the dock, pulls it downward, and I jerk back, letting it drop.

Tavish stands there, his cane-sword dangling from his fingers. Angry lines along his shoulder stream red, and a flap of skin and shirt near the top of his chest hangs loose, fluttering with each ragged breath. He shakes in a way that's not merely exhaustion, the shattering trembles working their way up from his pinkies, but when he shouts, the full force of his diamond voice is behind it. "Go!"

Teodor's rifle fires again, this time into the swarm that's crowded Luca. The aurora's whole body shudders. His two outer heads go limp, his middle one collapsing between them. With one great coordinated heave, the hippocamps pull his left neck into the harbor. The rest of his body begins to follow, weighted down by the bulk of him that's still beneath the surface.

I run. It feels like falling, like drowning, a little like dying, perhaps, but I charge Luca's middle head, veering straight under the half-gilded balcony. It groans as the coil he's clutched around it is pulled by the rest of his sinking body. Teodor curses and something topples.

The soft trail of glitter from the barrel of gold flakes she'd been mounting her rifle on turns into a storm.

In a gust of wind, the flakes billow around me. They blind my view, turning the world to molten gold and sticking to my wet skin. I charge through them, leaving me coated in gilding.

As the glimmering cloud disperses, I finally drag the ignation's power into myself.

The change is instant, the world shifting back into place in ways I didn't realize were broken. Colors return, my hearing sharpens, my lungs expand. A giddy surge fills my head so bright I could sing. After my deathly fatigue, the strength of the ignation is a brilliant, terrifying thing that makes me wonder what it must have been like to be an aurora before the ignit boon, when all that power was still hoarded inside them. Gods housed in quiet forms, sleeping deities more content to listen to the world pass than to move it along. Here we are, needing that power only now that it's too far-gone to truly grasp.

I slide to my knees before Luca's middle head, the last few flecks of gold still falling around me in a gentle flutter. As I cup his jaw in my palms, I feel the final slip of his consciousness, caught in a hazy realm somewhere between the fabric of our own world and the other; the beat of his heart and the vibration of his threads so dim that they sound as though they reverberate around me. He leans toward the power that now courses through me, pleading.

I let my head fall against his nose, offering him my threads, an open gift with the energy teeming from them. He tries to grasp it. But his strength slips further. His middle head skids from my hands, dragged back along the stone. It rolls once and drops into the harbor.

My scream resounds through myself, echoing in a way that must be heard by every aurora in a hundred miles. In the gap between us, a third heart suddenly returns, pulling the threads of us all together, driving the energy I offer into Luca like a conduit. I breathe it all out, letting everything I can soak into him. It has to be enough. It has to be.

Slowly, I feel a familiar, gentle vibration rise: a war cry. It grows, verse by verse, resounding into my chest with the same intensity that it floods the city. The rest of the hippocamps across the harbor—across the whole of Venalt— seize up in great shudders. They fling themselves toward the water, leaving their prey and stampeding over each other in their flight.

I sway, only a thin veil of energy left, but I root that last spark of it deeply into my core, fanning it like a flame. Creaks and groans and cautious shouts arise around the harbor as the hiding civilians emerge onto balconies and peek down stairs. Citadel guards pick themselves up, and Basilica medics rush to the injured, a pair of them swarming Tavish where he sits, shaking but conscious. Alvise, of all people, surges out from a building down the block, two babies in their arms, their jewelry clattering as a third child clings to their back. Someone cries softly from a channel alley, but it all feels hushed beneath expectation, as though the world is waiting for one final piece to slot into place.

Slowly, the harbor begins to roil once again. Luca's heads break through the surface—all three of them whole and functioning, though the rightmost bears scars and streaks filled entirely with aurora flesh, the ashen deadness tearing through feet to neck, where scales once were, and cutting straight through one of his eyes. He rises up from the water, fins flaring, and stares at the town in a way that would look like a strike about to happen if not for the slight cock I note in his outer heads, his irises wider than before. But Teodor—wherever she's gone—and I are the only ones who know this. The only ones who know *him*.

The hush of the harbor turns into a gasp. Then someone screams, edging back from Luca's monstrous form. More follow their lead. The medics with Tavish hastily pull him into the nearest building as others drag their wounded behind barricades. A Citadel officer—clearly not one who was on the ships—lifts his gun shakily, two of his team following his lead.

Luca's emotions blast into me so hard that I feel the ache in my own chest, like the love of my life has just looked me in the eyes and stabbed his cane-sword into my heart. A miserable acceptance follows—Luca knew this would happen—but it can't take away the pain, only makes it his fault, his stupidity for thinking maybe there was a chance they'd still love him even knowing what he has become, that he could be their aurora no matter the form he took. That their fear of him is only natural. Deserved.

I try to peel myself out of his emotions long enough to shout the truth: Luca is sensitive and wonderful and would sooner let them dash him to pieces than hurt a single one of them. And I see, in the moment between one breath and the next, that not everyone follows the crowd. A few people watch him with more suspicion than fear, their gazes lingering on his aurora markings—markings they've only ever seen on me before—as though trying to gauge whether this creature before them could truly be an aurora, too, could have protected them out on the water and back here in the city because he's *been* the one protecting them all this time. But some brave souls are not enough, and even they are too late.

Luca shies back like he's been hit, a wailing vibration ringing through his song, and drags himself back under the water. I feel every lurch and scramble of his long body as he bolts through the city, diving back into the safety of his tunnels beneath the foundation circle.

Luca, I call after him. But despite the energy I gave him, we're still only connected by one fragile thread, and my thought can't push through his current state of mind. I sway again, trying to swallow the nausea down. But as my gaze roams the streets, I can't hate these people any more than Luca can.

The wind dies for an instant, and the afternoon sun bursts through a tight gap in the darkening grey overhead. It lights up the edges of the cloud and pierces down on my spot of promenade and deck. Every fleck of gold still coating my body catches it as one, turning me into a glimmering star, just a hint of rainbow dancing through the cracks.

I can hear Alvise's inhale like a bullet. And as all eyes turn on me, I realize what they see: A savior. Their second prophecy, the one who's come to raise their sinking city into something glorious.

I am their golden one.

CHAPTER TWENTY-TWO

parental shift

NO MATTER WHAT I do, the wet gold sticks to me. The flakes slide along my skin when I rub at them, leaving me with bare streaks and gilded ridges like cross-hatching over my fishnetted aurora flesh. Just as it clings to me, so does the prophecy that I'll raise the city to a glorious pinnacle, until it seems like all of Venalt knows it whether they were near the harbor or not.

Its presence clings to me as I assist in the battle's aftermath, delivering the wounded to the hospital, and helping those rescued from the ships return to what's left of their families, and lining up the bodies that haven't been torn apart or dragged away. It comes with a tingling shock, but the attention itself is warming. Stares and whispers have been the standard all my life, from the hateful glances of the river people and the Murk dwellers and the world I came from before the mangrove, to the awe and fear and wonder of those who recognize me as an aurora.

The way these people look at me now is different though. Their bright gazes and timid smiles hold something unique. It's hope I see in them, I realize. They look at me with hope.

And that begins to fill me with dread.

After a while, I slip away from where Tavish gives orders from a stool while a medic stitches up his shoulder wound, and I apply myself to rolling the grounded hippocamp corpses into a pile off to one side as a few nereids drag the rest out of the channels. It's a small pile, all things considered: a little over a dozen of the creatures in total. With their eyes glazed and their tongues lolling, they look less like terrifying predators and more like victims. I cannot regret the ones I killed, the lives it saved in the process, but with the addition of each carcass, I still grieve.

It pains the Murk-born in me when they light a match to the oil-doused carcasses and cast the whole lot into flames. There had to have been some use for their bodies, for their deaths. Some way to carry their sacrifice on.

But these people, bleeding and mourning, parents and children alike wailing along the rows of the dead and searching the harbor as though their missing might suddenly swim back to them—these are not a people I can ask that of. Not today. Instead, I stand before the fire, so close I can feel its heat pounding through me, its light glistening off my coating of golden flakes, and I sign the most modified death proclamation I can: *Become one.*

It takes something out of me, not energy, but something deeper: motivation. I've only been awake for a few hours, but I feel like I need to fall face first back into bed, to cut out the failure of every life I couldn't save today and the responsibility of saving the rest tomorrow and just save myself for one gods-damned moment. But I'm afraid there's no amount of strength I can recuperate on my own that will fix any of this.

"How do you feel?" Teodor leans heavily against her cane. Her face is so tired she might have just pulled herself out of an emergency nap or else be about to fall into one, but the glow of the blaze seems to spark a flash of color in her eyes.

"I should be asking you that."

"It's pointless. My answer is always the same nowadays." She snorts, the sound turning into a quiet cough, then a hack, and back again. "But," she adds once her lungs finally settle, voice a bit rougher and lower, weaker, "that's not what I meant, and you know it. Golden savior."

A grunt clogs up my throat.

"It's a good color on you." Teodor wipes a fingertip over my arm. It just smears the gold around more.

"It won't come off."

"You wish it did?"

"It's not that, it's . . ." I rub the bridge of my nose, groaning into my palms. "Back home, our prophecies are instable predictions for the path of a single individual based on their current choices; this second prophecy, at least, makes more sense to me than the first or the third. I want to save the city. I want the second prophecy to come to pass. But I couldn't get Luca the ignits he needs or stop this attack. Prophesied or not, how am I supposed to prevent an entire city's annihilation? I'm not even from Venalt in the first place." But as I say it, I feel the welling of Luca's love in my chest, and his murmur of *home worlder*, and to say this isn't my home doesn't seem entirely true. "What if I can't do it?"

Teodor shrugs. "Then you're not the prophesied one. Then the Basilica is shitting us. Then someone else will save the city instead, or no one will. I figure the prophecies were always either going to happen or they weren't. The people who care enough are always going to try to make things better, and the people who don't will always find an excuse not to."

"You think the prophecies are meaningless, then?"

Farther down the promenade, an older boy bends over the layers of gold left pasted to the ground after they dumped on me. He swirls his finger across them and lifts it to his face, drawing a line of the flakes beneath his eye. A fierce smile grows across his cheeks, made sharper by the puffiness of his lids and the blood spattered on the cuff of his pants.

Teodor's gaze catches on him, and she rubs her own face like she's pulling off an invisible layer of the gold. "Fuck, I don't know. Maybe I'm just bitter and tired."

"That, I can understand." The flames before us slowly shrink, bone poking through the crisped flesh of the dead hippocamps. "Were you ever religious before you joined the Citadel?"

Her brows come together, lips bunching to one side. "I'm still religious—most of the Citadel is. And the Institute. The Divine Three are for everyone, even if the establishment that promotes them happens to be a branch of government that's single-minded and ostentatious, and some of their people are only there for the glory and power of it. I just never liked the whole destiny spiel that some of them go for. This is a lot of death for the gods to have foreseen and decided they were fine with it."

"It seems that would make the prophecies fabricated by the Basilica."

"Maybe. Or maybe a thing can be true without being a fact. You ever read a novel before?"

"Tavish keeps trying to make me, but reading's a lot of effort, and some days I'm just happy I can do it at all." It's such a raw admission, one that seems like it shouldn't be said in places like this, with their government named for establishments of knowledge. But it slips out, and I don't regret it.

"I was never big on books, either, truth be told. The letters always come in the wrong order for me." Teodor chuckles, but it sounds a bit more like a wheeze than a laugh. "Maybe that's why I'm dictating strategy at the Citadel instead of theology at the Basilica. Besides Luca, of course."

The world goes quiet in our little bubble by the fire, the warmth sizzling before us while the incoming storm tickles our backs. "The Murk gods are all about elements and phenomena, and the people who settled on the rivers brought their own gods with them, mostly. I'm not really sure when I started following them—in the beginning, it just felt like a rare piece of my own heritage that I could steal back from the people who didn't want me to have it, something to make me feel like I was still part of them. I'm not sure when I stopped following those gods, either, or if I have stopped at all. If they're just waiting for me back home, in a box. If they're in that box because the Murk confines them, or because I chose to put them there."

Teodor nods, but her eyes don't quite focus when they meet mine. I swear I can see her bones beneath her skin at that moment, pressing against her brittle flesh, trying to tell us both that she's already dead.

My chest feels numb. "You should rest."

"I should always rest." But she turns, slowly, giving me one last smile. "See you soon, golden one."

She calls for one of the gondolas the Citadel has commandeered, and when she's gone, it feels like she's left a layer of herself inside me.

The people of Venalt watch me with unbridled hope and expectation as I trek down the dock to where my discarded clothes from earlier now float in tatters beside a heap of luggage and a hundred bobbing oranges. My boots must have long since sunk into the depths. At least I still have the crisscrossing of my aurora fishnets, an eternal reminder of who I am, no matter what else I lose.

I fiddle with a fresh series of tears in the rim of my pants, where Matthia must have latched onto me in her seal form to drag me toward the surface after I passed out. A few loose strings hang off, and when I tug at them, it unravels the rest of the draw line on that side. The pants slip below my bony hips. It dislodges the hippocamp tooth I stashed there during their corpse collection—a thank-you to Matthia for saving me. With a curse, I catch it and drag the rim of my pants back up, bunching the fabric between my fist.

Tavish sits on a stool at the font of a small shop, his shoulder wound now bandaged and his shirt donned, his empty brooch pinned to its collar. I've known he's been here, safe, his gashes far from life-threatening, but that doesn't account for the knot that releases in me the moment I set eyes on him. He gives directions to a group of mixed Citadel and Basilica personnel in his diamond voice. A Findlay voice, with two Findlays to carry it once more.

Matthia looks like nothing the least bit sharp or hard right now though. She huddles off to one side, clutching her old book in her arms. She still wears Tavish's jacket, along with a pair of pants rolled twice at the ankles. Her drying hair fluffs up in chaotic waves and frizzes that nearly cover her little horns, and within them I catch the shine of red and copper.

She tries to slide between one official-looking government member and the next, reaching for Tavish without quite touching him, and clearing her throat a few times in a row, only to be shoved out of the way by the next adult before she manages to say anything. Looking defeated, she backsteps away. She doesn't smile at me when she notices my presence, but her brows come together almost pleadingly. Like seeing Tavish, her visible safety takes away a bit of the day's strain.

I wink at her and kiss Tavish's cheek, a quick peck that startles him only for a moment. He finds my hand to squeeze and then returns to his work.

The shop's contents are touristy knickknacks, snacks, and a section of supplies for dockworkers, most of it tossed to the ground in order to use the shelves to barricade windows and doors. I find a single pleated black skirt that ends in lace—probably the two-decade-old fashion disaster of someone trying to reuse a risqué party dress—buried in the back storage. It still seems preferable to losing my pants entirely, so I slip it on in their place and shove the hippocamp tooth into its waistband. I snag a straw boater hat with a lacy black veil thrown over the top to complete the look. It sits a bit crooked over my gilded braids.

With a groan, I slump to the ground beside Matthia. I don't say anything, mostly because I've forgotten every word in all three of my spoken languages, and most of the signed language, too. Instead, I tug a hippocamp tooth out and offer it to her.

A squeak leaves her. She grabs the long, oddly shaped thing, holding the spindly point with one hand while she examines the secondary tooth molded into it—a flat, molar-like piece that was hidden beneath the gum. "I knew it," she mutters. "The hippocamps aren't meant to be aggressive and predatory like this. See the tooth? It's all sharp here where it sticks out, but it was supposed to be like the flat one attached to it, like a cow's or a horse's for eating kelp. It just grew the new way because they needed to if they were going to take care of their families. They're not evil, they're just fighting to make good homes for their families, like us."

"I believe you." I hum, tipping my head back. "You said that the hippocamps swarm so every individual has just as much chance of acquiring food? There's not many creatures who do that—provide for the whole population instead of letting the weak starve in favor of the fittest. They're more considerate than a lot of people that way. But they *did* try to eat us. We can't let them hurt the people of this city under the hope that maybe they'll change."

"But it's our fault!" She wipes her nose, revealing a deep scratch that runs up the back of her hand and along her arm, an awful scab already forming. "One of those books you gave me has a chapter from a finfolk on the south coast who keeps a couple hippocamps in a part-underwater sea cave, and when she collected enough corelium for them during their mating season, their foals were all soft and docile, with teeth like these flatter ones. They didn't even eat meat if they had something else to feed on." She waves the two-part tooth in my face.

I gently steer her hand away before she accidentally pokes out my eye. "So you're saying we made them like this?"

"Yes!" She seems less enthusiastic and more frantic now, as though if she proves this thoroughly enough, it will fix everything. As though it will bring back all the people who've died. "The finfolk lady thinks it's the scarcity that makes something weird go on in their genes that makes them mean enough to keep surviving. If we let them have the corelium back and rebuild the city without it, then the next generation won't be dangerous anymore. They won't feel like they *need* to be dangerous."

A lump gathers in my throat, tight and stiff enough to thrust me into two. Neither half of me wants to acknowledge it, and it's not one of us, but our shared subconscious that pulls up Tavish's accusation from last night: confrontational; accidental arse. I swallow it down, the motion painful, and blink away the ache building behind my eyes.

"My mother was right," Matthia continues. "We should have let them have the city's corelium, we just should have done it a long time ago, little by little, before it got like this."

"We do seem to cause an awful lot of our own problems, don't we?" I try to turn it into a tease so it doesn't come as a sob. Somehow that makes it both instead.

I glance out the open door, past the bodies and the ships and the harbor's edge, to a lone gondola with a single passenger rowing frantically toward the distant coast. It confuses me at first that no one has stopped them. But then, I wouldn't have thought to stop them, either, didn't think anyone would be foolish enough to try to flee after knowing what happened to the boats. When the hippocamps finally rise up, their bodies look nearly like a wave, pulling the person seamlessly into the depths. It makes the blood and gore of the past few hours feel unreal.

I drag my hand down my face, crinkles of gold finally coming off now that I'm dry. "We can't leave. We have no more ignits, not unless we can find the ones that've been stolen—if they haven't been dumped into the abyss or floated off in the swarm. Pretty soon the hippocamps will have their corelium back, one way or another. The fight we just had will not be the last."

Matthia nods, her lips tight. She fiddles with the edge of her weathered book. Her next statement is barely a whisper. "I'm sorry you had to rescue me. I just needed one of the hippocamps' teeth to prove that they don't have to be like this, because then—then maybe we wouldn't have to fight them. Or we wouldn't have to kill them. We can't just—just keep killing, can we?"

Because every death now, every unnecessary death between bickering factions, is her fault. Because she already lost her mother and blames herself. "We all do foolish things sometimes, especially when we're desperate or in pain. The gods know I've done the same a hundred times over." The gods also knew I didn't have much room for mistakes at her age, and the combined forces of the Murk and the rivers kicked whatever foolishness I did have into a new shape, one of aggression and misery. Matthia deserves better than that. "You did put yourself in serious danger, though. A kid with a fantastic brain like yours should use it next time you're trying to decide whether or not to run straight into a terrible situation for a tooth. But you're safe still, and that's what matters most."

"You weren't!" She draws a ragged breath, shaking her head in a flurry. "I didn't mean to tear your pants, but you wouldn't move, and I—I thought you were dead."

"You saved me." I wrap my arm around her shoulders, cautiously, waiting to see if she'll pull away.

She dives into the warmth like she's been starved of compassion for months not days, sobbing against me.

"You saved me," I repeat, gentle and soft. "You were incredible." I don't push her, don't make her spill out the conclusion she might be too young to connect yet: the ways her fear and guilt and recklessness tie right back into her mother's death.

She cries until she's cried herself out, and slowly pulls back into her original sitting position, arms looser around her book and head held a little higher. She looks at me properly, eyes red and puffy. Between her sniffles, her nose wrinkles. "You're only half-dressed."

"But I'm covered in gold? That must count for at least three-quarters of an outfit."

Matthia huffs. She clicks her tongue and scoots onto her knees. From the toppled pile of touristy trappings to her side, she pulls a long, lacy ribbon off a basket. She makes me hunch so she can loop it around my neck and draws it into a messy bow tie. I'm not sure if it makes the aesthetic better or worse, but I love it.

I give her a full grin, canines bared, and waggle my eyebrows. "Well, now I just have to find myself a party."

Matthia giggles. "They'd throw you out."

"Only if they know what's good for them."

Across the room, Tavish laughs, a single sharp chuckle at something a Basilica woman says, returning immediately to his usual calm, composed voice. The longer I've sat here, the more representatives of various groups have come in to take his directions, Tavish acting as the intermediary and administrator between three government branches who are more likely to argue with each other than make decisions. Even Zuane pokes his head in to exchange news. He nods seriously as Tavish offers a vague instruction, then replies with a specification based on his own much more detailed knowledge of the city and their supplies, confirming with Tavish before leaving again. Every time there's a break in the flow, Tavish chews on his tongue, a little tremble rising up his pinkie.

The inside of Matthia's lower lip tugs in about as often, her jaw gently shifting as she gnaws on it. "Tavish is a selkie," she says finally.

I lift my brow. "And?"

"And . . . and I'm a selkie." Her cheeks turn a brilliant shade of red, and all in one go she blurts, "Is Tavish my dad?"

The laugh erupts from me, comes unbidden and entirely genuine, a blazing, full thing that reminds my lungs how close I came to drowning and my heart how much better and brighter life can be than this. Before Matthia can look too mortified, I manage to quiet myself, reaching out a hand to pet her head gently. "No, kid. As much as I'm sure Tavish would be honored to have a daughter like you, I think that's a bit impossible." I could tell her who her father is, but that doesn't seem like my place. I'm not her family; I never met Alasdair; I couldn't properly assure her that he might have loved her or tell her why he left, can't explain what it means to be a selkie or the weight that comes with the Findlay name. She needs Tavish for that. "I'm fairly sure Tavish *is* your uncle, though. You should talk to him about it."

He seems to be finishing with the last of the Citadel officers now with—for once—no one else awaiting his attention. Matthia carefully hands me her book and stands like she's a warrior queen on a mission, but she creeps into line with so much flighty shuffling that it ruins the image. As the officer leaves, she looks at me pleadingly.

Go on, I mouth.

"Mr. Findlay?"

Again, he flinches. "Yes—Matthia, is it?"

"That's me." Her chin lifts. "I'm a selkie," she says, like perhaps he's forgotten.

The tip of Tavish's nose wrinkles. "I heard."

"And you're my uncle?"

"Yes." It sounds like he's trying to end the conversation. He picks at his little finger, but the motion can't quite hide the tremble running through it.

"Can you tell me about—about everything?" Matthia's first question is timid, but once she starts, she doesn't stop, like she might never have another chance. "Who's my dad? He's your brother? I mean, of course he's your brother if you're my uncle, right? Where is he now? Does he look like me? I think you kind of look like me, maybe, but my hair is darker, and I mostly don't have freckles. Does that mean our seals look the same? Why do we need the fancy brooch to turn into them? Where do we come from—it's Maraheem, right? Rubem told me there's a city underwater and it's all selkies, and I—I think that's really cool. I think maybe we could go . . .?"

With each new question, Tavish seems to pull into himself, the trembling in his smallest fingers working into the one beside it and up through his suddenly shallow breathing. This is too hard on him, I realize with horror. He's just given up his ignation—his seal form—and now his dead brother's daughter is asking about the home he left behind. He must be experiencing grief compiled on grief with a side of conflicting emotions. As much as Matthia deserves answers about her past, she also deserves to get them from an uncle who isn't on the brink of an anxiety attack.

I scoot between them, patting Matthia's shoulder gently. "I think your uncle is a bit worn out. Maybe we should wait until everything's settled down?"

"But . . ." Matthia looks as devastated as she sounds. There's no time to comfort her, though, as the shop's door flings open once more.

"There he is!" Chancellor Alvise beams as they step into the room. Behind them lurks a Basilica party who looks much too formal for any kind of disaster relief, and I have one moment to hope that perhaps they're here for Tavish's guidance before the larger group's attention fixes solely on me.

Alvise's companions, at least, have the decency to hang back as their chancellor approaches. "Our golden savior! How are you?"

"Can we do this later, please?" I beg.

"Oh." Their exuberance fades, and beneath it is something that looks like elastic about to snap. "Sometimes it's too much, isn't it?" They sound as though they genuinely understand, their gaze, as always, not quite meeting mine. "As you wish, then. The prophecy will wait. Or it won't, exactly, but I will, and my waiting won't change it."

I hope they're right.

"Chancellor," one of the other Basilica officials interrupts from nearer the doorway.

Alvise waves at them with a shooing motion. "Go on, then, we can be useful to our people, can't we? That's what we're here for!"

It takes them a few moments of shuffling and whispering among themselves, but they back out of the space. A couple shoot Alvise uncharacteristically perturbed looks as they go.

"It seems I am the chancellor after all," Alvise mutters, their head feathers ruffling. "Some of them like that less and less now. I suppose it can't be helped, though. If I am to make my fellow officials perturbed, at least it will be for a good cause?" They look a little desperate as they say it.

"You're doing well, Alvise."

"Yes, thank you, I am," they agree, sounding steadier for the acknowledgement.

I think of what Tavish said of gender—that it was largely about feeling happy with how others perceived him and how he perceived himself—and I wonder if that's not true of everything, if being perceived and understood and still accepted is not the highest form of happiness.

Alvise's bangles jingle as they press their palms to their knees to squat in front of Matthia. "Now for you, child, are you all right?"

"Yes?" Her answer sounds more like a question, and she looks at Tavish, who's returned to pointedly ignoring her. My heart breaks, but I can't blame either of them. It's been a long day, and they both need time to recuperate.

"It seems your acting guardians are either missing or in critical condition at the moment. But I've set up a temporary adolescent care center for attack victims in the Basilica art wing. We have a space for you there." Alvise glances toward Tavish, but he seems suddenly caught up in adjusting his shirt. They shift their attention to me instead. "If she'll be needing it?"

I catch the implication like a punch to the gut, or perhaps not a punch but a knife cutting me open to carve out every emotion that's been building in me since realizing who and what Matthia is. But it's not a decision I can make without Tavish, and if he's too exhausted to handle the kid's questions, taking her in for the night isn't something I can ask of him. I force a weak smile instead and place a hand on her head. "You can trust Alvise. They know what they're doing. Are you okay going with them?"

Matthia nods slowly, her face transforming into that determined Findlay look. It chills my spine how much the expression makes her resemble her grandmother Raghnaid. She holds her tooth and her book a little tighter and follows Alvise from the shop.

The wariness I feel at letting her out of my sight again should be dampened by the knowledge that she won't be going back to the quiet apartment where her mother died with two people who clearly don't want anything to do with her. And with the hippocamps swarming between us and the mainland, there's nowhere better for her. So why does this still feel like tearing a scab before its time?

Her departure seems to take the very last of my energy, the last of my ability to be around all these people with their expectations and glances, this much noise and life and death. I catch Tavish's attention with a gentle touch to his wrist. All I can see through the tear in his shirt are bandages now, but the pain of his wound is apparent in the awkward way he turns toward me. His brooch looks lightless without the ignation in it, just a dull crown of silver.

"Tavish . . ." My chest feels all the emptier. "I know this has been a lot. Giving up your ignation, it was—"

"It's nothing. It would have died soon enough; I'm happy it's done with." The pinch of his face and the wobble in his pinkie speak to more than he's saying, but he charges onward before I can protest, clearly not interested in having this conversation now. "Are you all right? You were able to take enough of that energy for yourself?"

"Enough for now." I chuckle, a dry, thick sound that makes me want to cry. "But if I don't get a place to collapse here, soon that could change."

He pulls himself up without question. "We'll go back to the hotel. The immediate work here is nearly finished, and I think I may have instilled enough cross-branch organization to carry them through. It would require them to actually make sacrifices for each other, though, compromise somewhere."

"As long as no one will die if you leave."

Tavish cringes. "I think the deaths are already done for the day."

"Tomorrow will be a different story," I finish for him, and take his arm in mine as we head back for the hotel, trying not to let my gaze linger too long on the empty hollows of his brooch or the ones that mimic it inside my chest.

CHAPTER TWENTY-THREE

the bathwater and the baby

AS WE MAKE OUR way back to the hotel, Matthia lingers in my mind like the center of a whirlpool that keeps pulling at my thoughts. I try to focus on the walk instead.

Our meandering trip takes far longer than it should with the crowds that seem to have leaked onto the streets in droves since the attack. As the signs of hippocamp violence give way the deeper into the city we move, an excitable panic replaces them, the numbing grief of the harbor not real enough to breed sense into these people, only fear. The windows of a few shops have been shattered, and we pass injuries clearly caused by the city's own inhabitants. The most astute civilians are already hauling their essentials toward the foundation circle.

The clatter and stress of it all drain what little energy I have left, plucking at it with claws out, beaks bloodied. My consciousness feels like paper over a pit, like one wrong tear will leave me crumpled on the street, waiting for someone to notice I'm empty inside. If I'm not careful, I won't get out of bed in the morning no matter how much energy my aurora half can muster.

Tavish squeezes my arm and tucks himself a little closer as his cane bounces off the ankles of a passerby. He flinches away from the bang of a door, his breathing too shallow for my liking.

"We're only a few streets away from the hotel," I say pathetically, and it sounds almost like frustration. "Then we can both relax."

His brow tightens.

It *is* frustration: a crisp, sparking feeling that seems to eat up the rest of my paper exterior—frustration at myself, for not being enough for him right now. For knowing I can be better than this, usually, but that right now the strength isn't there. Right now, I don't want to comfort Tavish, don't want to be so close to his pain that I have to feel it myself; I just want to curl against the fur of a pet who has no wounds for me to heal, away from any sentient being, and drink until I meet oblivion. But I am feeling his pain.

And I'm thinking of Matthia again, her face pinched up with determination as the Basilica steward leads her away.

"Maybe we should have brought Matthia with us after all."

"She'll be safe with the Basilica," Tavish replies. "It's only a few days." He doesn't specify a few days until when. Perhaps it seems too ghastly to put into words. A few days until Luca runs out of energy. A few days until most of the city sinks. A few days until . . . whatever happens after that.

"But she's a Findlay—she has to be Alasdair's kid, she's got your mother's face and your Findlay voice. She's your niece, Tavish. Your family." Family. Tavish has family again. I try not to think of where that leaves me. This is good for him—good for him to have someone else when I'm gone. Good for him not to be alone if I follow Luca in the fading, no city to even bother begging ignits from.

"She has a great-aunt on the mainland," Tavish replies.

"Not a *selkie* aunt. Not someone who knew your family or your culture." My gaze catches on his empty brooch as I say it.

His fingers go to it, as though he knows, but the touch isn't fond, isn't soft or wistful. He looks like he might rip it off and toss it in the channel.

My gut clenches at the thought. Even without its ignation, this is the last piece of who he is—something just six weeks ago he grieved extensively at the thought of losing. Now he's flipping himself inside out to get away from everything it's connected to, even the child who just wants to understand that connection. And the person he's becoming isn't any better than the old one. Worse, perhaps, because he's distancing himself from the good in his heritage along with the bad. I come so dangerously close to pointing that out, but right now it'll only agitate him. With the last of my strength, I bury the impulse. What's left is a quiet terror. "You're all Matthia has." I don't say, *She's all you'll have someday, too,* but it resonates through every pore of me like a eulogy. "You need each other."

"She doesn't need *me*! Maybe she has the selkie genes, but we are a dying race. Once the ignits and the ignation are gone, there won't be selkies anymore. Matthia is a satyr and a Venaltan and the daughter of Fiordelise, and maybe that's all she should ever be."

"Tavish—"

"Did you ask if I wanted a child?"

"No, I . . ." I realize, numbly, that I had never thought to. Whether or not Tavish and I raise kids together had never been an issue for me; I had never imagined that far into our future, never imagined myself having that much of a future to begin with. But Matthia isn't just a *kid*. She's Tavish's family. She's *Matthia*. And Tavish still doesn't want her. "You're not interested in having kids?"

"Absolutely not." His tone is defensive, a stark, bitter vulnerability written across his features. His fingers tighten as though he can push the feeling into me the way Luca might. "A small person whose life I can lord over and ruin through any number of accidents or personal flaws? I ken that's a disaster waiting to happen."

I can feel myself pulling away, and I can't help it, no matter how much I don't want to.

Tavish snorts. "What did you think I would say? That we should settle here with Matthia and start believing in prophecies and having luncheons with the woman whose heart I broke? That we would drag her with us while we travel?"

"I don't know." I feel too many things at that, so many that I haven't processed a single one before my reply comes out, as though a part of me is trying to fill the space with something, anything to prove I'm not cracking in half, guts spilled on the pavement. Still, it comes out so soft, nearly buried by the sounds of the street. "I just know that she lost her mother, and she needs someone who will continue to love her." Between my gaps, my soul seems to shout: I needed the same and I didn't get it, and look how I turned out, sharp toothed and gold plated with nothing underneath.

"If you care so much, then you can be her family instead," Tavish grumbles.

"With you or without?" I swallow. He said that he was with me because he wanted to be here, and I don't doubt that—he's a manipulator, not a liar, and he's tried so hard to be vulnerable with me. But what if there's a change that pushes him too far? Is there a version of my life that he can't abide by? "Is this an ultimatum?"

He pales. "No! No, I don't know what it is."

Our conversation goes so deathly, his expression hollowing out the way my own chest does, that I nearly walk us right past the hotel, veering inside at the last second. The lobby passes in a blur, my feet taking me instinctively toward the stairs like they know the moment they stop, so will every other part of me. Still he says nothing. I'm ready to fill the space for him, bleeding out at his feet, when he finally gives a heavy sigh.

"I suppose it's that even if you choose to be a part of her life, I cannot." His brows pressed tight. "And I'm not certain that division wouldn't burn us both out in the long run."

"You're right. It wouldn't be fair to Matthia either." I groan, rubbing my face. Gold flakes peel off it in a shimmering rain. There has to be a compromise here somewhere, a way to at least secure us a place in her life—and her in Tavish's—even if we're not the ones raising her. "You don't know her, but she's a good kid with a head on her shoulders, and she's half-grown already. If you could just spend time with her, try to be her uncle, answer her questions—"

"But I don't *want* to be her uncle!" His diamond voice cuts right through me, the edge of his fingernail bleeding as he twists it into his brooch. "I am a Findlay, remember? We're all dead for a *reason*. I refuse to inflict that on her!"

Something nearly clicks, his whole argument almost sliding into place. There's more to his fear and fury, more than having kids or not, more than Matthia herself. But I am so tired, so wrung through and hung out to dry, that I can't pick it apart for him. I don't have the strength to be gentle with him right now, to be anything more than hurt and frustrated and so gods-damned exhausted. "Tavish . . ."

He trips on the first step. With a trembling breath, he squeezes his brooch. "We'll talk about this later."

It feels like he's shut a door in my face. With how much I want to hide away from everything, it should make me relieved, but the way my chest seems to crumble inward on nothing, it only amplifies my inadequacy, builds upon the pain I'm already siphoning off him, and I'm far too exhausted to pick it all back up again.

I grab the final half-empty wine bottle off the table. I shouldn't, I know, but that feels like it doesn't matter right now, not when there seems to be a hundred reasons why I actually should after all. It sloshes as I drag myself straight to the bathroom, shutting the physical door with nearly as much force as Tavish shut his metaphorical one. The water sputters into the footed metal tub, pounding, pounding. I hold my hand under it, but it never turns hot.

Right. The generator.

They must have been heating their water on electricity. With a sound more animal than human, I flop into the half-filled, room-temperature bath, one foot hanging out either side. The skirt's lace rises around my legs for a moment, floating there hesitantly, like it can't believe I'm this much of a mess.

I saved people. I helped Luca. I'm the second prophecy, or something. But it can't peel back the death and pain of the day.

If you care so much, then you can be her family instead.

I tug the wine cork out with my teeth and sip, low and slow, all but breathing in the dark, oaky alcohol. For a moment, it feels like it might be enough to transport me home, fanning out my simple house beneath me, the buzz of insects and the holler of parrots, one of my jaguars coming to nuzzle against my languid half hand. But there's not even Lavender here. A shout comes from outside the hotel, the racket too intrusive to let me daydream for long. I take another long drink.

Tavish moves through the main room, clattering and muttering to himself. I can't tell if he's louder than normal, or if I'm just more sensitive. Another drink. My faux bow tie feels constricting around my throat. I give it a few tugs, trying to remove it, but the odd, lacy material catches into a knot between my collarbones instead. Giving up, I close my eyes, tip my head back, and sink deeper, deeper, until the water rises around my ears, and the world turns into a gentle rush of blood.

By the time I pull my head up, most of my second-prophecy gilding floats in the bathwater. Tavish stands by the sink in his underpants, wiping the salt and grime off himself with a damp towel. His vacant stare is even less focused than usual, as though his mind is a faint blur of dark and light like his vision. Each motion is slow and repetitive.

With a sigh, I pull my feet into the water to brush at the gold that sticks to their tops. "You can use the bath. I'll get out."

Tavish freezes, towel hovering above his elbow. He exhales and returns to his scrubbing. "I'm meant to keep the bandage dry."

"Right." I should have thought of that. The wine bottle seems far too empty as I lift it again. I waver between downing the rest in one go or setting it to the side. It clicks against the floor, making Tavish flinch.

One of his curls sweeps into his mouth.

If you care so much, then you can be her family instead.

He didn't mean it like that, I think. *Didn't mean that I should replace him.*

'*What if he did?*'

We both think it, a tattered, guilty thought: he's done this before. Come with someone only so far and then cut it off at the final moment. And I am the sort of person everyone cuts off in the end.

I don't believe that of him, not truly. But I still feel the weight of the thought deep in my chest and the guilt of thinking it in the first place.

Another sigh escapes me, strangled out, the air feeling like it's leaving my chest for the last time. "At least let me wash your hair. There's a bit of blood in it, on the left, near your shoulder."

He lifts his free hand tentatively toward the area, only to wince as it moves his bandaged shoulder. "Aye, that would be—thank you."

I slip my legs underneath me, almost catching them in my skirt as I do. He kneels on a separate towel beside the tub and tips his head over the edge. His muscles go weak, then limp as I take his head in my hands, gently dunking his curls. I cup the water to where it meets with his skin, wiping the excess aside. Gold twinkles through it, sparkling softly where the crushed flakes stick in his hair.

I let the soap lather by rubbing it between his roots in methodical circles, supporting his head with my halved hand. The blood turns it pink around his ear, but I find no wounds beneath. Just the splattering from his shoulder, then. The suds disperse back into the water with each comb of my fingers, but the gilding remains, a twinkle of sunshine in his flame-hued curls.

Letting him go, I feel somehow a little better and a little worse all at once.

Tavish runs a hand through his hair, scrunching it. He fiddles with the ends. "Ruby . . ."

"We'll talk about it later." I think it almost comes out as gently as I mean it. "It's too much, and I'm too tired."

His shoulders sag, slight enough I would have missed it if he weren't so near, if I wasn't unable to take my eyes off him. A little emotionless twist lifts one side of his lips. "We both are." He stands, patting the towel twice before awkwardly setting it off to the side. "Rest. I'll join you when I'm done."

I didn't want him to fight me on it—I shouldn't want him to force me to talk when I know I'm still three wrong breaths away from saying something I'll regret. But I still feel the sink of disappointment in my chest.

I leave the skirt floating in the tub, the boater hat balanced on the spout, and take the wine bottle with me. It was already empty.

CHAPTER TWENTY-FOUR

tried and tired

I WAKE WITH THE dawn, Luca's song pulsing gently through me. I feel only slightly less dead than when I crawled into bed hours before sunset yesterday. My mind, at least, seems somewhat more centered—enough that I can grab it by the hazy grey mush it's made from and wrangle myself up with only a minimal amount of groaning and grunting. Despite last night's soak in the bath, I still leave a scattering of gold flakes on the sheets, marking my every toss and turn. Tavish's side of the bed looks equally messy, and the bathroom bustles with curses as he readies himself.

We have to talk still, but the more I think about it, the more daunting it feels. I try not to compare myself to Teodor, waiting to carry Tavish into a future he couldn't accept. This is a different situation at a different time and a different relationship. But I still feel as though a boat rocks beneath me, turning my stomach into a nauseous surf.

I shovel as much of an apple into my mouth as I can bear, hoping it'll be enough to fight down the incessant ache in my bones, and sluggishly don my spare clothes: the same tired, scarlet-trimmed outfit I'd been in when Lilias abducted me. A few more patches, a few more stains. Like me, I suppose.

The frantic atmosphere of the previous day sounds as though it's been riled twice as high. When I peek out the window, I can't quite glimpse the street below, but the channel beside it bustles with gondolas transporting supplies toward the center of the city. I wonder if Zuane's team is even still looking for the stolen ignits in this mess. It feels like something I should help with, savior and all.

I groan. Other than Teodor's personal theology, I've no idea how prophecies of the Divine Three function, whether these deities are all-knowing or merely offering vague predictions, if they even came from greater supernatural beings at all or just an ancient priest who wanted to inspire hope in future times of disaster. I should probably ask Chancellor Alvise about it—I did promise to talk to them— but I have enough crises going on; I don't need an existential one to top it off. What I do need is to check on Luca and Teodor.

Through the single thread that binds me to Luca, I sense his questioning presence. Compared to the comfort he felt with me before, commenting on my conversations and drawing off little slivers of my energy when he needed it, his reclusion seems like an impossible distance. But I'm glad he trusts me this much, at least. As I send him an acknowledgement that I'm awake, Tavish appears in his blue-grey suit and flower-embroidered scarf, his hair tucked beneath his cap and his cane-sword under one arm.

We'll talk soon, I tell Luca.

He pulls back, but I still sense him lurking, watching curiously as I give Tavish a quick peck on the cheek and head out. We haven't agreed where we're going yet, but he follows me all the same. It makes my heart twist.

If you care so much, then you can be her family instead.

Later. We'll confront that later. Later, when I really mean never.

There's no one at the front desk or the office, all the money cleared out.

"Perhaps they gave up once they realized that no one with sense would be seeking accommodations here for much longer," Tavish says.

It makes my skin tingle. "The foundation circle must be getting crowded."

The streets certainly are. We head deeper into the city—toward someplace they can put us to use—weeding through overfilled carts and an unusual number of nereids on their wheelchairs, all moving deeper into the city. As we squeeze along the channel, I can see the mirrored chaos beneath it as the nereids' undercity clears itself out. Between everyone's hurry and my lack of gilding, none of them seem to recognize me or even notice the aurora in my features. It leaves me with a surprising pang of disappointment.

I feel something of the thought echoed in Luca, his presence still hazy and distant. The more I focus on him, the weaker he seems. Or perhaps that's my own fatigue returning.

Whatever energy I gained from last night's rest abandons me so quickly that it feels like I haven't slept at all, leaving my legs aching and my lungs constantly out of breath. I slow as we skirt the edge of a large corelium plaza—the same one we bought lunch from a few days ago, I think. Now the sky has gone from sunny to a windy grey that speaks of tonight's storm. The vines along the rooftops and lines tremble in the breeze, and petals swirl off flowers, piling in corners and at the edges of waterways. The food carts have been packed up, Basilica medical tents and Citadel guard stations erected in their place. Institute workers carefully disassemble the front of a building across the way and pile the stones into boats that take off in the direction of the foundation circle.

I spot Zuane in his chair, talking to a set of officers, and Iseppa waving her hands at a battered-looking engineer. We've nearly reached them when Chancellor Alvise pushes through the crowds toward us. They tut to themselves, their eyes dancing warily and their arms tucked so tight to their sides that their plethora of golden bangles barely jingle, but their expression lights up when they spot me.

"Rubem! Our golden savior!" The broad, optimistic smile they give me makes my stomach clamp up, my gut twisting.

'Run?' half of me asks.

But that feels wrong, feels worse than the thought of standing here and accepting whatever this new role places upon me. If Venalt needs us, then we have to be here for them.

'And if we make things worse?' The human half of me pulls at our memories: him ripping me from my last host, the murders I committed in Falcre, the tangle of good we've done here mixed with all the ways that good has fallen apart, and a deeper and darker recollection that feels like pieces of me ripping apart, someone's sad, resigned statement, *Stirring up trouble like this is causing more harm than good.*

We've made things better before, too. A tingling feeling digs itself into my bones and buries beneath my sternum. Hope, maybe. Or want. *We'll just have to succeed here as well. Whatever it takes, we will be their golden one.*

I can feel his agreement by the way he slides into me, and me into him. As one, I smile back at Alvise, hoping it comes across as something more than a terrified grimace.

Alvise doesn't seem to notice my teeth gritting. "You were amazing yesterday—the children can't stop talking about it! Though, I do encourage them to focus on you, so that's part of it. It's easier for them to see the situation in light of the heroes who rescued them and not the people who couldn't be saved and the fact that most of this city is doomed. Much easier to think that heroes will rise for them again when— well, you know." Their grin turns sad, then shifts altogether to a frown. "We should have given the Citadel our ignits the moment they asked."

Across the plaza, a series of shouts ring out as a nereid in line for the foundation circle is shoved off their wheeler by an irate harpy to be met with the tired objections of two Citadel guards.

Tavish's unfocused gaze continues staring out over Alvise's shoulder, but he stills, his chin tipped as though listening to the squabble. His pinkie taps against the handle of his cane. "There is nothing to be done about that now. But we were hoping that we could be of use still, in whatever way is most needed."

"Well, I suppose it would be most useful to have the city raised to glorious heights," Alvise says in a half-joking tone that does nothing to quell the dread the words themselves ignite in me. "But until then, there's more than enough to be done to get everyone safely into the foundation circle."

"So we're giving up?" I snap. "We let the city sink and Luca die? After everything he's done for Venalt, we just abandon them both?"

"No, of course not," Tavish replies. "But, Ruby, there just isn't a good option here, you ken that."

"Would you be saying that if it were me in Luca's place?" The question comes out harsher than I intend, and meaner, too.

Tavish flinches. "I'm sorry, I didn't mean to imply that Luca isn't worth all our efforts. But there isn't a better option right now, not as things stand."

"Venalt's ignits could still be here," I mutter, though I know plenty well that if Zuane's team had no clues to go on yesterday, they aren't likely to have found anything new with all the chaos of the harbor and the city unraveling around us.

Someone in a Basilica tent shouts for Alvise. They bob on their heels, looking almost sheepish. "Oh, they want me! I'm the chancellor after all!" As they leave, they pause to press a hand to my arm. "You may be the savior, but this is not your burden alone. Whatever is to happen, a thousand choices will create it."

I can feel their touch long after they're gone, a tingle that urges me forward, as if enough distance might make me forget it. Despite their kind words, this *is* my burden. It will be my fault if I do nothing.

The officers around Zuane begin to leave, and I barge forward in their place. I fight the impulse to bare my teeth, to fully embrace the aggression that started our relationship off so hostile. Instead I think of the way he tackled that hippocamp yesterday, the danger he was willing to put himself in for this city. I breathe out, slowly, deeply, and give him a slight nod. "Commander Zuane."

His expression remains neutral, but one of his brows twitches up. "What is it?"

"The ignit search." I try to sound casual, but I feel like a piece of heavy machinery attempting to paint a mural. "Any progress since yesterday?"

Zuane shakes his head. "We've found very few so far. We'd just finished searching the foundation circle when the attack on the harbor hit, and the aurora consumed everything we had after he returned to the Citadel."

I grimace. I felt the slight spike in Luca's energy at the time, but it was so small, barely an ignit or two. "There has to be more. Maybe the perpetrator is waiting to bring them in when the storm hits? Can you get a checkpoint set up to search those entering?"

"We *have* a checkpoint. Just getting people to part with their nonessentials and designating them a space to sleep in an orderly fashion is taking so long that we'll have a mob on our hands here soon if we aren't careful," Zuane replies, his gaze flickering across the plaza to where a line of luggage-toting families is forming—one of the queues into the foundation circle, I imagine, though we're still blocks away from the nearest of the three entrances.

"So, you can't find a murderer, or a thief, *or* manage a crowd," Iseppa's high-pitched voice cuts in. The circlet of the Institute chancellor rests across her brow, its polished silver drawing out the dusky undertones of her dark skin. "Tell me, then, Commander, what are you good for? It certainly isn't the foundation's defensive measures."

Zuane's flat expression cracks at the edges, but he tightens his lips, seeming to pull himself back together with a breath. "You're the engineers," he says slowly. "It's hardly our fault that you built an indefensible city."

Iseppa wrinkles her nose. "I've had three walls erected today only for your team to demand them all moved. Commander Zuane, I think your people may be unclear on the fundamental purpose of a wall, but I will tell you, sir, that we build them *not* to be moved."

"If your people would wait—"

"Until the storm sets in? Or until the city sinks? Your little show of bringing civilians into the foundation circle won't matter if there are hippocamps hunting on the Citadel's lawn or swimming through the Institute's tunnels."

Zuane speaks through gritted teeth, every syllable flatter than the last. "I'd give you another damn defense consultant if *your* people wouldn't keep sending them back for, as they put it, 'being in the way.'"

Tavish looks an inch from butting in, but his attention keeps wavering, his fingers drawing up and down my arm as though he's thinking of carving me apart. After the events of the last few days, I know he very well could; he already holds my heart, and always will. I wrap my hand over his.

We've been awake for barely an hour, done nothing of consequence for Luca or Venalt, and already I feel as though I've swum the length of the Murk. Perhaps Tavish is right. Perhaps we've already lost the city.

But as I think it, I feel Luca lurking just beyond my consciousness, far more exhausted than I am, yet striving to protect Venalt with just as much dedication as ever, and I ache to do what I've come here for: to save him, or if not to save him, to at least save his city. Despite the prophecy's hopeful predictions, if the hippocamps enter Venalt, people *will* die under their teeth. The only way to stop that is by stopping the city from sinking in the first place. If there's any chance left, we can't give up.

Through the bustle of the crowd, a familiar Findlay voice catches my attention, as sharp as diamond and almost as disdainful as her grandmother's. "Excuse me, I have to get through!"

I tighten my grip on Tavish's hand. "Matthia!"

She shoves her way into view, her attention spinning toward me. One of her suspenders is missing, and the wind tugs at her wavy hair. In the dusky overcast of the encroaching storm, it looks fully brown, her light freckles washed out against her olive skin. I can't help but think of Tavish's objection to her.

If you care so much, then you can be her family instead.

My heart throbs, clenching at the back of my throat, but I have no time to think about that when everything around us is in such flux. With dread, I notice the way she clutches an old tome from Teodor's office under one arm, her misshapen plushie tucked beneath it. There's only one kind of news she's brought me from that book so far.

"What is it, kid?" I let go of Tavish to grab her gently, tucking her wild hair out of her face. "What's wrong?"

She shakes her head. "Nothing's wrong." A little smile bunches into her cheeks, growing the longer she stands there until she's practically beaming. "I've been thinking since yesterday, with the tooth you got me and how I'm a satyr but I'm a selkie, too, and I realized a thing." She takes a deep breath and straightens her shoulders like she's stepping up to a lecture podium. "I know what to do about the hippocamps."

CHAPTER TWENTY-FIVE

the love of a findlay

WE COULD SAVE THE CITY.

Even with most of Luca's attention fixed on his song, his attention still perks at Matthia's mention of the hippocamps. The single thread connecting us tightens around mine in curiosity, almost tugging, fear and hope pulsing off him. The same feelings vibrate in my own chest. Tavish's fingers find my back.

Both Zuane and Iseppa edge forward to hear.

Matthia glances at them, and a slight flush rises like twin spots on her cheeks. I swear her little finger wobbles. She's so much more like Tavish than I've yet realized.

I catch her gaze, giving her a reassuring smile, no teeth this time. "Matthia, what do you know about the hippocamps?"

She breathes in. "You remember how they're aggressive and armored right now because of the genes they've got turned on—the ones from not having enough corelium when they were born, right?"

"That's what you were telling me yesterday."

"Yeah." She bobs, catching her lower lip between her teeth once. "And selkies switch between being people and being seals because of their genes changing, right?"

It takes a moment, but I connect her points with a flutter of my stomach. "Go on."

"Tavish uses his brooch for it. It flips the genetics." She hesitates, and it feels like her whole being is hanging in that moment between the jump and the fall, where she can no longer stop what's to come but doesn't fear it any less for that. "Is it just selkie genetics, or could it, you know, be used on other creatures? Could you use it on the hippocamps to turn their genes around all at once? To make them like the docile ones with the flat teeth? Would it do that?"

Zuane's eyes narrow. "You're saying that we could make the hippocamps less aggressive?"

"Then we could kill them?" Iseppa asks.

Matthia shakes her head so violently that the wind pulls her hair into her face, catching it in her mouth. She shoves it out of the way with one hand, nearly dropping her book and plush in the process. "We can't kill them!"

"No." The flutter of excitement in my chest grows as I speak. "We wouldn't have to. If the hippocamps were docile enough to send out a boat, Tavish could collect ignits from the mainland, which would hold us off through the storm. It wouldn't save your aurora indefinitely, but it would buy us the time to round up the hippocamps in a safe manner and potentially uncover the ignits that were stolen from the Institute and the Basilica." I press my palm to Tavish's shoulder. "If it's even possible? Will a selkie brooch work on hippocamps?"

"Our brooch's technology is not merely for selkies," Tavish replies. "It will work on any person with secondary genetics. But—"

"Then I can't see why that wouldn't include animals too," I say. "We're all made of similar stuff, right?"

Matthia gives me a look so reminiscent of Raghnaid's condescension that I have to blink away a chill. "*Yeah.* DNA."

Tavish clears his throat. "Whether the technology would be functional for this is irrelevant. We used the ignation in my brooch to save Luca yesterday." His voice takes a twist I can't decipher, a hollowness beneath it, filled with all the painful, furtive emotions he hasn't put to words for me yet. "It's useless without ignation."

"Fuck." I groan, but the lightness of my chest doesn't seem to catch up to the knowledge. "And there's nothing else that might fuel it?"

I can see Tavish's response written across his face, his sadness almost desperate, as though he, too, hopes the answer will change in his mouth. "There's a rare ignit that we based the brooch's workings on, but if any were produced in this region, I imagine a shifter population would have grown up around them."

"Oh." Matthia tucks her book closer, pressing her chin to the top of her plushie's head. The harsh determination in her expression shatters, and in a single inhale, she seems like she might cry. "Sorry. I should have thought of it yesterday."

"It was still a brilliant idea, and you were so smart to realize it." I try to hide the breaking of my own heart as I say it. "Any other time, maybe it would've been enough. We just have bad luck for this one."

Matthia sniffles, but her lips rise, less with happiness and more with resolve not to be sad. "Bad luck," she repeats.

I don't have to thread myself into her the way I have with Luca in order to feel her emotions as my own, her disbelieving inflection the same one resounding in my chest. Somehow, this is still our fault. There was something we could have done. If we had been stronger, faster, bolder. If we hadn't sat back and let it fall apart. If I had invaded more offices and taken the ignits without asking and not taken no for an answer.

"Wait, but ignation is that silver stuff, right? That's what we need?" Matthia asks, her brows tight and her lips pursed in a way that makes my heart lift all on its own.

"Yes." I try not to plunge right back through the rise of optimism and the fall of despair again, even as Luca watches over my shoulder, contributing his every fluttering hope and fear. "It shines a bit like a rainbow is trapped within."

"I think Mom had some of that in a special box under her bed when I was a kid." Matthia's enthusiasm returns in an onslaught of tiny bounces that show just how much of a kid she still is.

"Goddamn my brother," Tavish mutters, but he laughs, soft and broken. "Alasdair must have truly cared for that woman to risk leaving it for her. Goddamn beautiful fool."

"Would she still have it?" I ask.

Zuane's lips tighten. "There was nothing of the kind in her office."

"She yelled at me for touching it, then hid the box in her room somewhere." Matthia shakes her head. "She didn't take it to the apartments, I don't think. Most of our stuff was all left in Grannie and Nanna's house. That's where we lived before Mom became chancellor."

"So it could be there still." I feel breathless, almost teetering. "We could do this."

"Aye, but a functional brooch is only the first step." Tavish rubs his hand against my back, like he's trying to tell me he'll catch me when I fall. "Mine requires the wearer to want the transformation in order to activate it."

Zuane snorts. "If you have a way to explain that to a hundred vicious hippocamps, I'd love to hear it."

"And there's only one brooch for all of them," Iseppa adds.

I remember the way the brooch thrummed against my skin, the song hidden within just waiting to burst out. Only one brooch, perhaps. But one vibration can cover a great distance. "There's only one aurora, but he keeps all the hippocamps at bay with his song. What if we could do something similar—he and I?" As I say it, I'm already reaching for him, his thoughts and mine overlapping through the small thread that connects us as we bounce the idea back and forth. "We would have to feel the vibrations of the running brooch and develop a song that projects them outward, but theoretically it should work."

Despite everything we would still need to accomplish to turn this into a success, the mere possibility of it feels like a flame in my chest. There is something we *can* do. This isn't over yet.

"Where's this house, Matthia?" I ask. "Can you bring us there?"

"I can take you to it, but it's all locked up. Mom had the key."

Iseppa flails her hands. "It should still be in her office with the others, if the Citadel didn't *take* them."

"We took evidence, not Fiordelise's personal keys," Zuane says, his flat words just terse enough to make his annoyance clear.

"I don't know what you people seem to think is evidence or not! Clearly whatever evidence you have gathered is—"

Keys. Ones from the same ring that would have opened the ignit cases? My stomach knots. "Where can we find these keys, Iseppa?"

She flutters her hands again. "My secretary would know. I'll have them sent for."

"Can't we just break in?" Matthia asks, the diamond edge gone from her voice as she tugs anxiously at her plush. "It's my house."

"See, the kid is the only smart person here," I say.

"Absolutely not!" Iseppa objects. "We *have* keys!"

Perhaps Iseppa hasn't proven herself to be a part of the scheme to sink the city, but I still don't trust her to collect them for us.

Tavish seems to pick up on my fears with a sigh. "There's enough chaos in this city as it is. I'll go with Iseppa. We'll be twenty minutes at the most."

"I can come with you," I offer.

"The fewer of us moving back and forth across the foundation entrance, the better." Tavish's fingers brush my wrist. "And you . . ." He knows just how tired I am. Of course he does. And the tight bunch of his brow pleads with me to rest.

I press both hands to my face with a groan. "Fine. Twenty minutes—no longer."

Even this allowance feels constraining.

Iseppa huffs, but she leaves with Tavish.

I feel antsy the moment they're out of sight. The growing crowd seems to close in suddenly, their voices too loud and bodies too near. Twenty minutes. Time we should spend helping with the relocation efforts, but I feel like all the energy has been drained out of me.

With Matthia in tow, I move toward the nearest channel. By the time we reach it, my legs protest every step.

I plop onto the stone, dangling my feet over the water. Matthia settles on the ground at my side, her leg brushing mine as she kicks mindlessly. The nereids here have almost finished clearing out, a few stragglers still hastily lifting their belongings onto the street across the channel. It's an odd sight: the city above so busy while the one below sits a ghostly remnant, only populated by the occasional rustle of sea grass in a window box and the soft tune of Luca's song.

The vibration still thrums solidly, a war cry, deep and fast and filled with dread, but when I push past it toward the aurora himself, the vague sense of him feels so much weaker than even an hour ago—weak in a way I've never felt from him before. His presence shifts tentatively toward me once more. The single thread connecting us doesn't carry his emotions with the same fluidity it once might have, but I don't try to weave more of mine into his, don't even offer him energy to try and tempt him closer, no matter how much I'd like to. He seems content to linger his presence here, close but not quite touching, his hope and mine running on separate but reflecting channels.

The longer we wait, the more signs of the battle I spot in the crowd, wounds and tears, amputations of limb and love, but other things, too: the streak of gold some people have drawn under their eyes and their little gilded horns for luck. My eyes fog a little, my chest tightening.

The emotion bundles in my chest, and I feel Luca take notice. *'You helped.'*

Not yet. Not enough. I came here to save you. So many attempts, and I haven't even managed that. Not wanting to burden him, I hold back my final thought: that this time has to be different. We're running out of options, and he's running out of life.

'Nothing you have tried has been wrong yet, though. Even when you have failed, you have seen the truth, always. About everything.' He hesitates, the echo of him vibrating unsteadily for a moment, before he adds, *'About Teodor, too. I love her, but sometimes I also don't know how to trust her. You were right about that, and it frightened me.'* The admission feels raw, like an offering. As loosely threaded as we are, he could keep the flood of it back if only he drew a little further away, but he stays with his attention fixed on my presence, as though his face is angled toward me.

What do you know about Teodor?

'I don't know—that is what makes me worry. I don't know what she does sometimes, and I don't like that. She is so weak, and I can't send things into her like I can you. Sometimes I wake up, and I think she has already faded away.'

My chest tightens. *Are you saying she's been up to something?*

His agreement writhes inside him, on the edge of fleeing. *'She is guilty. Or she feels guilty. I don't know why.'* The spin of my mind is only half-started when he butts back in. *'She is good though—she loves the city. She loves me.'* He says it like those two things are the same. To him, they are: a tangled mess he's trapped himself in, between his love for Venalt and his own insecurities.

She is *good, I think.* I'm not certain, and he'll know I'm not, but I open up my chest to let him see a deeper, rawer part of that. I don't know if either of us are truly good, not her and not me, but I care for her all the same. From the honesty, he pulls up something that seems ripped from my core, a fragmented thing made of pain and longing.

'You wanted her to be your sister.' Luca's words are faint but his wonder is clear. *'You want to stay here, to be near her.'*

She's like me, but we aren't related, I lash back, harsher than I mean. *I can't stay with her. I have a job—I have other auroras to save. And she's dying. Even if we were something, it wouldn't be for long.* With each word, I choke, bundling down a thought that's too large, too heavy, too mixed up in love and fear and the clutches of that bone-deep loneliness I felt in the Murk.

In its wake, my throat burns for a drink. I shove my hands restlessly into my pockets, and my fingers hit something hard. The paperweight from Fiordelise's office. I must have dropped it in there reflexively before we left the hotel. It fits between my fingers, the creature's tail wobbling from knuckle to knuckle as I twist and flip it.

With each consecutive roll of the little figurine, Luca's song drifts in time, a sad tune weaving through it. A small bundle of his threads weeds through the singular one he's given me. He offers them to me, too—fewer than he did last time, but still a show of trust. Of forgiveness.

I don't think I ever even apologized.

'You did,' he says. *'I felt it.'*

Cautiously, I offer him another few threads of my own in return, as small and fragile as the first. He pulls them into himself, pressing back with his own. As though we're two vines forming a bridge between trees, we remake the connection we had the day we met, a thick, sturdy stalk that lets me sense Luca's emotions crisp and clear, my energy and his shared between us like two streams running into one. We are stronger like this. I feel it.

Then his presence jerks back.

It's so sudden that I flinch, my shock almost blocking out his own. But beneath it is fear, strong and tense, and dread. Then sorrow.

'My friend.' His words hitch in my mind, jolting. *'I'm sorry. I'm so sorry.'*

What is it? I think I speak the question out loud, too, Matthia glancing up at me. *Luca, what's wrong?*

'You don't feel it?' He weeps, slow, internal bursts of misery. *'One whose home is the world: you're fading.'*

CHAPTER TWENTY-SIX

ash from rainbows

FADING: IT'S SUDDENLY A nonsense word. Not what I think it means. It can't be what I think it means.

But I can feel the exhaustion coiling in my bones. Even after a ten-hour sleep, my limbs feel heavy and my lungs like they won't quite open, and my brain moves a second slower than usual. Earlier, when Tavish dragged his fingers across my aurora flesh, his brow tight, as though he sensed it. A gust of chilled wind rushes through my hair, ruffling my full-length vest and the upturned collar on my shirt. Luca's sorrow buries into me, until I can't tell where his ends and mine begins.

I peel back my sleeve. Between my aurora, black with its glittering rainbows, run streaks of grey. They're tiny compared to Luca's, but they're there, sure as the sky is clouded.

I'm fading. It's still not a real word, not something that can apply to me, even with the proof before my eyes. It wasn't supposed to happen yet. Someday, maybe, but not yet. Not here. My rib cage seems to shrink in time with my vision.

Tavish—I have to tell him.

I turn to look for him on instinct only to remember he's not with us. How long has it been? I could ask among the crowd for a pocket watch, but I never checked what time he left. It can't have been the full twenty minutes though.

I force myself to stay put. I watch the water, the sky, the top of Matthia's head as she reads. I don't watch my fishnets, don't check whether the grey will spread before my eyes.

With every passing minute that Tavish doesn't reappear, my anxiety grows like the storm that's blowing in off the horizon, darkening my mood as it darkens the sky with something equal parts ominous and furious. He's not coming. Something happened, and he's not coming.

"We're going to find them." I burst to my feet. Matthia joins me without question.

The wind flares up the tails of my vest and twirls my braids as we push through the plaza. The crowd shoves right back. I hold tightly to Matthia to stop us from being separated, my already tired legs struggling to keep up with her. She notices and slips under my arm, propping her shoulder beneath mine; she might have her grandmother's aristocratic scowl, but she has her grandfather's long limbs. I avoid leaning on her—she's still small compared to my height—but just having her there for balance helps me conserve what little energy I have left. We keep moving.

Someone in the overflowing line grabs their belongings and begins sprinting past the waiting occupants, as though they're planning to charge the foundation entrance. Here and there people follow, cutting and thronging. Officers call over their heads. A shot fires, perhaps into the air, perhaps not. It seems to zip its way down my spine.

Someone shoves into me from my right so hard that it nearly rips Matthia out of my grasp. I pull her closer. We pass the tents where we first found Zuane and the interim chancellors, but none of them are there now, the remaining staff members overwhelmed and outnumbered by the people begging for their help. It feels like a bad omen. I shove my free hand into my pocket for the little hippocamp figurine just to have something to fiddle my excess anxiety into.

My fingers brush it, then paper.

I freeze. Slowly, I draw out the torn piece of a notepad, scribbled words across the top: *Mr. Findlay for the ignation. Tell anyone and he dies.*

A pale, blood-crusted fingernail has been taped below it, the size and shape of—

Bile surges up my throat. I lean over, trying not to heave as my mind blends memories—Lilias's boot in Tavish's side, blood painting his face, bruises across his ribs—and visions of his fingers splayed out, the tender skin he always picks at around his nails oozing.

Luca vibrates through my head, his threads twisting stronger around mine as he, too, panics.

'I'm scared,' he whispers, the words barely realized beneath the pounding of his emotions.

Of my emotions. I'm feeding it into him. The way he's fed me his love for Venalt, I'm giving him my love for Tavish and everything that currently brings with it, all the fear that he might suffer, that I might lose him. That whether he understood it or not, I was always his worst option.

I have to fix this.

Luca shudders beneath the weight of my determination. A whimper bursts from him, his threads struggling in my grasp. In horror, I realize that I'm drawing from his energy to give myself the strength to handle this. It hurts to pull back, to let go, but I force myself to as far as I'm able.

I'm sorry, I didn't mean to.

I expect him to jerk away, but he seems to stare instead, tight and anxious, and finally his threads tighten back around mine. *'We must save them.'*

He doesn't say whom, but I feel it, the breath of his love encompassing Tavish and expanding out to the far reaches of the city. All our fear still lurks beneath.

I try to wrap my emotions up in my chest. It just seems to rile them like a tornado, my guilt and panic combining into something worse. I shake with enough vitriol that I nearly lose the paper as someone else rushes past Matthia and me, their overstuffed bag shoving me off-balance.

Who could have known we were looking for the ignation? Tavish was with Iseppa, and she never returned either. Because she set this up or because she's trying to find Tavish, too? My suspicions churn in my gut, but there was such a crowd when we spoke to Zuane and Iseppa, and no way to know whom Iseppa or her staff told while looking for the key. It could be anyone. Anyone willing to torture the person I love most in the world to get to me.

"Rubem?" Matthia's voice is a tiny thing, nearly whipped away by the gusting wind. She stares at the fingernail. Her throat bobs. "They'll hurt Uncle Tavish?"

I want to say they won't, that it's an empty threat. But if there is any possibility that it isn't, then I have to assume it's the route they'll choose. "Yes. They'll hurt him."

"But the ignation . . ."

"I know." I feel on the brink of falling apart, but somehow Matthia's presence keeps my voice calm and gives my thoughts a semblance of rationality. So long as I have her to watch out for, I can't break.

"Why would they take him?" Matthia spits the words like venom, her tone so Findlay that it hurts. "They could just find the ignation themselves."

"I suspect they thought it would be safer and faster to hurt someone to get what they wanted." It stings just how often that method works, how often aggression is faster and easier than compassion.

She nods. "I have to come."

I grimace, but one look at the state of the crowd, and I don't see another option. Even if she gave me instructions to the house and descriptions of her mother's room, I feel even less comfortable leaving her in this place with the masses stoked nearly to a frenzy and the only government staff already drowning under their workload. If she's with me, at least I can protect her.

"You have to do as I say, you understand?"

She nods earnestly.

We run toward the Viscardi house.

Luca desperately desires to slam himself through the walls and meet me there, to find Tavish and cradle him the way he wants to cradle his city, his people's reactions be damned. But with each second that feeling grows, I sense the weakening of his song, its roar turning into static. He tugs at my energy as I did with his, the subconscious pull forcing me to cut him off after a moment.

You have to focus on the hippocamps. My fear trembles between us. I can't risk him losing control of his song. *I'll find a way to save Tavish without giving up the ignation. Just hold on.*

Luca wavers in thought. His presence shifts and his song falters, but it returns as he comes to a conclusion. *'I'll tell Teodor.'*

My stomach lurches. I don't want her brought into this. I don't want her hurt by this, too.

But Luca is already pulling away from me as his physical body courses through the foundation circle to wrap himself back toward the lagoon. I don't have to be woven into his consciousness to know this isn't something he'll back down on.

Matthia and I keep rushing, doing the best we can to push our way through the crowded streets. Every officer we pass, I fight the temptation to take their weapon or tell them to follow me at a distance, but either one will cause more trouble than it's worth. Why didn't I replace the pistol we lost in Roekia? My lack of a firearm, or at least a knife, seems like a terrible oversight. But my greatest strength has always been my aurora flesh. Until now.

I swear the grey woven through it aches, a tired, hungry tug that seems to pull the rest of me into it. I quicken my pace, shoving and darting between people as though I'm at risk of fading away before I can save Tavish. The streets grow denser the nearer I move toward the foundation circle, until Matthia pulls us down an empty, dead-end side street that wraps in an arc around the foundation circle, and the bustle turns into a hush.

Fancy stone buildings rise to one side, the gilded and ornate roofs of the Basilica peeking out behind them, and on the other, a central island of trees cuts along the channel, secluding the manicured porches and flowering balconies of the wealthiest of Venalt's residences. Even they aren't home, their houses dim and their luggage long gone, probably some of the first to be escorted into the foundation circle. However better this city treats its poorer citizens compared to places like Maraheem, greed still exists here.

I hold Matthia back as we approach the entrance to the residence with a placard labeled *Viscardi*.

Its brass knobs don't budge, but I keep pushing. Instead of snapping the lock the way I did at the Citadel holding cell, the action just pulls energy from me in painful drags that feel as though it's scraping away my marrow. I ease off, gasping as I lean against the door. Pressing my palm to the keyhole, I try to wind a piece of my aurora flesh through it, but the moment it peels up, the rainbows within the tendril's blackness turn into ash. I shudder. My knees wobble.

From the window to my right comes a crash.

Matthia stands beside it, scraping away the leftover glass with a statue nearly half her size, the base of its feet propped against her hip as she widens the hole she's made. She shrugs at me. "It's my house."

I chuckle, though the sound grates a bit against my throat.

We climb through the broken window, crunching the glass into the carpet on the other side. Thin white sheets drape the couches and conceal paintings that have been pulled from the walls, leaving the place a haunting realm of shadows and ghosts in the dim light. I look for Tavish's red curls around every turn, behind the spectral silhouettes of covered furniture and out the wide, dusty windows. He won't be here. But I still look.

I try to envision him and Alasdair twelve years ago, the chandeliers clean and sparkling above a younger, more carefree Fiordelise who laughs at Alasdair's jokes while her mothers introduce him around, Tavish constantly pushed to the side. Perhaps this was where Teodor came in, grumbling about parties and suggesting they find something better, the two of them slipping out as Alasdair flaunted the Findlays' ignation at everyone who would look.

Now Alasdair is dead, Fiordelise is dead, and Teodor is dying. I try not to see a pattern there.

Matthia leads me up the stairs and along a bridge-like landing over the foyer. Her mother's old room is spacious and just as covered in sheets as the rest of the house. I draw back one from the dresser to find perfume bottles arranged neatly beneath, half the drawers still filled with clothes. Matthia looks under the bed, shuffling through things as I open the closet.

What if it's not here? What if she got rid of it? The thought hurts so much that it splits me apart, half of me terrified of what that will mean for Tavish and the other half dreading what will happen if we can't power Tavish's brooch and transform the hippocamps. Tavish's brooch, which is still on him. But it's not as though I ever planned to let him go.

'We'll figure it out,' my human half says.

Like we've figured out everything else? He doesn't deserve the anger and the guilt any more than I do, but we're both feeling it with each box we tug down from the closet shelf and each drawer we yank open. *If we weren't so exhausted, or if we didn't let it get the better of us, then no one would have been able to kidnap him like that.*

My other half has no reply.

Matthia enters, pushing the door open wide enough to get a look at what I've pulled to the floor for her. Her brow knits, but she yanks open the next container I lower before I've even set it down. We peel through the memorabilia inside. Toward the bottom of the box, a black-and-white photo catches my attention. My breath trembles as I pull it out.

It looks just like my imaginings. Alasdair beams at Fiordelise's side, his hair slicked back on top and curling out around his ears, his face long and mouth large like his father, his lips a little crooked in a way that seems equal parts charming and devious. Fiordelise barely smiles, but her chin is lifted in a way that rivals Alasdair's smirk, and her hand lingers so close to Alasdair's that they could almost be touching. This picture must have been cut out of a larger version, because I can still see part of Tavish. It drops my heart out of my chest: his awkward, stiff posing, his cane tucked close, his head down, and his scarf bundled around his ears as though he might hide behind it. He looks about the weight he is now, but the teenage him seems to be trying to appear smaller where my Tavish now flaunts himself, taking up every bit of the space he deserves to inhabit.

But this younger, shier Tavish isn't entirely foreign, either. The longer my gaze refuses to tear itself away, the more I recognize of this teenager hidden within the man I first met in Maraheem. In the years between this picture and our first encounter, he took on the façade of a Findlay, but in the weeks since he killed his mother, he's become a Findlay fully—the kind of Findlay this world deserves, just as charming and exacting as Alasdair but wrapping his brilliance in compassion. Even if he can't see it for himself, I do.

And I love him for it.

A rim of moisture rises to my eyes so thick I have to wipe it away. I adore this perfect Findlay with everything in me, and someone had the cruel, foolhardy impudence to hurt him. As I set the picture to the side, a note slips from behind it, Fiordelise's name scrawled across the front.

I unfold it, reading as quickly as I can manage.

I tuck the note aside for Matthia and scramble through the last few items in the box, searching for the piece of Alasdair's heart—the ignation. But it's not here. Beyond the dried flowers and the cuts of twine and hair and a handful of other cards from people in Fiordelise's life, I find nothing.

No ignation.

I press my palms across my forehead, staring at the content we've emptied onto the floor as though that will make the vial Matthia found as a young child reappear.

"Where is it?" she mutters, her face pale.

Fiordelise could have easily thrown it out or given it away, stashed it somewhere in her apartments at the Institute or sold it off to the highest bidder. It could be miles away or dissolved into the sea, leaving me right back where I started this morning but with Tavish in the hands of a monster and Luca twice as weak as before.

No, no, it has to be here. I burst to my feet only to sway as a wave of exhaustion rushes over me. It brings an idea with it. Breathing out, I lean into my weakness, focusing on the way it drags me down, on how each breath seems harder to draw than the last, and it takes effort just to ignore the constant tugging in the back of my mind that tells me to give up, to drown myself in alcohol until the world slips away. Wine won't help with this, but something else would: ignation.

If I can just lean into that need . . .

As I move through the room, the nearby power tickles behind my eyes. For a moment, it seems like the ignation I'm seeking is in two places, both on the dresser to my right and somewhere across the room. When I try to focus on them, I feel something else, too: a subtle heartbeat, weaker than Luca's and nearer. It all cuts out as my hand slides around the dresser's third perfume vial. The power within it flares against my palm, begging me to get close enough to draw its energy into myself.

Carefully, I uncork the top. The liquid within shines a bright silver, its rainbow glimmer streaked ever so slightly in a grey like ash. It's enough to fill Tavish's brooch with some to spare. If I could just take a little for myself, there would still be some left; how am I supposed to rescue him if I don't have the strength to?

"Rubem?" Matthia's diamond voice breaks me from the spiraling thoughts, and I slam the cork back in place just as she tries to fold herself over my arm to see inside. "Is that it? Is that the ignation?"

"It is," I whisper.

We both jump as rain hits the windows.

"Come on." I take Matthia's arm in mine, trying not to lean on her more than I have to.

The house feels dimmer than it did even minutes before, so little light coming in that it could almost be dusk outside. It creaks in the storm, each silhouetted furnishing turning into a lurking fiend in the darkness. When we move to the landing that overlooks the foyer, even the giant two-story windows that show off the Basilica on the far side of the channel barely brighten the space. But what they do let in is just enough to highlight the two people stepping forth from the darkness across from us.

My eyes immediately go to Tavish, my heart launching itself against the front of my rib cage like it might break free and rescue him all on its own. His hands are bound in front of him, and a cloth gag fills his mouth. From the third finger of his right hand, blood has congealed where his nail should be, drops of it splattered down his pants. He's held from the side by a cloaked human, their cowl pulled down and their scarf covering the lower half of their face. They press a small knife near the side of his neck, his blood already staining it.

"Don't hurt him," I growl.

Tavish reacts to my voice with sharp, short sounds like he's calling my name, only his captor forces the knife harder against his skin, and he goes still but for the curling of his fingers, leaving a fresh red streak on his suit jacket.

"You have the ignation?" The speaker's voice is a high, rough form of androgynous that could be their natural speech or a purposeful modification. They aren't the person holding Tavish, but a figure cloaked by the darkness that obscures the top of the stairwell. The one in charge of this— perhaps in charge of all of it. They're keeping themselves purposefully concealed, I assume, but what are they hiding? Their height, their tentacle legs, their crest of feathers, or the lack thereof?

I bare my teeth despite having nothing to bite with, no threat to make. Or perhaps because of that. It's always been because of that. "I have it here."

"Show me."

I do, uncorking the perfume and holding it low enough that the glow of the ignation can be seen in the dimness. It calls to me so loudly that I have to close it again to keep from accidentally consuming it here and now and ruining any salvation it might provide Tavish or the city. "Why are you doing this?"

"To be rebuilt, Venalt must first sink."

"Is this about the fucking prophecy?" I almost laugh. "I can't raise it after, you know! When it sinks, it'll be gone. But we could save it with this. We could stop the hippocamps from being a threat."

"Venalt as it is threatens itself more than the hippocamps. They're a symptom of a deeper problem. It must sink."

It sounds like Fiordelise's reasoning, that the city needs to be rebuilt better whatever the cost. No wonder they joined forces. "You'd risk all those lives—all their homes—"

"It *must* sink." Like an exclamation point, a piece of metal hurdles out of the darkness. It clatters at my feet. "Bend it."

I pick it up. It's stiff and thick, perhaps the end embellishment to a curtain rod, and I see what Tavish's captors means to gain from this: they want me exhausted. The fact that I already am is the worst kind of irony. "I can't."

"You will."

Tavish draws in a sob behind his gag as the blade presses harder to his neck. I make the same sound, but lower and snarled. With whatever twinges of strength I still have, I bend the metal. The world splotches and blurs around me, my knees giving out. Matthia catches me with a yelp. She says my name, but it bounces listlessly off my ears for a moment before ringing back into focus.

Beyond her, the captor from the shadows says, "Roll the ignation to us."

"Tavish first," I growl, the contrast almost pathetic as I cling to Matthia to keep from falling the rest of the way to the ground.

"You do not look to be in a position to bargain."

They're right, and I want to murder them for it, if only my head wasn't swimming with quite so much vigor. I slip onto my knees and roll the ignation down the landing. It veers off course a little more with each revolution, bumping into the rail a few paces away from Tavish's captor. They let him go, darting to grab it before it can fall over the edge.

An oddly familiar sound breaks across the room, and it takes my brain a moment to piece it all together: the bang of a distant gun, the crack of the glass, the sudden inhale of pain all so similar to our first meeting with Fiordelise. This time no bloody wound materializes in the victim's stomach, but they jerk back, pressing a hand to their arm as they release a feminine shriek.

In the stone floor of the foyer gleams a little pink bullet.

I try to launch myself across the landing toward Tavish, but my knees buckle under me. Matthia screams my name, clutching at my shirt in a failing attempt to pull me back up. "Rubem, Rubem, don't die, please, you can't die."

I'm not, I try to say, but I think it's all in my head. All in our head.

'We're not dying yet.'

We force ourself back together, clinging to Matthia and the foyer-side railing. Tavish's captor—the one the ignit bullet nicked—drags him back toward the stairs. Their hidden companion joins them from the shadows. I still can't make out the speaker well enough to guess at their species, all three of them turning into fumbling blurs as they force Tavish down the steps toward the foyer. He screams through his gag. But I can't reach him.

As I lean there against the railing, Matthia frantically trying to hold the rest of my weight, my gaze latches to the pink ignit bullet buried in the foyer's stone floor. I can almost feel the hum of its power from here, can almost touch it. I *need* to touch it.

Better this than nothing.

With a heave that seems to rip pieces of myself loose from my bones, I drag myself over the landing's railing and drop. I black out before I hit the ground.

In the darkness, a song flutters through me, filling me, coming from *within* me. The sister from my aurora past echoes it. She sits beside me, her light so near to mine. A memory, I realize, or something like it. I'm still falling, or I've already fallen.

'Don't you get it?' she says. *'They will never understand you. They will never care about this place the way you do. They will never help you save it, because they don't want to.'*

I feel the dread taking root, then and now. But she's wrong. After all that I've done to get this far, she has to be wrong.

My sister flickers out as our song shifts. A whole chorus comes with it, pounding like the drums of war, like a human heartbeat in human ears. My dread turns into a visceral, painful thing, as though a blade is being stabbed through me, in and out and in and out. She was right. In the end, I fixed nothing of the world my aurora half has come from.

I failed that place.

We will not fail this one.

The cold of the foyer's stone floor lights up along my side, the first thing to return in a sea of numbing darkness. Within it, a little blaze of power churns. I reach. My fingers close around the ignit bullet.

Power explodes in my chest. It ripples through me, hot and bright, lighting me up from the inside. My muscles still ache, and my lungs protest every breath, but the room solidifies around me. I pull myself to one knee.

Tavish and his captors clamber down the final few steps. The one who held a knife to him earlier grips his arm while the other huddles behind him, hidden from view. They hold Tavish's cane, and with each step, it clanks as though they're putting weight on it. As though they can't walk without the added support.

The visible captor curses and pulls Tavish to a stop at the foot of the stairs. The great sitting room windows behind them turn their figures into shadowy silhouettes, but I catch the shine of the blade as they lift it once more.

I shout, "Cane, left elbow!"

Wrists still bound, Tavish shoves his elbow back and grabs the top of his cane right out of the hands of the captor behind him. He rips it free, sliding its hidden sword from its sheath as he spins. The captor with the knife keeps coming after him despite his weapon.

I spring at them, grabbing their wrist and twisting roughly. They yelp. The knife slips from their fingers as they try to writhe away from me, turning themselves directly into the path of Tavish's sword in the process. It slices into their stomach. Their former cry turns into a scream, and they drop to their knees, nearly taking Tavish and me down with them.

As they slump over, their cowl falls back and their scarf sags.

From the stairs, Matthia gasps. "But that's . . ."

It's Matthia's Basilica guardian. I don't even know her name, and all this time she's been one of the people trying to sink the city. But she wasn't the mastermind behind it all.

A crash echoes through the lofty space, and the wind gusts in, swirling my braids and pelting us with massive, chilled raindrops. I catch only the blur of Tavish's other captor as they dive into the channel, leaving their companion to bleed at our feet. Tavish slumps beside her.

He tears his gag free with shaking hands. "Oh, trenches, Rubem."

"She's still breathing." I shove my hands into her pockets, already wet with blood. No ignation. My fingers come away smeared in red. Fuck. "Hold a compress to her stomach. I have to go after the other one."

Tavish doesn't respond. He trembles harder, his breath coming in ragged gulps as he pats weakly at the woman's stomach wound. Matthia rushes in beside him. She grabs his hands, bunching up the woman's cloak and helping Tavish press it against the bleeding.

"We can do this. We can do this," she whispers like a mantra. When she seems to realize I'm still there, her head shoots up. Her voice turns into diamond as she snaps, "Go!"

I don't want to leave her here—I don't want her to have to go through this again, much less to be responsible for it. But I'm responsible for the whole city, and the key to its salvation is getting away. I take a step, but then I look back. "Are you sure—"

This time both of them shout together, two Findlays glaring at me with the same anxious scowl that could cut through anything, "Go!"

"Yes, fine!"

I race across the sitting room to the broken windowpane. A smear of a dark metallic liquid coats one of the long pieces of glass that still sticks out from the bottom. I tear it off and tuck it into my pocket. With one last glance back, I plunge into the murky channel beyond in search of the person who dared hurt Tavish, and Luca, and this entire city.

CHAPTER TWENTY-SEVEN

the goddess of wild shit

THE CHILL OF THE water hits me like an electric shock, overwhelming me for an instant before my aurora flesh warms to block it out. Beneath the choppy, wind-tossed surface, the hazy world is calm and quiet. On one side, the channel ends at the foundation circle, its tunnels barred by fragile gates. Along the other, the nereid-built versions of the wealthy homes hang down from the city's corelium supports. Twisting metal pillars hold their layers up, the smaller set atop the larger ones, crossed rods of glass in place of windows, and thin, plantlike curtains drifting in the gentle currents. With the electric lamps out and the storm choking the sun above, only the scattered bioluminescent lights still shine, indistinct twists of blue and green in the dimness.

My braids swirl around me as I float there, searching for Tavish's captor. I catch the last glimpse of their black cloak as they pull themselves under the massive metal enclosure of an underwater garden to my right, swimming in the direction of the main channel. I burst after them. My clothing flutters and catches around my limbs, slowing me down. I grab the garden's fence to pull myself under. Its coral boxes shimmer with the ornamental gold the Basilica favors, ropes of kelp tangling up the sides of the little encaged courtyard.

As I shove off the other side, I'm still so far behind Tavish's captor that they're a puff of dispersing blood and a billow of dark clothing.

They could still be anyone. But at the rate they're swimming . . . Iseppa was the most logical suspect until now, since she was with Tavish when he was taken. But she isn't the only one who knows where Tavish was going and what he was retrieving.

It's still too much conjecture though. I need proof.

Tavish's captor speeds toward a massive underwater structure hanging below the rest. Its glass windows flaunt breathable air within, and an elevator seems equipped to pull itself in and out of an upside-down tower off one side. Above me, the hull of a boat skims around the corner of the channel, moving the same direction. Through the shine of the surface, I can just make out the blur of the driver lifting something long and dark. They aim it toward my target.

A bubble trail bursts by my target's shoulder, just missing them. No pink ignit sinks into the sea below them—it must have been a regular bullet. But this is still clearly the same shooter from earlier. The shooter who killed Fiordelise.

They veer their boat away as they reach the path that wraps around the building above.

I ignore the ache in my lungs and keep swimming. Ahead of me, my target swims past the dormant elevator and into the upside-down tower. I follow them. Each kick grows harder the farther I move from the surface, my muscles protesting in fits of pain. But the longer my target is out of my sight, the more anxious I become, pushing myself faster and harder.

As I enter the inky blackness inside the tower, I shift to my aurora vision, outlining everything in silver. My desperate lungs scream at me to turn back—I don't know how long it'll be before this passage opens to the air again. But whomever I'm chasing, they'll have to breathe soon, too. Unless they're a nereid.

I finally break the surface and gasp. Through the veil of my aurora vision, I catch the final remains of a faint glow as it disperses into the water. A spark of power tingles along my skin, seeping into me, and Luca's presence mingled through mine immediately siphons it up. I don't want to blame him, but I can't help it as I'm forced to drag myself, tired and gasping, onto the landing where the elevator would have let out nereid passengers. My soaked clothes stick to me, and my sopping braids bounce against my back as I run down the connected stairwell.

It opens to the inside of the glass room I'd seen from the channel. The dim light from the water barely penetrates the space, its square viewing benches mere shadows against the windows. On the other side of the room, a second set of stairs ascends toward the street. It echoes with the sound of stumbling.

Teodor emerges at the bottom. She freezes at the sight of me, leaning heavily against her cane. Her brow lifts, and her lips part around her coughing gasps. The rifle strapped against her back bobs with each exhale.

All this time, Luca has been quietly thrumming with worry as he watches from a distance, but he blares a sudden wave of surprise at me. He warned her something had happened, hadn't he? Somehow, he got across enough information to bring her to the Basilica roof, to get her a clear shot at the people who worked with Chancellor Fiordelise: Matthia's Basilica guardian and the one I assume is their new leader. The one we just lost.

Teodor curls her fingers into a fist. My gaze flashes to it, and I don't need to see the pink glow that shines through the cracks in her fingers to feel the pulse of the inactive ignit she's clutching, small as a bullet but still burning with power.

Her gaze slips around the room. "Where are they?"

There are no other stairs or hallways, just a closed maintenance door. I try to drag it open, but it won't budge. "The handle's wet."

"It'll open with a key from the Institute."

"Fuck." This close to the brink of exhaustion, there's no way I can open it with strength alone. Luca's power sits at the edge of my perception, and for a moment, I almost reach for it, steal of his life in the hopes of saving it later. But as I step back, my foot hits something small and round. It rolls away from me. My heart leaps. I snatch the vial, but the moment my fingers find the top, the floor seems to fall out from under me. Empty. It's empty.

Of course it is.

The burst of strength as I broke the surface of the tower, the glowing sheen that quickly vanished from it—that was my ignation disappearing into the sea. Tavish's captor had just been waiting for the right moment to dump it out.

Luca responds to the knowledge with a low keening, and I feel pieces of his threads snapping off mine as he struggles to keep up with his song while still offering part of his attention to me. Gently, I wind myself deeper into him, giving him support where I can. I can feel the bulk of my power—the burning light that keeps me alive—drawing toward him. He draws toward me in return. But the closer he gets, the more his presence seems to tug like he might eat the whole of me alive without realizing it. I twist our threads to stop the progression. I'm too tired to give him anything, much less everything.

Too tired, and still failing this city.

If I were stronger or faster, I might be charging up the stairs, finding wherever the maintenance shaft lets out—and whoever comes out of it—in the crowded streets, or at least glimpsing their identity even if I couldn't catch them. But I am not that strong right now. There's nothing more I can do but this.

I drop onto one of the benches, releasing a sigh that sounds suspiciously more like a sob as I drag it back in. "Fuck."

Teodor settles on a bench farther down, her expression hidden in the shadows. Her fingers loosen around the ignit in her palm. "I guess I can give this to Luca now." An odd twist of emotion hangs in her rough voice, complex and unreadable. She is complex and unreadable, too, I suppose.

"You murdered Fiordelise, didn't you?" It feels like the wrong question, both for Teodor and for the city. I'm lost beneath it, but I don't know what else to ask, just as I don't know what else to do.

"Of course I did." All the tension seems to go out of Teodor, her posture wilting as she wraps an arm around her stomach. "She'd killed another chancellor and was going to kill my best friend—my only friend, since I've been sick—and sink my city out from under me, but I couldn't get proof. I had to do something."

The defense twists a knot in my gut. I glare out the great glass windows to the murky waters of the stormy sea. Through their haze I can barely make out the next line of nereid buildings, like shadows in the darkness. "I thought you said that wasn't your place, enacting justice without evidence."

"It isn't." Teodor drags in a breath like she means to add more, then lets it out slowly. "But I did it anyway," she says. "I was backed into a corner, and I made a choice. I did what I thought was best with the few options I had."

The memory of Fiordelise's stomach forming into its component parts makes me nauseous. My gaze tugs back to the pink of the bullet in Teodor's fist. "What you did was brutal. I saw her, it separated her into pieces—"

"She had passed out!" Teodor snaps. "Fiordelise always fainted at the first sign of an injury, it was a joke at the Institute. Her secretary could get a paper cut, and she'd be light-headed for the rest of the day."

I want to tell her that it doesn't make a difference, that she still did what she did. But my telling her won't make a difference either. Justifications trying to bandage a wound on a three-day-old corpse. I swallow, diverting to a new question instead. It's still not the one I need. "Did you know Tavish and I were there when you shot her?"

Teodor's shoulders droop a little farther. "She was supposed to be alone. I realized she'd brought someone back to her office with her, but I couldn't see your faces from where I was sitting. If I'd known you were an aurora, that you could destroy the ignit, I wouldn't have taken the chance." She draws her remaining ignit bullet up, twisting it in front of her face like she's looking for an answer in it. Or maybe the right question, like me. "I still should have waited, but I was tired, and at some point, Luca would have noticed how long I'd been gone."

"So you just shot her anyway? The whole Citadel investigation . . . Who knows you did it?"

"Only Zuane. He caught me just after I'd shot her."

It lines up, all the pieces rearranging in my head, the same evidence slotting into a new place. It's why he acted so suspicious, why he didn't want me to look into anything. He had been trying to thwart me all this time, not to harm Luca, but to protect Teodor. "He's been covering for you."

Teodor nods, slowly. "He hates the lack of justice." Her lips curl, but instead of a smile, they form a thing that's half guilt and half bitterness. "But my sickness has let him run most of the Citadel recently, and condemning me would force a new election for chancellor—someone who won't be him, not with how many people he's pissed off in the last decade—someone who will take over the chancellor's role in ways I haven't been doing for weeks. That's what I told him, anyway. It's probably even true."

That riles me somehow more than everything else—that this thing has spilled out from just three chancellors killing each other to affect so many others. "Fiordelise has an incredible daughter, you know that?" I bare my teeth, bright as the warmth that pounds in my chest as I think of Matthia. Luca echoes the sentiment, a little more numbly but with just as much love for this single, small member of his city. "She's a smart, brave girl who had to watch her mother die, who's going to feel like it was her fault for the rest of her life, no matter how often she tells herself there was nothing she could have done."

Teodor has the decency to grimace. "I'm sorry about that, truly." She tips her head, wiping at her mouth with the back of her hand. She stares at it a moment, as though it's wrong. It is wrong, I realize, smudged in darkness even though she never coughed. With a sigh, she brushes the stain away and slowly stands. "Any more questions?"

I rub my hand down my nose, digging into skin with the stumps of my fingers. My exhaustion feels complete now, as though this has taken my emotional energy the way my swim here took my physical strength. "What am I supposed to do with you?" I whisper. It's the right question, finally—I realize it the moment I say it, the words filling up my lungs then leaving them deflated after. "What do I do with you, my dear Teodor?"

A little laugh comes from her, joyless and maniacal, but it turns almost instantly into a cough that rattles her chest and leaves her hunched over, shaking. Tears slip down her cheeks. She doesn't wipe them away, only heads for the stairs.

I jog after her, taking them one step ahead. "Teodor."

She stares past me and continues to climb. At the top she pushes open the door to the exterior. The pounding rain and panicked shouts press in through the crack, elbows and shoulders and knees visible as those still trapped outside the foundation circle shove toward its entrance a block away. Teodor tries to leave. I put my arm out to stop her.

"Let me go, Rubem."

"I don't know if I can."

She looks at me, finally, rolling the ignit in her palm around with one finger. "Luca's going to die. Not in days now, but in hours. He shouldn't be fading like this; we always thought it'd be me first. It's too fast." She closes her palm so tight her ghostly knuckles strain. "He's all I have left. If I can't kill the people responsible for this, then at least I need to be with him when it happens."

She doesn't wait for me to respond.

With a shove far stronger and faster than I would ever have expected from her, she forces her way past me, into the crowd beyond. I stumble, gripping the side of the door to right myself, my mind struggling to catch up. She's too weak for this, *should* be too weak.

Her head bobs within the frantic throng as she moves deeper into the street. I could still catch up to her, see that she faces justice for what she did to Fiordelise. To Matthia.

'No.' Luca's voice is soft, drained. The weakness I've felt in him all day seems amplified now, his emotions barely a flutter against mine, even with our threads so tightly wound. *'Please,'* he whispers. *'She's still mine.'* I can feel the subtle twist of pain that comes with the statement. She is his, even when it hurts him. Even after she's done this behind his back, against his wishes, she's still his, in all her frustration and her lashing. Like Venalt, he will protect Teodor, whatever she's done, whatever it costs him.

I'll wait. What good would stopping Teodor do now anyway? She's already committed her murder, and the only other person she'd kill is the one person I already want dead. She can be dealt with after the hippocamps are, after Luca is gone. If there's even an after for either of us.

Without Teodor's presence, this empty place feels haunting—religious. Almost like a crypt, I think. A chill sets over me. My anxiety only intensifies as I slip into the crowd. I've left Tavish and Matthia for far too long already.

CHAPTER TWENTY-EIGHT

knives in the back

THE WIND TEARS AT me, rain plunging like tiny, angry needles into my soaked clothes, and the clouds seem even darker than when I went into the water. The crowd presses tight along the center walkway, thousands of people all herding their way toward the foundation circle. Gondolas pile up at the edge of the channel, knocking together as they push and shove. A nereid swims along them to try cutting into the line farther ahead, but the moment they climb onto the street, someone kicks them back to the water. The wind carries away their profanities.

I slip off into the quiet of the wealthy side road as soon as I can, and break into a jog. The front door of Fiordelise's house hangs open a crack. I fling myself through it, panting as I stumble through the foyer.

A pool of blood puddles in the center of the sitting area, the wind and rain howling through the broken window beyond it, but nothing else moves. The room is empty.

My heart pounds in my ears. I struggle to the stairwell, shouting for Tavish and Matthia. They must have left.

They're not dead. It's not even their blood on the floor. But it's so much blood, so goddamned much, and in it, I see every other drop Tavish has bled, every drop that's clung to him, the red smeared against his face from Lilias's boot and dripping down from his tortured finger. Bile curdles in the back of my throat.

Tavish isn't here, and turning circles won't lead me to him.

Luca's presence emerges within my panic, resonating against it so loudly that it feels like an echo chamber between us. But it's not just Tavish he worries about—I can feel the way he struggles harder with his song as his energy wanes. The threads he's wound through me leach my energy so slowly yet consistently now that he seems not to realize it. I feel bad every time I have to push him away, to conserve what strength I have left. Teodor was right. He's weakening at an alarming speed. It might not kill him yet, not if he stops singing for once, but I can feel from his determination that he'll drain himself dry before he lets harm come to his city.

Plunging back out of the house, I head for the foundation once more. It feels like running in circles. This whole week since arriving in Venalt has been that way, literal loops through bridges and stairways and metaphorical ones as hope for the city's future waxes and wanes. Two steps forward, three steps back.

I nearly trip over a man sitting against a low wall. His legs are splayed out before him, his eyes closed and his head tipped back. Bruises mark his arms, and his chest rises and falls in a lopsided, broken way. I worry that when I nudge his shoulder, he'll slump to the side, unconscious, but he grunts and his eyes open to slivers.

"Did anyone else come through here?" I ask. "A man and a child, perhaps?"

"Haven't seen anyone." He looks as though he wouldn't notice an entire swarm of hippocamps.

I set my palm on his arm. "We should get you to a medical tent."

"No need." He smiles, and the rain drips into his mouth. "The savior's gonna raise up the city soon. We'll all be ascending."

I'm pretty sure any ascending these people are meant to do is strictly metaphorical, but the harder I press him, the more he pushes back. I can't use up my energy saving a man who doesn't believe he needs it. His declaration follows me, though, sinking into each step I take.

What if there's still a chance to save the city, a way we haven't thought of yet? Each empty home that might be gone by tomorrow and every shout and cry of a person left behind makes me more certain: Whatever it takes, I have to do something. Whether it's Luca's love that fuels me or my own, I don't know, just as I didn't know whether any of this—this saving of the auroras—has been caused by my human half's devotion or simply the desires my aurora half supplied us both. I also can't decide how I feel about all this, this collection of loves; the way they ache inside me, demanding things I can't give.

Luca's presence in my mind pitches so hard that my grip on reality sways. Panic fills me. There are so many people still outside the foundation circle, so many preparations that still haven't been completed, so many deaths beyond his own waiting to happen.

Don't fade on us, please, I whisper to him, too soft for him to pick it up in his current state. *We can still fix this.* Not with Teodor's single ignit bullet, perhaps, but somehow. I'm not giving up yet.

I break into the most awkward, gasping sprint I can manage, stalling only when I hit the back of the crowd waiting at the foundation gates. It seems none of them are moving, more like me pressing at the edges, probing and shouting. They cut me off every time I try to step in. Even my most hostile teeth baring does nothing here, where there are more dangerous things than me coming. I wonder if Tavish cut through the crowd with his diamond voice, if he came this way at all. If I can't find him before the city sinks . . .

I un-wonder that, because it churns something in me that feels far too close to an eternal collapse.

As I near the front of the line, the chaos only increases, the aggression turning rampant. A barricade of tall metal sheets like person-high shields blocks most of the entrance, and the Citadel officers letting people in seem more focused on keeping everyone else off the barricade and out of the submerged tunnel to their right than on helping those at the front of the line. Through the few cracks, I glimpse another crowd beyond. So many people, so little room.

I reach for one of the officers. "I need to get in—"

"Step back!" She shoves her baton into my chest, knocking me away as she says it.

I struggle to find my footing, dragging in air through the pain in my chest. Clearly, she doesn't recognize me. "I'm the second-prophecy savior!"

"You and ten other people this hour."

"I'm also an aurora." I bare my teeth, willing the rainbows in my fishnets to shine past the grey streaked there.

She doesn't seem to notice, scowling at me through the rain. "Please step back and wait your turn like everyone—"

Fuck this. I can't wait—and I don't, not even for her to finish. With as much force as I can muster, I force my way through the Citadel line. Power fills me for a heartbeat, a rush of energy strong enough to help me yank free their sticks and slam aside their pistol barrels as they try to shift their aim. I sprint through them, charging into the foundation circle.

The power keeps coming.

Luca screams, dragging it back. His power, I realize. It's him I'm taking from, him I'm burning up to get through the guards. As I let go, he yanks, trying to balance us out again. I give him just enough, just enough that he can turn back to his song, desperate and frantic. Through the tension in this superficial push and pull, I can feel the deep energy we both still carry in the center of our beings. For how weak we are, we have so much power still hidden inside ourselves, as though the core of us—the thing sustaining our very consciousness—takes up many times the strength we use to fight and sing. It reminds me of the aurora who died in Maraheem, how the last of their waning energy was enough to break through dimensions.

Luca latches to the thought, tugging it toward him wordlessly. Tugging *me*. I follow.

Through the sea of pushing bodies, I catch the familiar diamond-edged clip of a Findlay's voice from farther down the street. It's just an instant of it, so distant it could have been an echo; then it's gone.

My heart skips.

The crowd just within the foundation center thins a bit as I keep walking, queues forming like snakes from the entrances of the government buildings on either side of me. A medical pavilion and some kind of evacuee registry have been erected at the split in the road between the Citadel and the Institute. Behind them, a series of makeshift civilian tents are in various stages of being put up or torn down, Citadel officers ushering their removal as the breeze turns into a gale. Even the medical pavilion is in the process of disassembly, I realize, a few patients being ushered out on stretchers headed for the Institute. I glance at them as they pass, searching for red hair and freckles, relieved when the only familiar face I spot is Matthia's Basilica guardian, passed out with an IV.

"Then bring the ship as close as possible!"

My heart stutters as around the corner walks Tavish, shoulders poised and a wrap across his neck and around his injured finger. He sweeps his cane in front of him as though he's prepared to knock down anyone foolish enough to step in his way as he continues berating an Institute administrator and a pair of high-ranking Citadel officers about the transfer of people from the foundation center to the two major Citadel ships. His curls are plastered to his forehead, dripping gently, and his coat is half-soaked through beneath the simple plastic shawl he's wrapped around his shoulders. He has never looked so at ease. So alive.

"Tavish." I might shout it, but it feels like a whisper, rough and uncertain, and it comes with a faint humming just within my skull, like my hearing is about to go out.

His head shoots toward me, his brow lifting. "Good fuck, Rubem." He exhales in a way that seems to let out his worries, and draws in a professional poise to replace them. "Do you have the ignation, then?"

"They dumped it into the sea." My voice sounds as decimated as my chest feels. I try not to let the emotion drown me, but the way Tavish's lips tremble with a shaky breath almost collapses me on the spot. "Who took you? Was it . . ."

I don't say her name, but Tavish seems to understand all the same. "Iseppa was distracted by one of her staff as we reached the foundation circle. I intended to go on ahead, but in the bustle, someone pressed a towel to my nose with a chemical that nearly knocked me out. The conspirator I stabbed was certainly a part of it, but we won't know whom she was working with until she recovers enough to wake."

It doesn't mean that Iseppa wasn't involved, but it still gives us no proof that it was her either. Again, it seems all our efforts are unraveling, no name for the villain trying to sink Venalt and no way to save it. "If this entire city doesn't collapse into the sea first."

"Aye, if that."

I drop my gaze from his face, and it catches on the empty rim of his collar. "Your brooch?"

Tavish lifts his fingers to its usual spot, as though he's realizing it's missing for the first time. He swallows. "They must have taken it as a precaution when they first drugged me in the plaza. I suppose it's no use to you without the ignation anyway."

"Tavish . . ." I don't know what else to add, not anymore. I can't convince him that his heritage is more than trauma and greed if he won't let me.

He hesitates, though, and the breath he drags in seems rougher than the last. But he shakes his head. "Without ignation, it was only a final connection to my family and our cruelty. I'm glad to be rid of it. I'm glad to be rid of *them*."

Our cruelty. It wasn't his, I want to say. Perhaps he ate at their table and tore himself to pieces for their love, but I see the ways that make him just as much a victim as anyone else they harmed. I don't know how to convince him of it, though. I rub my hands down my face. "Where's Matthia? This was her idea, I should be the one to tell her it won't work."

Tavish's brow tightens. "I sent her back to the Basilica, of course. With the other children like her."

"You did what?"

"What else was I to do?" Tavish snaps. "She's not my responsibility."

Of course she's not, and of course he would, but this still feels like a betrayal, like sitting on a boat, alone. I want to cry. It's such an irrational, senseless emotion that it almost gets the better of me before I blink it away, drawing in a steadying breath. The vibration in the back of my mind continues.

I had said we'd talk about this later, and he agreed, but my rebellious heart turns it into here, now, the wrong time and place and somehow the only one.

"She doesn't belong at the Basilica with the orphans. She *has* a family." The moment it's out of my mouth, I wish I'd just buried it all and pretended that I'm not scared half to death for us. This had to be the worst option.

"I can't take her, Rubem, I've told you this." He shakes his head as though the idea is the rain that slips down his face and pools in the dimple of his chin and he might flick it away the same. "She's not mine."

"She's your niece, Tavish! She's a selkie and a *Findlay*."

"Well she shouldn't be!" Tavish snaps. "We have the impeccable ability to ruin our family's lives and stab each other to death! I gave my all for that family, and all I ever—all we ever did together—was cause pain. I left Teodor, I upheld Maraheem's atrocious social structure, I killed my own mother. Matthia should stay as far from me as she can."

This is not about children; this was never about children. I can see it in his face, in his distant eyes clouding over, in the way his fingers flutter toward where his brooch should be sitting on his coat collar.

He sighs, a deep, strained exhale that breaks my heart in two. "If you want her this badly, perhaps we can make something work. But I told you, I can't be her family. She deserves better than that. She deserves someone like you. I hear the way you speak with her. You would be a fine parent."

"No." The vibration in the back of my head grows, like a constant ringing, the too-fast beat of a heart. "No, I wouldn't. I'm fading, Tavish."

"Oh."

The pain on his face is too much. I knew—I knew this would happen, back in Maraheem. I could have left him there, let him move on easier, when we were just a fling, and I was someone he hadn't fallen in love with. It makes me angry, at myself, at him, too—him who left Teodor on that boat ten years ago to be stuck with me as his only option now. "I need ignits to survive, and who is going to want to offer many of them to me? I don't even have a city to belong to, people to repay me for what I've given them. I'm not going to last very long. Matthia needs you. And when you don't have me, you'll need her, too."

"You cannot simply replace yourself in my heart, you ken that?"

"I know. But I love you, so I have to try."

The edge of his lips goes crooked. "We might not even live through this. Perhaps we will die here together instead."

It's not the response I want. Not the one I need either. And it leaves me hollow, brittle, caved in. I have nothing left to say to him, I realize. Not right now.

As the silence between us stretches, the last of the medical pavilion folding in on itself, the hum that haunts the base of my spine comes into focus, a grasping at my energy that's too weak now to siphon it off from this distance. My gut sinks. *Luca.*

He can't respond, not in words, but that faint, panicked hum leaps, pulling me toward him once more.

"I'm rounding up the chancellors and Commander Zuane to that stone structure at the foundation's center," Tavish is saying. "It seems the most logical meeting place; apparently that was its entire purpose once, to conduct forums between all three chancellors and other prominent leaders. If you could retrieve Teodor for me, if she's able to come . . ."

"I'll try," I mutter, already heading for the Citadel, my heart breaking a little more with each step.

CHAPTER TWENTY-NINE

mine and then some

THE PATHS NEAR THE back entrance to the Citadel basement are swamped with people waiting for access into the building. A couple families eye me suspiciously beneath their raincoats and plastic shawls as I twist the hidden lock and slip quickly inside, closing and sealing the door behind me. The sudden quiet beyond comes as a glorious relief. I feel ashamed for it when so many people still wait beyond the circle and huddle in the chill outside, but with the way Luca's consciousness slips and claps, his song vibrating in and out, if I let anything new distract him, it might doom us all. I'm amazed that his gentle leeching off my energy hasn't resumed now that I'm nearer. Amazed, and frightened for him.

He lies across the floor of the basement, breathing in long, tired heaves in the light of a low-burning torch. The translucent lids lift from three of his eyes as I approach, the others struggling and giving up. None of his heads move, only the slight part of his jaw nearest me.

I don't know where Teodor is now, but she should be here. With him. The three of us, despite our mistakes and misunderstandings, together one last time before the whole city collapses.

Luca . . .

'*Home worlder,*' he wheezes into me; even his voice in my head is painful and soft. '*Venalt cannot sink. They are mine, I have to protect them.*' I can feel the indecision in him, his whole being so weak that I can't quite reach beneath the surface of it to find the thoughts it comes with and address them specifically.

Instead, I kneel beside his head, pressing my palm to his nose, and wrap my threads through him, stronger, deeper.

He entwines with me in return, almost frantic. Tugging. Tugging at my energy. '*Help me save them.*'

The moment I feel my power wane, I stop him, tearing back a few pieces of myself in the process. It hurts me to do it, hurts me nearly as much as it must hurt him. *I can't give more than I already am. I'm fading now, too. I don't have enough for both of us.*

'*You must! For the city.*'

It won't help. You need too much energy, Luca. I've seen a lot of dying auroras, and what's happening to you isn't normal—at least not until the very end. The thought alone feels terrible, and the way it hits Luca is even worse, the truth of it mingling with what the ancient creature already knew but was too afraid to admit. *I'm sorry, my friend.*

'*No!*' His head trembles a little at the objection. '*No, I can still save them. With more strength, it will be enough. I will protect them.*'

I press against him with all the certainty and resolve I have. *I can protect them for you. I'm supposed to be their savior.*

'*The gold could have fallen on me!*' His wish that it did blasts me like a storm, like a sob. This was his right, his purpose all his life. And here I've stepped in to take it from him. '*You don't know how to sing. It is my song, you can't learn it. You tried.*'

You're right, I couldn't before. The vibrations coming from Luca feel different since my loss of consciousness at the Viscardi's house, some small, barely perceptible change, but the more I focus on it, the bigger it becomes. I remember the way my aurora half's light once fluttered as I spoke similar songs to life for my sister, gently teaching her the things our parent considered her too weak to learn. The memory pops as quickly as it comes, but the impression remains like a brand on my soul. Beneath every chord Luca sings, I can now sense the ten other blocks that build it, understand the way they interact and the strength of their purpose. *Let me try again. Help me through it.*

Luca recoils, his surprise as stark as his confusion. I feel the piece of him that wants to. The piece of him that hopes I can carry on in his place. The piece that's just as tired as I am, just as envious of the days when we could sleep and dream and die without feeling so drawn back to a world in need of saving.

The gentle thrum of his song spreads into me, deeper than the echoing version that has tingled in my chest since the beginning of this, a living, breathing thing that swells the light inside me. I catch it, every single tiny vibration, building it in myself and letting it go. It feels right—feels as though I'm the one singing. But as Luca pulls back, the chords vanish. Without him, they crash and fall, like the very knowledge of them is slipping from my mind. I reach for it, frantically.

Let me try again, I beg. *I'm still learning.*

But the softness is gone from Luca, blinked out beneath the larger whole of his territorial love. *'These people are mine. I cannot risk you failing them,'* he says, all his grief and all his resolve meeting in something that feels a little too much like guilt. *'We will both fade out sooner or later.'* His consciousness hardens, his threads stiffening with him. *'But at least I can keep them alive a bit longer.'*

My dread quavers in me, telling me to pull away, but Luca's threads tighten, refusing, pulling me closer instead. *Luca . . .*

'They saved me! I have to save them. I must save them.' His explanation comes frantic now, a pounding, roiling thing

like the storm outside and the hippocamps beyond the city limits—barely beyond, now, pressing in with every waver of Luca's song. *'They are mine, Rubem. And I am theirs—I have to be theirs—I will keep protecting them so they know, so they know I love them.'*

So they love me back, he doesn't say. But I feel it, the way I feel so much of him pounding inside my chest. Beneath everything, beneath my love for the Murk that I fought so hard to save even after they hurt me, beneath that, there's something deeper inside me, a place in my aurora past that was mine until the last breath, mine to save no matter how the people there hated me for it. And I wanted them so, so desperately not to hate me. *I understand.*

Luca quiets as he feels the knowledge. *'Perhaps you do,'* he whispers, a thin, aching thing that lodges in my marrow. It grows to a thrum, stiff and braced, a dam about to burst. *'So perhaps you will understand this, too.'*

He does not apologize.

His threads blast through me, into me, wrapping themselves like choking vines and hooked claws. I struggle, but with each twist, he presses deeper. I scramble my physical body away, but the otherworldly ties between us only lengthen to compensate, the size irrelevant of distance now that we're so firmly connected. He feels my panic—he must—but his consciousness is a hard, sharp thing now, unwavering in its course. This city is his. They are his.

With one terrible, determined breath, he pulls from me.

I have lost energy before, lost it as purely an aurora and as purely a human and as both, lost it quickly and slowly, to the weight of a spiraling depression, to sudden, physical overexertion, and to Luca's previous gentle tugs. That was the surface, the stripping down of a layer or two or three, and this is the core, dragged from the center out. My eyes roll, my body a husk held up by puppet strings. My consciousness bleeds.

Between the fraying edges, the strings of my being unraveling from me and into Luca, I understand: this is dying. He's killing me. At the end of this, when the last strand of me is gone, I'll be ash, drifting to the ground, the human and aurora alike dissolved into nothing. Not a savior. Not a lover. Not a guardian. Not anything.

But not yet.

I close in on myself like a fist, stalling Luca's vicious consumption. Someday, I'll be ash—someday, that will have to be fine—but not fucking yet. I have a city left to raise and a hundred thousand people to save, and a man whom I love with every fiber of my being. The vibration of my desire pounds through me, strengthening my threads as I rip myself back from Luca, piece by glowing piece. He thinks this love, this glorious, aggressive love, is his alone, but he's wrong. He thinks he's the only one whose pain can carry Venalt into the future, but he knows less heartache than me, has seen the rise and fall of fewer worlds. He thinks he can take my power to keep Venalt alive, to make them love him.

He thinks he can be strong, but I am stronger still.

I drag at the threads he's woven through mine and at everything he's taken from me, trying to siphon the energy of my core back. It flares behind my lids, but with Luca still gripping it, I can't quite bring it back into my center. I keep pulling, vicious yank after vicious yank. Luca flinches, hardens, and flinches again. Slowly—over an era or a heartbeat—his determination wavers. The solidity of his belief turns brittle. It breaks with a sob.

In a sudden panic, he releases his hooks, and a painful rush of remorse cascades through him. He tries to withdraw his threads back into himself, leaving the very center of my core energy behind but taking everything else with him. Everything that would have kept me fighting. He'd be leaving me alive, perhaps, but weak and useless. Not strong enough.

I grip him harder. Where he hooked into me, I hook into him instead. I pull, hauling the rest of that stolen energy back, cord by cord. He flails, his leviathan body trying to jerk away, but my physical fingers dig into the ashen stripes of aurora flesh on his head, pinning us together on both planes. His alarm turns into horror, then a ragged, feral fear. I feel him waver and slip, his consciousness fragmenting as the energy bundles into my chest. Then, he stills. A thought courses through him, so fast I miss it, but I feel its glow like the sun: love, a love so powerful it's jarring. With a flicker of warmth and a quiet caress, he stops resisting.

'Save them, then,' he whispers. And instead of pulling, he pushes.

The full sense of him bursts through me in flashes and in lifetimes.

I curl within a body of half-submerged sea grass, bobbing beneath the open sky and above the clear, shallow sea, dancing between dreams as I soak in the laughter of the people who love me. And I love them back. I swim through half-constructed tunnels and chambers as those people's tired descendants build the foundation for their new city, and though they flinch when they see me, I love them more still. I hear the cries of their children as the first hippocamp attacks, and I love them so much, that the next time, I drag the beast, still breathing, into my lagoon and weed my threads around it, trying to sense the way its smallest pieces vibrate until I can produce a song that goes against that exact motion, making future hippocamps incapable of approaching. They call me a monster, and despite it, I love them. I love them.

I feel the way every heart in my city beats, every life born, every laugh, and every tear, and I love them from a distance, even as they forget who I was and what I've become. And I suddenly feel split by the sight of one like myself—the other me, hosted in a human, walking up to my lagoon—a surprise. I love this one, too; I just forgot it for a moment, a moment turned into horror and grief and guilt, and then— nothing.

The depth of the emotion throttles everything I thought I knew of Luca's affection, the hints he offered me mere shadows compared to the fully realized thing, glorious as it is terrifying. I bend beneath it, a weight I can never live up to.

Take it back. My lungs tighten, and I shake, the understanding of what's happening hitting me finally. I push, trying desperately to return everything I've gained. But there's no Luca left to receive it. Beneath my fingers, his flesh melts to ash, the final shimmers of his rainbow shriveling up. His eyes stare at me, lidded and unseeing, as spirals of him go brittle and fall away until there's nothing left. A few flecks of gold linger, drifting more sluggishly, as though they haven't quite figured out how to fall yet. Gold from the harbor.

Luca. I shake, lifting my fingers. It seems there should be blood on them, but every hint of him is gone now, even the gilding twinkling itself out. *Oh gods, Luca.*

My sharp, tight breaths feel too small in the massive space. The frantic, wispy heartbeat of another aurora slides along the edge of my perception, looking for Luca. It doesn't find him, because he's dead. Because I killed him. I pulled so hard that he let go, he let it all go—gave himself to me.

I can't breathe, the growing knowledge seems to lodge itself in my chest, the room feeling too empty, too distant around me. I killed Luca. Oh gods.

A clatter breaks the silence.

CHAPTER THIRTY

the dying versus the dying

I WHEEL, SPURRED BY an energy in my chest that's equal parts terrible and intoxicating, to find Teodor standing in the entrance to the stairwell that leads to her apartments. There are no ignits in her hands this time, her cane rolling slowly away from her as she watches me in shock. For a split second, I hope that she didn't see it, doesn't know what just happened; hope it looked like Luca simply faded out, a natural, if terrible death.

But the guilt of it all rushes me, so hot it must sear across my face.

"How could you?" Teodor snarls, low and wet.

"He tried to take my energy. I couldn't . . ." I wave my arm uselessly, like that will make the feeble reply stronger. "I did what I thought was best." The same reasoning Teodor gave for her murder of Fiordelise. It twists in me. The pain is like a dagger, and I want to bow under it, let it break me into pieces. But I am all this city has left without Luca. I cannot abandon them. If not for the prophecy, then for Luca's sake, I have to save Venalt.

Teodor makes no sound as she approaches, the tears that slip down her cheeks dropping quietly as her face contorts. Her fists tighten, and I understand what the shift in her stance means from years of experiencing the same advances by people who didn't like who my human self was or what my aurora self stood for—not merely the threat of violence, but the intent of it. She should be far weaker than me, even without Luca's energy pounding inside me. But I recall her punch earlier, and I'm not so sure.

I stand, lifting my hands. "Teo . . ."

Two of her fingers dart in, wrapping around the back of my wrist. From them come a pressure so unexpected that I stagger as I realize what they are. Aurora threads, brittle and slim, but still the same otherworldly cords that Luca and I had talked through, shared through, fought through. The moment they connect with me, I can feel Teodor's presence the way I felt Luca's, like a gentle pulse, lower and slower, so small it's almost an echo at this point. The third heartbeat. The aurora I thought I'd sensed when we first arrived in Venalt, the one who helped me feed Luca the ignit power in the harbor, the extra presence that has pricked at my mind whenever I extend it too far.

It was Teodor.

The shock stops me from defending myself for only a moment, but it's enough for her to get a foothold, carving gracefully into me. Her threads move with a dexterity and foresight that I'm just beginning to possess. It thrills a part of me to entwine with her. This is what an aurora in a sapient host should become; where I'd be if I survived a few more years, each ounce of power stretched until it's a million times its strength, and each action perfectly calculated and understood, her emotions and memories contained effortlessly behind a barrier I can't break. If she were any stronger, she'd be practically a deity.

But however skilled Teodor is, she's still dying. So much of her is ashen that it seems like there's barely any healthy parts left. And I have the strength of two auroras cradled in my chest. I power through her elegant attacks with sheer force, plunging my threads straight into her. She seizes, her body going still and her consciousness rigid.

I slam her to the ground, tightening my grip on her core, sealing around it until just a pull would rip her energy out. I know what it feels like to have that much extra strength now. She's weaker than Luca, but she's still brighter than a dozen ignits—with the memory of Luca's song and her power added to it, I could hold the hippocamps off for days or weeks—press them back so far we could send help to the mainland. I could save Venalt. Be their second prophecy. Be theirs.

I feel their laughter like sunbeams, their admiration, their love. All I'd have to do is pull.

My threads ache to give one final tug.

Teodor stares up at me—even if I can't sense her emotions, she must feel my desire, my intention. I tighten my threads around her, muscles taut.

'Whatever am I supposed to do with you?' She's a whisper in my head, a phantom or a memory or a premonition.

My heart clenches. I could have been hers, hers and Luca's to love. A family, a thing more messy, more intimate, more beautiful than any other in this world. And I have ruined that already.

My threads shake, then roil, a scream running through them. The first inch I give, she takes back, a skilled kind of shimmy that flips the scales in an instant. I want to combat it, dread flaring in my chest. She attacked first. If I don't take her core energy now, she'll take mine instead. There will be no savior. There will be no me.

Again.

I force myself to loosen anyway. Quietly, gently, I let go of her, sitting my physical body up as I do. I let her dig into me. Her threads shoot and twist, hooking into my core as her body springs forward. She folds her arms around my back, her fingers tightening in the fabric of my clothes.

She sobs there, with her head on my shoulder and pieces of herself wound through the more delicate parts of my soul. Not killing me, not even mourning me, just crying.

I wrap her up, pressing my face into her hair and slivers of my energy into her threads. She could take the rest—she could rip me apart the way Luca tried—but she doesn't. I can't see into her soul or feel the train of her thoughts, but I think I know why. It's the same reason I didn't. Because my actions killed Luca.

He'd stopped fighting back; I could have let him go. And I didn't.

To destroy either of us who remain, for whatever gain or at whatever price, will always be the most terrible option.

We cry together, leaning into each other and letting the pain come. Her wall slowly shifts, glimpses of her emotions peeking through. They're not the impulsive, animalistic urges of Luca, or the hazy, dreamlike fluttering of the auroras with nonsentient hosts, but feelings as recognizable as any of mine.

As we both lapse into silence, the basement seems to grow emptier still. With a jolt of panic, I realize why. Luca's song. Of course it's gone—he's gone. I'm supposed to replace him.

Teodor bursts upright as I think it, her red-rimmed eyes going wide in her pale face, that hint of ash and rainbow just visible beyond her dark irises. She speaks aloud as well as in my head. *'Can you do it?'*

I respond by trying, using the knowledge I've gained of Luca's song from his final moments. With an ache I realize he did that on purpose, made sure to give me the pieces I'd need as I killed him, his love for Venalt still stronger than any anger or vengeance.

The song starts in a part of me that's purely aurora, each bundle of energy-filled threads in the core within my chest beginning to vibrate at a unique tone. Carefully, I break them into sets, like a new instrument being added to an orchestra, producing parts of the song from individual bundles, moving from two sets to four to ten. With each addition, I have to fight harder to keep them all on their own tune. It feels like trying to rub my human head while patting my stomach, but with a thousand heads and ten thousand stomachs and the motions as things entirely foreign to my human half's understanding. My mind shatters a bit trying to hold to a vibration so complex and resounding. It's not quite right still, a slip here and a shutter there, where a certain piece of the song falls out of line for a moment, muddling the whole thing. Even with all this knowledge, I don't have the skill to back it up—not in this body that's functionally only six weeks old.

Teodor weeds her fingers through mine, and in soft, steady beats, she matches the entirety of the song with bundles of her own threads. Her vibrations are weak—too weak, I think, even to leave this basement if she were singing on her own—but as I feel hers thrumming in time with mine, it's as though I'm a student who's gone from singing a note alone to having a teacher there to help me find the pitch. Everything falls into place as Teodor guides me, sharing in the strength I've taken from Luca until we both vibrate with a soundless melody that must reach near to the edge of the city, if not beyond.

It's a complete match for Luca's. Focusing on anything else while still holding it is harder than he made it look, and with every moment we keep up the song, it drains off far too much energy. But for now, between Teodor and I, we manage it.

She sits back, closing her eyes as she coughs into the edge of her shirt. Blackness comes out. Not blood as I assumed, but ash, her lungs turning into the stuff. No wonder she pushed aside my antibiotic idea. There really is nothing of this dimension that can save her now. That can save either of us.

"How long have you been like this?" I ask, using only my human vocals in order to keep from accidentally disrupting the song. I don't know how Luca could thread-speak so easily while maintaining it. My heart twists.

Teodor's lips pinch. "It's been about eight months since the fading started."

"And before that?" My gaze drifts from her eyes, across her pallid skin, to the lip of her high collar, always buttoned so tightly to the very top.

She undoes it, pushing aside the loops of bow-like fabric at her collarbone and worming apart tiny button after tiny button. As the front comes open, I see them clearly: thick and ashen and cutting through her skin like dark tentacles. "Four years now. The human part of me went searching across the mainland a few times before she found a place where they weren't properly guarded. It took my aurora part some convincing to actually bond."

"Me too—except it was my human half who was hesitant." I smile, a graceless, awkward thing that sticks in the tearstained crevasses of my face.

She mirrors it perfectly. I can see that very faint shine of the rainbow in her eyes better and better now that I know what I'm looking at. They're beautiful.

"Why didn't you tell me?" I ask.

"Luca was the one who trusted you, not me." It sounds like a joke, but there's a very serious edge to it, something that cuts right into my guilt and leaves it on full display between the threads she still has wrapped around my core. She looks to her fingers, sighing as she slowly buttons her shirt back up. "I hadn't told anyone except Luca, not the entire time I was healthy, and then when the sickness set in—months before Luca's—I had even less of a reason. I was dying. No use making connections that would break so soon. Though you just kept worming yourself in there anyways. You're trouble." She runs a hand under her eye, such a quick swipe that I can't tell if she's pushing aside old tears or new.

"How long had Luca known?"

"Luca was the reason I went to find an aurora in the first place. There's only so far you can get with a nod-once-for-yes, twice-for-no conversations, and I . . . wanted more." Her gaze wanders, skipping over the lagoon where Luca had lain and tucking back around. "For me, but also for him. I needed him to know there was someone who loved him that much."

She would have given him her core. Had I been a little later and her a little sooner, it would be Luca mourning her right now, and not the other way around. It's not a consolation, just another misery. So long as we were forced down this path, one of us was always going to die.

She laughs, the brittle sound turning into a series of coughs. "You know, I never told Luca to keep that I was aurora a secret? I'm a bit surprised it didn't come out by chance. His thoughts were always so loud and wild."

"He said he couldn't feel you the way he felt me. I thought he meant it was because you weren't an aurora and I was." I rub my halved palm along my nose, shaking my head. "But it was because you're more barred off."

She's not quite so barred off now, though, and I catch the faintest flicker from her: a teenager pacing the length of a boat, waiting for Tavish to arrive. To tell her that he loved her. It's gone in an instant, but the imprint lingers on my heart, leaving it to ache as though burned.

Teodor flinches, a physical retreat as much as an emotional one.

"There's a tradition among my people to give the dead and the living alike a blessing upon their passing," I say. "If you'd like, I can offer one for Luca."

"Please" is all she can seem to say.

I drag in one breath, then another. Luca has no corpse to make the sacred motions over, nothing left of him to give back to the world. It feels like a profanity. My hands tremble, but I run them quietly through the full length of the Murk's death proclamation, a whisper of the signs echoed between the two halves of myself. "We mourn for a life, both taken and given, for the dousing of a spark, unique, never to be replicated." There will truly never be another like Luca, or like Teodor and me, and that we found each other, even for this short time, is a wonder. "We mourn for the loss, the tear it forms within the world, the rip in the heart of each who feels the absence." I feel it now, the empty place where Luca's heart should beat. "We mourn for the love that was to come, for the dances cut short, the relationships severed by an unbreachable divide."

Teodor gives a strangled sob, but waits for me to continue.

"May you, Luca, protector of Venalt, may you find peace as full as the quiet of the womb. May the tears of those who weep for you become one with the foundation that bears this city aloft. May the fruition of your life, your love, and your loss carry those you left behind, guiding them into the future. We proclaim you ours, in life and in death." Ours, forever.

"Be at rest," I whisper.

"Be at rest," Teodor echoes within me.

In the thralls of our grief, the thrum of the song that bounces between us wanes as our energy slips. I feel it like an incoming collapse, my consciousness wavering on the edge for a heartbeat before it rights itself. I breathe, pressing my hands to the cold stone on either side.

Teodor coughs, her head shaking. I don't have to ask if she experienced it too. The real question is which of us it originated from, and Teodor answers that for me.

"I can't hold this for long."

"You can," I protest.

She cuts me off with a scowl. "I'm half dead already. Once we burn through Luca's energy, that process will become a lot less slow for both of us." Her eyes slip closed, her chin lifting as though she's looking into the sun, far above the basement roof and the darkness that drapes the city. But there are no clouds parting. Nothing coming to save us. "We just have to outlast the storm."

"And then what?" The words come with a vitriol I didn't know I possessed. "And then help will come? Did it come yesterday when our people were drowning between us and the mainland? Will it come tomorrow when the hippocamps are stronger and more vicious than ever?"

"Perhaps some of them can sail out of here, at least." It's a weak hope, a consolation prize at the price of thousands of lives.

I give her a miserable smile, all teeth and tears. "Yeah."

"Guess we can't just give up though?"

"Not a chance." I try not to sound as grim as I feel. "Tavish is gathering everyone important in the building at the middle of the foundation. We should find them. See if there's anything we can do."

Teodor grimaces, and I feel another wave of her pain, of her pacing on that boat.

I stand, but she strains to follow, pushing against her emotions as she fights not to think too hard about Tavish or to feel too strongly all the wounds from him she still hasn't been able to mend. Taking her hands in mine, I pull her gently up. "For what it's worth, I'm sorry. You deserved so much better than what Tavish did to you. And you have a right to be angry with him, and to hold this against him, but—" I catch a flash of her dread just as she starts closing off, and I bare my mind—my heart—wider to her in response, mirroring her defensiveness with vulnerability.

She hesitates. Slowly, she leans against me, her arm wrapped through mine just as tightly as her threads are. Her emotions peel open once more, a little softer now. A little more thoughtful. "I'm not angry. Or I am angry, but not that he ran back to his family. We were young and foolish, and the depths only knows we'd have fucked ourselves up eloping together like that. What hurt most—what still hurts—is that he didn't just tell me he wasn't ready. He could have explained it to me, and I would have been all right with that. I could have come visit him in Maraheem, sent him ridiculous love letters, even just been his damn friend—he needed one so fucking badly. But he didn't give me that chance."

"He didn't think himself worthy of that."

She freezes. "What?"

I don't have to have heard him say it, because I know him. I know the little spaces behind the cracks in his heart and the way he breathes when he's perfectly at peace. I know what lies beneath each scar he bears, and can picture the back of his hands better than my own. Because piece by piece, he's shown them to me in ways he's never shown himself to anyone else.

I gave my all for that family, he said, *and all I ever—all we ever did together—was cause pain.*

"He thought that if he told you, it would just end the same way—with him leaving and you never wanting to speak to him again—or, at least, he was scared that would be the case, that so long as he was still so attached to his family, what he had to give wouldn't be enough for you."

Slowly, Teodor cracks again, red eyes filling as she wilts against my side. They're softer tears than the ones she cried for Luca, a teenager's heartbreak finally let out. A wound cleansed and perhaps, finally, ready to heal. When she dabs her eyes, her emotions feel freer, like the air along the rivers after a hard rain, cleaned of all the soot and smoke and fresh as if the whole world had been given a new start.

I step with her toward the back door of the basement. Toward Tavish.

"Did he still have Sheona with him when everything in Maraheem . . . when it fell apart?" She doesn't ask if Sheona is dead. She must have known Tavish and his bodyguard's relationship well enough to understand that if they were still a pair, Sheona would never have let him come here without her.

"She was half the reason we're both still alive."

Teodor's eyes narrow. "She approved of you?"

"She said she'd cut me into little pieces and plaster me across the ceiling if I hurt him. I think that was her form of approval." My heart swells at the thought, and I have to brush aside a tear of my own as I imagine her here, the way she would have scolded us all for the trouble we've caused.

"Good." Teodor nods.

Now it's my turn to narrow my eyes. "Are you vetting me as Tavish's boyfriend?"

"Someone has to." One edge of her lips quirk. "Troublemaker."

I give her the gentlest shove in the shoulder. "Whatever am I supposed to do with you?"

"Take me to your boyfriend, I think," she says, and she doesn't quite smile, but something in her shines. "And help me save my fucking city."

CHAPTER THIRTY-ONE

her heart

THE LAWN IS BARE and dim beneath the black clouds. The crowd of windblown tents has vanished, the last of their occupants helped by officers toward the line that still huddles outside the Citadel's entrance. It's far shorter now, the weathered people eased inside by Institute staffers with a speed and calm that were missing when I passed by here earlier.

"Do any of your party need to see a priest or a medic?" an Institute staffer asks them. "Are you claustrophobic or have problems with tightly packed spaces? No? Then you can go to your left, inside. The emergency staff there will find you a space. Provisions will be given out once everyone is settled. Have hope; the city will rise."

After the chaos and fear of the day, I don't expect much from the civilians, but the group mutters a gentle, if tired response of "The city will rise," and a woman near the back lifts to her lips three of the little horns the people usually wear as singles, her head bowed. Through the cracked doors, I can just make out the echo of a small Basilica choir. I realize I've stopped only when Teodor wraps her arm around mine.

"It was so much worse before," she says.

And I think I know what changed.

The central building is lit by a series of lamps hung along the interior wall, flickering as the wind whistles softly through the little slit windows near the domed ceiling. Their light dances across tables set up along the floor's edges, each one bustling with a mixed group of high-level staff from all three government branches. So many maps, charts, sheets, and lists pass between them that I wonder how they moved it all out here so quickly. It's the same answer as everything else, I imagine.

It's Tavish.

He speaks with a Basilica staffer as he paces with his cane between the outer tables and a set of chairs at the room's center, where Alvise, Iseppa, and Zuane debate in low tones. His poise rests on him like a crown, a Findlay to the core despite his objections. My chest aches from the mere sight of him.

As we head for the other leaders, Teodor clears her throat, but her first word is lost beneath the room's noise, turning immediately into a coughing fit. I call for Tavish. His head shoots toward me, and his commanding expression wavers.

"Aye, I'm here." He shifts his hands, picking absently at a nail. "You have Teodor?"

"What's left of her," Teodor mutters between coughs, her strength fluttering. She still has all her threads bound into me, though, all my energy shared with her. It's as though her body can only hold so much of it at one time now, too little of her aurora still alive enough to function. A bit of ash stains the edge of her lips.

I wipe it with the corner of my sleeve, gentle and fast, and guide her toward the leader's circle. "Come on."

They don't seem to notice our approach, Iseppa tapping a pen to her chin. "That last transfer of patients and children to the ship should leave us with enough room in the Basilica's medical center that we could move the clinic out of the Institute."

Alvise shakes their head, not meeting Iseppa's gaze with a ferocity that feels like a stare. "If we pull medics from there, the injured within the Institute will have to be carried through the storm to the Basilica. Better to move a group of civilians to that freed space from the overpopulated west rooms."

"The guards I have returning from the ship could help with that." Zuane grunts.

Alvise's feathers ruffle. "Will there still be enough protection on the ships, then?"

"If we do this right," Tavish cuts in, "and sail them out just as the hippocamps enter the city, then they shouldn't need protection. The hippocamps' focus will be here, on the corelium and anyone who remains near it."

Zuane nods. "They'll be safer than us, at least." His gaze fixes on me. "Why is he here?"

Teodor scowls at him. "Because Rubem—"

Her voice cuts out as she bends over, clearing her throat with a cough that turns up a smear of ash on the back of her hand. I feel the explanation she means to give—that Luca is dead and we have taken his place—but it comes with a soft rush of emotion, a quiet hesitation to be known, even now. I send her back my assurance, pure and unbiased, hoping that she understands I will support her whatever she does.

She hides the ash, straightening a little against her cane. "Because Rubem is now the one keeping the hippocamps at bay. And because I fucking brought him here."

Zuane makes a sound deep in his throat, almost like a grunt or a growl perhaps, but he seems to swallow it quickly. "Right" is all he says.

It's Tavish with his brow tight, Tavish and none of these people whose wonderful, loyal aurora loved and lived and died for, who bothers to ask the question, "Why? Is something wrong with Luca?"

"Luca's dead," I whisper, though what I want is to strangle each and every one of these people. If any of them had sacrificed even a little for him, then maybe he wouldn't have needed so badly to take my energy in the end. But he wouldn't have wanted them judged, not even for this. So instead, I bare my teeth and say, "Your aurora died making sure this city lived."

I try to watch for the tiny shifts in each of the leader's expressions that might prove they were secretly hoping for this, working toward it, even, but there's so little light and so little time. Alvise lifts a set of three horns to their lips, and Iseppa inhales like she's been stabbed, while Zuane just sits in his chair, eyes hard and expression flat. There's a few flickers of gold glinting on his left cheek, not quite a smudge but just a light flutter of dust. Distress, worry, resignation— are they in the right amounts? I don't know anymore.

Tavish presses a hand to my arm, rubbing soothingly. "I am so very sorry, Rubem. And . . . and Teo. I'm sorry."

Teodor's gaze flickers to him. "Me too." She draws a breath and lets it out, not coughing through it for once. "But there will be no one here to mourn him if we don't live through the night. Rubem's channeling the vibrations that keep the hippocamps away, but it won't last for long. We have to be ready to defend the foundation soon."

"How soon?" Zuane asks.

"Real fucking soon."

"I don't know," I clarify for her. "Hours, a day, it's hard to gauge."

A fresh round of discussion arises from among them, shifting to the defense of the foundation and the underwater tunnels that breach its exterior.

"Perhaps with enough corelium to satisfy them, the hippocamps will leave us alone here?"

"They're aggressive predators who will see us as a high number of potential threats directly at the center of their new mating ground, and the moment their corelium destruction makes them hungry again, we're sitting ducks for their attack."

"How much barricade material do we have? There must be enough to form some kind of formidable blockade at the foundation entrances."

"We've brought in everything we can from the city outskirts. We've focused on the underwater tunnel openings, but it hasn't left enough to fortify all three aboveground pathways into the foundation."

Tavish lowers himself into a chair. "Aren't there gates around the tunnel openings?"

"They're made to stand against mer not hippocamps," Iseppa replies.

"Leave the barricades on them," Teodor says. "We have a better chance of keeping the hippocamps out of the foundation center above ground than we will by trying to pick them off in the water, where they're faster and more versatile. We'll just have to find another solution for the pathways." As the conversation turns to logistics, she rubs a hand down her face, and her voice drops to a mutter. "If we only had a way to run that brooch . . ."

Behind us, someone shouts, "Get off that pillar, kid. Where's your family at?"

It would be nothing, another voice raised over the wind and the rain, if not for the question that follows. "Isn't that the late chancellor's daughter?"

Matthia, goddammit, the little troublemaker. I'm about as impressed as I am frustrated when a Citadel guard drags her inside, their hand clamped around her arm. She's lost her favorite of Teodor's books, but she holds her plush so tightly that a burst of fuzz peeks through the unraveling fabric on its chest, the loosened thread bulging around the wound. She squirms under the guard's hold, and her cheeks flush as Iseppa squeals, "Matthia!"

At some point I'll have to explain that hunting me down during dangerous situations isn't always the best course of action. *Someday*, as though we will all get through this. As though she'll keep being in my life long enough for us to encounter future dangers together.

"She says her family is here?" the guard asks. "An uncle or something?"

I expect a new hippocamp revelation from Matthia, for her to reveal something we've missed about the hippocamps again. But the girl only stands there, brow tight. Her gaze moves from me to Tavish, her expression growing desperate with each moment of delay.

She came for us. For stability, for protection. Not to save us, not this time, but to be saved.

Her hands tighten around her plush, the mismatched creature nearly dry despite her soaked attire, as if she's huddled it against her chest while she ran. Her heart, she said her mother had called it. It seems to beat as she does, fast and uncertain and pleading, little strands of it ripping further and further as the moment stretches. It sings.

Tavish stares past her, his face pale. His jaw tightens, then releases, and his fingers follow suit, gripping the edge of his cane until they go white. He says nothing.

His denial fires me with indignation—how can he not see how much Matthia needs him, needs us—but in an instant, a storm of understanding puts out my frustration. All his objections to anything Findlay, his determination not to let his past haunt him even if that means removing the good parts of it, too, his rejection of Matthia, it's all coming from the same place.

I gave my all for that family, and all I ever—all we ever did together—was cause pain.

The instant he said those words, I should have told him how wrong he was.

I take his hand in mine, and he wraps his fingers in mine.

"Ruby," he says, like he knows I'm preparing to speak and needs it as much as he fears it.

Pressing my nose to his hair, my mouth to his ear, I lower my voice until only he can hear it. "I believe that you would be an amazing uncle, but if you're not ready for this yet, then that's all right. If you're never ready for it, that's all right, too." And it is, because I love him—love him too much to push him into something he hasn't chosen. "You're already enough for me. If you ever desire it, you will be enough for her, too, Findlay or not. You have become someone incredible, and there is no piece of you—nothing past and nothing future—that takes away from that. Perhaps you have made mistakes, but you are incredible, not despite your family, but because you have taken what it means to be a Findlay and turned it into something new. Any child would be lucky to have you as a part of their heritage."

Tavish's stiffness softens in an instant, like a dam breaking. He draws my hand to his chest, clutching it there as he releases a deep sob. I wrap my other arm around him, squeezing. But outside our little bubble, the world keeps turning so fast that it's hard to catch up.

Alvise waves at the guard, their bangles jingling and their head feathers in a fluff. "She's one of the orphans meant to be on the boat! Is it too late to get her there?"

"We haven't given them the signal to draw the gangplank yet, they should still take her," Zuane says.

The guard nods. "I can bring the girl if you need."

"No!" Matthia shouts, wiggling in the guard's grip. "I want to be here. Please—Rubem!"

Zuane waves at the guard. "Take her."

They grunt an acknowledgement and pull her back the way they came. She digs in her heels, wrenching against them, her efforts as useless as ever. Her plush falls as she struggles, tumbling across the floor toward us.

"Tavish," I whisper. "I have to go to her."

His hand tightens around mine. Then it releases.

"Wait!" I shout, sprinting across the room. I don't know what I mean to do—what I *can* do, when I'm not her legal family and I can only take her in myself with the warning that it won't be forever or even for long—but I have to do something.

The guard lets go of Matthia as I crouch before her, lowering myself until she's far too tall for me on her already teenage legs. I grab her by the shoulders, running one hand up her neck to clutch the back of it tenderly. "You're going to be safest on the ship. It's the best place there is right now." The only place where she's not likely to be torn apart by hippocamps by tomorrow. But I can't think of that, can't think like that's the only outcome. Not when we're all still here, fighting. "But I'm going to find you after—I'll find you, okay?"

Tears bead along her lower lids, but she juts her lip out, a comical expression on a kid as old as her. It reminds me ruthlessly of Tavish, and that break in my heart doubles. "You promise?"

"I promise." It's not a guarantee I can make, and I know it even as I say it. But, perhaps, neither is a prophecy. I almost kiss the top of her head, almost forget that she's not *my* niece, that even if I can return to her after this and help her find a new place in Venalt or elsewhere, this isn't my future. That I can't be another single guardian she loves and loses.

But then I hear the gentle swish, swish of Tavish's cane across the floor behind me. He looks so vulnerable, so hesitant, like at Matthia's first movement, he might run. His cane bumps into her fallen plush. He bends to pick it up.

I stand, reaching for the toy. "That's Matthia's—"

"The Underbed Monster," he whispers. It carries, the room almost silent with watching eyes. His hands glide over the old, tattered fabric, counting its seven legs, the odd horn that sprouts where its left ear should be, and the three button eyes, fingers catching finally on the gash in its chest. His face goes pale around the red in his cheeks. "My brother had a plush just like this—that's what he called it."

"That—that's it, that's its name." I breathe. "It was Alasdair's?"

"He'd kept it all the way through his twenties—Ailsa would make fun of him for it—until that last year we visited Venalt." He speaks like he's in a daze, a little tremble in his voice. "He said, 'It had moved on.' Those words exactly; he was rather adamant."

Matthia watches the plush, her expression going hard. Regal. Like a Findlay. "The Underbed Monster was . . . my dad's?"

Tavish runs his thumb over the top of its head, and his voice comes out a little hoarse. "Aye."

Slowly, he holds it out. Matthia rushes him, grabbing it like a lifeline. As she pulls, the loosened thread on its chest catches on a broken edge of Tavish's nail, tugging the rest of the seam free. Matthia fumbles to catch it as matted fluff spills out. From the gash pokes something stiffer and darker.

The Underbed Monster's heart, and Matthia's, too, Fiordelise had claimed, knowing the toy came from Alasdair, a selkie who cared for the baby he'd abandoned enough to leave her his favorite childhood toy, cared enough to leave her entirely, to be sure his family could never turn her into the wounded, unhappy people that he saw in his siblings. But from what I know of selkies, of their love for their home that rivals even the Venaltans, he would not have wanted her to be entirely without a piece of her culture either. And Fiordelise had known that, had forbidden Matthia from throwing out that scrap of fabric and fluff.

A piece of my heart, Alasdair stated in his note.

Perhaps it was sentiment.

Perhaps it was something more.

I lean closer, holding out my hand to Matthia. "Can I see what's inside it?"

She hesitates. Instead of handing it over, she flips it herself, tugging gently at the rest of the seam along its chest. She digs through the fluff like a surgeon, reverently pulling free a tiny bundle of fabric wrapped in a single string. It unfurls easily, a note falling out. And a brooch.

Revealed from the fabric, the gleam of the little star-shaped brooch's ignation shines a rainbow-laden silver against Matthia's palm, a single line of grey marring it. I can identify the faint draw of its power, the way it's been calling me all this time, making me pay attention to the plush even when there was no good reason to. Beneath that pull, I sense something else, too, something that tingles in my fingertips and rattles beside my heartbeat: a thrum, like a song just a little too low to hear.

Hope fills me, warm and bright despite my fears. I feel Teodor's presence as she moves toward us, her brittle threads tightening along mine. She presses my hope right back to me, her own just as giddy, just as wild.

Matthia holds the brooch up to us, grinning. "Now can you save everyone?"

"Maybe," I whisper. "Just maybe." And I lift my voice above the roar of the storm and the bickering of the chancellors. "We might not be able to stop the exterior city from sinking, but we can still save the people."

CHAPTER THIRTY-TWO

he whose home encompasses the world

NO ONE ASKS FOR Matthia to leave after that, even when Tavish backs away with the same hesitancy that he emerged. His mind hasn't changed yet, not about taking in Matthia, at least, but he seems a little less tense now, more thoughtful. He doesn't flinch at the sound of Matthia's name, and when she adds in notes about the parts of her plan I've missed, his mouth does a thing that's not quite a smile or a frown, but something in between, as though he's dealing with a complex equation he can't quite solve.

The other leaders take to Matthia's plan with less enthusiasm than I hoped, skeptical expressions, pursed lips, and Zuane's flat stare.

"Why can't we do the original strategy, where we send out a boat once the hippocamps are docile and bring new ignits back?" Iseppa asks. "We'd pay you to stay, of course, as long as it takes to round the hippocamps up."

"I don't think I can hold the hippocamps off long enough for someone to reach the coast, collect ignits, and return." I feel Teodor's agreement as I say it. However strong we feel now, it won't last. "I'm powering the song that keeps them away using the last of your aurora's core energy, but it's draining quickly. It won't be enough to get us through the night." I don't bother explaining what a core energy is, or that

I should never have had it in the first place. This isn't for them to know, not these people who cared too little to even know Luca's name.

"Then you're suggesting we kill these newly docile hippocamps when they breach the edge of the city?" Zuane asks, shaking his head. "I don't have nearly the staff to spread them that far. We would need a heavy militia force, and the people are already too exhausted to be trusted to fight in a storm like this."

"No, I'm not suggesting that at all." I take a breath, willing them to understand, to feel the warmth in my chest without threads to push it outward. "I'm suggesting we don't kill the hippocamps in the first place. That we let them have the corelium."

Iseppa balks, her hands fluttering in disgust. "This is our *city* they would sink. Our livelihoods, our homes—"

"Our art and history and culture!" Alvise puts in.

"I know." And I do—I ache for the city with the same violent love that Luca possessed, that he's given me despite everything. But that love makes me ache more for the people within it. "But if the people are safe, then someday all the rest can be rebuilt. It can rise again with the people who love it here to do so. And while it pains me to no end to admit it, Zuane is right. They'll be too hard to hunt down in this storm. This way, though, at least we minimize the danger and maximize the chance of rebuilding this city into something that won't ever face a threat from the hippocamps again."

"With what funds? What supplies? We will be losing *everything*."

"With the hippocamps!" Matthia shouts.

Iseppa scowls. "A bunch of murderous animals?"

"They're murderous because we made them that way. They're just trying to take care of their families too." Matthia replies with such force and poise that it cuts down the rest of the room's discussion, leaving her words echoing beneath the pounding rain.

Tavish clears his voice. "Go on, then, tell us your idea, Matthia."

A little wave of panic pinches the corners of her face as all eyes turn to her, but she takes a breath, and when she speaks, it's the same high, clear, diamond-edged voice that her uncle used to convince a room of the rich and powerful of Maraheem to follow him. I see it sink into this one before the words do, drawing these people to her like moths to a flame. "When the hippocamps aren't stressed into being predators, they're smart and strong, and they attract fish and produce a kind of protein-milk thing in their pores. With their help, you could pull back up pieces from the city after it's sunk, and ferry things to the mainland or around the sea. We'd have new ways to travel and hunt and a whole new kind of trade, and none of it would need the dying ignits, so the rest of the Nereidian Sea will want it too. We pulled all the corelium out of the ocean because we didn't think about anyone but ourselves, and it made this disaster. If we kill all the hippocamps now, it could just make another disaster in the future." She gives the chancellors a tiny scowl, her haughty disappointment far too grown up for a child her age. "Also, killing them is cruel."

Though thoughts churn and expressions change, there's a hesitation that stretches into their bones, and I realize: this won't be enough to convince them. I grab for Tavish's hand again. And he must've realized the same thing; even without seeing it, he must've felt it through me like conduit.

"Or, how about this?" He smiles, kingly. Dastardly. A man who's already won. "If you refuse to abide by the instruction that no docile hippocamp be harmed, then Rubem will refuse to turn them docile."

His words twist into me, and I'm not sure I could follow through with them—or I'm sure, with Luca's love still pounding in my chest, that I couldn't. But the way he's taken my blunt hostility, and with his voice and his wit turned into a fine-tuned instrument, makes me want to kiss him. I bare my teeth like I'm ready to eat this city alive, sharpened incisors gleaming. "What will it be?"

Outside, the rain pounds like a heartbeat.

Iseppa breaks the silence. "When the outer city sinks all at once like this, it will strain the foundation where it's joined. My team has been severing key supports to prevent bringing us down with it. They should be finished shortly. Other than that, I suppose we merely need to let the ships know, and then the hippocamps can come . . ."

Zuane grunts his acceptance and Alvise sighs, but nods. "We will hold a lamentation ceremony as soon as the storm breaks."

Teodor lifts an eyebrow at me. "Well? Do we try the transformation?"

"No time like the present," I grumble.

With all eyes on me, I turn my focus back to the brooch in my palm, feeling the musical thrum of it beneath my touch much the same way as I could Tavish's, back at the harbor. It's a hollow thing, but when I will the brooch to activate, it seems to come alive. The vibration it makes is less a true vibration—the kind that forms chords and earthquakes and heartbeats—and more the rhythmic flow of its energy, a wave that worms itself into my cells as though seeking something. It doesn't find whatever it searches for, not in my genetics. But it should when it touches the hippocamps.

With each roll of its power over me, I try to echo them, using the idle bundles of my threads. As I do, I feel the thrum of the song Luca created stutter, too many of the threads I designated to it trying to shift to this new song instead. I scramble to restore them, but in a cascade, they all stop entirely, like an orchestra passing out from a poisoned gas.

Teodor tries to take over the full strength of the song, attempting to thrum it loud enough for the hippocamps to hear. Her far weaker threads instantly snap out from exhaustion. She wavers at my side, descending into a fit of hacking, and I frantically press more of my energy into her. She quakes against it, but slowly she steadies herself from my grasp, her breath evening out.

I restart our original song. It takes me a moment to find it, so many tiny bundles of threads that need to be strummed at different paces in different ways and in different amounts, but feeling Teodor play the correct versions at me helps me tune in on them myself, until we're blasting the song across the city once more.

For the moment, we're safe.

Zuane's eyes narrow on me, but no one seems to realize that my aurora actions and her weakness are connected—no one can see our songs come and go without the aurora threads to feel their vibrations. They are all watching me, though, expectant.

"I think it'll work, but in order to test it out, we'll—I'll— have to stop making the vibrations that are keeping the hippocamps away." We'll have one chance for this. One chance to save Venalt. "How long do you need, Iseppa?"

"I should have final confirmation shortly."

"Tell me when you do."

The conversation around us moves to more subtle tones as those in the room turn their preparation inward, consoling each other with hopeful words and offering to spread the news among the rest of the staff. I shift to the edge of the building, feeling useless despite our preparations being nearly finished. The brooch seems to call to me still, equal parts siren song and taunt.

I can do this. I will save Venalt's people, even if the city must sink, for a prophecy perhaps, but for Luca far more.

I linger near one of the entrances, staring out at the rain as the swells blast soaking drops against me. It can only be late afternoon, but the dark clouds turn everything to shadows: the blustering trees and empty lawns and the packed government buildings hulking around their edges. I listen with my threads to the little piece of ignation-filled jewelry as though if I keep tracking through its song, it might turn my anxiety into confidence. Tavish works his way toward me around the edge of the room, but before he can reach my side, Teodor grabs his arm. Their canes knock against each other.

Tavish tries to pull away, snapping something too low to hear even in his diamond voice.

"Please, I have to say this." Teodor's words are just as soft, the pound of the rain and the wind nearly swallowing them up. Through our threads, I can feel more than I hear: her sense that this could be her last chance to tell him this, and that they both desperately need to understand it.

I step back, not wanting to interrupt, but her gaze bounces to me, and that slice of anxiety I felt from her returns tenfold. She wants me to hear this. She needs my presence. So I slip closer, leaning against the wall behind Tavish. I'm not sure if he knows I'm there, but I'm certain that he wouldn't mind.

His expression pinches, and he goes rigid in a way that I've seen before: with his mother, and his father, and the memory of his brother. "Then say it, Teo."

"You hurt me." It's small and a little sharp, a wound that's only beginning to scar. As she continues, though, her voice settles, just as determined in its new softness. "But you were a child, and your mother had claws buried so deep in you that you bled. It didn't make it right, but I can't keep blaming you. I refuse to keep blaming you."

Tavish shies away with a snort. "You *should* blame me. Whatever role my mother played, I'm still the one who let her turn me into that."

"Then, maybe, as a kid who couldn't have done better. And now that you do—"

"Her claws aren't out of me just because I killed her!" Tavish snaps, his diamond voice sharp enough to cut even as it trembles around the edges, and he presses toward her, like he can scare her off. "I'm still the mess she made of me. At this rate, I always will be!"

Teodor's lips peel back, returning his rage with her own. "You are brilliant sometimes, Tavish, but you're also a fucking fool, you know that? I see the way you command the other chancellors and Zuane with such integrity and assurance that they listen to you eagerly. I know how you love Rubem with so much of yourself, so passionately and vulnerably that it puts all my affection to shame. You're a different person from the one who couldn't face me on that boat. And this person is someone I'm so fucking proud to have loved—to still love, even if it's not our time anymore."

With each word, Tavish crumples further, until he's leaning against her shoulder, shaking, all the wrath returned to its origin: to fear. "I'm not any of that," he sobs. "I only left with Rubem because there was nothing for me in Maraheem. It could have been you all over again."

Teodor grips the back of his head, her brow tight and her chin tangled in his hair. "But it wasn't. You traveled across a continent with Rubem. You stabbed a fucking hippocamp in the eye. You helped save my city. And just because you pulled out the claws, doesn't mean the old wounds won't still hurt. You're not a broken piece of your fucked-up mom— you're you with some healing left, and you're strong, and brilliant, and damned beautiful, and even with your wounds, you're worth all the love of that ridiculous troublemaker you've caught yourself." She pulls back just a little, running her thumb along the side of his face as she looks into his unfocused eyes. "You're worth my love too." She presses her lips to the corner of his, soft and chaste, all the warmth in her chest filling mine as well; then she lets go.

And I love her for it, for all of it. That she can be the one to give Tavish this after so long of them both carrying around the pain of it. Even if she did just, technically, kiss my boyfriend.

"I . . ." Tavish sniffles, but as he wipes his eyes in the soft rain, his expression brightens a little. His fingertips drift over the spot where her mouth touched. "I am sorry. For all of it."

"Thank you," Teodor replies, warm and a little worn. She tips her head toward me, even though Tavish can't see the motion. "Now, I think your troublemaker of a boyfriend is waiting for us or something."

"That's rude," I grumble.

Tavish laughs at us, a sound almost sob-like in the storm. He reaches for me, and I pull myself against him, wet and worn.

"But it's not untrue. Everything Teodor said just now was right. Everything I said about you, too."

"I'm beginning to believe it." He shivers a little, but he lays his head against my shoulder and relaxes. Teodor smiles at us.

There's a moment where it seems that this is the life we are meant to lead, all three of us, just standing and watching the rain in comfortable silence. Then Iseppa announces the outer city's final dismantling has finished, and the peace falls away.

"We've done all we can?" Teodor asks.

It's confirmed that the foundation tunnels are barricaded and the supports to the rest of the city strategically broken. Both the Citadel's steamships wait in the harbor to carry the sick and elderly and unclaimed children toward the mainland as soon as we halt our song. There is, truly, nothing more we can do. Except this.

Through the threads between us, I feel Teodor's hope, but it's a small, flimsy thing, propped up by the way I keep echoing it back into her. We can do this. I want to shout it through our connection, but just maintaining Luca's old song already drains me too much to even try.

I press my palm to the back of her shoulder, her latched-up cloak wetted through and ever-crooked around her too-white shirt. If I look close enough between the flaps, I swear I glimpse the faint outline of her ashen aurora flesh. "It's now or never."

She grimaces. "How about *never*?"

"For that, I think you need a different prophecy." I fiddle with the brooch in my palm. "When we do this, I want to be out there at the edge to watch it fall. I think I owe the city that much. You can stay here. I should still be able to resonate with you from that distance." I lower my voice. "If this doesn't work—"

"Then I want to know I did everything I could, and that means being there with you."

I offer her something almost like a smile. Looping my arm under hers, I help her out of the foundation's central structure. Tavish's voice follows me, soft and probing, but it's not me he's talking to, I realize—it's Matthia. His lips quirk as she breaks into an explanation about hippocamp family structures, a flush coming over her cheeks. I almost reach out to them, but they look so relaxed together for once: two Findlays, two selkies, but more importantly, two people both trying to care about each other despite everything else in their lives that has fallen apart.

Besides, a farewell would feel far too much like these are our last moments together. I won't accept that. I need no good-bye, because this isn't the end. Finally, I am strong enough with Teodor at my side and everything Luca chose to give to me in his final moments. Together, we won't save Venalt. But we will save its people and its future, and that will be enough.

The wind tries to push us back, but Teodor and I shove onward, down the wide stone path between trees that whip and wail. We head for the most open of the foundation's entrances—the one between the Institute and the Citadel.

How big the buildings always looked. How small they seem now. Not enough space, not enough protection. I shiver and pull my gaze away, trying not to think of the thousands of people in each, thousands who will die if I get this wrong. Luca's love sits like a brick in my chest.

Teodor curls her fingers over mine. With her head tipped down against the rain and the darkness so thoroughly descended it might as well be night, I can't see her expression, but I can feel the sadness she offers me. Not alone. I am not alone in this.

We stop a hundred feet from the now-cleared entrance, giving us a full view of the street leading into the foundation circle and the channel beyond that. A Citadel officer comes up to us. I wave him back to his post behind the building's outer wall, where a group with weapons waits in case of the worst.

Teodor pulls a long knife from beneath her cloak. She seems to contemplate it, only glimpses of her emotions peeking through: fear, then resolve. Flipping the knife over, she hands it to me.

I don't protest.

There's no agreement that's passed between us. We just know. It's time.

I cut off Luca's song. It seems to echo as the vibration fades out, leaving the world a lifeless, chilling place, everything veiled in the pounding rain. Somewhere deep in the labyrinthine bowls of the Citadel, the Basilica choir starts again—or perhaps not the choir, but the whole building, taking up their mantle as one in a high, strong tune that feels like the end of a war, like the beginning of peace. The Institute joins in spurts and leaps before fully committing, and from the guards on the building's edges, rough and weary echoes rise into the night. Teodor hums quietly along, so soft it could be my imagination, and her emotions soothe.

I tuck the brooch firmly into my palm, activating it once more. The wind whips the rain against us in spurts, and I close my eyes, letting my world become only the sound of the storm and the choir and the soft pull of the power in my hands. I swear I can feel the hippocamps pushing their way into the edges of the city.

I squeeze the threads Teodor has wrapped through my core and sing with the people of Venalt—with Luca's people. I work as quickly as I can, building one bundle of the brooch's vibrations on top of another in my chest until the soundless tune it creates feels almost like a song. But something is wrong—I realize it as the melody comes together. The thing I'm creating doesn't have the fullness of the brooch's song, or the specificity of Luca's. It hits my cells as a dulled thing and rebounds like light off glass.

Every iteration I try, I don't seem to have enough threads to fill it out. The vastness of the brooch's influence is too great for me, too great for any dying aurora, much less the overly strained and weary pair Teodor and I make.

My panic spirals across my threads and into her as I clutch the brooch tighter, giving it one last, frantic try, then another and another, each time telling myself it will work. It will work. But it won't. She clutches me, her stabilizing presence tightening.

"How would he have done it?" She has to shout above the wind and the rain, but I feel the question, too, in every sliver of her being, like her whole self is quietly crying for Luca.

He would have been strong enough for this.

He would have been strong enough, but I—no. No. I pushed him, I retaliated, teeth bared as always, but he chose to give back to me, to the very same me who refused to roll over and die. He gave me everything he knew and everything he was for a reason. Even in those final moments, he chose to trust me.

I dive through the memories his death imparted, not a full life but the most important flashes of one. Arrival at the foundation. The first hippocamp attack—his confusion over how these were not the same prey creatures he'd once known, but with no guess as to what had changed them. Then, the creation of his song, his threads digging through the hippocamp's body, strangling forth the specific, unique vibrations their cells alone gave off. That's it, the piece I'm missing.

I focus not on the brooch, but the way it hits my body, each wave sliding between my cells like a seeking vine. Its song changes upon impact, parts of what the original brooch produces fading away while others seem to converge into a sharpened point, a single band instead of overlapping orchestras. They're focused enough for me to reproduce them perfectly. Teodor follows suit, one hand wrapped over mine, and our threads so close together that each piece of the tune seems to jump from my bundle to hers. The song we produce is made for me, though, not the hippocamps.

It'll do nothing to them.

We don't hear them come, the rushing of the storm and the choir surrounding us so loud that the thud of the creature's bodies and the scratch of their hooves can't penetrate. I barely spot the first one as it emerges onto the path outside the foundation circle, and even then, it's the flash of the signal light from a lookout atop the Citadel's roof that tells me I'm not dreaming them.

Luca's love for his people clamps around my heart, and I cling to it, letting it fill me. If we can catch one of the hippocamps and feel the way the brooch interacts with its cells, then we should be able to alter the song to a version that will work on them.

If.

The hippocamps continue their charge through the massive gap where the barricade shields were removed. Shots fire from guards, their blasts muffled by the rain. But between the wind and the hazy darkness, their bullets all miss. The hippocamps push onward, fifty yards away now: seven distinct forms in the gloom with the largest leading them.

This is it, Teodor and me against a small swarm.

If we can catch one, I amend, and *if* we survive long enough to sing through it.

I stand, one hand on her shoulder, the other on the knife. Someone touches my back.

I turn to find Alvise smiling at me, a massive, single-edged sword propped on their shoulder, which looks more ornamental than useful. Behind them stands Iseppa, a pistol in hand; Tavish, his cane-sword half-drawn; and Zuane leaning against his wheeled walker with one of his tentacle legs propped in a sling but his eyes shining with excitement. I want to tell them to run, that this is too dangerous, only Zuane has the training. But this is their city—their family— too. Their love that overflows, all of them, for once, in perfect agreement.

"Keep the smaller hippocamps off Teodor and me!" I shout, staring down the central hippocamp. "I just need to pin one . . ."

Our companions slip around either side of me, Alvise pushing Zuane along the Citadel's edge while Iseppa guides Tavish along the Institute's, both groups hollering and waving lamps that reflect off their weapons and the rain. The bulk of the approaching hippocamps split off toward them, but the one in the lead keeps its course fixed on me. Twenty feet.

Teodor stands with me, her grip on her cane changing. "Ready?"

Ten feet.

"No," I say truthfully, and let the hippocamp lunge at us.

Just before its teeth can sink into me, Teodor slams her cane into its head. I burn through a burst of Luca's energy to slip around its side. Around us, the sounds of other fights rage, guards falling into the fray as they realize what we're doing.

I grab hold of the hippocamp's neck and vault onto its back. Before I can press the brooch to its skin, the creature bucks. I tighten my knees around the base of its neck, but its slick, hard armor is impossible to grab. The brooch slips from my fingers. I don't even hear it as it hits the ground, its soft ignation glow reflecting off the puddles.

"Teo!" I shout.

She's already moving, snatching it off the stone with such speed that she drags a bit of energy out of me in the process. The hippocamp wheels and slams its tail into her. She buckles, struggling to get her cane underneath her. It pounces at her with such force it nearly throws me off. I stab Teodor's knife into the side of its neck, notching it between two slabs of its natural armor to get its attention. It reacts by twisting its head at the last moment, its teeth just missing Teodor's throat.

But she's still too far away to hand me the brooch.

She does one better: grabbing the side of its face, she slams the brooch onto it.

As the hippocamp bares its teeth to strike Teodor a second time, it falters. A shiver runs through it, starting small, but growing, building into something massive and racking. I press slivers of my aurora flesh against it, weeding into the top layer of its skin in order to catch the full force of the vibrations. They're so similar to the ones that rattled me earlier, but as they continue, I notice where they differ: a little chord here and there, a vibration that comes just a bit faster or slower.

I mimic the changes with one bundle of my threads at a time, getting faster with each new vibration I add, until I'm singing in perfect time to the brooch.

Below me, the hippocamp's teeth change first, the spindly, carnivorous sets pulling back as the thinly curving jaw bulks around rows of stubby molars. The rough plates of leathery armor beneath me seem to melt back into its flesh, replaced by a smooth, soft skin. A gentle ooze of blue blood seeps from around Teodor's knife. I yank the blade free and drop from the creature's back.

It looks at me curiously. With a small, grunting noise, it lifts one hoof, then the other. Even those have shifted, deadly points turning into a rounded surface that looks almost velvety in the dim light and pattering of rain.

As it pulls away from us, Teodor yanks back the brooch. Its vibration goes quiet, but the song it fed into the hippocamp still resonates within me, coalescing into a thing that rattles from my threads to my aurora flesh until I feel it in my human chest like I'm standing in the center of a drum circle. I wrap my threads so thoroughly around Teodor's that we vibrate in turn.

Together, we draw from the final reserves of Luca's energy and release the song outward. The hippocamps around us shudder as they shift. One by one, they turn from aggressive, armored beasts to docile, flat-toothed creatures.

They watch their once-prey uncertainly, a couple of them shying away a little skittishly while one snorts in Alvise's face and another tries to nuzzle a wary Iseppa. She shrieks and wraps an arm over her head. Slowly they each seem to take notice of the corelium. Most turn back toward the outer city on their own, but the one with Teodor and me takes a curious step deeper into the foundation. Zuane looks at the nearest guard with a firearm, but I shake my head.

We gently guide the hippocamp back toward the water with the others. Toward its future, and the future of its family.

There's a fresh ache in my heart, a tight, wonderful thing that's as scary as it is beautiful. My chest hitches with quiet, senseless laughter. Teodor mirrors me, half coughing, but still grinning. All of this, because an eleven-year-old girl cared.

Because we all cared.

CHAPTER THIRTY-THREE

the act of raising

THE RAIN CONTINUES TO slow as we regather in the eye of the storm. Alvise limps and Iseppa bleeds from a scratch across one cheek—already she seems to be fussing over it, waving her hands and muttering about scarring—but everyone is alive, looking brighter and less anxious than I've seen most of them in days. A shift in the wind pushes the clouds apart just enough for the light to catch in Tavish's hair, twinkling with the little gold flakes from the tub last night. I grab him and pull him toward me. He makes a soft noise as I press my lips to his, weeding my fingers into his wet curls and relishing in his warmth and presence. Because I can. Because we're alive, for now, even as my aurora flesh slowly turns into ash and the hippocamps reclaim their corelium in the city beyond, we are both still alive.

He returns the kiss in greedy, hungry mouthfuls that make me groan when I finally release him.

"Matthia?" I ask.

"Safe, at the—"

"Rubem!" A shout breaks through the crisp air, a gangly figure pulling up her fallen suspender as she sprints along the path from the foundation's center. "Uncle Tavish!"

The title makes Tavish's cheeks pinch, but they loosen into something soft, his jaw shifting as he chews his tongue.

"You did it!" Matthia worms through the crowd that's growing around us to watch the newly docile hippocamps mosey back the way they came.

I tense as she all but crashes into me, grinning so wide that the smile seems ready to explode off her. I lift Teodor's knife away from her bouncing head and sigh. "You want to go see them?"

Somehow, she lights up further. "Can I?"

"They seem pretty safe now." I'm barely through saying it before she lets me go, charging off toward the nearest hippocamp. I have to shout after her, "But don't leave the foundation circle!"

It seems she's not the only one, civilians and government staff alike drifting out the doors of the nearest buildings into the lightening rain and softening wind as the news spreads that the hippocamps are no longer a danger. Laughter and sobs echo across the foundation, guards slowly putting away their weapons and turning their attention to keeping the civilians from accidentally straying out into the city as they try to view the newly transformed hippocamps.

With the path filling around us, Iseppa waves both hands in the air. "What if we move to the landing?"

It seems no one else wants to go inside, either, because we all follow her toward the elevated garden patio that runs along this side of the Institute. An unusually skinny balcony extends over it, holding planters. The way the stairs to the landing swoop around the side makes it seem almost like they were meant to continue up to the balcony.

As we near the steps, Iseppa glances between it and the stub of a landing directly across from it on the Citadel building, an oddly blank wall above. She hums. "You know, this would be a good place for a bridge."

"Oh, they almost built one, three hundred years ago or so! One to the Basilica, too, with plans for another between it and the Citadel." Alvise's bangles jingle as they draw a line between the Institute's little half-bridge balcony and the start of it on the Citadel building. We all stare at them. Their feathers ruffle. "Does no one remember that?"

"Seeing as it was three hundred years ago, probably not," Teodor grumbles. Through our threads comes a softer, sadder *'Maybe Luca did.'*

With all our songs finished, it's easy to hear the thoughts she sends in clear, precise words, just as easy as it is for me to send back the weight those words build in my chest at our shared desire to reach for him and ask, and the void we'd find in his place.

"Well, I think it might be time to follow through on those plans," Iseppa says. "When we start rebuilding the new city, we'll want both the Citadel and the Basilica's help with the design, after all. Create something that's beautiful and defensible at the same time."

Alvise takes that as their cue to launch into all the artists they know would be thrilled to see their ideas incorporated into the new city. Teodor stops at the bottom of the landing steps, letting them go ahead of her. She smiles at me as I approach, and we walk together in silence, our exhaustion and relief balanced between us, keeping us aloft.

There is so much work still ahead for the people of Venalt, and whoever helped Fiordelise sink the city—efforts that are technically succeeding now—is still out there, or perhaps right here in our midst, still a potential source of aggression if plans for the rebuilt city don't align with their desires. But identifying them seems less important now that the people are safe and the deed has been done, and at least their partner is in our custody. Perhaps we all deserve this moment to rest.

A small blue flower dangles off one of the vines hanging from the balcony like the next strong breeze will tug it to the ground with the rest of its sopping and torn siblings. I rise on my tiptoes to snatch it free. The drizzling rain shimmers off its petals.

When Tavish joins us on the landing, I kiss his temple and tuck the little blue blossom behind his ear.

He touches it gently and then says the very last thing I expect. "We have to take in Matthia."

"Where did this come from?"

Tavish inhales and finds both my hands in his and prepares like I'm the one who needs convincing suddenly. "She's my niece, and she's a Findlay, and more than that, she's a good kid who deserves to have proper guardians who will care about her and whom she wants to be with. And you were right, you and Teodor. You were right about me."

"But you *want* this—you're ready for it?" I wish I could thread myself into him the way I have Teodor, the way I did Luca, to tell him once more that he is enough for me no matter what he chooses, and that if he does want Matthia, he will be enough for her, too. "I know that the idea of raising a kid after your childhood seemed like too much. You don't have to do this for me or for Matthia. It wouldn't be fair to us—and to you especially—for you to make a commitment that huge for anyone but yourself."

A single tear slips out of the corner of his eye, wiped away so fast in the dimness that it could have been nothing at all. "I ken that, but yes, I think I'm ready," he whispers, porcelain, too, but as he lifts his voice, the diamond edge returns. "I was afraid that with Matthia I would be only the pieces of me that my mother left behind. That we'd be two more Findlays in a terrible cycle. But I'm not that kind of Findlay, and neither is Matthia going to be." He draws another long, hard breath, and he smiles, genuine and full. "She's my niece. She belongs with me, and with you, too."

Despite his conviction, a little piece of my dread lingers, making me feel weaker suddenly. Hollowed out, just a bit. For a moment, I almost wonder if I'm wrong, that we'll fuck Matthia up the way our pasts have fucked us both. Who am I to grow my family when I know where it'll end up? Where will that leave Matthia in a month, or a year, or three, when the ignits run out or my aurora flesh refuses to accept them, and she's lost a guardian all over again?

Through the brush of Teodor's threads, I sense her understanding. But not her agreement. *'Would you rather you have never known me?'*

Her words feel like a breath finally exhaled. *Of course not.* Even knowing what's to come for her, what came for Luca, what'll take us all in the end, I'm still glad to have the people I do for the time we're allotted. But that's not solely my decision to make.

"I'm dying." It's not an objection this time, but a plea to take me anyway, to love me anyway, to go down this path with me into a fuller and larger future, even if I won't have the time left to see him through to the end of it. I don't know if the pain of losing me will be worth loving me until then, but I want him to take the risk for me anyway.

"I ken that," he says, like he knows it all, the said and unsaid alike. "But everyone is dying, just some slower than others. We'll get through it."

"I doubt our life will be stable. It won't be the easiest circumstances for raising a kid."

"Then we'll do everything we can to make it as stable as possible, and the rest will be what it is. As long as you're up for this?"

"I am if Matthia agrees." I glance over the landing, down the path to where she stands at the edge of the foundation circle, bouncing on the balls of her feet as she watches the hippocamps.

One of her suspenders has fallen, and her brooch gleams on her shirt collar. Teodor must have given it back to her already. It looks right there, as though she was always meant to be like this: a selkie brooch and her two little satyr horns. She looks up the moment I call to her, and when I wave her over, she barely even protests.

My heart sinks suddenly. "What about her great-aunt on the mainland?"

"Tavish has the closer claim," Alvise says. "Sorry, I was overhearing, I can't help it. And someone so old who never bothered to meet the girl in the first place? We never had much hope for that situation," they add, glancing at Matthia as the girl ignores the landing stairs in favor of scrambling up the side and pulling herself through the railing in such a useless but dramatic maneuver that I can't help but be proud of her.

"Hey, kid," I say as she settles, nudging into her with my shoulder. "I found you."

She grins. "I didn't ever go anywhere, so it doesn't count."

"Not fair." I pause, swallow, and then go for it. "Your uncle and I were thinking, maybe we can keep finding each other, stick together, you know? If you'd like to come with us when we leave Venalt, we could take over as your guardians."

For a delayed moment, the smile remains, her gaze bouncing between us. Then it drops, a pale, trembling expression replacing it. She shakes her head, taking a step back, then another. "No," she whispers, and runs.

As she sprints down the stairs, slipping and leaping amidst the slick stone and shallow puddles, Tavish cracks. "Oh," he says, the sound more like a sob.

I press a hand to his shoulder, sighing. "It's all right, I think I get it. Just give me a moment with her."

He looks as though he's trying to paste himself back together, but he swallows and pats my hand as though saying he'll trust me through anything, even this. I squeeze his fingers before following Matthia around the bend of the Institute. She sits with her back to the wall, her knees pulled to her chest.

She glances at me as I approach, then looks pointedly away.

I lean against the side of the building, my halved thumb tucked into my pants. "Can I join you?"

She stares at me, then nods.

I plop down beside her. For a moment, I say nothing, as though I've only come here to be with her and to listen to her breathe, because mostly, I have. The clouds keep softly crying, the breeze tickling our wet clothes. Along the path, a parent chases a toddler out of a puddle while their partner laughs at them. "Your mom was a pretty great mom, wasn't she?" I say.

"Yeah." Matthia presses her hand to her nose, watching her feet.

"We wouldn't replace her. No matter where you go now, or for the rest of your life, she will always, *always* be your mom." I try to be gentle with it but honest, try not to say all the things I wish I could, that as an adult, she'll wish she'd chosen this, that she was lucky to even have had the opportunity to find people who loved her again so soon, that she could have had uncles and aunts who refused to utter her name and an absent father whom no one still living ever knew—but she's a child, existing in her own moment, her own world, and mine will mean nothing to her when it feels as though hers is in the slow but steady process of falling apart. "And it's your choice whether you want to come with your uncle and me," I add. "We won't be staying here in Venalt, at least not while there's auroras out there to help, so maybe you'd rather live here, with a family your mom knew, or with someone that Chancellor Alvise could choose for you, or—"

"No." In the gloom, Matthia's freckles are faded out, the red in her hair replaced by dusky brown, but the determination that takes over her face is so unrepentantly a Findlay expression: the same poised, throne-worthy self-assurance that Tavish enters every room with. "I do want to stay with you and Uncle Tavish. I don't care if we have to leave."

From the outside, it looks like such a sudden change, but I figured the first *no* hadn't been a rejection at all, but a question she didn't know how to ask. I don't think we ever grow out of that, either, just get better at disguising it. "You sure?" I ask. "Uncle Tavish and I will never be your mom, but you'll still have to listen to us when we tell you not to go running into any giant fights on boats or sneaking into emergency government meetings, and probably a lot of other stuff too. Will you be okay with that?"

Matthia makes a face, lifting her shoulders around her ears. "If I have to."

I squeeze her against my side, both of us sopping. "I bet we'll see plenty of animals from your books."

"Yeah. That'll be good." She nudges me with her elbow, one edge of her lips lifting crookedly. It makes her look even more like a child, just a fragile, hurting kid playing at adulthood with her books and her theories. Delicate porcelain in the same places she's a Findlay diamond. Much like Tavish.

"Can we go tell my uncle?" she asks, as if she didn't just run shouting from him a minute before.

What have we signed ourselves up for? I sigh, but I'm grinning right back at her. "Yeah, let's do that."

We watch the hippocamps from the landing—Matthia and I, with Tavish at our side. The newly docile creatures still swim like arrows, darting through the channels and leaping onto pathways. Their long, tubular tongues dangle sloppily from their mouths as they regurgitate bile onto the corelium before slowly sucking bits of the degrading material up. A dozen Institute scientists pile after them in two gondolas with umbrellas held over their notebooks and collection kits in sealed bags.

"Can I go with them?" Matthia asks.

"When you're a scientist and you work for the Institute, absolutely."

She juts her chin at me and plants herself on the railing as close to the scientists' boat as she can. Her mauled Underbed Monster sticks out the back of her pants.

"Damn that child," I mutter.

"Is that affection I hear?" Tavish smirks. His fingers graze my hip and slip against my side, cupping there like it's where they were made to fit. "Eventually we will have to find a stable home for us all. I don't believe this place will be it."

"Well, it *is* sinking."

"You ken exactly what I meant."

I laugh, but I do know what he means. As wonderful as Venalt is, and as much as it should be a perfectly suitable place for us to remain once our traveling is over—and once it's rebuilt—there's something calling us onward. I press my lips to his hair. "We'll find our home someday. Until then, we have each other."

We linger like that, until Teodor calls Tavish over, Iseppa echoing her—there's some joint task force they're planning with Commander Zuane, and Tavish seems to know more about getting the two branches to work together than any of them do themselves. It leaves me alone at the railing, watching the people as they gather at the foundation's edge to witness their own city's annihilation.

The gold along their cheeks has all washed clean in the rain, but gilding still shines between them as some from the watching crowd lift little horns in sets of threes. Like the woman from earlier, it's their single pendants they've combined into trios to create something new. Something new to represent someone old. Others follow with three of whatever they can find, sticks and pens and utensils, and the rest with three raised fingers, heads bowed in salute. At the edge a teenager untucks a folded paper of a three-pronged neck, the end of each turned into the head of a serpent. It immediately begins to disintegrate in the drizzle.

Oh, Luca. How I wish I could split myself apart to reach wherever auroras go when we fade—if we go anywhere at all—to show him this. They love him. They have always loved him, I think, somewhere deep in their cores or their genes or whatever it is that made them yearn to be a part of this city—his city. He was just too scared to go looking for it.

And I was part of what took him away from this. We all contributed: myself, Luca, and the city. But the portion of responsibility I share in that will sting forever.

I breathe in and out, clutching Teodor through our threads. Her distant voice hitches in her conversation with Iseppa and Zuane, but she steadies herself, holding to me in turn. We linger like that, her focusing on the bright future of Luca's city, and me on its current destruction. Already it creaks and shifts as though preparing to plunge into the sea.

"So much for the second prophecy," I mutter.

"Oh, I don't think so." Alvise dangles their wrists over the railing, bangles jingling. "There are two translations, after all. It was written before the trade tongue had fully infiltrated the region, with a mix of the area's original dialect, and none of the spellings are standardized. One of the understandings is not as a raising up but as mere a razing. You saved the city—its people—and you razed its buildings, by which I mean you destroyed them."

I laugh. "If it's not rude of me to say, that seems like a pretty lenient interpretation."

"Oh it is—is lenient, I mean! Never rude." They beam.

"Then what's the point of it? If it could mean two entirely different things?"

"The point is that it exists." They wave a hand at the sinking city. "And through existing, it makes you see something different in the world and in yourself."

As I keep watching them all—the hippocamps and the people, the city glimmering with rain and the last of the light almost peeking through the clouds—I think I get it. "Even if we've failed ourselves, we are allowed to hold on to hope, and to give ourselves grace. The whole city needs a bit of both if it's going to reform itself into something new."

It still irks me that we haven't found the person responsible for all this destruction, for the theft of the ignits and Tavish's kidnapping. I can only extend so much grace; some things I still want justice for.

Alvise hums in acknowledgement. Their brow lifts, eyes darting toward mine for a moment. "Would you like to hear about our other prophecies?"

"There's more?" I groan.

"Oh yes. The six and the twelve are the other most well-known, but I favor the twenty-seven set, because the contradiction between the fifth and tenth line opens a whole host of diverging theological theories that prompt for reinterpretation of the other prophetic sets. But—oh, I'm getting ahead of myself, aren't I? Bother."

"It's fine." I chuckle. "Tell me about these weird lines. Tell me all the contradictions! I saved a city by sinking it, no prophecy can hurt me now," I tease.

Before Alvise can start, though, a Basilica medic rushes toward our group, holding a raincoat over their head to fight against the limp drizzle.

"Mr. Findlay!" they call, pushing their way through. "The woman you brought in earlier is awake." Their gaze darts through the little group, and they swallow.

"Well, did she say anything?" Tavish asks.

"She gave a name." They swallow again and glance between us all once more, from Tavish to Zuane to Iseppa, before landing on Teodor. "I—I have it written here."

My heart skips, and I feel the sentiment echoed in Teodor. This is it. The closing of a chapter. The opportunity for the city to move on from this mess and truly start fresh.

Teodor grunts. "Give it to Commander Zuane, then."

"No, I—I don't think . . ." The medic looks like they might choke on the words. Their gaze leaps back to Zuane, but Teodor is already upon them, silent as a ghost. She rips the paper from their hands. Her face goes blank.

And I know what the paper must say.

"Zuane," she whispers.

Something flashes across the commander's face, a bright, hot emotion, and he lifts his hands. "Now, be reasonable, Teodor."

His tentacle in the sling after Tavish's second captor was injured, the memo in Fiordelise's office that he didn't want me to share, the way he looks at Teodor now, he knows what's written on the note—it's too much evidence. And he must realize it.

He shakes his head, looking almost melancholy. "Fiordelise had great plans for Venalt, you know. She was a brilliant woman who knew what needed to be done and was willing to make it happen while every other one of you flailed about in your own muck."

I have always suspected it, hoped for it, even, but now it sinks through my gut like a weight. *He* killed Luca. Beyond the city as a whole, I have faces to attach to my fury and revulsion: Zuane's and Fiordelise's and all those who worked for them. I want to rage at him, but my own guilt pins me in place. Because it was not *just* them who killed Luca. It was also me.

Alvise overcomes their shock in a sputter. "How could you?"

"I could ask the same of you, and every other chancellor for the last three hundred years," Zuane says, his usually emotionless voice curling with ire. "You all let our city rot beneath us." He scoffs. "You thought we would bag the hippocamps and everything would be saved? As if pieces of the city weren't already sinking beneath the weight of the Basilica's grotesquerie and the Institute's arrogance? As if its defenses weren't relying entirely on ignit-powered vessels that will be useless soon? As if trade and tourism hadn't been dropping for years before the hippocamps even amassed? Stagnation isn't salvation. Fiordelise could see that, and so could I."

I remember our conversation in the café, his righteous dedication to help Venalt when no one else would. *The path this city has been on for most of my life isn't one it can maintain,* he'd said. *It has broken something fundamental within itself, and if its populace are unwilling to take the burden to change upon themselves, then it falls to people like me.*

His reply seemed so reasonable then, so relatable when I didn't know the cost of his actions. When I didn't yet see what the cost of my own would be.

"Zuane!" Teodor says it like she can bring him back to his senses weeks or months in the past, before he became convinced that this was the only option the city had left.

Tavish puts a hand to her shoulder.

"You might have killed Fiordelise, but her work still saved this city," Zuane snaps.

"Officers!" Teodor shouts, and for a moment, it seems like maybe no one will come. She calls again, louder. Across the street, two people in Citadel uniforms snap to a sprint.

Zuane shakes his head. "I'll come quietly. This is my city and I won't run from it. But I have one last piece of justice to see through." His sadness turns into a snarl. "For Fiordelise." He reaches beneath the uniform sash that bears his badge, and dives toward Teodor.

My gut sinks. I lunge for him, but he moves too quickly, too far from me and too near to Teodor. Launching off his wheelchair, he flings himself at Teodor. But even as I lunge after him, I know I won't reach him in time.

There should be a flash along his blade, the singing of metal, something to tell me he's pulled it free of its hidden holster, but there's just the collision—three bodies, not two— as Tavish steps in front of him, hard edges made of diamond. He wheels his cane.

It catches Zuane in the side of his neck. The disgraced commander stumbles, dropping onto his piled tentacles at Teodor's feet. Tavish raises the sheathed weapon up and slams it again, knocking Zuane down entirely. The commander coughs, a rough, wet sound, his focus going in and out, but Tavish brings the cane down one more time, a sharp crack across the bottom of Zuane's chin. He goes limp.

"I'll be having my brooch back now, you—you damned silt-breathing dobber," Tavish hisses.

My chest swells for him, just as it aches with Tavish. Across the landing, everyone is silent.

"It's a family heirloom," Tavish snaps, as though justifying himself. After a blush, he adds, "Zuane is still alive, aye?"

The Basilica medic bursts forward to check Zuane's body, nodding quickly. "He's alive."

Tavish's pinkie shakes around his cane, but only once. He nods. "Good—good. And Teodor . . .?"

As though her name cuts a pair of strings that have been holding her up, Teodor wavers. Her agony comes in a wave, pulsing into me through her threads. They tighten around my core, leaching energy in sharp, ragged bursts like her gasping.
Low in her stomach sticks the hilt of Zuane's knife, an ashen grey bleeding around it.

CHAPTER THIRTY-FOUR

the dying versus the death

ONE OF TEODOR'S KNEES gives out, then the other. I catch her in both arms as she curls forward, clutching her stomach. I feel her try to mend the wound with her aurora flesh, but the ashen stretches of it are too fragile and immobile. Moving them takes more energy than she has.

I push mine into her, not caring that I've run through all of Luca's power and am pulling from the dregs of my own now, but she pushes right back.

"It's not enough," she whispers hoarsely, ash clinging to the edges of her lips. A weak cough rattles her, and more of the grey silt seeps from the tear in her clothing.

"Venalt's ignits," I say. "They're still here somewhere—Zuane must have hidden them."

He makes a sound from where he lies on the ground with an officer binding his wrists.

I grab him by the shoulders, digging my nails into his skin and shaking him back to consciousness. "Where did you stash the ignits?"

He groans, his eyelashes fluttering. "Damn you," he mutters. "You could have saved Fiordelise."

The desire to hurt him makes me weak and strong all at once, but I know there's nothing I can do that will force the truth out of him, not when he can run me in circles around the foundation until Teodor is long dead, and I can't be certain any of his lackeys will know where he stashed them in the first place. There has to be another way to find the ignits he stole.

A city's worth of them. Where would Zuane hide dozens upon dozens of ignits—somewhere he had easy access to, somewhere no one else would think to look, somewhere on the foundation center that would be protected even if the rest of the city sank?

Teodor's comment from my first time in her apartment hits me like a sledgehammer. *Commander Zuane always says this place is so messy that you could hide a hoard of ignits in here and no one would notice.* Fuck.

I sprint across the street, skidding around the side of the Citadel building and tearing down the path to the basement's back entrance. My chest tightens, Teodor's phantom pain still burning between my ribs, lighter now as she pulls thread after thread of herself away from me, her walls slowly resurrecting. I fight the processes with every slice of my being. *Hold on. Just a little longer.*

She hesitates, and I feel the repetition of my own fears in her, the knowledge that she opened herself up to me, and now I will lose her. But I won't, not yet. Not if I'm right.

I tear aside the tapestry that covers the apartment's secret entrance, startling Lavender out of a dead sleep on a chair.

I woke to her hissing at that winged lion statue in the front parlor earlier, Teodor said.

Lavender, who cried when I tried to bring her into the detective wing of the Citadel—to talk to Zuane—who would have smelt his presence in the parlor after he stashed the ignits there. I scramble through the halls. As I round the final corner, I see it: the giant sculpture of a winged lion made of a dingy grey metal.

I run my hands down the side of it, shoving away a pile of ornamental fans and a giant satchel of costume pieces to find a little door in the back. It pops open as I press it. Power shines out. I shove my hands in, letting a few of the ignits seep into me for Teodor to quietly siphon off my threads. But this is a much slower transfer than the kind I've done with Luca—she needs me to be nearer, or else to touch the source of the energy herself.

Dumping the costume satchel out, I load the ignits by the handful.

Every step back to Teodor feels like a mile, every second an eternity as I keep feeding her as much power as she can take while I run. The rain has let up to a mist, the clouds breaking just above us to shine on the puddles, leaves and lost belongings blown, sopping, into every corner and crevice. The faint shimmer of a rainbow hangs behind Teodor.

Her fellow chancellors have gathered around her, and Tavish sits near her head, brushing a hand over her hair while a pair of Basilica medics kneel at her side. Her crooked cloak has been unlatched in the front and her shirt peeled off her ash-bleeding wound, but neither of the medics seem to have any idea what to do about it. She shouts them away with all the courtesy of an annoyed alligator, hacking between growled words.

I take their place, heaving the ignit satchel down beside me. Its contents clink together like a melody. I press her hand into them, feeling the pulse of the energy as it floods her, one, then another, and another. But nothing in her changes. She remains a black hole, an endless hollow. No matter how much energy she takes it, it's not enough.

Something sparks in the back of my mind, an aurora memory I can't quite hold on to. This has happened before, but differently. Reversed or mirrored or inverted. It hits me with the strongest sense of déjà vu, but no matter how much I dig into the feeling, I can't quite find the source. It doesn't matter, not as much as Teodor does.

I lace my hands over hers, helping her drag in more of the power with my own threads, but I understand her answer so deep in my bones before she even pushes the energy back at me. Gently, so gently, she takes my fingers and lifts them from the bag before pressing it closed.

'*Keep the rest for yourself. They can't save me now.*' The words come in faint trembles from her threads, her breathing so ragged I don't know if she can even utter them out loud anymore.

I sense Tavish on her other side, rubbing her shoulder and Alvise offering a prayer behind him while Iseppa tries to lead Matthia across the landing, but I can't really see any of them, can only see Teodor, can only clutch at her, wanting so badly for this not to be true and knowing so completely that it is, knowing it like I know my own death. *I'm sorry. I should have realized it was Zuane. I should have found a way to stop him earlier in the library. I should have—*

'*He was my right hand; if anyone could have seen it coming, it was me.*' She presses her assurance into me, though like the ignit power to her wound, it'll never be enough. I accept it all the same, cradling it like a gift. That she wants me to feel I've done enough, that I succeeded in every way that I could have, even when I failed in the end— that means something all on its own. She brushes her fingers against mine, and I can feel her own regrets, her own yearning. '*I would have liked just a little more time for the two of us to be astrals together. I had merely a childhood with my mother, and all your life you've thought you were alone. We should have had more time.*'

I can't stop how much I want that from filling me so totally that it pours into her, my hands squeezing around hers. But through the pain, there's warmth and something a little like love. *But I found you. I found you, and that's what's important. I wouldn't trade this for anything.* My chest aches, the sensation spreading behind my eyes and along my jaw and tightening in my throat, but that, too, I wouldn't trade away. In any reality where Teodor died, I want to be there with her. *I don't care what our ancestry says. We're siblings. Now and forever.*

The rush of joy that spills through Teodor is so bright it's almost blinding. She closes her eyes, a bead of liquid forming along the edges of her lids. *'Of course we are; we're the same kind of disaster, after all. I just wish we'd had time to cause a bit of trouble together.'*

I think we already did. I cup the back of her head and pull her against my chest, wrapping my arms around her as I turn our gazes to the streets and channels beyond the foundation center.

A rumble goes through the building as they tip and droop. A few distorted walls collapse into each other as others simply sink, slow and serene into the depths. Water rises up the sides of doors and windows, taking over homes and pouring across rooftops. Hippocamps dart and dive among the destruction, the once-dull skin along the ridges of their necks and backs now shining with the gold and reds of the corelium. Far beyond it all, the steam of the Citadel ships billows up as they chug their way toward the mainland, the eye of the storm protecting them.

We did this.

'It's almost beautiful.'

Almost, I agree. Rain drenches me in a renewed rush, concealing the tears that might have been pouring down my cheeks for moments or centuries, dispersing the salt of them.

Teodor flinches as another bout of pain overwhelms her, spilling into me with such force that I have to bite back the scream that collects in my lungs.

'You shouldn't have to feel me die.' As she vibrates it, she pulls free thread after thread, dragging them away from my aurora core, but I grab them back, wrapping through her with the same intensity that I grip her hands.

I want to. I'm going to be with you until the end. The way she should have had the chance to be with Luca.

She tips her head. Her eyes close, and she lets me hold her. The last of her walls fall. I feel the depths of her: the way she's awaited this, mourned this a thousand times over; the pressure of her grief for Luca and her hope for the city; her regrets over not following after Tavish and her peace at seeing him happy, finally; and me—the bitter, brilliant joy she's taken from discovering my presence, an astral and an aurora and a troublemaker all wrapped into one, wishing she'd been brave enough to reach out to me sooner and ecstatic that she had even the little time together that we managed.

In a heaving release, her brittle threads begin to collapse. They try to cling to mine in a final moment of panic, breaking themselves from the effort.

I hold her tighter, pressing my lips to her forehead. *It's all right. It's all right, I'm here.*

I don't know if she hears the end of it, because between our threads runs a spark like all the lightning in the world has torn us in two. It brings with it a sharp, excruciating pain. The sensation courses through my aurora flesh, tearing into my skin and burning in the back of my mind. My embedded fishnets spasm. I want to scream, but all that comes out is a whimper, lungs clamped shut.

Death. This is death.

I've felt it before.

Panic tears through me. It's too soon—too soon. Matthia—Tavish—my family—the world—I need more time.

Tavish's arms wrap around me, soft and warm, then stiffening, trembling as he holds me. He shouts my name— but it's not the right one—I'm not Rubem? He's here with me, screaming with me, his pain and mine overlapping into a beast that ravages us both. But my human, my Rubem, doesn't let go. He holds tight, sharing my agony in teeth-gritting determination.

The world fades to a pinprick. In that instant, I can feel the connection my threads make to the world I once came from, perfectly traced in agony. They wind like cords through a gap between this place and the other, mine and Teodor's and that of every other aurora left in his world, all strung between two different planes. The gap they fit into is wider now, suddenly, not the unreachable pinprick that I needed boundless energy to just view back in Maraheem, but a full tunnel. Through it, I see a familiar face, dusky-brown skin with a tinge of purple. Their head fins are a mess, their wide eyes pleading with me. Elspeth, I realize, through the numbing pain. Elspeth is alive.

And they're causing this. Something they're doing in the world from which we fell is—is—not killing us, not quite, but worse: it's setting us free.

"I'm sorry," they say.

The cords that tie us—every aurora across the globe—to that other plane slip and snap, breaking free, and for a moment—breath held and my heart beating with Rubem's, the two of us so caught in each other that we are as much an individual as a pair of beings from two different worlds—for a moment, it seems like it might be freedom. Memories flood into me in streams of light and emotion and wild, beautiful magic, all the memories of my life in the other world settling back into place. A home, a sister, a goal, a world to save. Then—

My existence implodes.

Without the other world to sustain me, it's as though the cords that bound part of myself to it unravel. *I* unravel.

We scream together, Rubem and me, Teodor and her aurora, every other aurora around the world, as a fresh wave of agony seems to shred through us. Us, Rubem and me, together, two people with two merging lifetimes, clinging to each other in a single body. In an instant, it all snaps out.

And I am Rubem, again.

The cold stone bites into my skin. Frantic questions and assurances come from Tavish as he holds me tight. Teodor lies in my arms, her breath heavy and her skin pale . . . pale and auroraless.

And inside my head I am utterly alone.

I die slowly enough to think three things—the three things that I've woven through my every thesis and essay and experiment. One: when an eruptstone hits an ignit, that ignit explodes, leaving nothing in its wake, not dust or ash, not your parent's final screams or the diamonds on their wedding bands. Two: nothing is created or destroyed. Three: then, logically, everything the ignit explosion destroys must go somewhere.

I might be dying. But I might be going somewhere, too.

All this hadn't even come down to an experiment, in the end. There I was, wrapped up in someone else's war again, the chaos of the fight already calmed, when the knife finally dropped. A literal knife, tipped in eruptstone, and not so much dropped as wildly flung at the glowing ignit I'd been trying to power off. It burst in the most spectacular blaze of light. Bursting me with it. A death sentence, or so every scientist has told me, usually while looking down their nose at my latest piece of research.

So here we are, with the dying.

APPENDIX

IMPORTANT FINDLAYS

Raghnaid Findlay: Tavish Findlay's late mother
Alasdair Findlay: Tavish Findlay's late older brother.

VENALT BRANCHES OF GOVERNMENT

The Institute: the branch governing infrastructure and technology
The Citadel: the branch governing policing and justice
The Basilica: the branch governing the humanities and religion

VENALT GOVERNMENT OFFICIALS

Chancellor Foirdelise: chancellor of the Institute
Chancellor Teodor: chancellor of the Citadel
Chancellor Alvise: interm chancellor of the Basilica
Chancellor Domenego: the late chancellor of the Basilica
Commander Zuane: second in command under Chancellor Teodor
Iseppa Collari: a high standing leader within the Institute

ACKNOWLEDGEMENTS

Thank *you* for continuing this journey with me! *Stronger Still* is my first "second book" to maintain the same point of view character and direct storyline, and I'm thrilled that you've chosen to stick with Rubem as I have. As an indie author, it's entirely through your support that this series is possible.

OTHER BOOKS BY D.N. BRYN

OUR BLOODY PEARL
Forty years ago . . .

After a year of voiceless captivity, a blood-thirsty siren fights to return home while avoiding the lure of a suspiciously friendly and eccentric pirate captain.

This adult fantasy novel is a voyage of laughter and danger where friendships and love abound and sirens are sure to steal—or eat—your heart.

ONCE STOLEN
The prequel to Odder Still . . .

An autistic, naga thief must guide a poisoned hero through his ex-homeland while fleeing cartel leaders, swamp monsters, and his own feelings in order to claim the hero's payment of precious stones.

This fun and fast-paced YA-style adventure comes complete with a hate-to-love romance and a boat-load of sass.

Explore a brand-new D. N. Bryn world of queer love and scientifically reinterpreted mythological species with . . .

Guides for Dating Vampires!

HOW TO BITE YOUR NEIGHBOR
AND WIN A WAGER

Feed and get out—that's Vincent's moto. But when his latest snack is hot, funny, and begs to be bitten, he can't help double-dipping. Little does he know, the man has an ulterior motive: a murder to solve, and a vampire's life to trade for proof.

D.N. Bryn is part of The Kraken Collective—an indie author alliance of queer speculative fiction committed to building an inclusive publishing space. For more adult fantasy titles featuring the diverse rep you love, check out the ones below!

THE XANDRI CORELEL SERIES
by Kaia Sønderby

Fascinated by complex water-based society and non-human races?

The Xandri Corelel series is all about alien diplomacy with intricate alien cultures—including symbiotic aliens in the second book! The series star a bisexual and autistic woman who heads the Xeno-Liaison department of the Carpathia, a Starsystems Alliance first contact ship. It's full of intrigue, alien accommodations and compassion.

CITY OF STRIFE
by Claudie Arseneault

Love Maraheem's ruling families and politics underpinned by deeply personal narratives?

City of Strife is a mosaical, epic novel with a large and majorly queer cast, a web of political intrigue, and a heart of gold, in which an elven noble's attempt to stop imperialist wizards from taking over his city will have repercussion from its richest towers to the homeless shelter at its very bottom.